THE MAN IN THE SHADOWS

He slid one arm around her shoulders and drew her close. His other hand grasped her chin firmly, and before she could utter a sound of protest, he pulled her across his lap and pressed his lips hungrily against hers.

Completely unprepared for what was happening, Amelia found herself momentarily paralyzed by the overwhelming spell of this disturbing man. Her senses, against all her control, responded to his touch, and it was only the warmth of his hand upon her breast which cleared her mind.

With a surge of strength that she had not known she possessed, she wrenched herself from his arms. Her voice and body shook from anger and humiliation—and an excitement she refused to acknowledge.

"I have never met anyone who would stoop so low as you, Matthew Laurence!"

MARINA MALCOLM

SECRETS IN THE SHADOWS

LEISURE BOOKS   NEW YORK CITY

A LEISURE BOOK ®

July 1991

Published by

Dorchester Publishing Co., Inc.
276 Fifth Avenue
New York, NY 10001

A love fulfilled illumines from within
And beams its light on all.

A love rejected builds inside a wall
To hold a pain so black it casts
A shadow on the sun.

Chapter One

The southbound train's shriek startled Amelia from her shallow sleep. Squinting against the glare of the Florida morning sun through the dusty window of the train, she saw another dismal, seemingly deserted village of weathered clapboard buildings and dirt streets. She shut her eyes against the ugliness, hoping to quell the sense of foreboding which threatened to engulf her.

"You not gettin' motion sick like Miss Maude, are you, Miss Amelia?"

Beulah's dark hands plumped the pillow behind Amelia's head, and even behind closed lids, Amelia could sense the anxious scrutiny of the rotund, kind black woman, who was Aunt Ursula's maid.

With eyelids still firmly lowered to shut out the squalor of the cracker village, Amelia shook her head. "Just resting my eyes, Beulah. Don't worry about me."

Amelia heard her move away in a rustle of black taffeta, clucking like a mother hen, and felt strangely reassured by Beulah's attention.

When Amelia opened her eyes again, the sun was blocked by moss-draped cypress trees rooted in stagnant pools of murky water. Although the temperature was rising with the sun, she shivered, filled again with uneasiness. The train's rocking rhythm and the now flat, monotonous landscape of scrub pines and palmetto bushes made her drowsy, but she could not sleep. In the distance she glimpsed an oasis of green, acres of orange trees neatly filed across the rolling hills. Their verdant foliage and branches heavy with fruit reminded her of Mr. Griffin's apple orchard, and a longing for home and the familiar blended with her sense of dread.

She laid her temple wearily against the window, grateful for its coolness against her throbbing forehead, and struggled futilely to hold back the rebellious tears slipping down her cheeks. With growing panic, she fought to control her churning emotions. Everything was so new and strange. In the past four weeks her entire life had been upended, and she knew that nothing would ever be the same again.

You have to get hold of yourself! she thought. *Don't just sit there feeling sorry for yourself. Get up and move!*

Taking a deep breath to calm her heart and to stop her tears, Amelia rose quietly, stepped past her elderly aunt, snoring delicately in the seat next to her, and made her way down the aisle of the swaying car to the ladies lounge.

The coach was crowded with vacationing families and their luggage, all headed for the Gulf Coast of Florida and Henry Plant's lavish resort hotel, the Belleview, completed just three years ago in 1897 on the large peninsula of land between the Gulf of Mexico and Tampa Bay. But the luxury of the carriage with its red plush seats and brass appointments, part of Plant's

Orange Belt railway, barely registered in her whirling mind as she hurried to avoid the curious glances of the other passengers and slipped into the lounge.

Amelia removed her stylish hat with its concealing layers of mourning veils edged with black grosgrain ribbon, then wet the corner of a towel and wiped away the tracks of tears on her smooth pale cheeks. Recapturing the stray curls that had escaped from the thick roll of her upswept strawberry-blond hair, she tucked each one neatly back into its proper place, wishing that she could restore order to her chaotic life as easily.

Her eyes caught their own reflection. "Perfect Carolina blue" her father had always called them, but now they were reddened by tears and ringed with the dark smudges of exhaustion.

Dear God, she prayed silently and fervently, *please spare me from anymore of the pain such as I have endured these past few months. I thought I was strong, but I am so weak and so alone.*

As she replaced her black hat and lowered the heavy layers of black tulle, she was amazed to see that she still looked twenty-one, even though recent tragedy had dimmed the youthful sparkle in her eyes. The initial shock and debilitating pain of that loss had subsided, and now she was left alone to pull her life together. Amelia was grateful for her aunt's care and concern, but rebellion rose within her. She must refuse to be dominated any longer by the demanding Ursula Hagarty. She would have to learn to make her own decisions.

With her thoughts a confused jumble of the past and future, Amelia started carefully back down the rocking aisle to her seat. As the train rounded a sharp curve, she felt herself falling. Suddenly she was in the firm grip of a passenger into whose lap she had tumbled. Looking up through the dark netting of her mourning veil, Amelia gazed into the most arresting pair of brown eyes that she had ever seen.

Like a butterfly caught in a spider's web, she sat motionless, entranced by the rugged beauty of the man who held her. The eyes of her captor searched vainly through her veil for a glimpse of her features, and the hint of laughter at the corners of his generous mouth jolted Amelia back to reality. She became embarrassingly aware of the masculine scent of his shaving soap and the pressure of his arm around her waist.

"Please excuse me," she said, leaping to her feet as quickly as the constraints of her fashionable skirts allowed, but she was undone by another lurch of the carriage. Thrown into the aisle in a heap, she struck her head against the brass fitting of the opposite seat.

Her head swam dizzily, and in spite of her best efforts, she could not clear her mind nor get to her feet. Suddenly she became aware again of the handsome stranger, who had scooped her from the floor of the aisle and now held her firmly in his arms.

"Can you hear me? Are you badly hurt?"

His breath brushed her cheek beneath the veil as he spoke, and she realized gratefully that he was speaking softly to avoid drawing attention to her predicament. He had returned to his seat on the aisle with Amelia in his lap, while the other passengers paid them no attention.

She attempted to struggle to her feet, but the man held her fast. Then, sensing her growing discomfort, in one fluid motion he rose, lifting her effortlessly in his arms and placing her lightly on her feet. Before she could continue on her way, the train lurched again, and Amelia was thrown against the tall stranger whose balance never wavered.

"Are you all right?" his rich baritone voice sounded in her ears.

Amelia nodded numbly, curiously shaken by the nearness of this disconcertingly handsome and self-possessed man and the pounding of her head where it had struck the seat.

"May I escort you to your seat?"

Unable to trust her voice, Amelia shook her head vehemently. Horrified to realize that he still held her firmly against his chest, Amelia pulled away from him, forcing from her consciousness the comfort which his embrace had given her. Chagrined that her recent bereavement had evidently affected her usual sense of propriety, she tried to wrest her hand from his firm grasp.

"Matthew Laurence, at your service." He bowed elegantly, as if in some formal drawing room instead of in a continually shifting fast train. He paused and looked at Amelia questioningly, waiting for her to give her name or at least to lift her veil so that he could see her face.

When she did not answer, dizzy from her own swirl of emotions as well as the knock on her head, he sprang into action.

"Come with me."

Before she could utter the slightest sound of protest, he had grasped her firmly by the elbow and was propelling her toward the rear of the car. When Amelia's head cleared, she found herself thrust into a chair in the dining car, staring at the stark white linen tablecloth in complete confusion.

"Steward! A large brandy, please, and be quick about it!"

The words brought her immediately to her senses. "What? At ten o'clock in the morning? You must be mad!"

"Strictly medicinal, my dear Madame X, since you refuse to give me your name. I'm delighted you've recovered enough to at least speak to me."

"Indeed I have. And you will not ply me with strong drink to get my name, either, even for the kindliest of motives."

Amelia's head was beginning to throb, but even through her pain, she was intensely aware of Matthew Laurence who stared at her so intently from across the table.

"Very well, Madame X. To assure you that my intentions are only benign . . . Steward! Forget the brandy and bring the lady hot tea. Now . . ." He returned his attention to Amelia. "You have suffered a bad fall and a nasty bump on the head. Are you all right, or should I try to locate a physician?"

Physician! The word twisted in Amelia's heart like a knife. Her father had been the finest physician Asheville had known, and now he was gone. Across the table Laurence awaited her answer.

"You're very kind, but I really am quite all right."

"Forgive me for saying so, but are you sure? You seem—dazed, I suppose, is the appropriate word."

"Dazed? Why, yes, I think I am. So much is happening all at once. But I shouldn't be here with you—"

"Nonsense, you are not alone. As you can see, the car is filled with people, anyone of whom would come to your assistance if you called out."

The steward set a tea service between them, and Laurence poured out a cup for Amelia, adding generous amounts of sugar and lemon without asking her preference. Then he pushed the cup and saucer across the table to her before pouring himself a cup of the fragrant hot brew. Amelia was fascinated by his hands. He had the long slender fingers of a pianist, or a surgeon, yet they were strong hands, too, and probably quite gentle. She gave herself a slight shake; she must have hit her head very hard indeed to be sitting drinking tea with a perfect stranger and going into flights of fancy because of his hands.

"Please drink your tea while it's hot," he pleaded. "You really did take a bad fall back there, and I want to be sure you are not injured. The tea will help revive you."

Obediently, Amelia sipped the hot liquid, finding that it did seem to restore her, although her head still throbbed. As she raised her eyes from the teacup, she saw Laurence scrutinizing her carefully. She had not removed her veil, but had merely lifted it to drink her tea, so he could not see her face. Amelia was relieved, because she knew she was still blushing at her indelicate situation. She was relieved that he would not know her if they met again.

When she raised her eyes to his, he smiled at her with a warmth that melted a part of the iciness that she had carried within her for weeks, but then Amelia saw also the amusement in his eyes, and her confusion turned to anger that the man had addressed and handled her so casually.

"Excuse me, sir"—Amelia placed her saucer on the table carefully lest he see that her hands were trembling —"but I must return to my aunt and cousin. Thank you for assisting me and for your refreshment, but you are a stranger . . ."

Every detail of the handsome and elegant Laurence burned into her mind: the striking planes of his high cheekbones; the warmth of his deep brown eyes; the manner in which his thick brown hair curled over the immaculate white stiffness of his collar; and the expensive clothes that complemented the strength emanating from his tall frame.

She shook her head, thinking that the blow had seriously affected her indeed, and finished weakly.

". . . And I must return to my aunt . . ."

He stood as she did and offered his arm, but she shook her head in refusal.

"I hope we will meet again soon, Madame X."

She tried to turn gracefully, but her steps faltered, and she avoided his eyes for fear of the laughter in them. Regaining her balance, she returned to her car, refusing to allow herself a backward glance. She could feel his eyes burning into her back, and even more upsetting, she could still feel the imprint of his hand at her waist and the pressure of his strong arms behind her knees.

Slipping quietly into her seat, Amelia shut her eyes and breathed deeply to release the tension in her chest. She silently berated herself for allowing a trifling incident and an arrogant man to have such an affect on her and attributed it to the physical and emotional fatigue that had plagued her for the past few weeks. She absentmindedly smoothed the wrinkles from the skirt of her traveling suit, thinking that the blackness of the fabric matched her mood, and she wondered if she would ever be happy again.

Aunt Ursula began to stir beside her, and across from her Cousin Maude sat, looking pinched and drawn. Maude obviously did not travel well, and Amelia pitied her her discomfort.

Throughout the car people began to gather their belongings as the train slowed. Glints of sunlight on wide expanses of blue water and the high gables, chimneys and dormers of the Belleview Hotel told Amelia that their journey had ended.

"We're pulling into the Belleview now, Aunt Ursula." Amelia smiled down at her as she gathered her coat and traveling bag. "I'll tell Beulah to get your things."

Amelia watched as Beulah, efficient and cheerful as usual, and Maude, gray-faced and travel-worn, assisted Ursula, whose painful rheumatism made it difficult for her to walk. As the others in her party left the train,

Amelia returned to her seat for her forgotten book of Tennyson's poems.

She paused before descending the stairs of the railroad carriage, her eyes taking in the impressive building. The Belleview sprawled before her, five towering stories of bay windows, balconies and verandas, built so that every one of its 145 rooms commanded a view of the water. The spacious shaded porches, furnished with white wicker filled with plump, colorful cushions, were arrayed with jardinieres of ficus and croton trees; hanging baskets of maidenhair and Boston ferns, suspended from the intricate gingerbread trim, gave the massive building a homey and comfortable atmosphere.

The lushly landscaped grounds with rows of stately palms along the avenues and beds of exotic shrubs and flowers could flourish only in a semitropical climate as this one. Having just come from the barren winter landscape and cold drizzly climate of the Blue Ridge Mountains, Amelia was entranced by the scene and the intoxicating smell of flowers mingled with the warm salty air. Her sense of foreboding vanished.

As she stepped off the car, a firm hand grasped her elbow. She spun around rapidly, losing her footing, and again found herself crushed against the hard broad chest of Matthew Laurence. Looking up into those same arresting brown eyes, she was struck speechless as his hands steadied her and restored her balance.

"Madame X, we meet again. Surely now you'll give me your name," Laurence said, the lilt in his voice matching the twinkle in his eyes.

He continued to hold her shoulders gently, as if she needed his support. Her heart leapt at the warmth of his touch, but the same look of amusement tugging at the corners of his mouth infuriated her.

"You startled me, Mr. Laurence. And please unhand me. I am not an invalid who needs your assistance," she replied indignantly, stepping back to release his grip.

Undeterred, Laurence continued to smile down at her. "At least you remembered my name. Now, if you would do me the courtesy of telling me yours. It seems only appropriate since we seem to be running into one another so often."

The teasing tone of his voice and the insinuation of his statement caused Amelia to blush under her mourning veil, and the heat she felt radiating from her face was not caused by the Florida sun.

"The time I have spent with you has not been by choice, Mr. Laurence."

Amelia realized that she neither felt nor sounded convincing. Aware that she was rapidly losing control of herself and the situation, she knew she had to leave this man's presence before she complied with his request for her name or in any way acknowledged the unspoken request shining in his eyes.

"At least tell me your aunt's name so that I can ask permission to call on—"

"Good day, sir," Amelia stated as firmly and angrily as her bewildered senses would let her.

She turned and walked steadily toward the broad steps of the hotel veranda to join Aunt Ursula and Cousin Maude. Her heart was beating fast and she wanted to run, but she forced herself to move with dignity. She knew that once again his eyes were watching her every move, and she would not betray to him that his very presence had shaken her to the core. She tried to assure herself that, if he wished, he would manage to have himself properly introduced, and she fought the small voice within her that urged her to turn around and tell her name.

"Amelia!"

Aunt Ursula's voice carried the imperative of royal command, the tone and quality of one used to having her way. Amelia hurried to catch up with her party, once again aware of Laurence's eyes following her.

"Quit dawdling, child, and catch up. For your dear mother's sake, I must see that you are properly chaperoned. Did I see you talking to a stranger? It just isn't done you know, even if you Southerners do have bizarre ideas of hospitality."

The vinegar in her tone was unmistakable, and Amelia attributed it to her aunt's discomforting rheumatism. Ursula's pride was such that she refused to use a wheelchair, preferring painfully, but proudly, to ambulate with the help of her ebony cane.

The elegant hotel lobby was so breathtaking that it drove all other thoughts from Amelia's mind. Its cavernous size was lighted by multiple crystal chandeliers hanging in rows across the length and breadth of the two-story ceiling. The January chill of the Florida morning was broken by roaring fires in the great fireplaces on opposite sides of the lobby. Several groupings of chairs, sofas, low tables with massive arrangements of flowers, and Oriental carpets patterned in soft pastels gave an air of intimacy to the immense expanse of the room.

Equally elegant were the dozens of guests who lounged in small groups or passed purposefully through the lobby, their casual vacation clothes carrying the stamp of wealth and importance. Uniformed bellboys and maids moved efficiently and silently through the crowd, their arms filled with luggage or linen.

Ursula settled herself on one of the sofas while Maude instructed Beulah and the bellboys to convey the luggage to their suite. The elderly woman was obviously exhausted and in need of rest. Amelia and Maude helped her to her feet and they began to climb the wide white stairway carpeted in green and lighted by floor-to-ceiling multi-paned windows on the landing.

A young man with a solemn expression hurried after

them. "I'm Mr. Carlisle, the manager, Mrs. Hagarty," he addressed Ursula. "Would you be so kind as to step into my office for a moment, please?"

Ursula waved her hand feebly, as if brushing away an insect, and resumed climbing the stairs. She was too tired to deal with underlings now. Amelia paused, but there was nothing she could do, so she merely shrugged and turned away. But the entire party stopped short at his next words.

"It's a telegram, Mrs. Hagarty, and I'm afraid it's bad news."

Ursula allowed Amelia and Maude to assist her down the stairs and into the nearby office, where she sank gratefully into the large leather chair opposite the desk. Like royal attendants, Maude and Amelia stood protectively on either side of her. Ursula held out an unsteady hand for the telegram then read:

JEREMIAH SINCLAIR DIED TODAY OF A STROKE STOP FUNERAL SERVICES DAY AFTER TOMORROW AS PER FINAL INSTRUCTIONS STOP PLEASE WIRE YOUR PLANS STOP DEEPEST SYMPATHY PHILIP SHERIDAN III.

"Grandfather!" Maude cried, bursting into tears and collapsing with her head in her mother's lap.

Amelia stepped forward to offer what comfort she could to her kinswomen, but the telegram acted as a piercing reminder of her own loss. She had been so preoccupied with her confused thoughts of Matthew Laurence that for a brief time she had forgotten her own grief, and now reality and all the pain that accompanied it came flooding over her. She stood still and silent, staring down at her weeping cousin.

"Maude, get off me, and Amelia, stop ogling, child, and get me pen and paper," Ursula snapped.

Mr. Carlisle handed Amelia paper and a pen from his desk.

"Take this down, Amelia. Telegram received Stop Am too ill to travel Stop Keep me informed Stop Ursula Hagarty.

"Now, children . . ." Ursula rose, leaning weakly on her cane. "I think you should see me to my room. Oh, Maude, do use your handkerchief and pull yourself together!"

Matthew Laurence stood with his back to the blazing fire in the lobby fireplace and watched the trio of black-clad women slowly mount the stairs. His eyes lingered on the slender figure on the right, "Madame X," whose face he had yet to see. As the women disappeared from the landing, Matt continued to gaze at the stairs where the young woman had been, and for the first time in several years, he realized that he was not bored.

Chapter Two

"Oh, no, Aunt Ursula, you can't mean it!" Amelia cried in dismay. "It's like being in prison!"

"Don't be impertinent, Amelia!" the older woman snapped. "We will remain in this suite until I say it is appropriate that we leave. You have recently lost your own parents, so you of all people should respect my grief and my wishes to observe my father's passing as I see fit. Beulah, draw the draperies, then advise the staff that we will take all our meals in our rooms until further notice. And, Maude, stop sniveling!"

"Yes, Mama."

Maude indelicately wiped her nose on the back of her sleeve as she sank awkwardly into the nearest chair.

Amelia, stricken with remorse, placed her arms about Ursula's aged shoulders. "Of course, I understand your wishes, Aunt, and I will abide by them. Forgive me. I was thinking only of myself."

"Hmpff," acknowledged Ursula, uncomfortable with

Amelia's show of affection. "Just leave me to my grief, child."

Amelia withdrew quietly to the seclusion of her own room. Thoughts of death and loss were still too painful for her, so she allowed her thoughts to wander. She was puzzled over her reaction to Matthew Laurence. Never in her twenty-one years had she ever been so affected by a man. Every detail of him was burned into her mind, and when she thought of him, the physical sensation was entirely new to her, a mixture of tingling anticipation coupled with feelings not unlike what she had experienced when she was coming down with influenza, feverish and lightheaded.

She had never really been in love before, but if this was love, she wasn't sure it was altogether pleasant. Besides, she had found him to be arrogant and insufferable in many ways, so how could she love him? Was it just because he was the most handsome man she had ever met, or perhaps hers was a natural response to someone who had been kind to her. Kind, arrogant and insufferable, an unlikely combination of traits. Well, it looked as if she was going to have a long time to consider the problem in depth. Who knew how long it might be before Aunt Ursula would release her from her confinement in the elegant suite in the Belleview?

Matthew Laurence found his frustration level rising daily. It had been over two weeks since his arrival at the Belleview, and although he had been constantly on watch, he had not caught even a glimpse of the mysterious Madame X.

Discreet inquiries accompanied by a liberal bribe had induced the desk clerk to tell him that the woman was registered with Ursula Sinclair's party, but beyond that he was able to find out very little, not even her name. Perhaps she was married. But where was her husband?

She was dressed in mourning. Was she a widow? The more he thought of her, the less he realized he knew, except that she was the most fascinating woman he had ever met.

He was sure he would know her if he saw her, even though he had not seen her face. The graceful carriage of her figure and the soft tones of her voice would identify her. His memories of the woman haunted him, distracting him from the business he had come to Florida to conduct and from any pleasurable recreation as well. Even his golf game was a casualty to his distraction.

"Sir, you're going to have to keep your mind on the game, or I will have to re-sod the entire course."

Angus, Matt's caddy, shook his head as Matt whacked at the golf ball as if he were killing snakes.

"Sorry, Angus," Matt grinned ruefully. "Have you ever had a woman drive you almost to distraction?"

Angus nodded in agreement. "Aye, sir, driven to distraction—and to marriage, and to tell the truth, I don't know which is worse."

"I saw this woman only once, the day she arrived more than two weeks ago and I haven't seen her since. I know where she's staying, but I haven't been able to think of an acceptable excuse to call, and even if I did—"

Matt whacked the earth again in frustration as Angus winced at the treatment of his world-renowned golf course.

"And what does this mysterious lady look like? Perhaps I've seen her myself."

"I don't know what she looks like, Angus. I've never seen her face."

"Excuse me for saying so, sir, but it sounds as if you've spent too much time in the hot sun without a cap. You say you haven't seen this woman you're so fascinated with? Then how do ye know you're fascinated?"

"I know it sounds crazy, but even though her face was veiled, the rest of her was magnificent, and she had the voice of an angel—and spirit. I like that in a woman."

The caddy scratched his head as if weighing whether to continue, then shrugged his shoulders and plunged on. "Ye could be lettin' yourself in for a nasty shock, sir. Under all those veils could be a face like my grandmother's cow, if you'll pardon my saying so."

Matthew threw back his head and laughed. "You could be right, Angus, but somehow in this instance, I don't think so. I have a feeling she'll be even more beautiful than I've imagined—if I ever see her again."

"I hope I'm not speaking out of turn, sir, but it sounds like what you need is a bit of diversion." Angus winked slyly at Matt. "Just say the word, sir, and I can have one of the South's loveliest delights appear at your door for an evening of, ahem, diversion."

Matt laughed again and threw his arm around the caddy's rugged shoulders. "I need a woman, Angus, but the woman I need is a very special one."

"Leave it to me, sir."

Matt shook his head. "Let's get back to annihilating this golf course, shall we?"

Amelia restrained herself from skipping down the wide stairs into the lobby. She had been confined for three weeks to the suite she shared with Aunt Ursula and Cousin Maude. Ursula had insisted that it was not appropriate for them to mingle with the other guests following Jeremiah Sinclair's death. So the women had been each other's only company in rooms darkened by closed draperies so that not even the bright winter sun of Florida could cheer them. Hidden away, they had dined, read, done endless needlework, played cards, or simply dozed in front of the fire in their parlor.

The anticipated arrival today of Ursula's attorney, Philip Sheridan, had finally given Amelia the freedom she craved.

"You run along, child," Ursula had insisted. "Maude will look after me, and Philip and I have a great deal of business to discuss. You can have the entire day to explore the hotel, if you wish. Take your time and don't hurry back."

Before Ursula could change her mind, Amelia had grabbed her book by Jane Austen, her boater and a shawl and hurried from the suite. She headed straight out the main entrance into the sunshine and stood for a moment relishing the clear clean air.

The day was mild with a warm breeze blowing from the Gulf, and Amelia was glad that she had left her black jacket behind. In her crisp white shirtwaist and soft black skirt she felt indistinguishable from the other female guests. Her own lack of self-consciousness prevented her from realizing that the fiery shade of her thick hair would call attention to her in any circumstances, but especially now with its highlights capturing and reflecting the brilliant sunlight.

Amelia stood on the top step of the veranda and watched the activity around her. Golfers, followed by caddies laden with clubs, strolled toward the course to the east, while groups of young people on bicycles headed north on the main drive that led from the hotel toward Clear Water Harbor, the nearest town. Another group in riding habits strode toward the hotel stables, and men with hunting and fishing gear lounged on the veranda steps, waiting for their guides.

Her eyes searched the crowds for a glimpse of Matthew Laurence, the man whose face and name had haunted her since the day of her arrival. During her confinement she had daydreamed about him continually, imagining herself cloistered away with him, rather

25

than with her aunt and cousin, in the dim candlelit suite. Amelia had tried to push him out of her mind, but every time she tried to distract herself with a book or a game of cards, into her memory would creep the touch of his hands at her waist and those deep brown eyes searching for a glimpse of her face.

Now freed from her rooms, she discovered that she was not free from her thoughts of Matthew Laurence, and she hoped that he would appear. As she scanned the crowd of golfers again, she remembered that he still did not know who she was or even what she looked like, so that if they ever did meet, it would be as strangers.

The refreshing salty breeze from the Gulf beckoned her attention to the water. Directly to the west, down the bluff from the hotel's main entrance, was a long pier that jutted out into the water for almost a hundred feet. At the end of the pier was a solitary bench, which Amelia, forcing hopes of seeing Matthew Laurence from her mind, decided would be the perfect spot for her morning's reading. She descended the steep wooden stairs that led down the bluff and walked slowly to the pier's end, savouring the fresh air, the cloudless sky, and the occasional silver flash of mullet jumping in the harbor.

She sat on the bench, propped her back against one of the pier pilings, and dug into her skirt pocket for the apple she had brought from the ever-present bowl of fruit in the suite. But her appetite for food and reading disappeared when she opened the book and saw the inscription on the flyleaf: "May you always be free of pride and prejudice. Love, Papa."

Tears welled in her eyes and rolled down her cheeks. She vividly remembered her father—his eyes, ever compassionate and as blue as hers, set in the most handsome face she had ever known, and his dark brown hair, graying at the temples, rich and full. She remembered him best with his patients, carefully attending to their complaints with his capable gentle hands, often with Amelia beside him. She had worked as his assistant, helping him both as an extra pair of skilled, sensitive hands and as a calming influence on nervous patients. Dr. Jerome Donelly and his daughter Amelia were well known throughout the county. They were a team.

It had been Jerome's dream and his daughter's to have Amelia join him in his medical practice and to help him start a hospital in Asheville. With his death that dream was dashed, broken to bits like the shells on the beach below her being pounded by the waves.

The screech of the gulls overhead broke Amelia's reverie. She knew she needed to focus on the future, not on the past, as thoughts of it were painful. But her future was too uncertain, and offered little comfort. She resumed reading but found that she could not concentrate.

Her thoughts drifted to her mother, the beautiful Emily, small and rounded, soft and gentle and smelling of lavender, so different from her sister Ursula with her sharp angular build and features, and her caustic manner. Her parents had complemented each other so well, her mother's gentleness and her father's patience, and their unending love for each other and for her.

Memories of her childhood filled her mind: the big white house with her father's office in the front parlor; the huge kitchen where she and her mother waited for Papa to return from what seemed to be never-ending housecalls; and the dinner table where the conversations were always lively and exhilarating. Emily and Jerome would discuss current events during the evening meal, taking opposing sides on controversial issues. As Amelia grew older, she participated in their debates, developing a quick wit and reasoning ability far superior to most children her age. From these informal arguments she had learned to approach issues with open-mindedness, a thirst for truth, and a horror of injustice.

After dinner, the three of them would gather around the piano as Amelia played and her father and mother sang. Even now Amelia could hear Jerome serenading Emily with "Believe Me If All Those Endearing Young Charms." She remembered the three of them gathered in front of the fire with the popcorn popper and apples to be roasted, reading aloud from her father's collection of the classics. They had always been short of money, for her father ministered to all who needed him, and there were many who could not afford to pay, except with an occasional chicken or a dozen eggs, but her family had been wealthy in love and learning and a zest for life.

But all of that had come to an abrupt and tragic end. She had been studying at her desk by the fireplace that November night when Dr. Will and Aunt Beth, her parents' best friends, appeared on the ice-covered porch. She could still see the shock in their eyes and hear the awful words that Dr. Will was forced to tell her.

"Your parents will not be coming home, Amelia," Dr. Will began haltingly. "There's been an accident. The ice from today's storm broke a limb from a tree as their buggy passed beneath it. The horse bolted. The buggy overturned. Both your mother and father were killed instantly."

That was the last thing that Amelia remembered until she awoke in her own bed the next day with Dr. Will and Aunt Beth standing over her. The terrible reality struck her, and she cried. Neither of them told her not to, for they too were weeping, and somehow their sharing her tears helped her to hold on to her sanity.

The next few days had passed in a glaze of pain; funeral arrangements, meeting with her father's lawyer, and the church services attended by hundreds of her father's patients, who all wanted to shake her hand and express their condolences. But not one of them, Amelia noted with an uncharacteristic touch of bitterness, offered to pay their bills.

It was after the funeral that Aunt Ursula and Cousin Maude had unexpectedly appeared. Ursula had sat in the center of the horsehair sofa in the drawing room with the late-afternoon sun throwing a nimbus around her white hair. A small, birdlike woman, she sat leaning forward, her arthritic hands clasped tightly on the gold ferrule of an ebony cane. She had the pink-and-white, unlined complexion of a young girl and her dark eyes narrowed as she studied Amelia.

Maude, a woman of about thirty with ramrod posture, stood by the mantelpiece, her elegant expensive clothes in stark contrast to her homely features. When she saw Amelia, she ran awkwardly toward her and threw her arms about her, kissing her on the cheek.

"I'm Maude, Amelia, and I hope we can be friends."

"Come here and sit by me, my dear." Ursula patted the sofa next to her as if it were her own parlor and she the one receiving guests.

"Yes, you're definitely your mother's daughter. I'd know that hair and those eyes anywhere, although you're much thinner than your mother was. She was always a plump little thing, too plump, I always thought."

Amelia had struggled to keep back the tears. How could the woman speak so casually of her dead sister? Then she reminded herself that Aunt Ursula had not seen Emily in over twenty-five years, so the loss was not as fresh to her as it was to Amelia. She sat down beside her.

"Now, child, you must know that we have come to help you in any way that we can. We are the only kin you have and I know that your mother would want us to be with you at a time like this."

Amelia was gratified at Ursula's concern and had begun to warm toward the old woman until she continued abruptly. "So tell me, what are you going to do? Are you engaged to be married?"

Amelia shook her head.

"Any prospects?"

Amelia shook her head again, outraged at the woman's boldness.

"Well, dear, just what are your plans?"

Her irritation at Ursula's manner subsided as Amelia realized that here was someone she could confide her financial troubles to, someone to whom she could unburden herself. She told them of her conversation with Lawyer Huffstetler, who had informed her that her parents' assets were modest. The sale of her father's medical equipment would pay off the bank loan he had used to purchase it, but all that was left to Amelia was the house and its furnishings.

Ursula spoke almost before Amelia had finished. "First, my dear, we will place the sale of the house and the auction of the furnishings in the hands of a capable agent and get your affairs here settled as rapidly as possible. Then you will, of course, accompany us to Florida where we will be spending the winter season at the new Belleview Hotel."

"Oh, but I could never leave Ashe—"

"The change of scenery will do you a world of good," Ursula had interrupted. "And you will have an entire season in the sun to decide what you want to do. I will not hear of your remaining here alone. Consider the matter closed."

Too overwhelmed by all that had happened to protest, Amelia had consented. The only home she had ever known and all its familiar contents had been sold. The modest sum remaining after her parents' debts and burial expenses had been paid was placed in the bank for Amelia's future use.

Aunt Ursula had insisted that she be allowed to provide a mourning wardrobe for Amelia's trip, and the intervening weeks had been filled with fittings as they waited to settle the estate. Then they had boarded the Orange Belt train for Florida.

How different these past weeks with Maude and Ursula had been from the warm and loving atmosphere of home. While her relatives were kind to her, they remained distant and cold, and Amelia doubted that any amount of time would change that. Aunt Ursula with her sharp tongue and commanding manner was already beginning to wear on her nerves and Maude's constant fluttering was difficult to tolerate, especially after three weeks of forced intimacy. Never in her life had Amelia felt so alone and discouraged. The tears rolled faster down her cheeks and made damp splotches on the starched bodice of her shirtwaist.

"Please allow me to be of assistance, ma'am," said an aristocratic British voice.

A large immaculately white handkerchief appeared before her nose, and Amelia looked up into a pair of twinkling blue eyes. An elderly gentleman with a thin, but kindly, face, impeccably dressed in Harris tweeds, thrust the handkerchief into Amelia's hands.

"Wipe your eyes, my dear. If there's anything that wounds me to the quick, it's the sight of a beautiful woman in tears. Forgive my lack of manners, but as

31

therc is no one else here to introduce us properly, I must introduce myself. I'm Hunter, ma'am."

He bowed gravely and with a wave of his hand and lift of his eyebrow asked permission to sit down.

Amelia nodded and the gentleman sat beside her on the pier bench. She felt so alone and afraid and his demeanor was so kind that her heart had warmed to him immediately, in spite of his formal manner, so she obediently dried her tears and gave him a weak smile.

"I'm Amelia Donelly. I'm here with my aunt, Mrs. Hagarty and her daughter, Maude. Are you a guest at the Belleview, too?"

"Well, yes, in a manner of speaking. Actually, I'm a 'gentleman's gentleman,' and my employer has a suite here. Every time he goes on an outing, I am given the liberty of doing as I please."

"Being able to do as one pleases must be the greatest luxury in the world." Amelia sighed and again her eyes filled with tears.

"Here now, this won't do at all," Hunter insisted. "I'm supposed to rescue damsels in distress, not make them cry. I am very sorry if I've upset you again."

"You're very kind, Mr. Hunter, and it's not your fault."

Amelia twisted the borrowed handkerchief with her long slender fingers and gazed at a flock of brown pelicans skimming low over the water's surface. She struggled to gain control of her fragile emotions.

"You must have a very good reason to be so sad on such a beautiful day and in such a beautiful place. Surely it is not Miss Austen's book."

"Oh, no, it is not the book itself, only its inscription," Amelia replied, her voice dropping to a whisper. "It was a gift from my father."

"Please forgive me if I'm intruding—"

"No, it's no intrusion, but it is a sad fact that my parents were killed in an accident just after Thanksgiving."

Amelia paused, swallowing hard to hold back the tears. "I still find myself grieving as though it were yesterday, when in reality it has been almost two months. I guess that I find it easier to grieve than to deal with living."

"You will discover, Miss Donelly, that the grieving will go on for a long time, but one must still enjoy life, despite the pain. Please don't think me presumptuous, but sometimes it does help to share one's predicament with a stranger who, being a stranger, can give you a very objective perspective on your situation. I have the entire morning free, it's a beautiful day, and I find your company charming, so I believe you would find me an excellent listener."

Amelia considered his proposal for a few moments, and she knew there was truth in it. Her own experiences as a compassionate listener to her father's patients brought home the realization that she needed someone to talk to.

Finding it easy to speak her memories aloud to Mr. Hunter, Amelia began. "My parents did not have an easy life, nothing at all like this," she said, indicating her surroundings. "You see, my father's family lost everything during the war, 'except our good breeding,' as Papa always said, but it really didn't matter to them as long as they had each other.

"Papa managed to scrape together the tuition for medical school at the University of Chicago. That was where he met Mama."

"Your mother was a nurse?"

"No, Mr. Hunter," Amelia continued. "She volunteered at the hospital, reading to patients, writing letters for them and such. She had become bored with the social life forced upon her as the daughter of Jeremiah Sinclair and—"

"*The* Jeremiah Sinclair, owner of Sinclair Stockyards?"

"Yes, you have heard of him?"

"He is, or was, one of the wealthiest and most influential men in Chicago. I am sorry to hear that you have lost your grandfather in such a short time after your parents. Please accept my condolences."

"I'm afraid I do not feel his loss as greatly. I never met my Grandfather Sinclair. You see, when Mama married Papa, a poor Southern doctor, her father was convinced that he only wanted her money. He threatened to disinherit her, thinking it would scare Papa off. But Mama married her doctor anyway. It's sad, but Grandfather Sinclair's pride would never let him take back his threat or admit his mistake, even though Mama and I wrote to him regularly. I don't think he could stand the thought that my mother could love someone more than him."

"I have heard that he was a very kind man, Miss Donelly. You should not judge the dead too harshly. Pride does strange things to men."

"Indeed it does," she replied, and for a brief moment a vision of Matthew Laurence's smiling face appeared in her mind's eye. With an effort, she pushed him out of her mind and returned to her narrative.

"But now, you see, my dilemma is that my financial future is rather dim. Papa was in debt for some new medical equipment, and all that is left of my inheritance is the proceeds from the sale of our home—our beautiful home."

Her eyes filled with tears again. "It has made my future quite uncertain."

"A beautiful woman like you should have no uncertainties about her future," Hunter said chivalrously, but the impatient look on Amelia's face told him that his reply had been a mistake.

"Thank you for the compliment, but my looks have nothing to do with my future. My father and I had made plans for me to join him in his practice—"

"As a doctor?"

"I see your attitude toward a female physician is the same as those of the men running the medical schools in this country," Amelia replied heatedly, the anger flaring in her eyes and coloring her cheeks. "I have met all their requirements. I graduated with honors from Woman's College in Greensboro. I made all the appropriate applications with the highest references. The only thing I don't do is wear trousers."

"My dear Miss Donelly, I did not mean to upset you further, but you must admit that a woman doctor is a somewhat rare if not unheard of phenomenon."

"Please forgive me. I should not take my frustrations out on you," Amelia replied in a calmer tone. "Aunt Ursula wanted me to use my time here to decide what I am going to do, but after three weeks, I have no more idea of what to do with my life than I did when I arrived. I no longer have a home, and I don't want to be forever tied to Aunt Ursula. At the risk of sounding ungrateful, I must admit that sometimes I find her quite overwhelming."

"If you will forgive my broaching the delicate subject of finance, it appears to me that money is the crux of the matter. If you were financially independent, you would no longer have to rely on your aunt, and you could go on to medical school."

Hunter looked at her questioningly from under his thick white brows to assess how she reacted to this bit of advice.

Amelia laughed bitterly. "Yes, and if wishes were

horses, beggars would ride. You make it sound so easy, Mr. Hunter."

"But it is, my dear. You said you have a small inheritance. Properly invested, the income from that would provide you with the funds you need."

"Thank you for your interest and suggestion," Amelia said, "but with the little I know about investing, I might as well take my inheritance and scatter it from the end of this pier."

"Ah, but that is where I can be of help. Oh, I don't mean myself personally, of course, but I know just the man you need." Hunter smiled, very satisfied with himself, and gave an emphatic nod to punctuate his statement.

"You see, the employer I mentioned is one of the foremost financiers in the world. In fact, he has advised me for years on my own small investments, and I now have such a tidy sum that I shall never have to worry about my old age. Yes, he is definitely the one to whom you should speak."

"But I couldn't afford his fees, even though I agree that he might be able to help me."

Amelia shook her head and returned to twisting the handkerchief. Her tears had dried and she began to think about the feasibility of Mr. Hunter's plan.

"Leave that to me, my dear. He owes me a favor or two and I am sure that he will be happy to speak with you at my request. In fact, I know that he will be working this evening. I am certain that he has no other engagement tonight. I'll tell him to expect you at, shall we say eight-thirty in his suite, number 245?"

"I can't impose on you or your employer like this," Amelia replied, sincerely feeling that she was imposing, but hoping with all her might that it could be arranged.

"Nonsense, of course you can. I shall be absolutely

insulted if you do not keep the appointment."

"Thank you, Mr. Hunter." Amelia smiled.

"Good day to you, Miss Donelly. You have made my morning memorable." And with a courtly bow and tip of his hat, he walked back down the pier toward the bluff.

Chapter Three

Amelia's heart pounded with new hope as she watched Mr. Hunter disappear into the deep shadows of the hotel veranda. Although his advice had been unorthodox, presumptuous, and somewhat frightening, it had at least presented her with a way to break out of the inertia which had gripped her since her parents had died.

Amelia again reviewed her financial situation. If she did not take Mr. Hunter's advice, she might miss the only chance she had to become self-reliant. But if she took his advice? First, it was not seemly for a single young woman to call on a man in his suite without a chaperon. But could she tell Aunt Ursula and Maude and ask one of them to go with her? She remembered the strained closeness of the last few weeks and immediately saw that as impossible. They would not understand, and, besides, she longed for the privacy of her own thoughts and actions. And what if Aunt Ursula forbade her to go? She would be forced to disobey or to remain with no options but a life of forced dependency on wealthy relatives.

The worst that could happen would be that she would decide his advice was unacceptable or inappropriate. And there was also the problem that if she followed his advice, she would be under an obligation to both men for their help. Then again, perhaps they were both just kindly old gentlemen who enjoyed assisting a young person in need.

Amelia's head spun with the hopeless muddle of the situation, and her initial surge of hope was assaulted from all sides by doubts and questions. She knew that she needed to assess her options in a more logical manner. She headed back to the hotel and to her room where she would organize her thoughts on paper in hopes that a solution would become clear. She was so deep in thought that she missed the admiring glance of the desk clerk as she climbed the wide lobby stairs to the suite on the second floor.

When she reached the door, a sudden feeling of claustrophobia swept over her at the idea of re-entering those rooms, every square inch of which she knew by heart. Equally oppressive was the thought of more hours spent in the stultifying company of her Sinclair relatives. She stood momentarily, taking deep breaths of the fresh air that blew through the wide French doors at both ends of the corridor, attempting to conquer the foreboding that had gripped her once more. Then her ears picked up the unaccustomed sound of a masculine voice inside the suite.

"So you were totally unaware of his plans? That isn't like him not to confide in you."

Amelia heard Ursula mumble something in a low, but angry tone to which the masculine voice replied, "I don't know how Jeremiah could have botched things so thoroughly. Have you told Amelia?"

This was followed by Ursula's sharp and clear retort. "No! It is absolutely imperative that she *not* be told. Do you understand that, Philip?"

Tell me what? Amelia thought, listening for Philip to reply. Then she grew embarrassed at her eavesdropping, knocked lightly at the door and entered.

"Am I interrupting, Aunt Ursula?"

Ursula looked up, startled, and Maude jumped from her chair, took Amelia by the arm and led her to the attorney.

"Amelia, this is Philip Sheridan. Philip, my dear cousin Amelia."

Standing at the bay window so that his face was in shadows was a tall, slender man. He had arrived late last night from Chicago to apprise Ursula of recent developments in the Sinclair holdings, and Amelia had been so anxious to escape this morning that she had left the suite before his arrival.

As Philip turned slightly toward her, the light struck his face and Amelia saw a man of classic handsomeness. The perfection of the lines of his forehead, nose and jaw appeared as if carved by a master sculptor. His hair and moustache were the color of bleached hay and the gray of his eyes reminded Amelia of the pussy willows that grew in her mother's garden. His build was thin and angular, and he towered above her. His clothing had the stamp of wealth and privilege, and he carried himself with the assurance of a man who knew how to handle any eventuality.

Amelia blushed as his eyes swept over her in an intense study, and she knew that she was flushed and disheveled from her brisk walk up the bluff, a stark contrast to the cool and impeccably groomed Philip. She was accustomed to the courtly manners of her father's friends, but never had one of them lifted her hand to his lips as Philip Sheridan was doing now, all the while looking deep into her eyes.

"Please accept my condolences on the tragic death of your parents, Miss Donelly."

At this, Maude compressed her lips in a tight line before curving them into a smile. She started to speak, but was interrupted by Amelia who had spent this time trying to retrieve her hand from the attorney's grasp.

"Thank you for your concern, Mr. Sheridan. I look forward to talking with you at length in the future, but I am sorely in need of freshening up. Aunt Ursula, if you will excuse me, I must change for lunch."

"Of course, child, run along. But keep in mind that Philip has invited us to dine with him tonight at eight o'clock in the Tiffany Room."

Amelia nodded her acknowledgment of the invitation and slipped into her room to change. Now she not only had the problem of whether to take Mr. Hunter's advice, but also the problem of how to keep her appointment, if she decided to do so. Mr. Sheridan had just made her complicated life even more complex.

She slipped off her wilted shirtwaist and dusty skirt and reminded herself to lay them aside for Beulah's care. Amelia wondered if she would ever accept as commonplace the luxury of a servant.

Going to the window, she threw back the heavy draperies and opened the doors onto the small balcony. Wearing only her camisole and petticoats, she stayed within the shadows of the room and luxuriated in the fresh air, hoping it would cleanse the staleness of the suite. Her eye caught a familiar figure walking toward the hotel from the golf course. His face was hidden by a golfing cap pulled over his forehead at a jaunty angle, but Amelia recognized the tall muscular physique in golfing tweeds and was amazed to discover how clearly this man had been etched in her memory. Her heart pounded and her face flushed as she recalled his arms about her on the train, and she found herself longing for him to look up so that she could have another glimpse of his tanned face with its generous mouth and soft brown eyes.

At that moment Matthew Laurence removed his cap and lifted his face to the sun. To Amelia, it seemed that he was staring straight at her and could see her even in the shadows. Flustered, she withdrew into the room and splashed her face with cold water from the porcelain basin, hoping that the freezing ablutions would drive away the unaccustomed heat radiating inside her. But even the shock of cold water could not quiet the timbre of his deep voice as it resonated in her mind.

I was in the sun too long this morning, Amelia thought. *It has to be sun sickness. The man is a complete stranger, and he was so—so—*

Even to herself she could not find the right word to describe his irritating behavior. She rubbed her face and arms vigorously with the fluffy towel, forcing her mind back to the dilemma at hand.

Yes, she decided, she had no choice. She had to take Mr. Hunter's suggestion and seek advice from someone who could help her. The luxury of her present life was intoxicating, but it was not worth the price of dependency on Aunt Ursula. She would surely die a slow and painful death if she spent the rest of her life in her relatives' company. Oh, she knew they had only her best interest at heart, but their world was so different than what Amelia had known. Somehow she had to return to her own world, her own life, and Mr. Hunter's idea seemed to be her only hope of accomplishing that. She had nothing to lose and might possibly gain a great deal.

Her decision made, Amelia put on a cool dress of deep lavender lawn and joined Ursula and Maude in the parlor of the suite as luncheon was being served, and Ursula was singing Philip's praises.

"I'm so pleased that Philip has joined us. He is marvelous company and such a help. And I always feel so much better with a man around that I can rely on."

Ursula laughed as she buttered a muffin. "Why, I remember Philip when he was just a little boy, such a charming well-mannered child. And now it's difficult to believe that he's in charge of the family firm."

"In charge?" questioned Amelia as she sat at her place opposite Maude.

"Yes, Amelia, Philip's father died last year and left him with the burden and responsibility of a large legal practice. Judging from his dealings with the Sinclairs, though, I would say he has met the challenge admirably."

"He has been and will be a comfort to you, I'm sure, Mama, now that he's here." Maude picked idly at her seafood salad. "And I'll be glad of an escort, too," she continued. "Even in such a fine establishment as this, it is almost impossible to meet the kind of man with whom one should associate."

She looked knowingly at Amelia, and Amelia flushed, wondering if Maude had observed her *tête-à-tête* on the pier with Mr. Hunter. Of course, he was only a servant, and she knew her relatives would consider him beneath them, but fortunately her own upbringing in Asheville had been less prejudiced and more democratic. Another indicator that she needed to escape this life for her own.

Nor had her experiences prepared her for life at the Belleview. Amelia would never become accustomed to having servants wait on her every whim. There was not only Beulah but the army of hotel staff, all standing ready to assist her. It was really quite stifling. *How on earth did the wealthy ever have any time to themselves?* she wondered.

That night as she dressed for dinner, she silently thanked Aunt Ursula for having insisted that she have a mourning wardrobe fashioned before she left Asheville. Even if the behavior of the wealthy was foreign to her, she could at least dress the part. Her dress of heavy black patterned silk was perfect for dining in the Belleview's magnificent hall. The low-cut bodice highlighted Amelia's smooth white skin and the curve of her breasts, and the fitted waist accentuated her slimness. The voluminous skirt was pulled tautly across her stomach and slender hips into a bustle with a velvet bow at the back. Her only accessories were long, black kid gloves and her mother's cameo on a thin ribbon of black velvet around her neck. Beulah swept her fiery hair up into a bouffant crown and arranged long wisps of curls at her ears and nape, finally pinning all the luxuriant mass in place with a spray of delicate black feathers.

"Um, um," she clucked. "Miss Amelia, you is one fine-looking woman."

"Thank you, Beulah."

Impulsively Amelia threw her arms around the maid and hugged her. Beulah was the one person in the entire Sinclair entourage who had shown any glimmer of affection for Amelia, and Amelia loved her for it. Very much alone and very much in need of someone who cared for her, Amelia was happy that the older woman returned her embrace. No one else had touched her with kindness since she had left Asheville; that is, no one else except Matthew Laurence. Try as she might, she could not rid her thoughts of the man.

Ursula drew in her breath with a sharp hiss as Amelia joined them in the parlor. "You look stunning, my dear. I can see that my money was well spent."

"Why, thank you, Aunt Ursula," Amelia replied, unaccustomed to compliments from that quarter.

Ursula couldn't help but compare her niece to her daughter. Amelia managed to make mourning look smart and stylish, but black only made Maude look ill.

Shaking her head and leaning heavily on her ebony cane, Ursula allowed the two younger women to assist her to the dining room.

In spite of her crippled walk, Ursula commanded attention with her regal carriage, the fashionable beaded jet of her sweeping dinner gown, and the small veil of black lace pinned like a mantilla atop her thick white hair. Heads turned as the impressive trio entered the Tiffany Room.

Amelia had thought herself inured to the opulence of the hotel, but the dining room was stunning. The arched ceiling of the great room soared two stories above her, inset with panel after panel of Tiffany-stained glass in jewel tones. Red and yellow lilies and other hothouse flowers in a rainbow of colors decorated the tables, and the scent of flowers blended with the aromas of roasting meats and steaming soups.

The women, like lovely hothouse blooms themselves in their colorful gowns and glittering jewels, contrasted with the elegant simplicity of the men's evening clothes. The flames from a thousand candles were reflected in the lead crystal, and above the muted conversations and the clink of silver flatware against fine bone china, Amelia could hear the hotel's chamber orchestra playing a Vivaldi concerto. It was a majestic setting for a young woman from a small town in the Blue Ridge Mountains, and Amelia felt like a princess.

The *maître d'hôtel* welcomed them respectfully and escorted them to Sheridan's table. Sheridan, tall and perfectly at ease in formal attire, rose to greet them and graciously assisted Ursula into her place beside him. Maude was seated on his left and Amelia directly across the table from him.

"It is a privilege to dine with three such beautiful women," Philip said, but his eyes rested on Amelia. She was relieved when the waiter handed her a menu so that she could hide from his obvious scrutiny. Although she tried to concentrate on selecting her meal, her mind was grappling with the problem of how to get away to keep her eight-thirty appointment.

"Shall I order for us all?" Philip suggested graciously.

"Oh, yes, please!" Amelia blurted out in obvious relief, evoking a studying look from her aunt.

By the time the waiter brought the first course of Coquille St. Jacques, Philip and Ursula were deep in a discussion of Chicago society, and Amelia found her thoughts wandering to the haunting image of the man on the train.

Trying to appear inconspicuous, she looked around the large dining room, hoping to catch another glimpse of him. She caught her breath when she saw a beautiful young matron and two teenaged children sitting with whom she presumed to be Matthew Laurence. As the man turned to gesture to the sommelier, she recognized her mistake. But by then her heart was racing, and she wondered at the violence of her reaction to the possibility that Laurence might be married and have a family. Over the pounding of the blood in her ears, she heard Philip addressing her.

"And how do you find the social life in Asheville, Miss Donelly?"

His voice was cultured and pleasant and held a note of sincere interest with only a touch of condescension.

Amelia, embarrassed to have forgotten her host, made a valiant attempt at giving him her full attention. "You'll probably think me a country bumpkin, Mr. Sheridan, but my social life at home revolved around my family and our church, and my studies often had to take precedence over social occasions. Our life was very quiet, I'm sure, compared to the whirl of activities you describe, but we were very happy and never bored."

"I can't believe anyone capable of boredom in your

company, Miss Donelly," Philip replied gallantly.

"Philip, do tell us of your plans for your stay here."
Maude spoke too loudly, injecting a discordant note into
the otherwise refined atmosphere.

"I hope you're not going to spend all your time
playing golf," she almost whined.

"I must admit the prospect of nonstop golfing on the
courses here is tempting, but as it would rob me of this
delightful company, I intend to engage in other pursuits
as well."

He paused and looked about the table, making sure
that he had caught the interest of his female trio.

"In fact, I was thinking that a picnic on the island the
day after tomorrow would be beneficial for all of you.
You need fresh air and a bit of recreation. You can't be
expected to spend all your time in your suite."

Maude nodded happily and looked questioningly at
her mother for a response.

"If the weather is mild, I believe it will be an excellent
idea. Thank you, Philip, for being so solicitous of us. Life
will be so much more pleasant now that you are here."
Ursula smiled affectionately at the young man.

Amelia could barely follow the rest of the conversation; her mind was on the passing time. It was now well
past nine o'clock and there seemed no hope of her
getting away soon. Anxiety had tightened her throat
until she could not swallow, and she looked up to see
Philip's concerned glance as he realized she was not
eating.

"Is anything the matter, Miss Donelly?"

Amelia knew that this might be her only chance to
escape. Her mind raced to find a suitable excuse to
leave, as her heart raced at the thought of lying to her
aunt.

"Everything is delicious, but I must have stayed in the
sun too long this morning. I have a terrible headache. If

you will please excuse me, I will return to my room."

Guilt lay heavily on her. She had never been a deceitful or dishonest person, and she felt sure the others would see through her facade.

"Oh, Amelia, what a shame!" Maude's loud statement made Amelia cringe.

"Yes, my dear, you must go back to your room and lie down. Perhaps you can have Beulah rub your temples. That always helps when I have a headache," her aunt suggested kindly.

Amelia felt relief wash over her as both Maude and Ursula continued to express their concern and urge her to go back to her room to rest.

Philip rose and pulled back her chair. Taking her arm, he escorted her to the door of the dining room. Amelia took great care to avoid his eyes as they bid each other good night.

"I regret that you are unwell, Miss Donelly, and look forward to our next meeting in hopes you will be in better health. Do you want me to see you to your suite?"

"No, thank you, Mr. Sheridan," Amelia replied a bit too hastily. "Please return as quickly as possible to my aunt. She enjoys your company so much that I would not deny her your presence. I regret having to leave our little party early."

"But when may I see you again, Miss Donelly?"

"Oh, any time, any time you wish."

She spoke impulsively and too emphatically, willing at that moment to promise him anything to be rid of him. Had she seen the look of radiant hope that sprang to his face at her words, she would have regretted her impetuousness, but now her only thoughts were of escape.

"Good night, Mr. Sheridan."

She turned toward the lobby and felt a twinge of conscience at having deceived both her relatives and

Philip Sheridan. She hoped the quality of the advice that she would receive tonight would justify her subterfuge. She was aware of Philip watching her, so she climbed the lobby stairs languidly until she was out of his sight. Then hiking her elegant silk skirt to her black-stockinged knees, she raced up the remaining stairs in a most unladylike gallop.

She ran along the deserted second floor corridor toward the westernmost suite atop the carriage portico entrance of the hotel. But when she reached her destination, she stood hesitantly before the door in the dark hallway, catching her breath, smoothing her rumpled skirt, and gathering her courage to knock. Quickly she said a silent prayer that Mr. Hunter would answer, then lifted her hand and rapped firmly.

The door opened with a rush of air and Amelia's apology for her lateness froze in her throat. There on the threshold stood Matthew Laurence. His eyes widened as he saw Amelia, her lovely face flushed pink from exertion. As he pushed the door open, she could see the empty room behind him and no Mr. Hunter in sight. Her hopes fell and her mind grappled to understand exactly what was happening to her.

"Come in," he said.

She was sure that he was leering at her.

"I really didn't think you would be coming at all tonight, but I'm very glad you're here."

Matthew Laurence stepped forward, placed his arm around Amelia's bare shoulders and led her into the room. With a casual kick of one booted foot, he closed the door behind them.

Tonight he was even more attractive than Amelia had remembered him. Every corded muscle of his body was accentuated by the tan jodhpurs and cordovan riding boots he wore. The powerful expanse of his chest was exposed by a collarless white shirt unbuttoned to the

50

waist, and his searing gaze was framed by a shock of thick fine hair that had fallen across his brow. He smelled of saddle leather, horses and fine Kentucky whiskey. Amelia saw the glass in his hand and the half-empty bottle on his desk and concluded that he was more than slightly drunk.

"Please excuse me, Mr. Laurence," she stammered in confusion, "I seem to have come at a bad time. I hadn't intended to be late—"

Laurence threw back his head and laughed mockingly, his words slurred. "Oh, it's never too late, but I must admit you're not at all what I expected, even though I did think Angus was only joking. But where are my manners? Please have a seat and I'll pour you a sherry."

Amelia's confusion deepened. She assumed that Angus was Mr. Hunter, but why would he treat her as a joke? Suddenly she was stricken with a terrible thought.

"Is it possible I have the wrong room? Does a Mr. Hunter work for you?"

"Of course. Hunter has worked for me for years. But what has that to do with anything?"

Now Amelia was even more confused. Time seemed suspended as her senses were bombarded from throughout the room. The masculine scents of sandlewood and whiskey assaulted her nostrils, the crackling of the fire and the beating of her heart filled her ears, and the deep brown eyes of Matthew Laurence filled her vision. Her mind raced frantically for the words to explain why she was here, because Mr. Hunter evidently had not.

Matt met her gaze, and this time she did not detect the least hint of laughter at the corners of his mouth as she had on the train. Try as she might, she could not read the meaning in his look, which bewildered her even more.

Clumsily, Laurence sat down and pulled her onto the

sofa beside him, drinking in her loveliness. Her agitation had produced a rosy glow that began at her high wide forehead and spread to the curve of her breasts visible above the decolletage of her gown. The only light in the room emanated from the embers in the fireplace, casting golden highlights in her upswept hair. He could even detect the pulsing of a delicate vein in her throat against the velvet ribbon. Her blue eyes were wide with questions, and he knew at that moment that he never had seen so beautiful a woman in all his thirty-five years.

He slid one arm around her shoulders and drew her close. His other hand grasped her chin firmly, and before she could utter a sound of protest, he pulled her across his lap and pressed his lips hungrily against hers. Amelia, startled by this unexpected and audacious move, opened her mouth to protest, but Laurence, interpreting this as compliance, crushed her to his bare chest, roughly stroking her naked shoulders and the swell of her bosom before slipping his hand into the low bodice to caress her breast.

Completely unprepared for what was happening, Amelia found herself momentarily paralyzed by the overwhelming spell of this disturbing man. Her senses, against all her control, responded to his touch, and it was only the warmth of his hand upon her breast which cleared her mind.

With a surge of strength that she had not known that she possessed, she wrenched herself from his arms. Striding toward the door, she turned to Laurence, who still sat uncomprehendingly on the sofa. Her voice and body shook from anger and humiliation—and an excitement she refused to acknowledge.

"I have never met anyone who would stoop so low as you, Matthew Laurence, unless it's that seemingly kind Mr. Hunter who serves as your procurer. If I do not file charges against both of you, it will be only out of concern for my own reputation and my family's, certainly not because I don't believe that someone like you belongs behind bars!"

As she stood defiantly in the middle of the room, her entire being vibrant with anger, she was even more beautiful than she had been before. Drunkenly, Matt moved toward her, thinking of nothing but his desire to have her in his arms again. With all the strength that she possessed, Amelia struck him across his tanned startled face with such force that he staggered from the blow.

"And if you so much as look at me again, so help me God, I will have you locked away!"

Whirling away from his grasping hands, Amelia tugged the door open and rushed out, running squarely into Mr. Hunter.

"Why, Miss Donelly, how nice to—"

"No, it isn't, Mr. Hunter," Amelia shouted angrily. "There's nothing *nice* about this situation at all!"

She threw him a withering glance and hurried down the corridor to her room. She was in such a fury that she did not look back to see Hunter standing in the hallway, watching her retreat with an expression of complete puzzlement.

Chapter Four

As she entered her room, Amelia stripped the silk gown off as quickly as she could, not caring if she ripped it. Soon she stood naked in the center of the room, so angry that her thoughts were jumbled; she felt as if she were moving in a fog. Going into the bathroom, she drew a full tub of hot steaming water and slid into it so that only her head showed above the bubbles.

Taking a large sponge, she scrubbed as hard as she could. Her skin grew red and raw, but she still could not erase the taste of his lips from hers or the heat of his hand from her breast.

As she scrubbed, her thoughts ran riot. What kind of woman did he think she was? And how could she have been so wrong about him? All of her romantic day-dreams and illusions crumbled. Matthew Laurence had proven to be the most despicable of men. Behind his warm brown eyes and generous mouth lurked the mind and heart of a cad.

What a fool she had been! For a woman who considered herself of above average intelligence and well-educated, she had a great deal to learn when it came to judging men's characters. Why, even the kindly considerate Hunter had proven to be false, and she had been taken in by every bit of their scheming, idiot that she was. She was only extremely lucky that the evening had not ended even more disastrously. She dropped her head as tears of frustration and humiliation dripped down her cheeks.

Beulah found her an hour later, fast asleep in the tepid water.

"Lawh, chile, you gonna catch your death of cold," she exclaimed. "It's lucky Miss Ursula told me to come see how your head is. Now you git outta that tub this minute."

She picked up a large white towel from the basket on the floor by the tub and held it for Amelia. Shivering with cold, Amelia stepped out of the water and Beulah wrapped her in the fluffy softness of the towel.

"I'm going to get that fire started in your room, chile. You jus' dry off good and get in a warm gown as quick as you can."

Amelia took her heavy flannel gown from the hook on the bathroom door and slipped it over her head. She had never experienced such complete exhaustion and wondered where she would find the energy to put herself to bed. But her body responded with a rush of adrenaline as she heard a sound so familiar and frightening to her from her walks in the Carolina mountains: the dry, husky rattle of a snake! Moving only her eyes, she glanced at the flat basket of towels by her ankles on the floor by the tub. Coiled menacingly there was a pigmy rattlesnake!

Trying not to move, Amelia called softly to Beulah in

the next room. "Get help, Beulah, there's a rattlesnake in here."

Standing motionless for what seemed forever, Amelia kept her eyes on the snake, wondering how it had entered her second-floor room.

Suddenly Beulah burst through the bathroom door, her speed and agility amazing for a person of her size and weight. Above her head she brandished the fireplace poker, which she brought down with a loud whack. Again and again, she struck the serpent, until it lay battered and still on the bathroom floor. Then slipping the poker gingerly beneath the carcass, she lifted it up and carried it away.

When she returned, Amelia was collapsed in a heap on the floor, crying hysterically. "Dear Lord, Beulah, what else could go wrong tonight? I am such a fool." Her sobs came in long choking gasps. "All I can think is that I want my mother, and I'll never see my mother again."

Beulah placed her arms gently around the weeping young woman and helped her to her feet. After she had led her to bed and tucked the covers around her tenderly, the kind, old black woman smoothed Amelia's hair until her crying stopped.

"You jus' go to sleep, Miss Amelia, and I'm gonna sit right here in this chair until you do."

Beulah began to hum softly as she rocked. The tune of the lullaby was unfamiliar, but its soothing sound gradually calmed Amelia's jangled nerves, and slowly even her ragged breathing returned to normal. The sight of Beulah rocking in the chair by the fire was the last thing Amelia saw before she fell into a deep sleep.

Beulah, pulling open the long heavy draperies, was also the first thing she saw when she awoke the next day. From the angle of the sunlight streaming in the high windows, Amelia knew that it was well past noon. And then she smelled the roses, hundreds of them. She sat up and looked about her in confusion, certain that she must be dreaming, for every surface of furniture in her room, the wide cherry bureau, the matching nightstand, even the polished cedar mantle, held large vases of deep red roses. On the coverlet of her bed was a nosegay of pink sweetheart roses and baby's breath with an envelope attached. She saw another envelope propped against the Tiffany lamp on her bedside table.

"Chile, you done caught somebody's fancy. I never seen so many flowers in one room 'less somebody died." Beulah chuckled. "You read your letters while I get you some breakfast."

The masses of roses had distracted Amelia upon waking, but now all the ghastly memories of the night before crashed over her. She gave a low moan and dived beneath the covers, pulling them over her head to shut out the reality that daylight had brought.

But Beulah would have none of it. She pulled the covers back, plumped the pillows against the headboard, and pulled Amelia upright.

"Now you listen to ole Beulah, chile." Her dark eyes, wise and clear, stared into Amelia's blue ones. "I don't know what happened last night, but I know you well enough to know you didn't go to pieces over some ole snake. You is made of stronger stuff than that. But I do know that crying over what's past don't help none either. So you jest sit up and enjoy this beautiful day and thank God for the sunshine, and you'll see. Whatever was wrong last night, it'll sort itself out. Now you read your mail, and no more hidin' while I'm gettin' your breakfast."

Amelia stared in amazement as Beulah stomped from the room. She had never heard the woman speak so long or forcefully before. Beulah had mothered her, and it was just what Amelia needed. For the first time in a long time, Amelia didn't feel quite so alone.

Amelia picked up the nosegay and unpinned the letter. Her name was handwritten in a bold dark script. When she opened the envelope, a small white card fell out, engraved with the name "Matthew Porter Laurence." All the anger and humiliation of the previous night returned in a rush. She paused, her hands trembling as they held the smooth linen paper. Only her innate curiosity prevented her from tearing the letter to shreds instead of reading it. Slipping the single sheet from the envelope, Amelia unfolded it slowly and read:

Dear Miss Donelly:

Words are inadequate to express my horror at the terrible mistake I made last night. Please believe that I mistook you for someone else or I would never have behaved toward you as I did. I know it is expecting too much to ask you to forgive such shameful conduct, but I hope that you will find it in your heart to do so. Please accept these flowers as a token of my regret at having treated you so unchivalrously.

Please allow me to meet with you again so that I might apologize in person and perhaps make amends by giving what advice I can as to your financial situation. I also beg that you not blame Hunter for what happened, as all fault lies completely with me.

Your devoted servant,
Matthew P. Laurence

Amelia's dignity and pride had suffered wounds too deep to be healed by flowers and a mere note, however eloquent. Angrily, she threw the paper aside. She reached for the small bouquet on the coverlet and instinctively held it to her nose. Its pungent sweetness activated her senses and she remembered the sandlewood scent of Matthew Laurence's shaving soap as he had kissed her so passionately the night before. She felt a twinge of regret that only strong drink and mistaking her identity had evoked that response from him and not her, and then she blushed at her shameless thoughts.

Well, she would be safe enough from such thoughts in the future, she assured herself, because she would have nothing more to do with Matthew Laurence. Even if he did wish to see her again, her embarrassment and his would prevent her ever being comfortable in his presence. Conflicting emotions of anger and inexplicable sadness struggled within her as she opened the letter that she retrieved from her bedside table.

Also addressed to her, but in an elegant spidery handwriting, it was from Mr. Hunter and requested that she meet him on the pier the next morning so that he might also apologize and explain to her in person.

Who had Laurence thought she was? Amelia pondered. And how could she possibly face Mr. Hunter after last night?

Maude's entry into the room delayed her deliberations. Her cousin's black mourning dress and raven hair accentuated the sallowness of her complexion. Despite the faint touches of rouge on the skin drawn tightly over her high cheekbones, she looked more tired and paler than usual.

She brushed a light kiss on Amelia's forehead and sat on the side of the bed. Her hands fluttered in the air as she spoke. "Oh, Amelia, I am so sorry about your terrible experience last night! You must have been absolutely petrified!"

Amelia sat up with a shock. Who had told Maude

about her visit to Laurence's suite? Did the entire hotel know?

Her reply to Maude was prevented by Ursula's arrival. The old woman hobbled in painfully and eased herself carefully into the bedside chair, sighing gratefully as she removed the weight from her arthritic feet.

"I'm so relieved that you're unharmed, my dear. I've already made my complaint to the management. They have apologized profusely, although all these roses were quite unnecessary. A dozen would have done as well. They think the snake must have crawled into the basket of warm towels at the laundry and was inadvertently carried into the bath. This part of Florida is still mostly wilderness, and rattlesnakes are common here. You must both wear stout boots if you plan to do any walking off the hotel grounds.

"I must say, Amelia, that the excitement seems to have been good for you. You look prettier than ever this afternoon."

Her tone was more annoyed than complimentary, as she cast a sideways glance at her own homely daughter.

But Amelia didn't notice. She leaned back against the pillows, weak with relief that the shameful escapade of the night before remained a secret and that Aunt Ursula believed the roses were from the management. Ursula's inaccurate conclusions saved her from embarrassing explanations.

"Thank you both for your concern. And particularly thanks to Beulah, that snake never had a chance."

Amelia smiled as Beulah placed a tray laden with an omelette, toast, orange juice and tea across her lap. She winked at the beaming Beulah, and Beulah, moving out of Ursula's line of vision, winked back as she left the room.

"You must rest this afternoon, Amelia," Ursula insisted. "I'll have a light supper sent up to you so that you can recoup your strength for our outing to the island tomorrow. Philip has already inquired about you this morning and expressed his concern over your scare last night. He is looking forward to your accompanying us on our picnic, so you must take care of yourself."

An amused Beulah re-entered the room carrying an enormous bouquet of yellow roses and day lilies. She handed the card to Amelia and cleared a space on the bedside table for the flamboyant flowers. Amelia opened the card under the curious eyes of Maude and Ursula.

"They're from Mr. Sheridan," she explained with a blush.

The card had read: "To remind you that you are in my thoughts constantly—Philip," but Amelia felt reluctant to share that with her relatives, so she simply tucked the card into the bouquet.

"How thoughtful of him," Ursula uttered in a tone filled with irritation. "Come along, Maude, we must let Amelia rest now so she can fully recover from her harrowing experience. Take care, my dear."

"In a moment, Mother."

Maude walked to the bedside table and buried her face in the flowers Philip had sent.

"Oh, Amelia, these yellow roses are magnificent and they smell divine!"

Then she carefully rearranged the blooms, glancing casually at the card. Her curiosity was so blatant that Amelia had to suppress a giggle. She didn't want to offend her solemn, but nosy, cousin.

"Here, Maude, I'll have Beulah take some of these roses to your rooms. Then you and Aunt Ursula can enjoy them too, and I'll feel less like the guest of honor at a wake."

"Why, thank you, Amelia dear. You're very kind. And again, let me say how happy I am that you're unharmed. Rest up now for our outing tomorrow."

With a fluttering wave, she left the room.

As Amelia watched Maude retreat after Ursula, she speculated on the evidently strained relationship between mother and daughter. How different it was from the loving atmosphere she had known at home. Obviously, Ursula felt sorry for her plain daughter, which created a distance between them. And Maude went through the motions of being loving and caring, but it seemed to Amelia that all Maude's fluttering was to brush away Ursula's pitying glances. What could cause such a state between mother and daughter?

Beulah interrupted her thoughts.

"Which ones of these do you want me to take, Miss Amelia?"

"Some of the red ones, I guess, Beulah. And take some to your room, too. You should have them all after what you did for me last night."

"That's mighty sweet of you, chile. From the looks of things, you gonna have to find lots more people to share flowers with, now that you got two gentlemen friends sending them to you."

Her large body shook gently with its deep-throated chuckle as she began removing flowers from the room.

Amelia picked up the note from Matthew Laurence and wondered if she should answer it and thank him for the flowers. No, she would leave bad enough alone and forget the entire incident—and Matthew Porter Laurence.

Rising from her bed, she tore Mr. Hunter's note into fragments and dropped it into the wastepaper basket. But as she started to do the same with the note from

63

Laurence, she hesitated. Instead, she took down her copy of Jane Austin's *Sense and Sensibility* and folding the letter carefully, placed Laurence's note gently between the pages of the book before returning it to the shelf.

Chapter Five

Amelia had intended to follow Ursula's instructions to remain in her room and rest, but the brilliant sunlight streaming through the windows and the salty breeze rustling the curtains were too tempting. Besides, she had already spent too much of her time confined to the Belleview suite.

Determined to escape once more, she dressed in her lavender lawn with its high-necked bodice and long-fitted sleeves to protect her delicate skin from the hot afternoon sun and donned a wide-brimmed straw hat, anchoring it with a flowing lavender chiffon scarf tied in a large bow under her chin. The shadows created by the hat and scarf concealed her face from any but the most direct observer, and she hoped that she could get out of the hotel without seeing anyone she knew. Taking a matching ruffled sunshade, Amelia crept silently from her room and down the back stairs.

Once outside, a glance toward the water verified that

her bench on the pier was empty, and a survey of the area showed no signs of either of the gentlemen she wished most heartily to avoid. A sudden lightness filled her heart as she leisurely descended the steep stairway down the bluff and walked to the pier's end. Perhaps the strong breeze would help clear her thoughts.

She reveled in the glorious seascape before her with the sun dancing on the water, producing small explosions of colored light on every ripple of the surface. To the west lay the barrier island, misty and green in the midday haze. To the north she could see the piers of Clear Water Harbor and the long narrow bridge that connected the town to another barrier island where the residents swam and picnicked. To the east was the magnificent Belleview, and to the south, wooded hills rolled back from the bluff as far as she could see.

The woods reminded her of the rattlesnake in her room and she shuddered. Amelia had never been fearful of snakes before, although she had always treated them with respect and caution. She decided that it must have been the emotional tensions of other events that had produced the unfamiliar squeamishness and fear. She had always been cool-headed and imperturbable, the ideal temperament for a career in medicine, or so she had thought. But last night she had behaved like the stereotypical hysterical woman, a type she had always disdained, and she began to doubt if she was truly suited to a medical career, especially now without the all-encompassing support of her father.

She began to assess her situation with the logic that her parents had taught her. There were reasons for her atypical—although perfectly understandable—behavior. There was her bereavement over her parents' deaths, and her unwanted dependence on the austere

Ursula; but more than that, there was her undeniable fascination with Matthew Laurence. She knew that he was not the kind of man for her, a man of wealth and power with no respect for women, but she could not drive the thought of him from her mind nor the longing for him from her body.

She knew that what she needed now more than ever was to put the greatest distance between her and this place, but she was without the funds or means. She was certain that if she asked, Dr. Will and Aunt Beth would take her in for as long as she wished to stay, but she could see no advantage in moving from one dependent situation to another. She sat down, spreading her skirts across the bench and adjusting her parasol to block the sun. Perhaps if she put her mind to it and kept her emotions in check, she could come up with a solution.

From the window of her suite, Ursula looked down on the harbor. She had recognized Amelia instantly as she walked down the pier, her long coltish stride purposeful and smooth. Ursula closed the draperies against the sun, but Amelia was indelibly impressed on her mind's eye, the mirror image of her mother, Emily. Ursula sighed deeply to defuse the rage that was building inside her.

For twenty-five years she had enjoyed life unencumbered by the lovely and spirited Emily, Jeremiah's favorite, and now it was as if the clock had been turned back and Ursula must live once more in the shadow of her younger sister. But what was she competing for? Jeremiah was dead.

For the first fifteen years of her life, Ursula had held the enviable position of being the only child of Jeremiah and Margaret Sinclair, and she had been her father's darling. She remembered his strong arms as he had swung her up on his shoulders and her squeals of delight as they galloped at breakneck pace up and down the marble stairways of the family mansion on Chicago's Lakeshore Drive, while the formal halls reverberated with their peals of laughter.

On cold winter days, her governess, Miss Trenwith, would dress Ursula in her red velvet coat and fur-trimmed bonnet, so that she could accompany Jeremiah in the glistening black brougham for their Sunday-afternoon drives. Jeremiah would bow gravely to her as if she were one of the most important ladies in Chicago society as he assisted her into the carriage.

"This is my princess," he would boast when he introduced her to his business and social acquaintances.

As she had grown older, he had taken her to his offices and, just as if she were an adult, had begun instructing her in the business which had made their fortune, treating her as he would the son he never had.

Her mother had always been very frail. Ursula's strongest memories of her had been of the dim and silent chamber where her mother had spent most of her time in bed, smelling of peppermint and oil of wintergreen and propped up by dozens of lace-trimmed pillows as she read or received visitors. Ursula had found the sickroom atmosphere oppressive and was relieved that her mother did not require her presence often, for her father's attention had more than compensated for her mother's lack of involvement in her life. Then tragically, when Ursula was fifteen, Margaret had died giving birth to Emily, and Ursula lost her father's complete devotion.

From the moment of Margaret's death, Jeremiah had consoled himself with the small pink-and-white Emily, who would laugh and gurgle as he held her. Ursula, the awkward and insecure teenager, could not command the attention or affection that baby Emily drew from her father with no more than an infant's toothless smile. And as Emily grew into a toddler, her infectious giggles and comic antics made her father roar with laughter and approval.

Entering young womanhood, without the guidance and nurturing of a mother, Ursula withdrew into a shy and clumsy adolescent. She suffered terribly from Jeremiah's neglect and felt that she must have done something very wrong for God to punish her by taking away her father's approval and her mother at the same time. And her feelings of resentment toward Emily grew immeasurably.

With no mother to oversee her introduction into society, Ursula did not make the usual contacts that a young girl of marriageable age would have made, and so at the age of twenty-five she was still unmarried. She had no desire to marry. Men frightened her, and all she required for happiness was to remain with her father, but it was not to be. Perhaps she was being punished for her resentment toward her sister, for it was about that time that Jeremiah saw that Ursula needed a little push if she was to leave the well-feathered nest. Casting about for a likely husband for the shy, but pretty, spinster, Jeremiah settled on Daniel Hagarty, a rough handsome newcomer to the meat-packing industry with whom Jeremiah had had some business dealings. He presented Hagarty with the marriage proposition, including a sizeable dowry, and Ursula found herself married to a man she hardly knew.

As it had turned out, the less she knew of her husband, the more she liked it, for Hagarty was a man of raw appetites and unpolished manners. Ursula swore that if her father had been less preoccupied with Emily, he would never have married her off to such a lout.

Just three months after her wedding night, Ursula discovered that she was pregnant and was overjoyed at the excuse to bar Hagarty from her bed; just the sight of the man sickened her. He was never to come to her bed again, for the night after Maude was born, Daniel Hagarty was shot to death by the jealous husband of Ursula's best friend. With great relief, Ursula and the infant Maude returned home—to Jeremiah Sinclair.

Her new maternal status had instilled confidence in Ursula. Upon her return to her father's house, she had assumed the role of hostess for Jeremiah, entertaining his business friends and edging her way into the whirl of Chicago's social life, as well as picking up where she had left off in the study of business, now that she had her late husband's interests to manage. But regardless of what she did, she could never quite regain Jeremiah's total affections.

Ursula saw to it that Emily received the guidance and instruction necessary for a girl of her age and position, and on Emily's eighteenth birthday gave a spectacular ball for her debut. This attention was not entirely unselfish on Ursula's part. The sooner she could get Emily married, the sooner she would have Jeremiah to herself. But she was careful to conceal her motives from her father. Emily, however, was in no hurry for matrimony.

"Why should I be?" she would laugh. "Especially since I've never met a man who could compare to Papa."

Jeremiah would bristle with pride and Ursula would fume inwardly. It seemed she would never be rid of her baby sister. Emily loved her life in Chicago and flitted from party to party interspersed with the occasional volunteer work that was considered every privileged young woman's duty. It was at the hospital she had met Dr. Jerome Donelly during his residency.

Just as Ursula had felt it an act of God when her mother died, she also viewed Emily's elopement with Jerome Donelly as heaven sent. God had rewarded her for all her years of perseverance by removing Emily not only from home, but also from Chicago—Asheville, in fact, seemed like the ends of the earth—and finally from her father's affections as well. Ursula was well aware that Jeremiah had thought Jerome Donelly an opportunist who would disappear when he learned that Emily had been cut out of her father's will, and Ursula was equally aware that Jeremiah had never really expected that Emily would leave him. Ursula took full advantage of the situation, encouraging her father in his disinheriting Emily and continually emphasizing Emily's desertion and lack of loyalty, while she, in stark contrast, remained ever present and steadfast.

Unfortunately, as Maude grew up skinny and homely and with her mother's inbred shyness, she was such a contrast to his beautiful Emily that she was a constant reminder to Jeremiah of what he had lost. As a result, he had not been fond of the child and had guiltily compensated for his lack of affection by allowing her to run undisciplined and by granting her every wish.

When she had reached marriageable age, he had even allowed that unforgivable, though brief, engagement to that rogue, now long gone. Consequently, Maude now at thirty was unmarried, spoiled, and without friends. In fact, Ursula found her difficult to bear, and tension formed the basis of their unhappy relationship.

Ursula's brow wrinkled into a frown as she remembered Jeremiah's distress on receiving the telegram of Emily's death. He had sobbed as if his fragile heart would break.

"I've been an old fool!" he had proclaimed, suffering pangs of relentless remorse at the loss of his younger daughter.

Unexpectedly, he had turned on Ursula, too. "And you're as much to blame as I am, for you encouraged this estrangement from the first, with never a kind or reconciling word for your sister—"

He would have gone on had he not turned red in the face and begun to cough and sputter for breath until Ursula, fearing for his life, had sent for the doctor.

Ursula remembered how Jeremiah's pride had not allowed him to go back on his word and resume contact with Emily after her marriage, but he had always looked forward to her letters and Amelia's and had worried when one was late. Now the opportunity for reconciliation with Emily had been taken from him forever, but Jeremiah had felt that at least he could take care of Amelia.

"I cannot, but you and Maude must go to her," he had insisted. "The poor girl hasn't any other family. Help her to get her affairs in order, then bring her to the Belleview when the season opens in January. I'll meet you there. It is time I met my Emily's daughter. Above all, Ursula, you must assure Amelia that I will take care of her."

Jeremiah's voice had trembled, as much from age as emotion, for at eighty-six he no longer enjoyed the robust health that he had had all his life.

Ursula had no choice but to obey his wishes, but upon reaching Asheville, her possessiveness had not allowed her to convey to Amelia Jeremiah's message. In fact, she had not mentioned the child's grandfather to her at all, and Amelia in her grief had not appeared to notice.

And now Jeremiah would not be meeting them at the Belleview. He had been committed instead to the frozen ground of a Chicago cemetery. Well, at least now she wouldn't have to worry about Amelia pushing her into second place in her father's life as Emily had done before her. Now she had only to worry about what to do with Amelia, and how she was going to find a husband for Maude while her beautiful cousin was in the picture.

Oh, Maude, what am I to do with you? the old woman wondered.

She loved her homely daughter, but she had to admit that she did not like Maude very much and the responsibility of her lay upon Ursula like another penance from God.

Ursula's spirit sagged under the weight of her problems. Perhaps she should just leave it all in God's hands; after all, He'd managed her life fairly well up until now. She lay back wearily on the silk-covered chaise longue and was sound asleep before Beulah could cover her with her shawl.

Amelia stayed on the pier until the sun began to set, watching the play of light upon the clouds and marveling at the intensity of colors. At its zenith, the sky was pale pink, gradually increasing in intensity until it glowed deep orange at the horizon above the teal blue waters of the harbor. She thought that if she were to paint a perfect copy of those colors, they would appear unrealistic, frozen on canvas.

The wind had picked up and breakers from the bay were crashing on the beach beneath the bluff. As the sun dropped below the horizon, she was chilled by the cold air and she shivered in her lightweight dress. Although she was reluctant to leave the scene before her, she knew that she must get in out of the cold, and she remembered that soon Beulah would be bringing her supper to her room. She had spent hours in contemplation but she was no nearer to a solution to her dilemma. However, catching cold would not help, and the thought of more confinement to her hotel room made her anxious to get inside.

As she turned to leave, she was startled to see a man reclining on the bench. She had not heard him approach over the sound of the waves.

When he saw that she had spotted him, Philip Sheridan stood and removed his hat.

"I didn't mean to startle you, Miss Donelly. I hope you don't mind having shared the sunset with me. Why, you're shivering."

He quickly removed his woolen jacket and placed it about her shoulders. "I'm surprised to find you here," he continued. "Mrs. Hagarty told me that she instructed you to rest in your room."

"Thank you," Amelia replied, grateful for the warmth of his jacket. "I can't resist coming here because I find it so beautiful."

She remembered her manners. "In fact, the colors of the sunset reminded me of the magnificent flowers you sent today. They were thoughtful as well as beautiful." Amelia stopped, flustered, as she recalled the personal note that had accompanied them.

"May I walk you back to the hotel?"

Philip offered Amelia his arm as they walked slowly back down the pier. Neither of them spoke, listening instead to the rhythm of their steps on the wooden planks, the dry rattle of the palms in the wind, the lapping of the waves and the screeching of gulls diving for their dinner.

As they stepped off the pier onto the steps that led up the grassy bluff, Philip stopped momentarily for a look back at the now dark expanse of water.

"You're not the only one who finds this place beautiful, Miss Donelly. It was its beauty that brought the first settlers here."

"I'm not surprised. It seems almost like a paradise

sometimes," Amelia noted, and added to herself, *and a prison at others*.

While she was woolgathering, Philip had continued speaking. "Excuse me, I didn't hear what you just said. The gulls are making a frightful racket this evening."

She hoped her excuse covered her inattention. It was difficult to concentrate on small talk with all the weightier matters on her mind.

Philip, undeterred, cleared his throat and continued. "Captain Charles Wharton Johnson 'discovered' this bluff, so to speak. He was captain of a vessel that sailed regularly from Cedar Key north of here to Fort Myers in the south. This spot caught his eye every time, and he had always intended to come ashore one day, but like so many of us, he kept putting his dreams aside."

"You don't seem like the procrastinating type to me, Mr. Sheridan."

Amelia smiled up at the talkative attorney, and Philip returned her look with a warmth that made her wary.

"There is much about me that you don't know, Miss Donelly, and much I don't know about you, but I look forward to some instruction in the matter."

Amelia dropped her eyes to avoid his intense look and reverted the conversation to the safer topic they had been discussing. "How did Captain Wharton come to this place then?"

"Fate took a hand in that. In 1870 the captain and his son were shipwrecked not far from here. He liked the countryside so much, he brought the rest of his family here. Two years later he had built a house and planted a citrus grove where the Belleview now stands."

"Where are the Whartons now?"

"The soil in this particular location isn't suited to citrus and the groves failed. I believe the family located further inland where their citrus crops have been more successful."

"You seem to know a lot about the area, Mr. Sheridan. Is it that you come here so often or is history your hobby?"

"The latter, well, both actually. I have been coming here since the Belleview opened in '97, but I have always found it interesting to learn about the places I visit. I suppose I inherited my inquisitive nature from my father. He loved history so much that he became a well-respected historian. He was very good at everything he did."

The hint of bitterness in his voice was unmistakable.

"Aunt Ursula told me about your recent loss," Amelia commiserated. "I understand what you must be feeling. My father and I were very close, too."

"We were not close, really," Philip replied, almost as if talking to himself, the planes of his classic face set like stone. "We were more like competitors than father and son—and he always won."

The subject of his father seemed to draw him deep in thought, so Amelia picked up the conversation. "History has always interested me, too, Mr. Sheridan, except my particular fascination is with the ancient Greeks and their search—"

"Why would you ever wish to fill that beautiful head with Socrates and Plato?"

The fiery look that Amelia shot at Philip evoked an immediate apology.

"Forgive me, I had forgotten about your academic achievements and aspirations. I must admit I find a highly educated woman a bit frightening. I do not understand it, and I am not quite sure that I approve. However, I will withhold my judgment until I can get to know Doctor Donelly better."

The charm of his boyish grin dulled Amelia's anger. "Thank you for not dismissing me out of hand," she responded, thinking of all those who already had done just that. "I am not Doctor Donelly yet, but I am quite serious."

"Yes, I believe you are—and so am I."

His meaning could not be missed as his gray eyes met hers. But Amelia chose to ignore it, and their return to the hotel continued in companionable silence.

As they reached the foot of the lobby stairs, Philip turned to Amelia. "Thank you for your very pleasant company, Miss Donelly. I look forward to our outing on the island tomorrow with you and your family."

Again, as on the day they met, he lifted her hand and brushed it lightly with his lips.

"Thank you for a very . . . educational walk. Goodbye, Mr. Sheridan, until tomorrow."

Amelia turned to mount the stairs, only to find herself suddenly face to face with Matthew Laurence. The unexpectedness of the encounter stunned her and she was speechless. She stood entranced for a moment, gazing into his eyes before her anger from the previous night washed over her. Then stepping carefully around him, she climbed the stairs without a word of recognition or acknowledgment. She heard him call her name, but her anger kept her going as if she had not heard.

Upon entering her room, she found herself shaking uncontrollably. The strength of her feelings for that man, an incredible mixture of wrath and desire, frightened her. Part of her was glad that she had not spoken, yet another part had longed to thank him for his note and roses, and more than that, to reach up and lay her hand against his tanned cheek. She felt as if she were losing her mind. She must be mad to have any kind of positive thoughts for such an animal as he had proven himself to be. She was still shivering when Beulah entered the room with her supper tray.

"Miss Amelia, you gonna kill yourself yet, out in that night air in those thin clothes. You get some of this hot soup in you and I'll fix your fire."

Amelia sat obediently at the small table and sipped the hot consomme until her shivering stopped, but even then she continued to see a pair of brown eyes into which she could look for a lifetime and never tire.

If this be madness, she thought, *I can only pray that it is transitory*.

She found that she had spent the afternoon trying to solve her dilemma, only to find it had deepened instead.

After supper Amelia was too restless to stay in her room. She had tried reading and also writing a letter to Dr. Will and Aunt Beth, but her mind continued to wander from Matthew Laurence to her indecision and lack of independence and then back to Laurence again. Throwing down her pen in disgust, Amelia dressed in a practical warm dress of soft black wool, wrapped a thick black shawl about her shoulders and left her room.

Most of the guests were at dinner, so she was able to pass unobserved through the lobby. She turned down the west corridor and went out onto the veranda of the carriage portico. Choosing a location sheltered from the wind, she perched on the railing and leaned back against one of the intricately carved columns. Her eyes were on the harbor, but her mind was on the room almost directly above her head, and conflicting feelings over what had transpired there the previous night, which now had developed the unreal qualities of a dream, warred within her. A long shuddering sigh escaped her.

"Excuse me, my dear, but are you all right?"

A soprano voice with upper-class British intonations addressed her from the shadows of the porch.

"Oh, I didn't know anyone else was here," Amelia stammered in surprise.

"I find this a perfect time and place to escape the crush of people and activities."

The voice moved closer. At that moment a lamp was lighted in a room off the veranda and a large golden rectangle of light fell across the porch floor. Centered in the light was a small woman of regal appearance. She appeared to be in her late forties but her figure had the slimness of a girl's and her carriage was at once majestic and natural. Large green eyes and an infectious smile dominated her round face framed by a bouffant coronet of salt-and-pepper hair. She wore a cranberry velvet gown elegant in its simplicity, decorated only with an edging of schiffli lace at the bodice.

"I'm Caroline Fraser."

She looked at Amelia questioningly.

"Amelia Donelly. And I'm sorry to have intruded on you, ma'am."

"Nonsense, girl. Come sit here next to me. It will be a pleasure to talk with someone young. I've been surrounded by too many prattling old people lately. Don't the young in America ever go on holiday?"

Her question seemed rhetorical so Amelia did not reply. The white wicker chairs creaked as they sat down opposite one another.

"Is this your first season at the Belleview?" the woman asked.

"Yes," Amelia replied. "I'm here with my aunt, Mrs. Hagarty, and her daughter. It's my first visit to Florida as well, Mrs. Fraser."

"Actually, it's Lady Caroline, but I like American informality, so please call me Caroline. This is my first trip to Florida, too, although I've visited New York and Chicago several times. I'm visiting my son who lives here now. I find this area exhilarating, almost a wilderness, and surely as wild as your Western states are said to be. I look forward to visiting them someday. Do you ride, Amelia?"

"Why, yes, I do." Amelia was surprised by the sudden change in subject. "Although I ride only Western style. I've never mastered the sidesaddle."

"A barbaric custom, but better than not riding at all, which is the case with so many of you American women except, of course, the Virginians. I understand they are quite civilized. Oh, dear, I do sound horribly toffee-nosed, but I am very passionate about horses. They were an interest my late husband and I shared."

Even in the dim lamplight, Amelia could see the glistening tears in Lady Caroline's eyes. She leaned forward, patting the older woman's hand comfortingly. "I understand how you feel. It was my father who gave me my first pony and taught me to ride." Amelia's voice cracked with emotion. "And now it saddens me to know I'll never ride with him again."

Lady Caroline squeezed Amelia's hand, tossed her gray curls, and shook away her tears. "This will never do, my girl. At the Belleview we are to enjoy ourselves, not sit about weeping in our teacups. The stables here are excellent. Why don't you join me for a ride someday soon?"

"Why thank you, Lady—I mean Caroline. Neither of my relatives has shown any interest in riding, so I will enjoy the chance for an outing. If you will leave me a message at the desk, I'll ride with you.

"Splendid!" Lady Caroline clapped her hands in approval. Then she was off in another disconcertingly swift change of thought. "And I also want you to meet my son. I'm sure you two will find much in common. You might even be great friends. Good night, Amelia."

She rose gracefully, and with a swish of velvet skirts, disappeared into the hotel.

What an amusing woman, Amelia thought.

She smiled wryly at the thought of meeting Caroline's son. All she needed now was another man to complicate her life!

Chapter Six

The morning was bright and clear with a delicate breeze creating a dry rustle in the fronds of the palm trees lining the walkway to the boathouse where the hotel launch was docked. Overhead, a flock of egrets wheeled and turned in their flight across the brilliant blue of the Florida sky, then dropped like bits of white confetti toward the mangroves near the shore.

Maude pushed Ursula toward the boathouse in a bath chair and Beulah followed, bearing a gargantuan load of blankets, sunshades, and a massive picnic basket. Amelia breathed in the tangy salt air and smiled up at Philip, who walked beside her. After so many weeks of confinement, she felt like a prisoner who had just been released, and her sense of freedom was intoxicating.

"This is a wonderful day for an outing, Mr. Sheridan, and it is very thoughtful of you to include us."

"Your being here is my pleasure, Miss Donelly. I will

83

enjoy showing you the flora and fauna of the island. You'll find them quite different from those of your North Carolina mountains. The climate here is semitropical, which allows for species too delicate for our northern latitudes."

He adjusted the strap which held a pair of binoculars across his shoulder and strode forward to assist Beulah with her burden.

The hotel launch was trim and freshly painted. A small forward cabin housed the wheel but the rest of the boat was open to the sun and air and lined with wide benches stacked with soft overstuffed cushions for the guests' comfort. The two-man crew lifted Ursula carefully into the boat and settled her onto the widest bench. She raised her black parasol to shade her face, which showed the most color and animation that Amelia had seen since Jeremiah's death.

The crew stowed away Beulah's picnic supplies and assisted her into the launch, no small feat for a woman of her size. Her eyes were round with apprehension, for Beulah's stout legs had never before left land.

Philip lifted first Maude and then Amelia from the pier into the boat with an ease that told of hidden strength in his tall slender form.

"Philip, dear, come here and sit by me," Ursula commanded. "I haven't seen much of you since your arrival. You must convince me you haven't been avoiding me."

Obediently Philip settled on the bench next to Ursula and soon the two were locked together in quiet conversation. Maude sat as near them as she could, obviously listening carefully to all they had to say while at the same time leaning precariously over the side of the launch, attempting to trail her hand through the salty water.

Amelia moved to the bow of the boat, longing to feel

the wind and spray on her face, and longing as well for a few minutes away from her ubiquitous relatives. She had made a pact with herself that just for today she would put her dilemma aside and give no thought to her future or to Matthew Laurence. Today she would enjoy the pleasures of the moment, and perhaps a day's respite from her thoughts would provide her with new energy and insights when she tackled them anew tomorrow.

The crew cast off from the dock, backing the boat slowly in the water and making a wide arc, then heading it west toward the center of the barrier island opposite the hotel.

"There she goes," Matt groaned to Hunter as he watched the party board the boat. He let the draperies fall back over the window of his suite where he had kept watch as Amelia, Sheridan, and her relatives had set off on their outing.

"Amelia Donelly has to be the most stubborn young woman I have ever met! She passed me on the stairs last night and looked right through me, as if I wasn't there. Not that I blame her. But how can I ever set things right if she won't let me at least speak to her? And in addition, she seems to be spending a great deal of time with Philip Sheridan."

Matt paced the floor in frustration. For someone who was always in control of every situation, he felt helplessly out of his element now. It was one thing to behave so stupidly, but it was worse being unable to rectify it.

"Well, help me, Hunter. Don't just sit there looking mournful. She's angry at you, too, you know, and we've got to clear this whole thing up. Don't you have any ideas?"

Hunter blotted the paper he had just signed and rose from behind the large desk where he had been working since early morning on Matt's correspondence. He crossed to the window and stared out at the boat as it traveled farther and farther away from the hotel. He was worried about Matt. Never had he seen him so distracted or distraught. Yes, there had been that other matter in Chicago that still left some untidy ends undone, but that would be taken care of soon. At least Matt had finally come to a decision about that. But this was a different matter altogether. Matt had been obsessed with Amelia Donelly ever since his encounter with her on the train. Hunter had never known him to be so single-minded about a woman. Well, if Amelia was stubborn, in this case she had certainly met her match.

Hunter was worried, too, about the young lady. She had already so much to deal with that it was a shame for such a terrible mistake to have happened to her. He would have to think of some way to help the two of them. Matters could never be cleared up between them if Amelia refused to listen, and she had been adamant in that regard.

The boat had reached a point halfway between the hotel and the island, so far away that its passengers were indistinguishable one from another. Hunter turned from the window, studying Matt who still paced the room like a caged lion. There was no helping it. This was a situation that called for desperate measures. He sighed, weighing the consequences of what he was about to suggest.

"Perhaps in order to get her to listen, you must have a captive audience?" Hunter recommended.

Matt looked thoughtful for a moment then his eyes lighted and he laughed aloud. "Get your hat, Hunter! We have work to do. We can't waste any more time."

The wake of the boat, a churning froth of salt water, trailed behind them back toward the hotel, and as

Amelia watched the path they had made, she noticed several smooth gray forms break the surface. She moved astern and pointed out the sea creatures to the others.

"Porpoises," explained Philip. "They're harmless creatures and very friendly. They are even said to have rescued swimmers by pushing them back to shore when they have swum too far out and tired."

The porpoises followed the launch across the sound, turning away only when it docked at a small pier extending from the east side of the island. The shoreline was overgrown with mangroves, broken only by the dock. As the party disembarked, a large gray anhinga floated down onto one of the nearby branches and spread its massive wings in the sun to dry. On a flat of wet sand near the pier dozens of fiddler crabs scurried about in what appeared to be purposeless motion. Amelia's attention was divided in a dozen directions at once by the variety of creatures and foliage. She felt like a child again, exploring the creek behind her home. Then she experienced a sharp pang of loss, remembering that she no longer had a home.

Philip thanked the crew and arranged for them to return for their party at four o'clock. That would give the picnickers time for luncheon, rest, and exploring the island.

They left the pier, taking a path of deep sand across the island to the sparkling white beach on the gulf side. Philip carried Ursula in his arms, because using the bath chair and walking were impossible for her in the soft sand.

The island was narrow in width, so they did not have to travel far before they reached the gleaming expanse of fine white sands and the brilliant blue waters of the Gulf of Mexico, so clear that the bottom sands and passing fish could be seen easily. Tall clumps of graceful sea oats fringed the beach. A large shelter, constructed of weathered upright poles and a high peaked roof thatched with palm fronds, had been built at the edge of the dunes for the convenience of the guests, and the party stopped there to spread their blankets in its shade.

Philip kept up a running commentary on the island's wildlife. He pointed out the large nests of ospreys in the spars of dead pine trees and warned against the raccoons that would try to steal their food if they did not watch it carefully.

"If we're fortunate on our walk after lunch, we may see some of the small deer and wild pigs that live here. There are also strange creatures called armadillos which look like possums wearing armor plating. It's said that the Timacuan Indians who lived here hundreds of years ago found them tasty morsels, but I doubt if you will ever see them on the menu at the Belleview."

They seated themselves on the carriage blankets and cushions, and Beulah spread a large linen tablecloth before them on the sand. Maude helped Beulah unpack the basket, and Amelia watched, amazed at the chef's idea of a picnic lunch. In Asheville it would have been ham or fried chicken, potato salad and deviled eggs, bread and butter pickles, and homemade chocolate cake with cold tea or apple cider. But spread on the cloth before her were such delicacies as fresh tomatoes stuffed with crabmeat, an ambrosia of fresh citrus fruit and shredded coconut, a chafing dish with thinly sliced tongue of beef over fresh spinach with a Gruyère sauce, Canton ginger, candied kumquats, Neufchâtel cheese with water crackers, and several bottles of dry white wine.

The salt air and exercise had made the entire party hungry and they attacked the feast. Maude and Beulah both kept refilling Amelia's plate until she had to beg them to stop. When they had finished their meal, they were sated and drowsy and reclined comfortably on the blankets and cushions under the shelter making desultory conversation. Amelia mentioned meeting Lady Caroline, and Ursula made a clucking noise with her tongue.

"That young scamp of a son of hers will be the death of that poor woman. Since her husband died three years ago, she's had no control over Bernard at all. She had hoped that by sending him to Florida she could keep him out of trouble, but ever since William Coe opened the gambling casino just north of the hotel here, Bernard has all but lost his inheritance. Fortunately, her older son, Charles, inherited the title and family estate or Bernard would have lost that, too. Bernard had rooms in Clear Water Harbor until his mother arrived for the season. He's staying in her suite at the Belleview now, so she can keep an eye on him, I suppose."

Ursula shook her head disapprovingly. She knew what it was like to have troublesome relatives.

Amelia remembered Caroline's saying that she and Bernard might have a lot in common, and with this new knowledge, she wondered if the remark had been meant as a compliment.

"Well, I find her very interesting," Amelia countered, "and she has invited me to ride with her soon."

How had Aunt Ursula learned all about Lady Caroline? Amelia thought. Caroline did not acknowledge knowing the Sinclairs at all. Either Lady Caroline was very forgetful, or more likely, dear old Ursula was a bit of a gossip, Amelia smiled to herself.

"Then I hope you're an excellent horsewoman, my dear, for Lady Caroline sits a horse as well as any woman in England," Ursula warned.

"I should like to ride, too," Maude said. "I would like the exercise and the opportunity to meet Lady Caroline myself."

Maude's voice held all the petulance and whine of a

spoiled child, but Amelia knew her life could not be easy, tied as she seemed to be to Ursula's apron strings; Maude must have some diversion, too.

"Of course," Amelia replied, "I'm sure she would be happy to have you join us. She is really a very pleasant woman."

"Perhaps you'll ride with us also, Philip," Maude invited, but Philip shook his head.

"Thank you for the invitation, but I'll need a bit of a bribe to seduce me away from the golf courses," he answered, grinning at Amelia.

Beulah had finished packing the remains of their luncheon and had given the white linen cloth a vigorous shaking before folding it and placing it atop the basket. Ursula reclined against the cushions and was soon snoring softly. Philip placed his finger to his lips to signal silence and motioned for Amelia and Maude to join him. They began walking south along the beach, stopping frequently to study starfish and horseshoe crabs or to pick up sand dollars and colorful shells.

Suddenly Amelia was stricken with a wave of nauseating dizziness and collapsed on the beach. She convulsed with violent stomach cramps and shivered with chills. Philip and Maude rushed to her.

"It must be food poisoning," Amelia groaned.

In a state of semiconsciousness, she felt Philip lift her in his arms and carry her back to the shelter. But she was barely aware when Beulah wiped her face with a damp cloth and leaned her back on the cushions placed behind her head. She had seen many cases of food poisoning on rounds with her father, and she knew enough to know that whatever had affected her was indeed serious.

"She needs a doctor, Philip," Ursula insisted. "But how are we to return to shore without the launch?"

A soft moan escaped from between Amelia's

clenched teeth as she fought against the debilitating pain.

"I'll run back to the dock and see if I can attract a boat or somehow signal the hotel."

Philip was tearing off his tweed jacket as he spoke. "Perhaps if I wave this above my head, someone will see it."

"Here, this is better." Beulah shoved the white linen tablecloth into his hands, then turned her attention to Amelia, whose moans of pain had increased.

Philip headed across the island at a loping run, stumbling occasionally in the deep soft sand. Ursula watched until he was out of sight.

"Loosen her bodice and skirt, Beulah. Perhaps you can make the poor child more comfortable."

The three women sat in an uneasy silence, all realizing that Amelia's condition was worsening and that there was no sign of help. The minutes passed in agonizing slowness before they heard the sound of someone running up the path across the island. Onto the beach burst two men, Philip and Matthew Laurence.

Amelia saw their approach through a haze of pain and was too ill to feel any embarrassment at Laurence's presence.

He gathered her up in his strong arms and spoke to Philip. "Hunter and I will take her back to the doctor's. You stay with these ladies and I'll send the launch back immediately in case anyone else is stricken."

Amelia's eyes were closed, but she could feel the palmetto branches slap against her face as Laurence carried her across the island to the dock. The violent cramps still wracked her body and she wished that she would die rather than have to endure such agony. She heard the sound of feet on the wooden dock and felt herself being lowered gently into another pair of arms.

"You take the tiller, Hunter, and I'll look after her,"

she heard Laurence say as he scrambled down into the boat. Then she was transferred to Laurence's arms again.

She felt the boat heel to one side as its sails snapped and filled with wind and could tell from its sound as it cut through the water that they were moving swiftly. The motion of the boat accentuated her nausea. Using all her strength, she lifted herself from Laurence's arms and leaned over the side, violently sick until she felt that her body had been turned inside out. She sank weakly back into Laurence's embrace and in her delirium thought she heard him praying, "Dear God, now that I've found her, don't take her from me."

Then blackness engulfed her as she lost consciousness.

Chapter Seven

Amelia lay pale and still in Matt's arms as the small sloop knifed its way through the waters of the bay, guided by Hunter's skillful hands. Matt watched every shallow breath she took, wishing that he could breathe for her, wanting desperately to restore the color to her ashen cheeks. She was even more beautiful than he had remembered, and had he not been so afraid for her life, he would have kissed her—and more. She shivered violently. Matt removed his jacket, wrapped it gently about her and held her close to him, trying to warm her with his body heat.

Her hair smelled of sunshine and flowers, and he buried his face in its curls, praying all the while for her to live. His greatest horror would be to lose her, made greater by the fact that she still thought of him in light of his unforgiveable treatment of her in his room.

"We're approaching the dock, sir," Hunter called. "I'll find a carriage while you wait with the young lady."

Matt nodded, never taking his eyes from Amelia, anxiously watching the faint pulse in the delicate slender column of her neck and the barest rise and fall of her breasts as she struggled to breathe. When Hunter returned, he reluctantly handed her up to him, then reclaimed her once he was on the dock, running with her to the carriage where Hunter appeared before him to open the door and assist them inside.

Holding her close to him to absorb the jolts and swaying of the carriage, Matt heard her moan softly.

"Hold on, my darling Amelia," he begged. "Don't leave me now."

The carriage had taken the road from town toward the Belleview, and although it seemed a lifetime to Matt, it was only a matter of minutes before they turned into the drive of a large home set back along the bluff overlooking the harbor.

A handsome young woman with hair like flames ran out to meet the coach as it stopped at the door.

"Food poisoning," Matt called to her as he lifted Amelia from the carriage. "Is the doctor in?"

Panic was evident in his voice, and the young woman, obviously accustomed to emergencies, spoke in low soothing tones. "Dr. Winston will see her right away. Bring her in, please."

She led him into a foyer that seemed dark after the brilliant outdoor glare, then into a sunlit room with an examining table. A short, stocky man with a kind face and a gentle voice entered the room. His words and manner radiated calmness.

"Lay the young woman here on the table," he directed. "Then go with Sarah for a cup of tea . . ." He looked closely at Matt, quickly assessing the state of his alarm. "No, I think tea won't do in this case. Sarah," he addressed the red-haired woman. "Fix the gentleman a large whiskey, settle him in the waiting room, then come back to assist me in my examination."

Sarah took Matt by the arm and led him into the next room where he found Hunter awaiting him. He shrugged in answer to Hunter's quizzical gaze and paced the floor until Sarah's large whiskey, which packed a blow that Matt had not expected, took effect and he slumped semiconscious onto a leather sofa. Hunter, refusing the dubious comfort of alcohol, waited anxiously for news of Amelia and watched diligently over his employer and friend.

Soft murmurings broke into Amelia's consciousness first, but she could not identify the words or the voices. The next assault on her senses was the smell of antiseptic and the melange of odors so familiar to Amelia from her father's office. At first she thought she was back home in Asheville, but as her mind cleared she remembered her attack of illness on the island. She also remembered vaguely something about Matthew Laurence and Mr. Hunter, but she was too weak to recall clearly anything that had happened after her collapse on the beach.

She felt a cool hand lift her wrist to take her pulse and she attempted to open her eyes. An aurcole of light from a lamp beside the bed was reflected in the gold-rimmed spectacles of a middle-aged man as he studied his watch. He gave her a reassuring smile and patted her hand before tucking it back beneath the coverlet. Amelia had glimpsed someone sitting in the shadows by the window and heard the bespectacled man speak.

"She's out of danger now, sir. There's no need for you to stay. Sarah and I will keep good watch over her through the night."

"I'd rather stay, Doctor. Not that I don't believe you, but for my own peace of mind."

Amelia knew the voice, but she could not place it. All

she knew was that hearing it and knowing that its owner would be there was somehow comforting.

She awakened to full consciousness the next morning to see Matthew Laurence asleep in a large wing chair by the window. His eyes were smudged with tiredness and his tanned face was darkened by the shadow of a beard. His white flannel trousers and navy-blue blazer were rumpled and creased, and his soft cravat was loosened at the open neck of his white shirt, exposing the demarcation line of his deep tan. His thick brown hair tumbling down over his eyes gave him the vulnerable appearance of a sleeping child.

He awoke with a start as a young woman bustled into the room with a breakfast tray. Amelia reluctantly switched her scrutiny to the new arrival.

"William—that is Dr. Winston says you're to eat as much of this as you can, Miss Donelly, but especially to drink the tea as you're probably dehydrated from yesterday. I'm Sarah, the doctor's sister."

As she arranged the pillows for Amelia to sit up and placed the tray of soft-boiled eggs, toast, and tea across her lap, Amelia studied the girl. Her complexion was a mass of freckles and her hair the reddest that Amelia had ever seen. Her trim figure was covered in a sensible navy-blue dress and a stiffly starched white apron, but there was nothing stiff about her manner. She emanated cheerfulness and efficiency, and Amelia thought her perfect for assisting in a sickroom.

"Good day, Mr. Laurence."

Sarah closed the door quietly behind her as she withdrew from the room.

Laurence stood and stretched, raking his fingers through his thick hair in an effort to restore order to it but only caused more disarray. Then moving with the grace of a natural athlete, he walked to the bed and sat down on its edge. He looked searchingly into Amelia's eyes as if assuring himself that she was truly out of danger.

"You gave us quite a scare yesterday. It's fortunate that Hunter and I happened along when we did."

"I owe you my gratitude for such a timely appearance. Who knows what would have become of me if you hadn't brought me here so quickly? It was lucky for me that you were on the island."

Amelia sank back against the pillows, still weak from her ordeal, as well as breathless from the confusion that reigned inside her; attraction and anger toward Laurence waged war in her heart.

"It wasn't entirely luck, though," Matt assured her. "When you didn't meet Hunter so that he could apologize, he was very upset. We had watched you depart for the island and thought perhaps that if we could corner you there as a captive audience, you would give us both a chance to explain. So we rode into Clear Water Harbor and rented the sailboat. We had just begun tacking toward the island dock when Sheridan appeared waving a large white cloth."

"Philip! Is he all right? Was anyone else affected?"

"It's very strange that you were the only one stricken, since all of you shared the same food, but Hunter reported to me last night that your entire party had returned safely to the hotel, shaken but in good health. You didn't eat any berries or fruit or nibble any twigs or foliage on the island, did you?"

"Of course not. I'm not a city girl, Mr. Laurence. I know better than that."

Amelia was indignant, angry not only at his implication that she would have done something so foolish but also at the seed of suspicion he had planted in her mind. The foreboding that she had felt on her journey to Florida washed over her again, and she turned her concentration to the handsome man at her side to drive away the fear that someone might wish her serious harm.

"I didn't mean to insult you, Miss Donelly. I'm just trying to make sense of some very strange circumstances. Now, you follow the doctor's orders and eat your breakfast while I make the speech I had prepared for you yesterday. I'm not sure that it has improved with the delay, but since I did come to your rescue, the least you can do is hear me out."

Amelia nodded her consent, although still somewhat wary of being alone with the same man who had used her so shabbily. Surely the kind doctor and his sister would not leave her with someone who would do her harm. Still very confused, and not knowing whether to be angry or glad, she motioned for him to speak and began picking disinterestedly at her food.

Realizing that she was not going to eat, Matthew removed her tray and sat down on the side of the bed. He picked up both her hands and held them clasped in his. "Please promise that you will listen carefully to what I have to say, Amelia, because these are the most important words I have ever uttered in my life.

"Hunter had told me that you would be coming to the suite at eight-thirty that night and he waited there with me until shortly after nine to introduce you. I must admit that I have had some worrisome personal matters in my life lately, and that evening I tried to forget them by drinking too much. However, the drinking alone was not the reason for my behavior. I never would have forced myself upon you in that way.

"As I mentioned earlier, I've had some personal worries and unhappiness lately. One of the reasons was a beautiful woman who fell into my lap on the train and then seemed to disappear from the face of the earth. You see, even though I had not seen her face, I knew that more than anything else, I wanted to meet and know her. I loved her, just from that brief encounter.

"I had been very despondent because I thought I had lost this woman forever. Angus, my golf caddy, suggested that what I needed was some female companionship. He jokingly said that he would send someone up to my room to keep me company that night. I really did think it was a joke until you arrived."

"You mean you thought I was—" Amelia gasped. "Why, that's horrible! I would never—"

"Yes, but I mistook you for someone—something— else only because by that time I had drunk too much to think clearly. All I could think of when I saw you was that you were the most beautiful and desirable woman I had ever seen. It wasn't until you stormed out of my suite and Hunter returned that I recognized the magnitude of my compounded mistake. Not only were you Hunter's friend, but from your voice and fiery exit, I realized you were also the woman from the train, my Madame X, and I was afraid that now you would hate me forever. Do you hate me, Amelia? Can you forgive me?"

Amelia paused before giving her answer. She knew that this was a smooth and experienced man, and that she had no expertise in matters of the heart and was therefore doubly vulnerable. But the look in his dark brown eyes melted away her misgivings.

"I could never hate you, Mr. Laurence, especially after your help in bringing me ashore to the doctor when I was so ill. And as for forgiving you for the other night, it seems to have been a comedy of errors that is best forgotten by us all."

His relief was visible in the wide smile that lit his face. "In that case, I have two requests. First, will you have dinner with me tomorrow evening? Dr. Winston has assured me that you should be fully recovered by then.

And second, would you drop the Mr. Laurence and call me Matt?"

Enchanted by his charm and the sincerity of his apology, Amelia had only one answer. "Yes, Matt, I look forward to dinner with you tomorrow evening." She looked up into his eyes but found it necessary to lower her gaze, so shaken was she by the depth of feeling she read there. "And thank you again for rescuing me."

"Good-bye, Amelia, until tomorrow." Brushing a soft kiss upon her forehead, he departed.

She lay back on the pillows, feeling that she was taking part in some distorted dream, part nightmare, part fantasy, and that soon she would awake in her own bed to hear her mother calling that it was past time to get up. But her mother would never come to awaken her again, and Amelia wished her mother were there to advise her what to do. With both her parents dead, she would have to rely solely on her own judgment from now on. She hoped that the decision she had just made to trust Matthew Laurence was not one that she would regret. Physically and emotionally exhausted, she closed her eyes and drifted back into a light sleep.

Dr. Winston was standing by her bed when she awoke again. "How are you feeling, my girl? You certainly had a nasty touch of something."

"I'm much better, Dr. Winston, just still very weak." Amelia smiled back at the plump little man.

"Another twenty-four hours of bed rest should take care of that. Strange case, yours. Can't understand why the rest of the folks weren't ill, too. Ghastly stuff, whatever it was. Might of killed your aunt at her age and with her condition. The only thing that saved you was emptying your stomach over the side of the boat."

Amelia paled at the thought of how close she had come to death. Several weeks ago when her parents had died, she would have welcomed an escape from living, but now she felt that she had someone to live for, and life had become very precious indeed.

"It's very strange that no one else was affected," the doctor continued. "Do you have any allergies, to shellfish, for instance?"

"No, I'm not allergic to anything that I know of. I don't have that kind of constitution."

"Well, perhaps it was only a brief upset of the stomach, caused by an illness you may have contracted from the other guests. Don't let it worry you, my dear."

Amelia reflected on her confinement, a type of quarantine as such, of the past weeks, and knew that it would be highly unlikely that she had caught anything from the guests. And if it was an illness that had been transmitted through their food, then Maude and Ursula would have been stricken as well. No, she knew too much about medicine not to recognize that whatever had affected her had been swift and deadly, almost certainly contained in the meal that she consumed on the island.

"Poison?" Amelia asked.

"Ahem, well, that's a pretty strong charge." Dr. Winston's brows knitted in thought above his gold-rimmed spectacles. "Besides, a pretty young girl like yourself surely can't have that kind of enemy. And you were with your family, weren't you?"

"Of course, Doctor, the idea of poison is absurd. Perhaps the chef at the Belleview used some exotic ingredient in his cuisine that I've never had before and my system reacted violently."

"Yes, that must be it." Dr. Winston agreed too heartily and too quickly. "Now you must try to put the entire matter from your mind. And I have just the trick for that. You have a visitor, if you feel up to it. Lady Caroline is here to visit her son. When she heard you were here, she asked to see you. May I send her in?"

Amelia nodded. Dr. Winston left the room and only seconds later Lady Caroline entered. She wore a traditional black riding habit, and although her stride was youthful and energetic, her face reflected her age this morning. Her eyes looked puffy and tired, and there were noticeable furrows between her brows.

"My dear girl, I'm so sorry to hear of your frightful experience. I came to see Bernard. He was in an—uh—accident last night, and Dr. Winston told me that you were a patient also. But you look splendid! How do you feel?"

"I'm almost recovered, thank you. And how is your son? I hope his accident was not serious."

"A few cuts and several unsightly bruises, but he'll recover. Somehow my Bernard always manages to land on his feet."

She sighed deeply and a look of grave concern momentarily replaced her cheerful expression. Then her smile broke through again and her eyes twinkled as she rose to leave.

"I know my sickroom manners well enough not to tire you, so I'll be on my way. I hope your recovery is swift and complete, my dear. We must ride together soon. The only way to appreciate this country is on horseback."

She squeezed Amelia's hand affectionately, crushed her hard black riding hat with its flowing veils firmly onto her gray curls and left in a whirl of skirts.

After Lady Caroline had gone, Amelia dozed fitfully. She had a recurring dream in which she felt threatened and afraid and kept calling out for help, but there was never anyone in the dream to answer her cries. She awoke at lunchtime enveloped with a sense of uneasiness and dread precipitated by her nightmares, and the mood stayed with her in spite of her practical admonitions to herself in broad daylight that she had nothing to fear.

Dr. Winston brought her lunch, and she spent the lunch hour talking with him about his practice and sharing some of her experiences from her father's rounds. He commiserated with her on her difficulty at being admitted to medical school, but expressed the prevailing male viewpoint that as soon as she married and had children, she would forget about medicine and a career. Amelia was growing accustomed to this patronizing attitude and knew that he genuinely believed it; besides, she was still too weak to argue, so she merely smiled and murmured that perhaps he was right.

Her next visitor was Philip Sheridan. In his arms was a large clay point containing an orchid plant covered with exquisite tiny yellow blossoms. He placed it on her bedside table and pulled up a chair beside the bed.

"You look wonderful, Miss Donelly. I was so frightened for you yesterday. I was afraid you were dying, but now you look as if you had never been ill. Are you feeling better?"

"Yes, I seem to be on the mend. You are very kind, and I thank you for your help yesterday. I'm very sorry that I spoiled our outing. The island is such a beautiful place."

"Then we'll plan to go again, as soon as you're feeling up to it. Dr. Winston said you would be able to leave tomorrow morning. I'll bring a buggy from the hotel to take you back. I know your Aunt Ursula and Maude will be relieved that your recovery has been rapid and complete. They would have come to see you themselves, but the excitement yesterday was too much for Mrs. Hagarty, and Maude felt she must stay with her."

"I understand," Amelia replied. "And I'm sorry to

103

have caused them any worry. They have both been so good to me since Mother and Father died."

Philip seemed uncomfortable with the subject of her parents' deaths. He rose from his chair and walked to the window from which he could see the dormers of the Belleview in the distance. He stood for several minutes as if studying the landscape before he turned back to face her. "Miss Donelly, I hope you don't think me presumptuous, but I would be very honored if you would dine with me tomorrow night. I will ask your aunt for her approval, of course, but—"

"I appreciate your invitation, but I already have an engagement for tomorrow evening."

Philip gave her a puzzled look. "I didn't realize you knew anyone else at the Belleview."

"Matthew Laurence has asked me to dine with him," Amelia said.

She was astonished to see his eyes flash with anger and the hard lines of his face made it look as if it were cast in stone.

"I'm sure your aunt would not approve."

His tone was cold and disapproving, and Amelia felt annoyance building within her. This was the second man who had patronized her today.

"I am of age, and whether my aunt approves or not is of little consequence to me. She has been kind to me and I am thankful, but not to the point where I will allow her to choose my friends." Amelia's eyes blazed with defiance.

"Amelia, you are making a terrible mistake in going out with that man. I strongly urge you—"

"I don't need your approval either, Philip," she snapped back, then suddenly feeling very weak, she lay back upon the pillows.

"Very well, if that's the way you feel, then I bid you

good day, Miss Donelly." He turned on his heel and abruptly left the room.

There had been poison in Philip's glance as he departed. *Poison.* Amelia shuddered. Even thoughts of tomorrow with Matthew Laurence could not chase away the desolate loneliness that engulfed her. And now that loneliness had a companion—fear.

Chapter Eight

Philip Sheridan's behavior was punctiliously polite but cool and distant as he assisted her into the buggy for her return to the Belleview. His handsome jaw was set in a firm line and his gray eyes refused to meet hers.

But Amelia would not allow his fit of pique to diminish her pleasure at being alive and out in the open air. Her fears of the previous day had vanished in the sunlight, and her avid curiosity took in every detail as they approached the Belleview.

The winding road ran between an avenue of stately pines, whose needles formed a carpet on the road and deadened the sounds of the horses' hooves and the buggy wheels. Emerging from the pines, the road then passed between massive stone pillars bearing the gates which marked the beginning of the hotel grounds. The ornate bridge, which crossed a shallow creek in a deep ravine at the entrance, included several small shops built within its supporting arches, and Amelia hoped to explore these. As the road curved up a hill toward the hotel, it passed several cottages, three-story Victorian houses with ornamental turrets and gingerbread trim, which could be rented by families for the entire season.

Not until the buggy pulled under the west portico did Amelia become aware that Philip had said very little during the entire journey from the doctor's house to the hotel. He gave her his hand as she alighted, but he still would not look directly at her. She was undaunted by his attitude. Nothing could spoil this perfect day for her. Tonight she would be with Matt, and everything else held little significance.

She thanked Philip for bringing her to the hotel and hurried up to her room. She was still weak from her ordeal, and she intended to spend the day recuperating so that she could enjoy the evening to the fullest.

She was greeted solicitously by Ursula and Maude and crushed into an embrace by Beulah whose cheeks were wet with tears.

"Lawh, Miss Amelia, when that Mr. Laurence carried you off that island, I never thought I'd lay eyes on you alive again. You was one sick girl!"

"Not anymore, Beulah." Amelia laughed. "Give me a good long nap this afternoon, and I'll be fine. If I oversleep, be sure to wake me by five o'clock. Mr. Laurence is taking me to dinner."

Hurrying to her room, she did not see the long look that Ursula and Maude exchanged behind her back.

The deep violet taffeta of her dinner gown rustled about her as Amelia pirouetted before the full-length mirror. The simplicity of the high neckline and softly draped sleeves of illusion was the perfect foil for her youthful beauty. She pinned the spray of creamy white camellias in her hair and reread the card that had come with them: "Amelia, I have waited a lifetime for tonight. Matt."

Everything was perfect—almost everything. When she had awakened from her nap, she had been summoned by Ursula.

"Sit down, child," she had commanded. "I feel a great responsibility for you, my late sister's only child, so I will be quite frank. I do not approve of your association with Matthew Laurence. As you have already accepted his invitation for this evening, and in light of the fact that he saved your life by conveying you to the doctor when you were so ill, I will grudgingly allow you to dine with him. But tonight is the end of it, is that understood?"

"But why, Aunt Ursula? What is it that makes him unacceptable to you?"

"My reasons are my own, Amelia, and need not concern you. What must concern you is that after tonight, you will not, you *must* not, spend any more time with that man. Do I make myself clear?"

"But, Aunt Ursula—"

"Quiet! I will not be crossed in this matter. Will you show your gratitude for all I have done for you by flouting my wishes?"

Amelia bit back an angry retort. Obviously now was not the time to reason with Aunt Ursula. Later when Amelia felt stronger, she would remind her aunt of her independence and her right to choose her own friends.

"I don't wish to appear ungrateful, Aunt. I do appreciate everything you've done for me."

"Then let that be the end of our discussion."

"Yes, Aunt," Amelia agreed, but only for the moment. Later she must assert herself so that she did not have to live under Ursula's thumb as poor Maude did.

A knock on the door of the suite sent Amelia rushing into the parlor. Ursula and Maude had gone down to dinner earlier, but Beulah was there to answer the door. Matt stepped inside, resplendent in formal black and white, even his tousled mane under control for the occasion. He bowed to Amelia, offered her his arm, and led her out into the hallway. As the handsome couple descended the wide stairs into the lobby, heads turned to stare at them. Even among the beautiful women and attractive men so common at this resort, Matt and Amelia were outstanding, not only in their physical attractiveness but also in the aura that surrounded them. They walked through the lobby and down the corridor to the Tiffany Room, oblivious to everything but each other.

They lingered for hours over a dinner which they barely touched. Hunter had told Matt much of Amelia's story, but there were gaps that needed filling, and Matt, wanting to learn all that he could, plied Amelia with questions.

"You have me at an unfair advantage," she insisted. "You now know the story of my life, but I know almost nothing about you. Tell me about your family."

"You would love my mother. In fact, you're like her in many ways. She's a Southern belle, too."

He smiled across the table at her and the candlelight glimmered in his brown eyes.

"My Grandfather Porter raised horses in Kentucky, and my mother, Catherine, was his only daughter. My father was an officer in the Union cavalry during the war and was headquartered at the farm. Father was one of the few men Grandfather had ever met who understood and loved horses as much as he did, so that even though they had their political differences, they at least agreed on the important things in life—good horses.

"When the war ended, Robert Laurence, my father, asked Catherine to marry him. Grandfather had died shortly before Appomattox and had left the stables to my uncle, John. Times were hard in the South after the war, so Father took Mother back to Chicago. He always said it was a place with a future.

"Unfortunately, there wasn't much future left for my father. Not long after I was born, Father was killed trying to rescue some children trapped in a burning apartment building near the bank where he worked. Mother became a dressmaker to support us.

"Things would have been a lot rougher for us if it hadn't been for Phineas Dayvault, president of the bank where my father had worked. He saw to it that I received an education and gave me a job at his stables after school and on weekends. One Saturday—I must have been about sixteen then—Mr. Dayvault's regular caddy at the country club was ill and I was called on to fill in. I soon began caddying regularly. That's where I learned to love golf and also learned a great deal about investments by staying very quiet and paying attention.

"Mr. Dayvault liked me and I must admit that I admired him greatly. He paid my way through the University of Chicago with the understanding that I would work for him after I finished my degree. With my income from the bank I began a careful program of investments in stocks, land and commodities and was surprisingly successful. Others noticed my success and began to come to me for advice. With the blessings of Mr. Dayvault, I opened my own investment counseling firm and have lived comfortably ever since. But a fortune is not always a blessing, Amelia. When everything you want in life comes too easily, nothing has much meaning. Or at least it didn't until I met you."

Amelia blushed under the intensity of his gaze and shook her head. "Perhaps it is boring to have everything," she replied, "but it can't be as frustrating as wanting something with your whole heart and not being able to have it."

"Anything, Amelia, anything at all. You have only to say it and I will see that it is yours."

With other men, such a declaration would have seemed pompous, but Amelia felt his strength and knew that he did not make empty promises.

Matt's hand reached across the expanse of white linen for hers. Their eyes met and locked, and in that moment the strength of their emotions grew unbearable, forcing Amelia to look away.

Unable to bear the emotional tension any longer, Amelia stammered, "But you haven't told me about your mother. Where is she living?"

"Mother stills lives in Chicago, no longer dressmaking I might add. When I made my fortune, I had a beautiful townhouse built for her, exactly as she wanted it, and I live there with her. However, Mother and I are not speaking to one another now because—" He stopped short, as if suddenly remembering something he wished that he had not.

Amelia, not wanting any unpleasantness to mar this enchanted night, quickly changed the subject. "And where did you meet Mr. Hunter?"

"Now that is a story in itself." Matt laughed. "I met him on a cold, blustery Christmas Eve in Chicago. I was hurrying home from work to change for a party for which I was already late. There had been an unseasonable thaw that day, and careening around a corner, I ran directly into a strange gentleman and was knocked flat on my back into a mud puddle in the street. I was furious! The gentleman was very drunk, but he pulled himself up in a very dignified manner and informed me that I now had a spot on my suit. It struck me as funny and I laughed, until I noticed that the man had no overcoat and was shivering violently in the rapidly dropping temperature. So I took him home with me.

"He never would share much with me about his

background, but when I asked him what kind of work he could do, he informed me that all he knew was how to be a gentleman. I hired him then and there as my valet. That's been ten years ago and he hasn't touched a drink since. He's also turned out to be the best friend I have."

Matt looked across the table at Amelia. Her hair shone like gold in the candlelight and her skin had the same translucent creaminess as the camellias in her hair. The smoldering emotion in his face made her tremble. Her hand shook as she raised her wine glass to her lips.

"You're trembling." Matt placed his hand over hers to steady it. "Are you overtired? Should I take you back to your room?"

"No!" Amelia shook her head vigorously. "I feel better than I have in months. But I mustn't keep you from your work."

"Miss Donelly, if for one moment you believe that I would rather spend my time with dry dull financial reports instead of with you, you must think me a very deranged man indeed. What I had in mind, if you're sure you're recovered enough, is some dancing in the ballroom. Do you waltz?"

"Certainly, Mr. Laurence—"

"Matt. Remember your promise."

"Very well, Matt, I find the prospect of dancing with you delightful."

Amazed at her immediate response, Amelia thought she must have gone mad. Never in her life had she flirted so outrageously with a man. What had happened to the sensible smalltown girl she used to be?

As they walked up the corridor to the ballroom, they could hear the hotel orchestra playing "Roses from the South." The ballroom was a mass of whirling color and humanity.

Matt turned to her with open arms. "You see, Amelia, I'm a very devious man. I have found a perfectly legitimate and acceptable excuse to hold you in my arms. Shall we?"

Amelia slipped into his arms as if she had been born there. The pressure of his hand at her waist was at once comforting and disconcerting and the long slender fingers of her right hand were cradled in his. She resisted an overwhelming desire to lay her head on his shoulder and instead looked up to find him studying her closely.

"So you're here at the Belleview primarily to play golf?" Amelia hoped the introduction of a mundane subject would help to calm the fierce beating of her heart.

"That's one of the reasons, of course, but another has to do with business, some very unsavory business."

A hard glint shone in his eye, and Amelia felt a slight shudder, hoping that she would never do anything to provoke that look. But then his look softened and he gazed down at her.

"But land fraud does not concern me now. This, Amelia Donelly, is where you belong, and I promise to do everything in my power to keep you here with me always."

Amelia could not trust her voice, but the light in her eyes answered for her.

They were the last couple to leave the ballroom, and the tall case clock in the lobby was striking two o'clock as they entered.

"It's been such a glorious evening, Matt, and I'm not the least bit tired. Let's not have it end yet," Amelia protested.

"I am yours to command," he answered.

Matt took her arm and led her to the south corner of the lobby where a grand piano stood in front of the tall French windows.

"Do you play?"

Amelia nodded and sat down on the wide bench. She played a few measures of a Chopin etude, then struck the opening chords of her father's favorite song. Matt sat beside and began to sing softly.

> *"Believe me if all those endearing young charms,*
> *Which I gaze on so fondly today,*
> *Were to change by tomorrow, and fleet in my arms,*
> *Like fairy gifts fading away,*
> *Thou wouldst still be adored as this moment thou*
>   *art,*
> *Let thy loveliness fade as it will;*
> *And around the dear ruin, each wish of my heart*
> *Would entwine itself verdantly still!"*

His rich baritone voice caressed her as he sang. She began the second stanza and sang with him:

> *"It is not while beauty and youth are thine own,*
> *And thy cheeks unprofaned by a tear,*
> *That the fervor and faith of a soul can be known,*
> *To which time will but make thee more dear!*
> *No, the heart that has truly loved never forgets,*
> *But as truly loves unto the close;*
> *As the sunflower turns on her god, when he sets,*
> *The same look which she turned when he rose!"*

When the song was finished, she turned to him with tears glistening on her cheeks. She knew that her father would have approved of this man. "Oh, Matt," she whispered.

He enfolded her in his arms and pulled her close, brushing her lips with a tender kiss. Then his embrace tightened and his mouth sought hers, crushing her to him in a surge of passion. Amelia felt herself losing all control, the only reality of time and space was the strong arms which held her and the kiss which touched her to the core and enflamed responses that she had never known that she possessed.

Suddenly Matt pulled away. "Forgive me, Amelia. I don't want you to think that this is a repeat of the other evening. I haven't had too much drink to use as an excuse, although I am intoxicated by you. But I keep forgetting that you have been ill and should have been in bed hours ago. I'll take you to your room."

And with a flourish, he picked her up and carried her slowly up the lobby stairs. She nestled her head against his shoulder, entranced with the happiness of the moment. Outside the door of her room, they stopped.

"Thank you for the most wonderful evening of my life, Amelia. Rest well, and I will call on you tomorrow."

He kissed her gently on the lips before she slipped inside the door, then walked down the corridor to his suite, whistling softly under his breath.

Amelia had completely forgotten Ursula's edict, and had she remembered, it wouldn't have mattered.

Chapter Nine

The trilled cadenza of a mockingbird awakened Amelia early that morning to the heat of the famous February Florida sun that had warmed the room, making a fire unnecessary. A warm glow spread through her as she remembered her evening with Matt, and she looked forward to seeing him again today. Amelia threw back the covers and climbed out of bed. She thought of her parents, and for the first time since they had died, she did not find herself overwhelmed with sadness; instead, her happy memories comforted her.

She stretched energetically, thankful for the youthful resilience that had enabled her a swift recovery from the food poisoning and had allowed her to dance until the early hours of the morning with no ill effects. After hurrying through her morning bath, she braided her long hair and coiled it in a crown around her head, then pulled on a fresh white shirtwaist and her black bombazine skirt.

When she entered the parlor of the suite where Maude and Ursula were already having breakfast, she knew immediately that she must spend as much time outdoors today as possible, for her old feelings of claustrophobia had enveloped her again.

"Good morning, Amelia," Ursula returned her greeting. "I was just informing Maude that you girls must be on your own today, as Philip and I have a great deal of business to attend to and will need to use the parlor. I'm certain that with all the activities available to you here at the hotel you will find some way to pass the time."

"Of course, Aunt Ursula." Amelia struggled against sounding too relieved. "I plan to find a comfortable spot and curl up with a good book."

"Goodness, Amelia, you'll ruin your eyes with all the reading you do, but suit yourself."

Her aunt seemed distracted with other matters, and Amelia did not want to call attention to herself. She especially did not want Ursula inquiring about her evening or making any more pronouncements about Matt, so she quietly finished her breakfast as quickly as possible, hoping that Maude would not ask to accompany her.

"Amelia," Maude began, and Amelia's heart sank. "I'm sorry I won't be able to spend the day with you, but I believe it best if I stay close by, in case Mama needs me."

Amelia tried to look disappointed and failed.

"As long as you aren't underfoot, Maude," Ursula agreed. "You must stay in your room unless you're called."

"Why, of course, Mama." Maude nodded.

Amelia felt a twinge of pity for the woman, shut away in her room for another day, even if it was by her own choice. She excused herself from the table, returned to her room for her hat and book and slipped quietly out her door which opened into the hallway. She wanted to get safely away before either Maude or Ursula changed her mind.

Running lightly down the stairs and through the lobby, she fled to her bench at the end of the pier, anxious for solitude in which to relive every exciting moment of the night before. Her original instincts had been right all along, she reassured herself. Matthew Laurence was a most wonderful man, and Hunter truly was as kind and gentlemanly as he had seemed.

Adjusting the brim of her straw boater to keep the sun off her face, Amelia leaned against the bench and closed her eyes, hearing again the lilting waltzes of the night before and remembering Matt's arms about her as they danced.

For the moment, the problem of Ursula's prohibition against her friendship with Matt threatened to burst the bubble of her morning's happiness, but Amelia thrust thoughts of Ursula away. She would deal with her later. For now, after so many weeks of pain and grief, it was magnificent to feel happy again, and she reveled in the sensation. Her reverie was broken by the snap of luffing sails.

"Ahoy, Amelia!"

She opened her eyes to see Matt easing a sailboat next to the pier and throwing a line about one of the dock posts.

"Matt, how did you know I'd be here?"

"I didn't know. I went into Clear Water this morning to rent the boat and had planned to come and get you when I returned. Now you've saved me the trouble, for here you are. You must have read my thoughts. In addition to your many other talents, you're not telepathic by any chance?"

Matt was laughing as he climbed onto the dock, securing the boat before settling next to her on the pier bench.

"How would you like to spend the day exploring the coastline by sailboat? We could sail north toward Anclote Key and then back, perhaps with lots of fascinating stops in between? Are you up to it after your late night?"

Matt's boyish enthusiasm was contagious. A day with Matt, especially one miles away from tiresome relatives, was Amelia's idea of heaven on earth.

"I would be crazy to turn down such an offer. When do we leave?"

"As soon as we take on supplies. In fact, here they come now."

Matt pointed to the top of the bluff where Hunter was directing two members of the hotel staff, both laden with baskets, flasks, and cushions, toward the pier. Hunter hurried down to meet them, tipping his hat courteously to Amelia.

"Good morning, Miss Donelly. I'm delighted to see you looking so well after your ordeal of a few days ago."

"I owe you my thanks for your part in my rescue, Mr. Hunter. Had you and Matt not been there, things might have ended differently."

The sight of the picnic hampers revived memories of her near fatal experience, and Amelia gave an involuntary shudder. Her preoccupation with Matt had removed all thoughts of poison and mayhem from her mind, but now they came tumbling back.

"Please," Hunter insisted, "I did not mean to inject any unpleasantness into your day. The weather is beautiful, the chef has outdone himself in packing your picnic lunch, and you are in the hands of a most capable seaman. I bid you *bon voyage*."

"Thank you," Amelia replied, shaking away gloomy

thoughts at the prospect of the adventure before them, and accepting his hand as he assisted her down into the boat. Matt was already on board and rigging the sails.

"Yes, thank you for taking care of all this, Hunter. Now if you would also see to those reports for me today and that other matter I can enjoy myself with a clear conscience," Matt called as the boat glided away from the pier.

"Consider it done, sir."

The wind caught the sails as they moved away from the dock, and the boat picked up speed, cutting silently, but swiftly, through the crystal-clear waters of the bay. Matt tacked carefully to guide the craft through the narrow channel between the two offshore barrier islands and into the Gulf of Mexico. Then he headed the boat north, parallel to the shoreline, which was mostly pine forest and palms, varied only by an occasional house set back into the trees or a small dock.

Amelia settled back on the cushions on the deck, luxuriating in the feel of salt spray and sunshine on her face. She looked at Matt, who caught her gaze and smiled from his seat at the tiller. She was perfectly happy. There was no need for conversation, for the two shared the comfortable companionable silence of those who find joy simply in each other's presence.

The winds were favorable and within an hour they were in sight of the lighthouse on Anclote Key. Its windows gleamed in the sunlight above the tall pines, and at its base beyond the mangroves along the shore stood the cracker house of the lighthouse keeper with its stilted foundation and wide, covered veranda that encircled the structure.

Matt lowered the sails and ran the boat onto the beach at the island's north end. Removing his shoes and stockings, he rolled his flannel trousers almost to his knees, then jumped overboard into the shallow water to push the boat even further ashore. The tide was at low ebb, so he secured the anchor in the sand to keep the boat from drifting away with the incoming tide.

Then he held out his arms to Amelia and carried her to the beach. He spread a canvas from the boat in the shade of a stand of pines at the beach's edge and conveyed the baskets, cushions and flasks to their picnic spot.

"Here you are, my girl, all the comforts of home." He grinned at Amelia. "What is your pleasure? Have lunch first and then explore the island, or vice versa?"

"The island first, please."

They walked leisurely from the island's northern tip to its south end and back again, collecting colorful and exotic shells, watching the adjoining woods for signs of wildlife, and marveling at the great colonies of seabirds of all types and sizes.

As they passed the lighthouse keeper's dwelling, Amelia studied it carefully, taking in its foundation of stilts, high peaked roof, and its wide wraparound verandas.

"Why do they call these 'cracker' houses, Matt? I've heard the word used often in reference to many things here in Florida, from people to houses to cooking, but I can't figure it out."

"It puzzled me, too, until one of the grooms at the Belleview explained it to me. Most people, myself included, are not aware of how much cattle are raised in Florida. The central part of the state particularly has great herds of them, and the cowboys who manage these herds use huge bullwhips that they crack in the air over the animals' heads to move them along. Hence, the name 'cracker.' Now the term has come to be associated with anything native to the state."

"Cattle in Florida," Amelia marveled. "What a multitude of surprises this state holds."

"And you, my darling Amelia, are its most lovely surprise of all."

He pulled her to him as they stood among the dunes, tasting the tang of salt on her lips as he kissed her gently at first, then with a growing desire as he molded his body to hers.

Shaken by his intensity, Amelia pulled away. "Right now, Matt, I'm starving. Let's attack the picnic baskets, shall we?"

Reluctantly, Matt released her and headed back up the beach. If one hunger could not be assuaged, at least he could appease another.

When they returned to their campsite, Amelia unpacked the hampers of lunch, happy to see that the chef had prepared plainer fare for this luncheon than for her previous picnic.

"So tell me, Amelia, how did you come by this passion for medicine?"

Matt waited for her answer as he polished off his third piece of fried chicken.

Amelia leaned back on the stack of cushions at the base of the tree, watching a flock of pelicans diving offshore as she worded her reply. Having Matt understand how she felt about becoming a doctor was terribly important to her, so she was careful to express herself well.

"Without question, it's all tied up with my father. I wish you could have known him. He was such a gentle and caring man, but the foundation of all that care and gentleness was an unwavering strength and dedication.

"When I first began accompanying him on his rounds—I was still a little girl—I noticed that when my father would arrive at a house where there was sickness or injury, the atmosphere would almost immediately change. People would become less grim, tensions would ease. It wasn't until I was much older that I realized what was happening. My father's very presence, as well as his skill and bedside manner, drove away fear. He taught me that many times it is our fears that kill us, not accident or disease. We give in to terror or despair and we are lost. He knew how to drive that fear away.

"And now that I am old enough, twenty-one to be exact, that is what I want to do for people, not only alleviate their physical sufferings, but ease their mental anguish as well, so that they can draw on their own inner resources to aid in their recovery.

"The worst thing in the world is to be sick and frightened, so I want to rid the world of as much fear and illness as I can."

Amelia took her eyes from the diving birds and looked at Matt. The look of love and admiration in his eyes embarrassed and discomforted her, so she immediately changed her tone. "However, since I have no money to attend medical school and would have great difficulty, being a woman, gaining acceptance even if I had the tuition, there is not much chance of my following in my father's very large footsteps."

"Oh, but there is, Amelia. Hunter told me of your small inheritance. With the proper investments, you could probably make enough to pay for your books and tuition. Would you consider allowing me to work up a portfolio for you?"

Amelia found it difficult to believe her ears. Her father had been the only man she had ever known to encourage her in her career, yet here was Matt encouraging her as well.

"Yes, I think that might be a very good idea indeed!" Amelia laughed with delight at the thought that her dreams of medical school might actually become reality.

Matt found her more beautiful than ever when she laughed. Her cheeks and the bridge of her nose were pink from the sun and wind, and although her golden hair was coiled in braids at the crown of her head, small tendrils had escaped, softly framing her face. Her blue eyes sparkled like sapphires with laughter, and her lips, soft and full, begged to be kissed.

He swept her into his arms and kissed her passionately, wanting never to let her go, pressing the soft curves of her body into his with an urgency he had never known. He felt her stiffen slightly beneath his touch and knew that he had gone too far. For all her intelligence and her twenty-one years, Amelia was still inexperienced in the ways of love. He must be careful not to frighten her away. Reluctantly he released her, running his fingers gently across her cheek and down the slender column of her graceful neck before turning away.

"Forgive me, I had no right—" he began.

"You have every right," Amelia replied, "because I believe I've fallen in love with you, Matthew Laurence."

"And what do you know of love, my innocent Amelia?" Matt queried. "How many broken hearts have you left in your wake, you of the sapphire eyes and golden hair?"

"Are you making fun of me?" Amelia's temper flared.

"No, I am very serious when it comes to you," Matt insisted. "Now tell me truly, is there no one waiting for you to return to him in Asheville?"

"There was once, but not anymore," Amelia admitted. "Robbie and I grew up together. His family lived next door. He always swore that he would marry me, but he couldn't reconcile himself to a wife with a college education. He married Cordelia Johnson while I was away my first year of school."

"I'm sorry."

"Oh, no, you mustn't be. Robbie and I were great friends as children. We rode together and explored the mountains behind our homes, and I helped him with his homework. But we wouldn't have made a good marriage. We both knew that."

"Why not?"

Matt thought the young man in question must have been foolish indeed to have let such a prize as Amelia escape him.

"When I marry, it must be to someone I can love as my parents loved one another. They had so much in common. They enjoyed the same books, shared a sense of humor, took pride in each other's accomplishments. Robbie is a fine young man, but he'd rather play checkers with the men at the smithy than read a book. And when he kissed me, it was never—" Amelia stopped, embarrassed at the turn the conversation had taken.

"Yes?" Matt encouraged her with a twinkle in his eye.

"Well . . ." Amelia swallowed hard and plunged on. "He never kissed me as you do."

Matt needed no further prodding to kiss her again.

Amelia, weakened after a moment by the tumult of her own senses, pushed him away with a question of her own. "Matt, I have a favor to ask of you."

"Anything, dear."

"Aunt Ursula has forbidden me to see you."

Matt sat up and his voice was sharp. "Did she say why?"

"She said the reasons needn't concern me, that I should only do as I am told."

She was so engrossed in her problem that she did not notice that Matt had visibly relaxed at her reply.

"But," Amelia continued, "as my presence here today proves, I will not let my aunt run my life. However, my relationship with her would be so much more pleasant if she approved of you, and I know she would if you would only go to her and speak with her—"

"No!" Matt spoke so fiercely that Amelia jumped.

"No," he repeatedly softly. "I don't think that would be a good idea. There are some things I need to tell you, Amelia. I don't know how to explain. I can only ask that you trust me for a while longer, even if it means deceiving your aunt. And as soon as I can, I will explain everything to you. Will you trust me?"

Deceit was foreign to Amelia's nature, and Matt's request was puzzling and worrisome. What was he hiding? But as she looked up into the dark brown eyes pleading silently with her, she could give only one response. "Of course, Matt. I won't let Aunt Ursula know that I'm seeing you, not for now, at least."

A gust of strong wind shook the pines above them, and Matt looked to the northwest to spy a line of menacing gray clouds of a rapidly approaching squall.

"Grab everything you can, Amelia. We have to beat this weather back to the hotel or we're in for a drenching."

Talk of love and deceit was forgotten in the rush to load the boat and outrun the storm. Once they were underway, the howl of the wind made communication impossible except by shouting. The boat heeled to one side, pushed by the strong winds, and Amelia looked down into the churning green waters as she held on tight. She found the entire experience exciting rather than frightening as she watched Matt's expert handling of the craft in the strong wind and rough seas. By the time they reached the Belleview, the sky had darkened overhead as the storm caught up with them and large drops of rain began to fall.

"Get into the hotel before you're soaked, Amelia."

Matt turned away, working hurriedly to secure the boat, and abruptly dismissed, Amelia raced up the bluff and into the shelter of the lobby.

"Amelia! Mama sent me to find you. She was worried with the storm coming."

Maude met her as Amelia was ascending the stairs, fluttering about in her usual nerve-wracking manner.

"She wants us to have dinner in our rooms tonight. Her session with Philip today has tired her out."

Maude stopped fluttering long enough to study Amelia as she climbed the stairs beside her.

"Where have you been, Amelia? You're all windblown and"—Maude gave a horrified little gasp—"sunburned!"

"Of course I'm sunburned. I've been walking on the beach most of the day," Amelia replied with irritation, not sure if her unease was with Maude's inquisitiveness or her own secretiveness. Everyday brought new complexities to her life, but at least she had the compensation that along with them had come Matthew Laurence. Smoothing her tousled hair, she followed Maude meekly into the parlor to face Aunt Ursula and dodge her questions.

The next morning Beulah slipped a note to Amelia as she arose, requesting she meet Matt at the stables. She dressed hurriedly in riding clothes, asked Beulah to convey to her aunt that she would be riding most of the day, and slipped away before having to face any interrogation from her relatives. She had gotten off easily the night before. Ursula had been so preoccupied with her business with Philip that she had shown no curiosity at all about her niece's whereabouts during the day.

The day had dawned clear and cold after the storm, which had washed the foliage clean and added freshness to the air. Matt was waiting for her at the stables.

"They'll be bringing the carriage round in a few minutes. I thought you might enjoy a view from land of the surrounding countryside today. That is, if you have no other plans." Matt smiled down at her. "Even though the weather has turned cool, the sun will be out and we should be very comfortable in an open carriage."

"It sounds wonderful," Amelia agreed. "I've told my relatives that I'll be riding most of the day. Will that give us time for exploring?"

"Enough." Matt nodded. "But not as much time as I'd like."

Amelia had to look away from the depth of emotion in his eyes. The groom brought the carriage around, and Matt lifted her into it.

"We'll head east into the groves and then back to Clear Water Harbor," he explained as he turned the horses down the avenue and through the stone pillars at the hotel gate. Within a few minutes, they had left the hotel behind and were riding through a forest of pines and moss-draped oaks.

"What is that heavenly fragrance?" Amelia asked as the wind wafted a perfumed scent their way.

"You'll see." Matt smiled.

Around a bend they came to cultivated land, row after row of glossy-leafed citrus trees, some bearing golden globes of fruit while others were covered in blossoms.

"It's the orange blossoms you smell," Matt explained. "The orange crops are unusual in that different varieties bloom at different times, so sometimes a grove will be thick with fruit and blossoms at the same time."

Matt stopped the carriage and jumped out, going to a nearby tree and picking an orange, which he sliced neatly into sections with his penknife and offered to Amelia. She bit into the luscious fruit and its juice ran down her chin, but Matt came to the rescue, wiping her face with his handkerchief.

"It's magnificent!" Amelia exclaimed. "Not at all like the fruit we have back home."

"You can't beat tree-ripened fruit for its sweetness," Matt explained. "You know, I've never thought of myself as anything other than a businessman, but I think I would enjoy working the land, raising a crop like this."

"And give up Chicago?"

"Chicago and all that goes with it—with the exception of my dear mother, of course—has bored me for years. In fact, it's only since I met you, Amelia, that I have lost that boredom. Even everyday matters are exciting to me again."

He gave her chin another tender wipe with his handkerchief and clucked at the horses to continue. They passed through a small community with a general store and a tiny church, saw homesteads in the distance set back in orange groves, and eventually arrived on the outskirts of Clear Water.

Matt handed her down in front of a pleasant, but plain, boarding house, explaining that they would be able to have lunch there. They were met at the door by a smiling woman with a red face and sleeves rolled to her elbows. She showed them to a table by the fire and left to prepare their meal.

"Matt, I know you have asked me to trust you, but when can I tell my aunt that I am seeing you? This creates a very awkward and uncomfortable situation for me."

A look of such pain crossed Matt's face that Amelia was immediately sorry that she had asked. "Never mind, I shouldn't have mentioned it. Let's enjoy our day together."

"Tell me about Asheville, Amelia," Matt requested, relieved at the change of subject.

"Oh, it was a wonderful place to grow up, Matt." Amelia's blue eyes sparkled as she spoke of home. "The town is nestled in a small valley surrounded by the Blue Ridge Mountains. Living there is like living in a separate world, apart from everything else. But our wonderful secret is getting out. Boarding houses are springing up all over town where people can come for the summer season, or for their health, if their doctor recommends mountain air.

"It's a close-knit community. Everyone knows everybody else—and their business. But they are good-hearted, friendly people. Except for the Biltmores, none of them is very wealthy. They all work hard for their living—" Amelia stopped abruptly, embarrassed by the implications of what she had just said. But Matt only laughed.

"Don't worry, my dear, there's no offense taken. I had always thought of myself as a hard worker, but next to the people you described, I'm sure to appear quite the man of leisure. That probably accounts for my boredom. In fact, I've been thinking lately how a new line of work—hard work—might be just what I need.

"Amelia, my love, you make me see things about myself in ways I've never thought of before. You're very good for me, don't you know?"

"Yes, Matt." Amelia looked at him with eyes alight with love. "I believe we're very good for each other."

With heads close together, they ate the plain, delicious fare the boarding house offered, talking of books they had read, music that they enjoyed, and all the trivial things about one another that people in love share. The hours passed so quickly that Amelia was surprised to see that the sun had sunk low in the western sky.

"I must go back now," she said reluctantly.

Matt released her hands that he had held lightly in his, tracing the lines in her palms as they talked. He sighed resignedly.

"Yes, it's time. But there is something I want you to have before we go. I had Hunter locate this for me yesterday. I was insistent that you have this, even if he had to send a messenger to Tampa to find it—which he did."

He withdrew a small package from his coat pocket and handed it to Amelia. Blushing with pleasure, she turned back the tissue paper to reveal a rosewood box, the top of which was inlaid with other woods in the shapes of a floral bouquet. Lifting the lid gently, she exclaimed in delight as the tinkling music of "Believe Me If All Those Endearing Young Charms" filled the air. But there was more. Attached to the velvet lining of the lid was a tiny brass plaque engraved with the words from the song, "The heart that has truly loved never forgets."

"Oh, Matt, it is so beautiful. How can I ever thank you?"

"There is no need for thanks, Amelia. Just being with you is thanks enough for me. And now I must get you home before you incur the wrath of Aunt Ursula." He made a mocking, scowling face.

Amelia laughed with delight. Her life had never been so happy. Inadvertently, she remembered her readings of Chinese superstitions and hoped that the gods would not be jealous of her joy.

Chapter Ten

"Miss Amelia, are you sure you knows what you're doing chile?" Beulah asked as she helped Amelia pull on her riding boots the next morning.

"Whatever are you talking about, Beulah?"

"Don't you go all innocent-eyed with me. It's Beulah you're talking to. Don't I know you ain't been off by yourself these last two days? Don't I know that fancy music box didn't just spring outta thin air? Be careful, chile. You're still all heartsore from losing your mama and daddy. Don't go jumpin' into sumpin' you gonna regret."

Amelia lifted the lid of the music box that sat on her dresser. Its pure notes filled the room as she finished putting up her hair.

"You're a love, Beulah." She smiled and kissed the old woman's cheek. "But you needn't worry about me. I know what I'm doing."

The maid shook her head sadly. "Younguns . . ." she

muttered under her breath. "You can't tell 'em nothing. Why'd they always have to learn the hard way?"

"I'm going for a ride this morning, Beulah. If any messages should come for me, please don't let Aunt Ursula or Maude see them, will you, dear?"

She ran her finger lightly over the inscription before closing the lid of the music box gently, picked up her hat and gloves, then whirled out the door, leaving Beulah behind, shaking her head sadly at the whole state of affairs.

Amelia had decided to have breakfast at the buffet in the dining hall to save time. She had a euphoric feeling that today was going to be a very special one, and she didn't want to waste a minute of it. She slowed to a ladylike pace as she reached the stairs to the lobby, moving as quickly as she could without sacrificing her dignity.

She restrained an impulse to descend the stairs two at a time, crossed the crowded lobby and entered the dining hall. It was a glorious day; in fact, every day that had Matt in it was a glorious one.

Lady Caroline was seated at a table near the door, and when she spied Amelia, she waved her over. "Fill your plate, my dear, and come join me."

Amelia was ravenous and remembered sheepishly that she had barely touched her dinner the night before, having been so engrossed in her memories of her days with Matt. As she filled her plate with sausage and scrambled eggs, she surveyed the room to see if he was there. Not seeing him, she decided that he must either be still asleep or out on the golf course for an early tee-off time.

As she sat next to Lady Caroline, a waiter filled her coffee cup and placed a large glass of freshly squeezed orange juice at her place. After yesterday, oranges would always remind Amelia of Matt. She wished she could share her love for him with Caroline, but she honored her promise to keep their meetings secret.

"I see you're planning to ride today." Caroline observed. "I wish I could join you, but I promised Bernard that I would keep him company. He's very self-conscious about his appearance and won't leave the suite."

"He is recovered then?" Amelia asked.

"In all but his pride. My Bernard is a very foolish young man, Amelia. Gambling had become an obsession with him, and now he is indebted to a very unsavory character. His 'accident' was a dunning notice, a threat that he must pay what he owes or they will do him even worse harm. The thugs beat him unmercifully. Most unfortunately, we can't go to the authorities without implicating Bernard and his dubious borrowing activities. I'll never understand how that young rascal manages to get himself into such messes."

Lady Caroline looked so unhappy that Amelia felt sorry for her. She reached over and patted her hand. Caroline's face brightened.

"Why don't you join Bernard and me in our suite for tea at four o'clock today? He has been so peevish at being shut in, but he refuses to let the other guests see his dishonorable bruises, so he keeps himself shut away. Your company should be just the thing to cheer him up."

Amelia had been hoping to spend the afternoon with Matt, but she could not tell that to Caroline, or to anyone for that matter; nor could she bring herself to disappoint this woman who was fast becoming a friend to her.

"I'd like that very much," Amelia said, thinking that she could leave a message with the desk clerk to tell Matt her whereabouts.

They drank a second cup of coffee and talked of

upcoming events on the social calendar at the Belleview, including a performance by the hotel's opera company and also the spectacular costume ball held every year at Mardi Gras. Amelia noticed an outdated copy of the *London Times* folded by Caroline's plate.

"Do you get homesick for England, Lady Caroline?"

"Not yet, my girl." She laughed. "Robert Browning knew what he was saying when he wrote, 'O to be in England, now that April's there.' Only a fool or someone who delights in misery would wish for London in February. Well, I must return to Bernard, and you should be off if you're to ride this morning."

They left the dining room and walked together into the lobby where their path was blocked by a barricade of trunks, portmanteaux, and hat boxes. Bellboys, the desk clerk and the resident manager were hurrying about, solicitously accommodating the registration of a new guest.

Standing to one side watching the hubbub with a look of cold disinterest was a tall, statuesque young woman. She was dressed elegantly in a sapphire-blue traveling suit which accented the beauty of her pale blond hair. A large hat of matching blue with several ostrich plumes and a flowing veil partially obscured her face, but even from a distance Amelia could see the high cheekbones and full bow-shaped mouth. The long coat of her traveling costume was molded to her voluptuous figure and emphasized her ample bosom and tiny waist. Across her arm, she held a boa of ermine and with a flick of a well-manicured hand, she directed several maids in the disposition of her luggage.

"Who is she?" Amelia whispered to Caroline. "Even royalty doesn't get that kind of attention around here."

"She's Diana Barrington, and her father is one of the wealthiest men in Chicago. She's probably here for a visit with her fiancé, Matthew Laurence. I hear their engagement party last year outdid even Mrs. Potter Palmer's reputation for . . . What is it, Amelia? You look ill."

Lady Caroline's announcement had struck Amelia with the force of a physical blow, and she found that she could not speak. She felt as if all the air had been compressed from her lungs, and she could not breathe. All that she could think of was escape. She had to get away from there before Matt came to welcome his bride-to-be. How could she have been such a fool! She had assessed him correctly that night in his suite. Why had she ever let him change her mind? She was still standing there in shock when Caroline's voice broke through.

"Amelia? Amelia!"

She could not speak, so she simply shook her head and ran back down the corridor from which they had come and out the east door toward the golf course. All she wanted was to place as much distance between herself and the hotel as she possibly could. Stumbling across the lawns, she reached the stables at last and demanded a horse from one of the grooms.

"And be quick about it!" she screamed, frantic in her need to flee.

Pacing up and down while the horse was being saddled, she castigated herself for her foolishness. Matt had never indicated that he was engaged. Was that why he wished to keep their meetings a secret? Of course! And just as clearly why he refused to speak to Ursula, for she would know of his engagement. Oh, he must have thought it clever to distract himself with Amelia when his fiancée wasn't around. It was clear now that he had seen her only as a romantic dalliance during his vacation before he returned to Chicago and the bonds of matrimony. The night he had accosted her in his suite, her body had felt dirty and used, but now she felt that he had sullied her soul.

Oh dear God, I'm hyperventilating, she thought as the first wave of dizziness struck her. She sat quickly on a nearby bale of hay and lowered her head between her knees, trying to control her breathing and her temper. A groom approached her warily and announced that her horse was ready.

Swinging astride the mount which the groom held for her, Amelia felt the urge to ride as far and as fast as she could so that the wind would scour the hurt and stain from her heart. She headed north on the road toward Clear Water Harbor and gave the horse its head.

The rush of wind against her face dried her tears as they fell, but they kept coming. Amelia cried until her lungs ached from sobbing and still she rode. She slowed momentarily to pass through the city blocks of the small town, turning her head to avoid the boarding house where they had spent much of yesterday, and continued on. Finally she realized that the horse was beginning to tire, and as she reached a bridge that crossed a wide inlet, she dismounted and walked the horse while it cooled down.

Tasting the water of the inlet, she found that it was fresh and allowed the horse to drink. She wet her handkerchief and wiped her face. Tying the horse to a palmetto bush, she sank down onto a bed of needles beneath several large pines and leaned back desolately against one of the trunks. She tried to think clearly and logically about her problem, but the pain that was swirling inside her would not let her. Her heart was a battleground for the love and hate that she felt for Matthew Laurence, and she found no easy resolution for the conflicting emotions. She sat, transfixed, unable to cry another tear, yet also unable to move.

To Amelia, the passing time seemed like a few minutes, but in actuality, the sun was now on its downward
course and a chilly breeze was blowing off the water.
The wind awakened her spirit, and she knew that love
had won the battle. She also knew that there was
another battle to be fought, and fought daily. For
although she loved him, he belonged to that goddess in
the lobby, and Amelia would have to live without him.

In the distance she heard a masculine voice calling
her name softly. She could see only the shadow of a man
silhouetted against the sun. For a moment her heart
leapt within her as she thought it was Matt, but as he
moved toward her, she realized that it was Philip
Sheridan.

"Amelia, I've been searching everywhere for you.
Lady Caroline was worried when you ran off without
speaking, and she asked me to look for you. What in
heaven made you run away like that?"

Embarrassment and shame caused Amelia to blush,
and she could not meet Philip's eyes. Now she understood his objections to her friendship with Matt. She
had thought him patronizing, but he had only been
observing the appropriate social mores and perhaps
had even been concerned for her reputation. A proper
young woman doesn't have dinner alone and go dancing
with a man who is engaged to someone else.

"I'm afraid I owe you an apology, Mr. Sheridan. You
were correct in your disapproval of Matthew Laurence.
I thought you were meddling, but now I know that you
were only being kind. I saw his fiancée today. He hadn't
told me that he was engaged."

Amelia spoke between clenched teeth, trying desperately to hold back a new onslaught of tears. Anger and
sadness battled inside her as she forced herself to look at
Philip.

"I guess I came very close to making a complete fool

of myself." She forced herself to smile.

"You don't need to apologize to me, Amelia. I know the last few months have been difficult for you and you haven't been yourself. Let's forget about Matthew Laurence and start over. Shall we? Now, we need to get you back to the hotel before your aunt begins to worry."

His boyish smile was so understanding and nonjudgmental that Amelia wanted to cry all over again. She nodded her agreement, touched by his concern and the warmth of his smile, while a voice within her screamed that she would never forget Matt, not if she lived to be a hundred and fifty and forgot everything else she'd ever known. But then another inner voice asked where was her pride, and she knew then that no matter what else happened, even if she continued to love him until her dying day, she would never let Matthew Laurence see how much he had hurt her.

Philip offered his hand and pulled her to her feet. She brushed the pine needles from her skirt, while Philip retrieved her horse and held it as she mounted, then gracefully swang into his saddle. They rode at a slow walk back to the Belleview. Amelia struggled to block Matthew Laurence and the pain he had caused her from her mind and to concentrate on Philip. He must have sensed that she did not feel like talking, for he attempted to entertain her with bits of local history as they returned to the hotel.

It seemed to be one of Philip's quirks to ramble on about history when no other subject seemed safe, but Amelia welcomed his control of the conversation and found herself escaping into his story to forget, however briefly, the pain she was feeling. Just south of Clear Water, he pointed out where Fort Harrison had stood during the seven-year Seminole Indian War.

"It was built in 1841 primarily as a place where sick

and wounded soldiers from other forts in Florida could come to recuperate. I'm sure you know full well the healthful benefits of this climate as well as the restorative properties of the view overlooking the harbor."

Philip smiled down at Amelia only to notice that she still seemed quite withdrawn and was only half listening to his narrative.

"After the war ended in 1841," Philip continued gamely, "the Indians were still on the warpath, so Congress enacted the Armed Occupation Act. Any settler who would come armed to defend and live on the land for five years was given 160 acres. That's how much of this county was originally settled."

Amelia looked at the oak groves draped in Spanish moss and thought of hostile Indians lurking there. She shuddered, and Philip, perceptive of her reaction, changed the topic to the development of the citrus groves and some of the local flora. Suddenly he stopped, dismounted, bent to the ground and returned with a tiny red wildflower.

"Legend has it, Amelia, that if you place this Valentine flower under your pillow, you will dream of someone you love, even though he may be faraway."

"Thank you, Philip. It is so delicate . . ." Her voice trailed off to a whisper, and she was once again overwhelmed by her thoughts of Matt.

It is beautiful, she thought, *but I will not need magical flowers to keep Matt in my dreams.*

Philip, ignorant in the ways of love, did not immediately notice that he had only conjured up the painful events of the morning. Flustered at his own stupidity, he asked if she would have dinner with him that evening. This time she did not refuse.

When she returned to her room, she found a note in Matt's handwriting and a dozen red roses. Without reading it, she tore the note into tiny pieces and hurled them and the roses into the fireplace. She grasped the music box from the bureau top, ready to hurl it into the fire with the note, but she could not bring herself to destroy it. She would keep it as a penance, as a symbol of her own foolishness and vulnerability.

Then she remembered that she was to have tea with Lady Caroline and Bernard. If she hurried, she would have just enough time to bathe and change clothes and still be there by four o'clock. She had no desire for socializing, but her fear of being alone with her memories and pain outweighed her reluctance to keep her appointment. She began to draw water for her bath.

Although she had eaten no lunch, Amelia had no appetite for the delicious array of cakes and sandwiches that Caroline tried to tempt her with. The desolation she felt made her stomach revolt at the thought of food, and the constriction in her throat made swallowing anything other than the strong hot tea impossible. She turned her attention to Bernard, hoping that by studying him she could drive the images of Matt from her mind.

Bernard was an attractive young man about her own age, slight in build and with his mother's merry green eyes. At least one of them was green. The right one was still swollen almost completely shut as a result of his encounter with the thugs. His left arm was in a sling, but he assured Amelia that it was not broken, only badly sprained. He showed no embarrassment over his injuries but seemed to accept them as payment for his own foolhardiness.

"Mr. Coe's casino is a very fine establishment, Amelia, and as honestly operated as games of chance can be. It was when I began borrowing money from those characters that hang out there that I created my own trouble.

I've been promised more of the same if I don't pay up soon, but at their exorbitant interest rates, I can't afford to pay up, and I'm not about to bankrupt Mama. I despise the thoughts of this happening to anyone else. Once I'm able to leave this suite, I'll keep both eyes open to get some clue that will lead me to the head of this operation. Then we can turn them all in to the authorities."

"But aren't you running a terrible risk?" Amelia asked.

"Perhaps, but I don't see that I have any other choice."

"Well, enough of this dreary talk," Lady Caroline interjected. "I want to know what plans you've made for the Mardi Gras Ball that's coming up in a few weeks. Have you decided on a costume, Amelia?"

"No, I haven't, for I don't think I will be going."

Amelia felt as if she would never dance again unless, of course, it was on Diana Barrington's grave. She horrified herself with the viciousness of that thought. It wasn't Miss Barrington's fault that her fiancé was a cad. With difficulty she focused her attention on Lady Caroline.

"Why, my dear, it's the high point of the social season here. You must go! It's an extravaganza that you won't want to miss. Everyone tries to outdo everyone else as far as elaborate costumes are concerned. Some take it so seriously that one ball is barely over before they start planning for the next."

"Mama is planning to go as Queen Elizabeth this year. I was going to be Sir Walter Raleigh, but with these new facial decorations, I'll have to choose a costume that includes a more elaborate mask." Bernard laughed.

Amelia tried to enter into the spirit of the conversation, but she could not shake the gloom that had enveloped her since Diana Barrington's arrival that morning. As soon as she could do so politely, she excused herself, thanking Lady Caroline for tea. She promised to come soon to read to Bernard while he remained confined to his room, then departed.

When she reached her room, she threw herself face down on her bed, too sick at heart to cry and too physically exhausted to move. Thoughts swam through her mind in a jumbled mass, but the one emotion that finally pushed itself to the forefront was self-pity. As she lay there, the feeling of pain had given way to humiliation, then pity, and finally, to anger, not at Matt, but at herself.

Amelia sat upright on the bed and caught her reflection in the mirror on the cherry bureau.

"Amelia Sinclair Donelly," she admonished herself aloud in the empty room, "how dare you let such a cad of a man affect you so! You will not allow him the satisfaction of thinking he has hurt you! Where is your pride? Tonight you will dine with Philip Sheridan as if you haven't a care in the world."

She dressed carefully in her black silk dress, pinning up her hair with the spray of black feathers. As she placed her mother's cameo on the velvet ribbon around her neck, she forced from her mind the memory of the last time she had worn it. She pinched her pale cheeks to bring color to them and picked up her black lace shawl.

Maude and Ursula were seated in the parlor of the suite. The small table was set for dinner and a waiter was removing chafing dishes from a cart to the table.

"Amelia, you look lovely," Maude said in her typical fluttering fashion.

"Yes, you do look lovely. I just am not feeling well enough for formal dining tonight. Maude has agreed to dine here with me. What would I do without you, my girl?" Ursula smiled enigmatically at Maude, who helped her to the table.

"You run along and have a good time, Amelia. We will probably retire early this evening."

Beulah opened the door of the suite for Philip. He greeted Ursula and Maude and presented Amelia with a corsage of gardenias which she pinned to her black jet bag. Bidding her relatives good night, he escorted her out the door.

Amelia took a deep breath, lifted her head high and gave Philip a dazzling smile. If she could carry this off tonight, she thought, she really should consider a career on the stage.

As they passed through the lobby, her heart began to beat rapidly, fearing that at any moment she would see Matt with his voluptuous blond fiancée on his arm, but she recognized no one except the desk clerk, who nodded to them as they passed.

The Tiffany Room was crowded, but here also Amelia saw no one she knew as her eyes scanned the room, and relief surged through her. She might make it through the evening after all.

"You are more lovely than ever, Amelia," Philip complimented as he gazed across the table at her. "There is not a man here tonight who doesn't envy me the company of such a beautiful woman."

Amelia thanked him with a smile, thinking how good it was to have a friend like Philip, especially now when her self-esteem had been so cruelly shaken. She still had no appetite, so she asked Philip to order for her. As he did, she studied the self-confident, capable man before her. There did not seem to be any situation that he could not handle with ease and finesse, except possibly rejection, she thought, reminded of the first time he had invited her to dine with him alone. No wonder Aunt Ursula relied on him so heavily.

As their waiter had served their roulade of beef and filled their glasses with burgundy, Amelia felt herself begin to relax. Perhaps she would be able to enjoy the evening after all. But her calm was quickly shattered as she heard Matt's voice at her elbow.

"Good evening, Miss Donelly, Sheridan. May I present Miss Diana Barrington?"

Philip stood and bowed politely. "How nice to see you again, Miss Barrington. Did you just arrive?"

"Yes, this morning, after an impossibly long and boring train ride, even though Matt was kind enough to provide his private car for me." She spoke in low husky tones that matched her sensuous appearance.

Amelia kept her gaze on the Tiffany panels at the far end of the hall, all too aware of Matt's proximity. She felt her throat closing up again and was unable to speak. All she could manage was a polite, but cool, nod to Diana before the couple moved on to their own table several yards away. Amelia feared she was going to hyperventilate again and directed all her attention to regulating her breathing. She wanted to give Matt no indication that he had affected her in any way; no, she would not give him that satisfaction.

Philip sat down and gave her hand an encouraging pat. It was as if he sensed her inner turmoil and she felt herself responding to his concern. Looking up, she gave him a thankful smile. In turn, he lifted his glass to her in a toast. "To Amelia, the loveliest woman at the Belleview," and his eyes were warm as he sipped his wine.

She studiously avoided looking in the direction of Matt's table, even though she remained achingly aware of his presence. She kept her attention on Philip, who entertained her with stories of growing up in Chicago. He kept his voice soft and low so that Amelia had to lean forward to hear him. She did not see Matt's constant stare at the two heads bowed close together in the candlelight, or Diana's look of fury as she noted the object of Matt's concentration.

When they had finished dining, Philip asked Amelia if she would like to walk in the rose garden. The night air was balmy and sweet, a potpourri of fragrances. Toward the west, the half moon cast a silver path across the water of the harbor. Amelia wrapped her lace shawl around her shoulders and took Philip's arm. They strolled lazily along the garden paths and down the bluff to the waterfront.

Amelia forced her thoughts away from the three nights before, which now seemed to be an eternity ago, when she had waltzed in Matt's arms. Perhaps she should have been warned by the intensity of her happiness that it could not last. It was like phosphorus that burns hot and bright and then disappears.

Turning her thoughts from Matt, she attempted to focus on more practical matters. She knew that she must begin thinking realistically about her life. Her dreams of a career in medicine and founding her own hospital were impractical, and impossible without Papa, she admitted to herself. But if not that, what?

Philip intruded on her thoughts. "Amelia?"

"I'm sorry, Philip, my mind was wandering over what I am to do once the season ends here. I can't continue being dependent on Aunt Ursula's hospitality, but I can't seem to formulate any plan of action."

"I've advised Mrs. Hagarty for many years, Amelia, and I believe she has been well pleased with that advice. Give me some time to think on it, and I will be happy to advise you, too."

Amelia laughed self-consciously. "But I can't afford the fees you charge my aunt, Philip."

"The only payment I'd expect from you, my dear Amelia, would be the pleasure of your company. I can't remember when I've spent so enjoyable an evening as tonight. We must do this more often."

Even in the moonlight, Amelia could see the light in his eyes as he looked down at her, and she knew that she was unready for any relationship other than that of simple friendship. Suddenly a wave of exhaustion swept over her. The tumultuous emotions of the day had taken their toll, and she felt drained and tired.

"I have enjoyed spending the evening with you, too, Philip, but suddenly I find that I am very tired and really should return to my room."

Philip apologized for keeping her out so late as they climbed the bluff back to the hotel. When they passed through the lobby and ascended the stairs, Amelia did not see Matt and Diana emerge from the corridor. Matt watched with an unreadable expression as the couple climbed to the second floor and disappeared from view.

Philip said good night to Amelia at her door. She went quietly inside so as not to disturb Ursula and Maude, removed her dress, leaving it in a mound on the floor, slipped on her warm gown and climbed into bed. Sobbing softly, she fell asleep.

She slept so soundly that she did not hear the key turn in the lock or the door to her room open softly later in the night as a dark figure entered and stood at the foot of her bed, gazing down at her. Hatred shone in the eyes that watched her, and strong hands gripped the bedpost until their knuckles gleamed white in the moonlight. If violent thoughts could kill, then Amelia would have never stirred again. The menacing visitor reached forward, fingers flexed at Amelia's slender throat, but a noise in the adjacent parlor stopped the intruder's movements. A look of cunning caution crossed the snarling face. Then quickly, having cast the full force of its malevolence on Amelia's sleeping form, the intruding figure slipped out as quietly as it had come.

Chapter Eleven

Matt's eyes followed Amelia longingly, and even after she had disappeared around the landing with Philip, he continued to stare at the space where she had been. His feeling of helpless frustration at his situation made him want to lash out and smash something. Curbing his inherent quick temper, he reminded himself that the only way to extricate himself from this dilemma was one strand at a time until he had unraveled the Gordian knot that had tied up his life and he was again free to act as he wished.

The most constricting strand now clung tightly to his arm as if trying physically to hold on to what she must know that she had already lost. Turning to Diana, his mouth set in a grim line, Matt shook his head wearily.

"I need to talk with you in private, Diana. Either your suite or mine, it makes no difference, but we must talk seriously now. I have played your little game of chitchat all evening, but now there are things that must be settled."

Diana chose to misunderstand him. "Why don't we go to my rooms, darling? I can get rid of my maids much easier than you can be rid of Hunter. Then we can 'talk' all night if you wish."

She looked up at him with that gaze that he had seen so many times before, an invitation that had only one meaning.

Matt sighed. He had known from this morning when he had received word that she had arrived that this would not be easy, and he cursed the day that he had allowed himself to become entangled with Diana Barrington.

He remembered that spring day as if it were yesterday. He had decided not to attend the dinner party being given by the Potter Palmers that evening; he was sick to death of the repetitious round of business, luncheons, business, dinners, business, and parties. Everything was done with the ulterior motive of improving one's contacts and increasing one's fortune. *But to what purpose?* he wondered.

For the last few years he had suffered from an overwhelming ennui in which life had no meaning or purpose except the treadmill existence of making more money. He already had more money than he could ever use in his lifetime, so the business of making more seemed pointless indeed. Wealth and power had lost their fascination for him, and there was nothing in his life to fill the void left by that loss.

The only time he really seemed to enjoy himself was on horseback or negotiating the purchase of new stock for his stables. He had inherited his father's and his Grandfather Porter's love of horses.

Perhaps if he would marry and have the care and attention of a loving wife, he would find life more pleasing. Perhaps, too, if he had children to whom he could leave his fortune, he would enjoy his work more. His mother had already exhausted every avenue she could find to locate a suitable young woman for him, but so far Matt had shown no interest in any of them. That day Catherine Laurence broached her favorite subject with renewed vigor at the breakfast table.

"Matthew Porter Laurence, you put down those newspapers and listen to me," she had insisted after the maid had withdrawn from the breakfast room. "I can't stand to see you continually unhappy as you've been lately."

Matt lowered his paper and gave his mother his attention as she attacked the issue of his marrying head on.

"Won't you please give some serious thought to settling down and raising a family? I think that's just what you need to get yourself out of this rut you're in."

Matt smiled indulgently at his mother. At sixty she was still a beautiful woman, and he never tired of the graceful Southern drawl of her speech which still lingered after so many years in Chicago. She looked even prettier when she was agitated, as she was this morning. Her flashing hazel eyes and the bright spots of color in her cheeks made her look years younger.

"I've told you many times, Mother, that I believe you're absolutely right," Matt reminded her. "But I have yet to find a woman whom I feel I want to spend the rest of my life tied to."

Catherine sighed. "I never thought I would say this, Matt, because you know I loved your father better than life itself, and it almost killed me when he died, but perhaps you should forget about love and just look for someone suitable to raise your children and take her place in society with you. Maybe some folks go through life without ever experiencing the kind of love your father and I had. Perhaps you'd be smart to find a compatible partner and leave it at that. Then your children, at least, might fill the void you find in your life now. Besides, I'm not getting any younger either, and I would like to spend some time with my grandchildren before I'm too old to enjoy them."

Matt felt annoyance building inside him, but he recognized it as frustration with his own predicament, rather than irritation at his mother. Catherine had never been the type to meddle in his affairs, and he knew that for her to take so bold a stance now was only an indication of how much she cared for him.

"You may be right, Mother, and I'm certainly not getting any younger either. But how do you suggest I go about selecting this 'compatible partner'? Put an advertisement in the Chicago papers?"

Matt was teasing Catherine, but underneath the humor the idea was taking hold with him.

"It could be that the very best place to begin looking would be at the Palmers' dinner party tonight. There are always several unattached young women of marriageable age at these affairs, as you would well know if you didn't spend all your time in the smoking lounge discussing finance and horseflesh.

"Oh, Matt, you know I don't mean to nag, but I do worry about you and your happiness."

Her voice ended on a quivering note and a small tear rolled down her cheek. She blotted it quickly with her linen napkin.

"Mother, you really do fret about me too much."

Matt knelt beside her chair and put his arms about her. His mother was the most important person in his life; she had been both father and mother to him since his father had died when he was small, and she had provided and cared for him all on her own. He could not remember a complaining or pessimistic word from her in all those years, so her distress now moved him to action.

"If it will set your mind at ease, I'll go tonight and check out the prospects. Would you like to place a special order for your daughter-in-law now?" he teased. "Blonde, brunette, short or tall, stout or slim?"

"You are impossible, young man," Catherine smiled through her tears, looking very satisfied with herself.

That evening at the Palmers, Matt remembered his mother's advice, but the only eligible women he saw were either immature and empty-headed debutantes who made him feel like an aging uncle, or spinsters whose unfortunate appearances or unpleasant personalities explained their single status. He chuckled silently as he pictured himself checking out the teeth of any possible candidates, much as one would do when selecting fine horses, and made a note to share the image with his mother, who always enjoyed a good laugh.

Having surveyed the prospects, he had pushed the subject from his mind and was answering Potter Palmer's questions about land speculation in Florida when Mrs. Palmer approached, accompanied by a stunning young woman whom Matt had never seen before. The sensuality of her appearance, from her full pouting lower lip to the daring cleavage of her gown, evoked a physical response in him, and he listened attentively to Mrs. Palmer's introduction.

"Miss Barrington, may I present Matthew Laurence? Matthew, this is Diana Barrington. Her father, Orville Barrington of Barrington Armaments, has just moved his family here from Hartford. They're our new neighbors on Lake Shore Drive."

Diana murmured a demure greeting, but there was nothing else demure about her. Every voluptuous curve

155

of her body was evident in the crimson silk gown that she wore. The creamy flesh of her abundant breasts strained against the fabric of her tightly fitted bodice which emphasized her tiny waist. Her ample hips were accentuated by the clinging cut of the cloth, and as Matt raised his eyes from his appraisal of her physical charms, the glance that met his was at once challenging and knowing.

"Matthew, would you be so kind as to escort Miss Barrington in to dinner?" Mrs. Palmer asked.

"Of course." Matt offered her his arm as the butler announced dinner. As he escorted her into the formal dining room, he felt her fingers caress the inside of his forearm, sending a wave of sensation over his body like an electric shock.

He discovered as he sat beside her during the innumerable courses that she was not much of a conversationalist; in fact, from the blank expression she assumed at times, he questioned the extent of her vocabulary and comprehension. But she more than made up for the lack of stimulating talk with an occasional suggestive glance or double entendre. Once he even felt the firm pressure of her knee against his thigh under the concealing linen cloth. Matt's eyes opened wide in amazement, but she simply smiled at him innocently and turned to speak to the person on her left.

Such sensuality in a woman of his own class was an entirely new experience for Matt. He had known sexually agressive women before, but always women for whom sex was a profession. Certainly he had never encountered such a blatantly flirtatious and openly sensuous female in the formal drawing rooms of Chicago's high society.

The novelty intrigued him. Perhaps he should consider this woman. She came from a good family and moved in the same circles of society as he did. From her physical characteristics he could tell that she must certainly be good breeding stock, and her definite appreciation for him as a male was infinitely more appealing than the giggling debutantes or withered spinsters he had encountered. He remembered his mother's encouragement of the morning and decided to venture further in his investigation of Miss Barrington. As the women rose to withdraw while the men enjoyed their cigars and brandy, Matt asked Diana if he could see her again.

"I was hoping you would ask, Mr. Laurence. Please call on me tomorrow afternoon—for tea."

Matt could tell by the look in her eyes that tea was not what she had in mind, and her next words assured him he was right.

"But don't come to Daddy's. I have my own suite of rooms at the Astoria. I'll be there at four tomorrow. Don't be late."

Her expression as she held out her hand to bid him good evening was full of unspoken promises.

Nevertheless, Matt almost did not keep his appointment the next day. In the far corners of his mind alarm bells warned him against any association with the wiles of Miss Barrington, but his curiosity and male appetite won out over the warnings, and he arrived at her suite shortly after four.

Diana answered the door herself, and he was soon aware that they were alone in the apartment. Conveniently it was her maid's afternoon off. She wore an afternoon gown even more revealing than her dress of the previous evening, not more daring in cut, but fashioned of transparent batiste that left nothing to the imagination.

Matt glanced around the elegantly appointed parlor but he saw no tea service.

"Tea, Miss Barrington?" His eyebrows arched with his query, a smile widening his lips.

"Later, Mr. Laurence," Diana whispered, pulling his head down to hers.

She wasted no time on formalities but pressed her body against his and lifted her full red lips to be kissed. Matt obliged her without hesitation, reveling in the sheer sensuality of the encounter. But even as his body responded automatically and enthusiastically to her lead, the warning signals still flashed and a detached portion of his mind registered that this woman was not only knowledgeable, but also highly practiced in the physical act of love.

If only he had stopped there, instead of carrying her into the bedroom. By the end of the afternoon her seduction of Matt had been complete. Lying among the lace-trimmed sheets of her bed with Diana naked above him, Matt had yielded to his senses while his reason took leave.

Their afternoon trysts became a habit of Matt's life, easing for brief interludes the boredom which had plagued him for so long. Finally, his practical turn of mind told him that life would be simpler if he just married Diana and moved her into his home. Then they could have the grandchildren that his mother wished for. Besides, Diana's hints of marriage had been none too subtle and were beginning to irritate him. If he married her, it would stop her hints and prodding and perhaps give him some peace.

Diana was elated by his proposal, and her family gave a vulgarly extravagant party for the announcement of their engagement. But it was then that their relationship began to sour. Instead of the willing and enthusiastic partner that she had been before, Diana became as petulant and demanding as a child. She refused to consider moving into the mansion Matt shared with his mother and insisted that he build her a place of her own. She also expressed a definite aversion to children and told Matt that she didn't care if they never had any. In the face of this whining personality, even Diana's physical charms lost their attraction for Matt.

His mother, of course, had been horrified after her first meeting with Diana. That had been an encounter Matt would not soon forget. He had taken Diana home to tea. Immediately upon seeing his fiancée seated next to his soft-mannered, cultured mother, he had been forcefully struck by Diana's contrasting coarseness and vulgarity.

"Why do I want to marry your son, Mrs. Laurence? Why, for his money, of course. Matt will buy me anything I wish, and that's what's important in life isn't it? Having all the things one wishes?" She had thrown back her head and laughed too hard, her voluptuous bosom almost bursting the tenuous restraints of the plunging neckline of her bodice.

Matt had to give credit to his mother. Catherine had tried.

"But my dear Miss Barrington, how do you spend your time? Do you help with any of the many charities in Chicago?"

"Oh, I have no time for such things," Diana replied airily, "especially as I spend so much of my time in bed."

"Oh my poor child, I didn't know that you are ill," Catherine murmured sympathetically.

"I'm not," Diana stated bluntly, smiling provocatively at Matt, who by that point had wished for the floor to open up and swallow him.

He ushered Diana out as quickly as possible, knowing that it was already too late.

"Matt, you can't be serious about marrying that woman," his mother later insisted.

The dreadful girl was everything that Catherine's genteel Southern upbringing said a woman should not be. And as if that was not enough, Diana had developed a definite aversion to his mother as well.

"Don't ever ask me to visit that horrid woman again, Matthew. She does nothing but sit there oozing through every pore how superior she feels she is to me. Why, she's no more than a self-righteous Southern prig!"

"Diana," Matt shouted angrily, "I will not have you speaking of my mother in that tone!"

"Have it your own way, Matt darling. If I can't speak of her in that way, then I simply shall refuse to speak of her at all."

And Catherine, panicked that Matt might follow through on the disastrous course he had chosen, continued to press Matt to end his engagement.

Matt, his patience stretched to the breaking point by Diana's whining and feeling none too pleased with himself for his own stupidity, roared at his mother for the first time in his life.

"Leave me alone, Mother! If you hadn't pushed me, I wouldn't be in this mess in the first place."

He had left the house, slamming doors as he went, and had not returned, sending Hunter instead to collect his belongings.

Matt and his mother had exchanged their first harsh words over the engagement. As Diana's tantrums and complaints increased, and Matt finally realized what a terrible mistake he had made, his anger toward his mother grew. He irrationally felt that she had pushed him toward matrimony, and that without her prodding, he would not be caught as he now was with a woman he could no longer stand to be near.

After a very strained and unhappy Christmas season, when Matt had visited his mother briefly, he told her that he felt he had to get away to think things over. He had been pleased that Catherine had understood that his going would lessen the tension between them.

Diana, on the other hand, had been less understanding. Having been outrageously spoiled and catered to all her life, it was impossible for her to comprehend that Matt could lose his fascination with her. When he told her that he needed to get away from her to think about their relationship, and that there would be a very strong possibility of his breaking their engagement upon his return, she only laughed.

"You'll come running back to me, my darling, after a few weeks of long lonely afternoons without—me."

Before he left for the Belleview, Matt had generously placed his private railway car at her disposal in case she wished to visit friends while he was away. It had never occurred to him that she would follow him to Florida.

The morning after his carriage tour of the area with Amelia, he had awakened early and breakfasted in his room. He turned immediately to the reports he had been studying. Potter Palmer had contacted Matt when he learned that Matt was going to be spending the season in Florida. Potter wanted him to investigate a fraudulent land investment scheme involving false deeds for land on Florida's central west coast that had duped many of his friends and business associates.

This particular morning Matt was reading the reports of two private investigators he had hired in Tampa to check into these schemes. He also had Pinkerton men from Chicago working on the case. They had discovered that the frauds had always been operated by front men, and the reports Matt now read seemed to indicate that the leader of the operations, although still unknown, must be headquartered in the area.

It was then that the bellboy brought the message that Diana had arrived.

"Damn and blast!" Matt roared, furious that she had

ignored his desire to be alone and also worried that Amelia might find out about Diana before Matt could explain.

"What do I do now, Hunter?"

Hunter, for once at a complete loss for words, shot Matt a look of total helplessness and beat a hasty retreat, leaving his employer to face the Barrington tiger alone.

Matt threw up his hands in frustration. He had already dispatched a note and roses to Amelia's room much earlier, but he decided that this was something he must explain himself. He straightened his collar and tie, pulled on his tweed jacket, and hurried down the hallway toward Amelia's room. There was no answer, however, when he knocked on the door of the Hagarty suite.

Returning to his room, Matt sent word to Diana that they would have dinner that night and talk, that he had come to a decision on what he must do. All day long Matt tried to contact Amelia, but neither he nor Hunter was able to locate her.

Matt did not see Amelia until dinner that night in the Tiffany Room with Philip Sheridan, and he knew by her pallor and icy silence that she knew about Diana and believed the worst of him. His meal with Diana was interminably long as she prattled on primarily about herself and occasionally the trivia of Chicago society.

Upon leaving the dining hall and seeing Amelia again with Sheridan, Matt knew he must have it out with Diana right away.

When they entered her suite, Matt sat down in the Morris chair by the fire instead of sitting next to Diana on the loveseat which she patted invitingly. Her blatant sexuality that had once fired his blood was now like a drenching of ice water. He had lost all patience with her and knew that he would be cruel not to end it now.

"Diana, I told you I was coming here to reflect on our

relationship, and I have. I have decided that a marriage between us would be a terrible mistake. I do not love you, and I have discovered that love is what I must have for the woman I marry. Rather than cause you any embarrassment by my breaking the engagement, I think it would be better for you to announce that you have terminated our betrothal. You can do that immediately upon your return to Chicago."

Diana's lower lip stuck out in an exaggerated pout. "You don't know what you're talking about, Matt. We really are good for each other and you know it. Besides, it's not fair of you to drop me like an old shoe. The least you can do is give me a chance to restore our relationship. I'm sure if you'll let me stay, at least through the Mardi Gras Ball, and not break our engagement yet, that you will change your mind. If for some reason after that you still wish to call it off, I'll agree and leave quietly."

Her voice had held its usual childish whine, but now it deepened with a threatening venom. "But in the meantime, you must promise to do nothing more to embarrass me like you did tonight making cow eyes at that little twit of a girl with Philip Sheridan."

Matt's fists clenched in anger, but he had dealt with Diana before, and he knew that if she had any idea of his feelings for Amelia that she could be vicious and cruel, so he said nothing. He also knew that she could be the most stubborn and obstinate person he had ever met, so that arguing with her at this point would be futile. In addition, he considered it a point of honor to grant her the little time she had requested. Then she might be more willing to accept the fact that nothing she could do would change his mind. He knew now that he would never marry her, and by the time Mardi Gras had come and gone, Diana would have to admit it, too.

"Very well, Diana," he said as he stood to leave, "I'll give you that much time. But I tell you now that my mind is made up. When the time has passed, you will realize it, too. Good night."

His thoughts were on Amelia as he left Diana's suite. To be fair to Diana and to save Amelia from bearing the brunt of Diana's bad temper, he knew it would be better if he did not see Amelia until the time was up and Diana had admitted defeat. Then he would be free. His only worry was how Amelia would deal with this situation in the meanwhile. Had he seen the look of rage on Diana's face after his departure, his worries would have doubled.

Chapter Twelve

The next day passed for Amelia in a blurring numbness. When she awakened, she could not believe that a mere twenty-four hours could change her attitude on life so drastically. It took an almost superhuman effort to make herself get out of bed. All she wanted to do was pull the covers over her head and pretend that everything that had happened in the past three months had been just a bad dream. Her emotions were as fragile as crystal, and she felt as if she would shatter into a million pieces if she had to withstand any more pain.

Listlessly, she bathed and dressed and joined Ursula and Maude in the parlor for breakfast. She was glad she did not have to enter the hotel dining room this morning. She intended to use every excuse she could think of not to go there at all. She must spare herself the heartache of seeing Matt with the woman he was going to marry.

"You look ill, Amelia," Ursula observed, more disapproving than caring. "You're not coming down with something are you?"

Amelia managed a weak smile. "No, just too many late nights. I must begin following your sensible example and going to bed at a reasonable hour."

Maude nodded her approval. "We really haven't seen much of you, Amelia. We all must spend more time together."

A few days before Amelia would have cringed at the idea of more time spent with Maude and Ursula, but now the prospect offered her a safe retreat.

"You're absolutely right, Maude. I have been remiss as a guest. We must plan more activities for the three of us."

"We shall try to include Philip, too. After all, he's almost like one of the family," Ursula added. "Are you sure you're not ill, my dear? You've hardly touched your breakfast."

"I'm just not hungry after that elaborate meal last night, Aunt Ursula."

"How was your evening with Philip?" Maude's question was blurted out, but she then blushed and added, "I'm sorry, Amelia, I hope you don't think I'm prying."

Amelia smiled to ease Maude's discomfort. "We had a lovely time. He was telling me all about Chicago and what it was like to live and work there."

"You didn't talk about your grandfather?" Ursula asked sharply.

"Why no, I don't believe he mentioned him at all. All that I know about Grandfather Jeremiah is what Mother and you have told me."

Ursula's sigh of relief was audible, and it aroused Amelia's curiosity momentarily, but her thoughts were interrupted by Maude.

"I know we are still officially in mourning, Mama, but

do you think people would consider us horribly gauche if we attended the Mardi Gras Ball in costume?"

Her eyes were bright and the animation gave her face an almost pretty appearance. She waited nervously for Ursula to answer, demolishing her toast into a pile of crumbs on her plate.

Ursula's expression was so disapproving that Amelia felt certain that Maude's request would be denied. Amelia had no desire to attend the ball; any type of celebration or social event would be an ordeal for her, but for Maude's sake, Amelia hoped that Ursula would consent. The homely spinster had so little joy in her life that Amelia's heart went out to her.

Suddenly Ursula's countenance broke into an unaccustomed smile which she lavished on her waiting daughter. "It certainly would be inappropriate for me, my dear, but you two are younger, and the old customs are less binding today. So I see no reason why you should not attend, so long as your costumes are tasteful and not flamboyant. I shall ask Philip if he will be so kind as to escort you."

Maude clapped her hands with the delight of a small child who has been promised a treat.

"There, Amelia," she said. "That will give us something to do. We must plan our costumes right away, and then we must ride into St. Petersburg to the dressmaker's so that she will have time to complete them. Perhaps Philip will take us there."

Amelia nodded absently. She did not want to squelch Maude's obvious enthusiasm at the upcoming event, but it was impossible for her to generate enthusiasm for anything. Her mind still wrestled with the problem of what to do. Part of her longed to return to Asheville and the familiarity and security of Dr. Will and Aunt Beth. Another part of her insisted that it would be extremely ill-mannered to cut short her stay with Aunt Ursula and

Maude. Besides, Aunt Ursula was so adamant about their stay that Amelia knew it would take a colossal battle of wills for her to leave the Belleview, and Amelia didn't have the emotional stamina for such a contest. So all that she knew to do was to endure. After all, the season ended the Monday after Easter, so it was only a matter of nine more weeks. But how was she to avoid Matt and Miss Diana Barrington for all that time? Her head ached as the options boiled through her mind.

"Please excuse me, Aunt Ursula, but I have a terrible headache. I must have drunk too much wine at dinner last night. I think I'll lie down in my room until lunchtime."

"Of course, dear. Use a cold compress on your forehead and close the draperies. That should help. Maude and I will stay here to read the morning papers and catch up on our correspondence."

Amelia lay down in the darkened room and tried to sort out her feelings. Homesickness and grief for her parents pressed on her like a heavy weight. If only her father were here so that she could ask him what to do. So many times in her life his counsel had helped her to make decisions. She remembered him sitting at his desk, his feet propped on the desk top as he filled the large briar pipe that he smoked in the evenings after dinner. As a child, she had sat on the ottoman by his chair.

"Amelia," he would say, "to make a good decision, you must gather all the facts and information that you can. Then think of all the possible alternatives. List the pros and cons of each one and using these, select the plan of action that seems most feasible. Approach the problem one step at a time. Once you have decided what to do, stick with it unless you find incontrovertible evidence that you have made a bad choice. Otherwise, you will spend your entire life vacillating from one course to another and find yourself old with nothing accomplished."

She knew that she hadn't been very good at following her father's advice lately. She also realized that the Belleview's exotic setting was not conducive to clear-headed, rational thinking. Living in a fantasy world of luxury and beautiful people made dealing with reality difficult. What she needed was the pure thin air of the Blue Ridge Mountains to clear her head.

Very well, she thought. She'd play out the fantasy while she was here. She'd attend the operas and balls and mingle with the wealthy and the privileged and enjoy this dream world, if for no other reason than not to let Matthew Laurence know that he'd hurt her. In fact, she would make him believe, if he saw her, that she was having a wonderful time. Then after Easter she'd go back to Asheville and make her decisions. In the meantime, she'd do her best to enjoy what Aunt Ursula called her season in the sun.

Having reached that conclusion, she arose to write a letter to Dr. Will and Aunt Beth before luncheon. She told them to please expect her the week after Easter, if it would be convenient for her to stay with them for a while. Sealing the letter, she picked up some pennies to purchase stamps at the desk and passed through the parlor on her way to the corridor. Ursula was nowhere to be seen and Maude was at the escritoire.

"Do you want me to mail anything for you?"

Maude shook her head. "I haven't finished with these yet, but thank you all the same, dear."

Amelia nodded and walked out into the hallway, closing the door softly behind her. She purposely avoided looking to her left in the direction of Matt's suite, and she paused for a moment at the top of the stairs, remembering the possibility of meeting him in the lobby.

Reassuring herself that he was probably on the golf course at this time of day, she took one step down. At that moment she felt a rush of air behind her. Before she could turn around, strong hands shoved forcefully against her shoulders and she felt herself beginning to fall. She tumbled down the stairs until she was stopped short on the landing by a pair of cordovan riding boots. Gentle hands helped her to her feet and she looked up into Matthew Laurence's concerned face.

She tried to wrest herself from his grasp, but her trembling knees buckled beneath her, and she found herself holding on to him for support, afraid now that if she let go, she would pitch forward down the remaining flight of stairs.

"Someone pushed me!" Her eyes and voice were both angry and fearful, and she didn't know at that moment whether she was more angry with Matt for being the one to catch her or more frightened by the unknown person who had pushed her.

His face darkened and she could read anger in his eyes, too. "Are you sure? Perhaps you only tripped and fell?"

"Of course I'm sure. So sure that I know you can probably see bruises on my shoulder blades where someone hit me."

Then she blushed, hoping he would not request a viewing of the evidence.

"After that tumble, I'm sure you'll have bruises in quite a few places. Did you get a glimpse of who pushed you?"

"None at all. One second I realized someone was rushing up behind me and the next second I was on my way down."

For a moment Amelia had forgotten about Diana Barrington and Matt's deception. He seemed no different than he had been yesterday, but she would not let herself be fooled again.

"But I'm perfectly fine now, Mr. Laurence. Thank you for breaking my fall. Now I have some letters I must mail."

She attempted to step around him on the landing to continue downstairs, but again her quivering muscles refused to respond as she wished. Before she could fall again, Matt grabbed her arm and held her fast.

"Don't be a little fool, Amelia! At least let me help you down the stairs and into the lobby before you do serious harm to yourself."

Without waiting for an answer, he half walked, half carried her down to the bottom of the stairs, where she stopped, hugging the newel post for support, refusing to take another step with the man at her side.

"Amelia, I must talk with you."

The coldness of her look made him release her, and the frostiness of her voice was unmistakable as she replied, "I can think of absolutely nothing that you might say that would be of the least interest to me."

She turned away quickly before he could see the tears in her eyes and squeezed the newel post tightly to hide the trembling of her hands. He studied her for several long moments in silence before turning to ascend the stairs. She looked up to see him watch her carefully from the landing before he disappeared up the stairs.

When she felt sure that he would not return, she walked with shaking limbs to the nearest chair and sat quietly, trying to regain her composure. When the trembling in her muscles had eased, and her desire to burst into angry tears had passed, she walked testily to the lobby desk, choosing a route that threaded itself among several sofas and chairs in case the weakness from her fall and fright returned.

Gaining the desk without further accident, she purchased her stamps from the desk clerk and attached one to her letter before dropping it in the mailbox nearby.

She was so lost in her thoughts that it was not until the desk clerk touched her arm that she became aware of someone calling her name. Looking in the direction of the voice, she saw Lady Caroline striding across the lobby toward her.

"I am going to accept your offer to spend some time with Bernard, dear girl. Please come by after lunch. We'll have a lovely visit and you can stay for tea. Please say yes."

Lady Caroline was so enthusiastic that Amelia could not refuse. Besides, Amelia reasoned she would be less likely to run into people whom she wished to avoid in the safety of Lady Caroline's suite.

"I look forward to it. Will two o'clock suit you?"

"Splendid! Now I must get back to Bernard. I only came down to check the mail. Ta–ta!"

Amelia couldn't help smiling as she watched the bundle of cheerful energy that was Lady Caroline bustle up the stairs. With a pleasant companion like her to spend time with, perhaps the next nine weeks could be endured.

At two o'clock she knocked at the door of Lady Caroline's suite and was admitted by Rose, Caroline's gaunt dour-faced maid. Bernard rose to greet her and she noticed a definite decrease in the swelling of his eye from the day before. Lady Caroline entered from her dressing room and embraced Amelia.

"You are so kind to spend your time with us. I know there must be dozens of other activities you are giving up for this."

"No," Amelia answered truthfully. "At this moment there is no place else I would rather be."

"Good heavens, girl, is that a bruise on your cheek? You haven't had a meeting with Bernard's 'friends,' I hope!"

Amelia shook her head and recounted to them the disturbing fall she had taken that morning.

"You have now had two accidents too many, Amelia. I find it difficult to believe that they are just coincidental," Caroline insisted.

"I'm sure that coincidence is exactly what they were," she replied, refusing to consider that they might be anything else. "Food poisoning on a picnic is an all too common occurrence, and it was probably just a mischievous, misguided child who pushed me down the stairs. Why, even the rattlesnake in my room could be explained in a perfectly logical way."

But even as she spoke of the logical explanations for her accidents, Amelia again experienced uneasiness and dread and an involuntary chill raced down her spine, causing her to shudder. Could there be a real cause for alarm? Amelia mentally shook away the thought. She knew no one who would want to harm her, nor any reason why someone would try. Coincidence was the logical answer.

"Rattlesnake!" Lady Caroline's eyebrows shot up in twin peaks, as Amelia told them the story of the snake in her bathroom and its destruction by Beulah.

"Well, my dear," Caroline insisted, "you are very fortunate indeed to have such a staunch protector as your Beulah."

"Perhaps you've just had a run of bad luck, Amelia," Bernard said, "and since bad things supposedly occur in threes, then I would venture a guess that your bad luck is over."

"I hope you're right, Bernard. It seems not much has gone right for me in the last few months, so I'm due for a change."

"Do you think you should have Dr. Winston look at that bruise?" Bernard suggested.

"Oh, I'm sure it will be fine," Amelia answered, but the growing aches in various parts of her body told her that she would feel the effects of her recent fall for a few days at least.

"Bernard, you are so transparent, my boy." His mother laughed. "I really do think you are more interested in news of the doctor's delightful sister than in Amelia's bruises."

"Sarah is a lovely and refreshing young woman, Mother, and if I did not look so ghastly, I'd be calling on her myself."

Lady Caroline gave Amelia a conspiratorial smile and raised her eyebrows again, which gave her a pixie appearance. "You heard it here first, my dear. This smacks of infatuation to me. And I couldn't be more pleased. Sarah is a charming young woman and with more common sense in her little finger than Bernard has in that large noggin of his."

Bernard playfully tossed a silk-fringed sofa pillow at his mother, who dodged it easily. "You're right, of course as always, Mother. This whole nasty episode with those moneylenders has made me realize that I need to settle down and do something constructive with my life. But I'm afraid that the aristocratic life of leisure that I've led has left me eminently unsuited for employment. The only thing I really know well is horses, which I've learned from you. Once we get this mess straightened out, I'm going to look about for a good breeding farm or stable that might need a manager. And once I'm gainfully employed, you will find me settled down with a wife and possibly a houseful of redheaded children."

It was a long speech for Bernard, who was usually very quiet in the presence of his loquacious mother, and he leaned back on the sofa looking tired but very pleased with himself.

The remainder of the afternoon passed pleasantly and quickly and Amelia almost forgot about Matthew Laurence. It was not until she returned to her rooms after tea that she remembered his look as he had held her on the landing. Why had he been so insistent on speaking with her, she wondered? Did he really think she might continue seeing him when she knew not only that he was engaged to be married but also that his fiancée was staying under the very same roof? How could a seemingly decent man be so devious?

Stiffly, she removed her clothes and ran the deep tub full of hot water, added fragrant bath salts, and eased into the water for a good long soak, hoping the heat would draw out the achiness she was beginning to feel from her fall. She knew that she had been extremely fortunate not to have been seriously hurt. The complete surprise of it had not given her time to tense her body. She shuddered as she realized she might have broken her neck or back. Refusing to admit that it might have been maliciously intentional, she decided that she must keep watch for the naughty child who had pushed her.

She was reluctant to leave the soothing warmth of the bath, but she knew she must dress if she was to be on time for dinner. She would be dining in the suite tonight with Ursula and Maude. Afterwards they would play a few hands of whist, then Amelia could retire early and do some reading. Not a very exciting way to spend an evening at the Belleview, she thought, but one that she hoped would at least cause her no pain.

Chapter Thirteen

The next few days provided the calm that Amelia's wounded heart desired. Her time was spent either in the seclusion of the Sinclairs' suite or Lady Caroline's. Ursula and Maude maintained the same quiet pattern to their lives that they had established upon their arrival. Just a few days before, Amelia had found it difficult to understand her relatives' desire to keep to themselves in such a place, but now she was thankful for their reclusive routine, which meant that Amelia did not have to suffer the pain of seeing Matt or Diana.

But the pain of being alone with her thoughts frightened her now more than anything else. She found it impossible, especially in the quiet hours of the night, to keep her mind's eye from focusing on visions of Matt and the euphoria and ensuing pain those visions brought her. Each night as she would drift into a fretful sleep, she could see the love that had shone for her in his deep brown eyes. But then the vision would change, and a laughing Diana Barrington would appear, jolting Amelia from her fitful rest. Only by forcing her thoughts on a happy moment of her life, at a time long before she had known that Matthew Laurence even existed, would she finally be able to fall back asleep in the wee hours of the morning.

When the appointed time for Ursula's nap arrived, Amelia, fearing the waking dreams that solitude brought her, sought Caroline and Bernard's company. She looked forward to the jovial mood that prevailed in the Frasers' suite, a welcome change from the serious atmosphere of her own rooms. She was happy to be spared seeing Matt with Diana, but she began to chafe at the confinement and longed to be outdoors in the bright Florida sun.

"Steady on, girl, you're pacing like a tiger in a cage," Lady Caroline observed. "Let's go for a ride so you can work off some of that energy."

"No!" Amelia answered much too quickly. Her heart raced and she felt her terrible tendency to hyperventilate start to take control once more. She wanted to escape from the confinement of the hotel, but she still could not face the prospect of seeing Matt. She saw Caroline's puzzled expression and tried to make amends.

"It's embarrassing to admit, but I'm still a bit bruised from the fall I had, and I don't think riding would be the most comfortable of activities for me right now, so if you'll excuse me, I believe it would be best if I return to my room. And thank you for a delightful afternoon," she added flatly as she slipped out the door.

"I'm worried about that girl, Bernard," Caroline remarked to her son after Amelia's uncharacteristic departure. "I don't know what's happened to her recently, but it's as if someone drained all the spirit out of her. And all those strange mishaps . . ."

178

Her green eyes beneath her knotted brow were filled with concern.

"We'll have to keep a special eye on her, my boy. She needs friends right now."

Returning to her suite, Amelia kept her eyes downcast, studying the patterns in the hall runners and hoping to avoid contact with Matt. She was so lost in her private pain that she was startled to be greeted with an embrace and a squeal of delight from Maude.

"Oh, Amelia, Philip has agreed to escort us to St. Petersburg for a few days. Isn't it wonderful!"

An escape from the Belleview. Amelia's unhappy face immediately assumed an expression of relief. She even managed a smile for Philip who was there with Maude.

"Why, that is wonderful news, Maude. Philip, Aunt Ursula, how soon can we leave?"

"Give me a day or two to make the arrangements, Amelia." Philip did not bother to conceal his amusement at her eagerness.

Amelia, embarrassed at her almost zealous desire to leave, responded as calmly as she could. "A day or two would be perfect, Philip."

Maude immediately launched into a discussion of preparations for their journey with more animation than Amelia had believed her capable of. After a few moments of Maude's monologue, Ursula suggested that they ask the Frasers to accompany them so that Lady Caroline might serve as chaperone.

Beulah was immediately dispatched with a note and returned quickly with an affirmative reply.

"Well, that's nicely settled," Philip said.

"Oh," Maude interjected suddenly, "but what about you, Mama? We can't just leave you here alone."

"Don't be foolish, Maude," Ursula snapped. "Beulah will be here with me. And I am perfectly capable of taking care of myself, as I managed for many years before you were born."

"Yes, of course, Mama," Maude agreed meekly.

"We'll leave in the morning, day after tomorrow," Philip announced.

"Yes, and we shall all have a wonderful time," Amelia sighed.

In the moment that followed, everyone in the room silently agreed with her, but for different reasons.

The party boarded the train early that morning from its terminal on the hotel grounds, and they would arrive in St. Petersburg before lunchtime. The group was in a festive mood as they settled in among the other passengers. Bernard joked about his injuries, which were now almost healed.

"I do believe I can go about in public now without frightening the children."

"Let's test that hypothesis," Lady Caroline chimed in, looking about the car for a nearby boy or girl, and the group pealed with laughter.

The sights of their journey were similar to the ones Amelia had experienced before reaching the Belleview: pine forests, huge moss-covered oaks, wide still lakes and orange groves.

However, unlike the silent, almost mournful trip to Florida Amelia had endured with Ursula and Maude, this time the journey was alive with chatter. Lady Caroline dominated the conversation with tales of Bernard's mischievous exploits as a boy, which Bernard, used to his ever-doting mother, bore in tolerant silence.

"I should have known you'd never change," Caroline clucked, but her eyes and voice were filled with love, not reprimand.

Amelia had seen that look in her own mother's face,

and for a moment she was back in Asheville, sitting at the huge walnut kitchen table with Mama. How she wished she could talk with her mother now.

"Look, Amelia," Philip interrupted her thoughts, and pointed to her left.

Through the window she saw a field filled with rows of low plants with sharply spiked leaves.

"They're pineapples," Philip explained. "I'm always amazed at the variety of fruit this area produces. It's a veritable Garden of Eden."

With its fair share of serpents, Amelia thought, remembering the rattler in her room—and Matthew Laurence. Were there others of whom she was unaware? She directed her attention back to Philip.

"I've never tasted a pineapple," Amelia said, but before she could continue, Caroline jumped in.

"Beware, Amelia, a gentleman in England became so enthralled with that fruit that he built a mansion in the shape of it."

"How silly." Amelia laughed, noting out of the corner of her eye that Maude, once again suffering the throes of motion sickness, could manage only a wan smile.

Amelia loved St. Petersburg on sight. Despite the wide and dusty dirt streets, it was a sparkling clean city with well-kept homes and businesses. Its business district was located on the Tampa Bay side of the peninsula.

Alighting from the train, Amelia could see a pier built out into the clean clear waters of Tampa Bay with a two-story pavilion and slide down into the water constructed at its end.

"What is that?" Amelia asked.

"It's the bathing pavilion!" Bernard shouted with all the excitement of a six-year-old. "Follow me, and we'll take a closer look."

Ignoring the awaiting carriage, he motioned to the group to accompany him. Walking north along the block, the party followed the porters, who carried their luggage to the nearby Detroit Hotel, a three-and-a-half story building in unmistakenly Russian style.

"The best view in town is from the hotel's tower," Bernard told his entourage. "Let's climb up and have a better look."

"I'll wait for you here," Lady Caroline said, sitting down in one of the chairs on the hotel's shaded veranda and fanning herself with her handkerchief.

"We'll collect you on our way back down," Bernard called over his shoulder, up one flight of stairs already.

Agreeably, Amelia, Philip and Maude followed up the steps of the seventy-four-foot tower that graced the side of the hotel.

"It's so lovely, exotic even, in its own way. Like Venice or Florence, only more wild and rugged," Amelia said, taking in the panorama before her, the waterfront and the city.

"Have you been to Italy?" Philip stepped up behind her, placing his arm around her waist as if to keep her from falling.

"Oh, no, but I've read of it and seen paintings. I wish I were a painter so that I could put this magnificent view on canvas," Amelia exclaimed.

"Perhaps I could take you to Italy someday and show you all those things," Philip suggested to Amelia in a low voice that the others could not hear.

Amelia was saved from a reply when Maude stepped up and took her place opposite Amelia on Philip's other side.

"It's so Russian," commented Maude, referring to the architecture of the railroad depot and the minaret that graced the hotel entrance.

"Interesting observation, Maude. It reminds me of a story about this place," Philip began, turning his head to make sure everyone could hear.

"The hotel or St. Petersburg?" Maude chimed in, obviously recovered from the train ride.

"Both, actually," Philip continued, enjoying his role as tour guide. "Most of the land in this downtown area belonged to a Mr. Williams, but the railroad at that time belonged to Peter Demens, a Russian immigrant. In order to build a city, they needed each other. When the time came to name the city, each thought that he should have the honor. The story goes that they decided to draw straws, and, as is obvious from the name, Demens won the draw and the city was named St. Petersburg after his native city. Williams then built the first hotel and named it the Detroit after his hometown," he finished, indicating their place of residence for the next few days.

Maude and Amelia shared a room on the second floor with Lady Caroline next door and Bernard and Philip across the hall. They met in the hotel dining room for a light lunch, then went out on foot to explore the city. All along the sidewalks up and down Central Avenue were brightly painted benches sporting advertisements for the various business establishments.

Amelia smiled up at Philip. "I remember reading a report in one of Papa's medical journals that this is supposed to be the ideal 'health city.' I didn't think anything could surpass the clean, clear air of the mountains, but now that I'm here, I may have to change my mind."

"Look, Amelia, there's the dressmaker's," Maude interjected. "It doesn't look very elegant. Are you sure that's the place we want, Lady Caroline?"

"The very one. Don't worry, Maude. It isn't like your Chicago salons, but you will find it very adequate for our needs," Lady Caroline assured her. "Excuse us now, if you will, gentlemen. We have work to do," said Caroline as she bustled the young women into Mrs. Gifford's shop. "We'll meet you on the pier in two hours."

A tiny woman, wearing a large pin cushion tied round her wrist, came forward to greet them. She pushed her steel-framed glasses up the bridge of her nose and looked them over with an experienced eye.

"You're from the Belleview, I see."

"How can you tell?" Amelia asked in amazement. She could see nothing extraordinary about them that should give them away.

"It's the cut and quality of your dresses, Miss. Only rich folk dress like you, and most rich folks this time of year are at the Belleview. Don't take no detective to figure that out."

But the large smile showed that she was pleased at the accuracy of her deduction.

"And I bet I know what you're here for, too. Want some costumes for that fancy dress party they have there every year, doncha?"

Her mouth widened into a grin, for she could tell by their expressions that she was correct again.

She directed them to a large table covered with fashion magazines and artists' sketches and invited them to browse until something struck their fancy. Lady Caroline giggled like a girl over some of the costumes and insisted that except for modesty's sake, she would enjoy a night as Cleopatra or Scheherazade. She discovered what she was searching for in a sketch of an Elizabethan gown with an elaborate ruff and laced bodice and a skirt worn over a farthingale. And she chuckled again when she explained to the girls that she would put a henna rinse on her hair to complete the effect of the Virgin Queen.

Maude decided to go as a Pilgrim, thinking that the subdued colors of the gown and the primly starched apron, neckerchief and cap would be most appropriate for her mourning status.

Before Maude had voiced that decision, Amelia had been studying the sketch of a gypsy dancer and admiring the riotous colors of the bodice and layered skirts. She pictured herself with her fiery locks unbound and large gold hoops in her ears. She might even carry a tambourine tied with multicolored streamers to complete the costume.

Her choice brought opposite reactions from her two companions. Maude was horrified.

"Oh no, Amelia, whatever would Mama think! She expressly said nothing too flamboyant. That won't do at all!"

"Don't be so priggish, Maude. It's a costume ball, not a wake," Caroline cried. "I think it's a marvelous costume, Amelia, and suits you splendidly."

Amelia felt the fires of independence surge in her veins. She knew that her parents would rather she enjoy herself than to mope about grim-faced in dull clothing for a prescribed period of time. She could even imagine their delight at the audacity of her costume. She made up her mind to have it.

"I'm sorry you don't approve, Maude, but this is what I've decided upon."

"Well, I can assure you right now that Mama won't pay for such boldness," Maude answered with a whine.

"Maude, I refuse to let you bully Amelia. Mrs. Gifford, put this young lady's gypsy costume on my bill."

And with a firm nod to the saleswoman, Lady Caroline indicated to all that the subject of Amelia's costume selection was closed.

The moment of tension passed and the women relaxed again in their discussion of fashions and fabrics. Mrs. Gifford took the necessary measurements and guaranteed that the costumes would be sent by train to the Belleview well in advance of the ball.

Returning to the hotel, the women watched wagonload after wagonload of oranges being taken to the train station for shipment north.

"But they're all green!" Maude exclaimed with a frown.

"Of course they are. Otherwise they'd be rotten before they reach their destination," Caroline instructed.

"That reminds me of something one of my father's patients told me," Amelia began. "He used to grow peaches in South Carolina. He said the first peach growers had a terrible time marketing their crops until they discovered that the peaches traveled well in the kind of baskets the French used for transporting bottles of champagne. I always thought of champagne after that whenever anyone mentioned peaches, an elegant combination."

"You're making me hungry," Caroline said. "Here's a tearoom where we can order lunch. But I doubt if they'll have peaches or champagne."

That night at dinner the women shared with Philip and Bernard their choice of costumes. The men had gone to the haberdasher's and placed their costume orders. Philip was to go as the notorious pirate Jose Gaspar and Bernard had decided to attend as an Indian. He reasoned that the war paint would cover any remaining marks or bruises from his "accident."

Philip turned to Amelia who sat on his right. She wore her dinner gown of deep violet and the day's activities and her high spirits had brought color to her cheeks.

"You're even more beautiful than ever tonight, Amelia," he said.

Amelia thanked him for the compliment. Then Philip, ever the gentleman, noticed the crestfallen look on Maude's face.

"It's a privilege to dine with three such beautiful

women," he said as he raised his wine glass, and Bernard joined him in a toast.

Throughout the many courses of the dinner, Philip regaled them with tales of Tampa Bay history, including the feats of Jose Gaspar whose crew had captured Tampa across the Bay. As he ended his story, he noticed a concerned look on Bernard's face.

"Something wrong, old man?"

"I hope not, but your talk of cutthroats reminded me of the two seedy-looking characters who seemed to be following us this afternoon."

"I'd forgotten all about them until now. They're not the same two who roughed you up before, are they?"

"No, I'd never forget those faces!" Bernard's mouth twisted with anger. "But it would be just like them to send in a second team, now that I know what the first two look like. In fact, if you hadn't been with me this afternoon, I may have been in for more of the same."

Lady Caroline, who up until now had seemed to treat the entire episode lightly, blanched noticeably. "Dear Bernard, you must promise me that you will not go out alone."

"Don't worry, Mother, I'm not ready for another dose of their medicine. I shall do everything in my power to avoid them."

"Yes, you mustn't worry, Lady Caroline," Philip assured her, "I'll keep him company, and I'm a good man with my fists if the need arises."

"You are most kind, all of you." The energetic Caroline, now evidently weary, slumped back in her chair. "Now, as this has been a most exhausting day, I will ask to be excused and retire. Good night all."

Bernard rose to escort his mother to her room, and Philip accompanied Maude and Amelia upstairs to their door where he bade them both good night. The two women removed their evening finery and prepared for bed. As Amelia sat at the dressing table brushing her long thick tresses, Maude sat up in her bed, her knees hugged to her chest, watching her beautiful cousin closely.

"Do you like Philip, Amelia?" she asked suddenly.

Amelia was taken aback by the unexpected question since her thoughts had been entirely of Matt, so her answer was flustered and delivered with a blush. "Of course I do, Maude! Philip is a very charming and entertaining man, and his manners are excellent. His company is always enjoyable."

Maude pondered this for a moment before she replied with a complete change of subject. "Do you know that this is the first night in my life that I have not spent under the same roof with Mama?"

Amelia turned to look at her in surprise. As close as she had been to her parents, there had been many nights that she had spent away from them, either visiting friends or the months on end when she was away at school in Greensboro. She found it difficult to believe Maude's statement, but she knew it must be true. She was struck again by the fact that Maude was one of the most puzzling women she had ever met. As much time as Amelia had spent with her over the last few months, she still felt that she never really knew how Maude felt about anything or what she was thinking.

"Are you homesick then, Maude?"

Maude gave a short laugh that sounded like a snort. "Never! This is the most fun I've ever had. I don't care if we never go back to the Belleview."

And with that she lay down, turned her face to the wall and pulled the covers snugly around her, leaving Amelia to puzzle over the curious relationship of Aunt Ursula and her only child.

Although tired from the long day, Amelia hesitated before climbing into bed as her cousin had done.

Maybe a little more fresh air will put me right to sleep, she thought optimistically.

Wrapping a shawl around her shoulders, she stepped out onto the balcony outside her room, where she watched the moonlight shimmer in silver ripples on the waters of the bay. Amelia let the shawl drop to her feet as the warm breeze caressed her skin, molding her night clothes to her body. She yawned and stretched out her arms to the beautiful city.

If only Matt were here, she thought. *No, if only Diana Barrington didn't exist and Matt were mine.*

It would be another long sleepless night.

As she turned to leave the balcony, the flare of a match on the street below her caught her attention. From its glare and the light of the moon, Amelia could see Bernard, who obviously was enjoying a last cigarette before turning in. Stealthily two other figures appeared from the shadows, one on either side of her young friend, and although she could not make out their words, she could hear the menace in their voices as they addressed him. Her heart was pounding in her throat as she wondered how she might help him, when suddenly a voice called out from the darkness below her.

"Bernard, how about a last drink before bed?"

Philip stepped from the shadows toward the trio, and the two strangers moved away. Taking Bernard's arm, Philip led him back inside, glancing up toward the second-story balcony before entering the hotel.

Amelia, shaken by Bernard's close call, returned to her bed. It never occurred to her that Philip had not followed Bernard, but had been instead watching her all along from the street below.

The next morning Amelia had already decided not to say anything about what she had witnessed the night before. It appeared, she hoped, that everything was

189

under control. Besides, she did not want to alarm Lady Caroline on such a beautiful balmy day. By the time the party had finished breakfast, the temperature was well into the eighties and the day promised to be a scorcher. Bernard's face was crinkled with mischief as he made his suggestion.

"Let's all go down to the bathing pavilion, rent bathing costumes and go for a swim!"

"An absolutely topping idea," agreed Lady Caroline, who was looking wilted in the unseasonable heat.

Amelia had opened her mouth to agree when Philip spoke up.

"Somehow I don't think it would be quite the thing to do. There seemed to be a rather common lot hanging about there yesterday, and I'm not sure Mrs. Hagarty would approve of Maude and Amelia participating in such an escapade."

"You're right, Philip," Maude chimed in. "I have no intention of making a fool of myself at a public attraction."

Amelia felt rebellion stirring inside her again. It sounded like a great adventure to her, and she loved to swim. She gave Bernard her brightest smile. "Count me in!"

"Splendid," said Caroline. "We'll go immediately. Philip, you can keep Maude company while we enjoy ourselves."

Philip looked disapproving, but he knew there was no gainsaying the impetuous Lady Caroline.

The entire party walked out to the end of the pier, and while Amelia, Caroline and Bernard changed into their bathing costumes, Philip and Maude waited atop the pier to watch the spectacle. Amelia felt encumbered by the clumsy shapeless bathing suit. She remembered the secluded lake at home where she had swum naked and felt the velvet smoothness of the water against her skin.

She wondered how she would be able to stay afloat weighted down by all this fabric.

They joined Bernard at the top of the slide, and feeling like small children at a playground, slid rapidly down the two-story slide with screams of delight before they hit the cold water with a breathtaking gasp. The water was too cold for them to endure it for very long, so after a few more trips down the slide, and some playful splashing and ducking, they returned to the dressing rooms to shed the wet suits for their street clothes. As Amelia and Lady Caroline were dressing, the latter made an observant remark.

"It appears that our Philip is obviously very fond of you, Amelia."

Amelia looked up in surprise and dropped the laces she had been threading through her dainty boots. She had never thought of Philip as anything but a good friend, a kind older brother, and she wasn't sure she liked the idea of him as a romantic interest. She had more than she could handle in that department now in dealing with her feelings about Matt.

"I'm fond of him, too, Caroline. He's been like a brother to me, and I'm very appreciative of his many kindnesses."

She pulled the laces tightly and tied them and stood with a shake of her skirts to close the subject.

The bathers, now dry and dressed, rejoined Philip and Maude at the top of the pavilion. They enjoyed the view of yachts, fishing trawlers and shrimp boats with their nets spread to dry and watched the comical aeronautical maneuvers of sea gulls as they battled for bits of food thrown to them by tourists. Then they turned back for a leisurely stroll up Central Avenue with a stop at the milliner's for ribbons and veiling for Lady Caroline before returning to the Detroit.

They had just entered the hotel lobby when Bernard

caught sight once more of the two men who had been following them. They had all enjoyed their visit, but on this ominous note, they were glad to be returning to the Belleview the next morning.

Amelia, relieved at the chance to be alone, went up to her room to rest before dinner. Maude and Philip had joined Caroline and Bernard for a game of cards in one of the hotel's public rooms. The past two days had been a relief for Amelia, because she had not had to worry about Matt or Diana, but that would all end when she returned to the Belleview. She wondered if she could keep up the appearance of indifference toward him, when her desire for him ached within her. If she were lucky, the couple might return to Chicago before the end of the season and spare her a great deal of misery.

Lucky? she thought. When Matthew Laurence returned to Chicago, she would never see him again. She laughed silently and bitterly.

And I call that luck!

Chapter Fourteen

The same morning that Amelia's train left St. Petersburg for its return to the Belleview, Matt and Hunter were closeted in their suite studying reports about the fraudulent land scheme which had been delivered by the Pinkerton detectives Matt had hired. While reading one of the documents, Matt was glad that he had chosen the Belleview as a command post for their investigation since it was near the land in question.

"Damn and blast!" Matt exclaimed, throwing the sheaf of papers down on his desk in frustration. "This fellow's as slippery as a snake in the grass."

"Are you implying Mr. Rousseau, sir?" Hunter inquired dispassionately.

"Yes, I am. But I don't have the proof. I just feel it. But if I'm right, why can't I find the facts to confirm it? Let's start again with the latest report from Pinkerton's people."

Hunter removed a pince-nez from his vest pocket and

balanced it delicately on the bridge of his nose. Clearing his throat, he began to read from the sheaf of papers on the table before him.

"The first advertisements appeared a year ago in the Chicago papers. They were for 'prime acreage on Florida's West Coast, perfect for development or agriculture.' For a small fee and postage, those interested could obtain pictures of the land for sale. With a twenty-five per cent deposit, they could hold the option on the land until they wished to purchase or sell their option to someone else. If they decided to complete purchase, they simply mailed their certified check to the same address, Florida Sunshine Land Company, at a post-office box in Tampa and the deed was mailed to them, complete with what appeared to be official document stamps with everything in order.

"Many Chicago investors would have been leery of such dealings, except for the fact that Edward Rousseau, the prominent Chicago banker, made a purchase, came to Florida and inspected the land. He then returned to tout the merits of the offer and encouraged participation in it. Others followed suit, thinking to hold on to their land as an investment. It wasn't until a friend of Potter Palmer's came to Florida himself last fall to inspect his land that he found it under two feet of water in a cypress swamp and sounded the alarm. By then it was too late. Several others had already invested hundreds of thousands and discovered their land to be worthless."

"Wasn't that Rousseau I saw at dinner here last night?" Matt interrupted. "It can't be just coincidence he's here now. There must be some connection."

"He's at the Belleview for the season. Pinkerton suspects, as you do, that he is involved, deeply involved in this and has been watching him very carefully for any signs of complicity. He is either involved himself, the report says, or is the innocent bait for setting up the scheme."

"Hardly. There is nothing innocent about Edward Rousseau. All of his dealings have a distinctive stench about them, including this one. He didn't become one of the nation's leading bankers by being an unsuspecting dupe," Matt reasoned.

"No, sir, I believe he married money," Hunter replied dryly.

"Please continue," Matt requested, trying to hold his dislike of Rousseau in check. "Sorry for interrupting, Hunter. Carry on."

"When the detectives went to Tampa to locate the Florida Sunshine Land Company, they were unable to find any firm doing business by that name. However, they picked up from street talk that there is a loan company, known as Florida Sunshine Loan, that has been lending large sums of money at inflated interest rates to wealthy gamblers who hit a run of bad luck at gambling houses in the area, including Coe's just north of here. They have no office, only roving agents who make loans and control collections, although extortion might be a better term. And their collection techniques are nasty and life-threatening. One of their most recent victims is Bernard Fraser, Lady Caroline's younger son, who was severely beaten when he did not meet their demands.

"The detective agency seems to think that there is a banking connection somewhere, because these large amounts of money seemingly disappear and are untraceable. Rousseau, of course, would be a highly likely and qualified suspect because of his banking expertise and the opportunities he would have to secret away these funds."

"The real estate, the banking, the extortion, all smack of Edward Rousseau, but he simply has not made any mistakes that will allow me to nail him," Matt complained as he stared out the French doors at the island in the distance.

"You must be extremely careful, sir," Hunter warned, "and not make any accusations unless we find incontrovertible evidence. Rousseau is a very ruthless man. If you even hint of his involvement in this scheme, without the proof to put him where he can harm no one, he will ruin you, or even worse. Be careful."

Matt turned and observed the grave expression on Hunter's face and knew that his advice was sound.

"So, in a matter of words, our search has reached an impasse at this point, eh, Hunter?"

Matt looked over the last sheet of the report. "The Pinkertons have identified four of Rousseau's 'bill collectors' and are keeping close watch on them. If we're patient enough, one of them may lead us to Rousseau. So all we can do now is wait."

Matt stood and stretched, easing the tension in his neck from the hours of reading. Tiny lines around the corners of his eyes indicated his weariness. For the last three evenings, Diana had demanded that he escort her to dinner with dancing afterwards, and the strain was beginning to wear him down. He was more emotionally fatigued than physically tired. The conversation each night was always the same. "When we are married, darling . . ." Diana would whine, repeating her litany of expensive and selfish requests.

And every night she would make her now repugnant attempts to seduce him, which aroused his disgust with her—and himself—all the more.

"Matt, please come in," Diana had begged pathetically last night as she dug her fingers into his arm. He had no choice but to enter her suite to avoid creating a scene in front of other guests in the hallway. Expecting her anger to rise again at his obvious disinterest in her charms, Matt was surprised when Diana fell to her knees before him as soon as the door was shut.

"Matt, what have I done? What has changed? I can't bear your indifference toward me a moment longer. Just tell me what it is, and I will change, I will do anything. Only don't say that you won't marry me," she pleaded pitifully.

But Matt knew from the tone of her voice that her speech was insincere, that this was just another of her well-rehearsed theatricals. As he looked down into her tear-filled eyes, his anger began to rise as he recognized another of her manipulative ploys. He stepped aside to extricate himself from her grasp.

"Diana, there is nothing you can do to change my mind. Don't you understand? It is over. As I promised, I will maintain this charade, but only until Mardi Gras when *you* will break our engagement. If you do not, *I* will."

Hadn't he suffered enough for his own lust and stupidity? Matt had thought as he returned to his suite, ripping off his white tie and casting it aside, wishing he could cast aside the blond thorn in his side as easily.

Well, Mardi Gras was only three weeks away. He had counted the days gratefully. And then, if she held to her part of the bargain, he'd be rid of her.

Returning to the present and pushing thoughts of Diana aside, he sighed as Hunter pulled off his riding boots. Then he stretched his tall, muscled frame out on the settee and turned his thoughts to Amelia, happy that the blond witch down the hall could not read his mind, and soon fell asleep.

Hunter quietly gathered up the reports, stowed them neatly in a briefcase and left the room. He carried the briefcase down to the lobby, sought out the manager, and requested that the briefcase be secured in the hotel safe.

As he returned to the suite, his mind was filled with the dangers of their investigation, and he was worried about Matt. He knew that the people with whom they were dealing would stop at nothing to protect themselves. And he knew that they would both have to be vigilant if they were to come through this safely. After he entered the suite, he turned and locked the door firmly behind him.

When Amelia returned to the Belleview again after her St. Petersburg visit, she could not help remembering her first arrival there and how much had happened to her in those few short weeks. She had made new friends in Caroline, Bernard and Philip, she had been plagued by a chain of inexplicable accidents, and she had fallen deeply and disastrously in love with Matthew Laurence. Even now her pulse quickened as she contemplated the possibility of seeing him again. Her pride still smarted from the way he had used and deluded her, and she felt herself shaking with anger once more. How long would it take, she wondered, to be able to forget this episode in her life, or at least to be able to remember it without getting weak in the knees and short of breath? She forced Matt from her mind as she became aware that Bernard was speaking to her.

"I say, Amelia, be a sport and ride over to the Winstons' with me this afternoon. You could say you've come to thank the doctor for his good care of you, and while you visit him, I'll be able to talk with Sarah."

His boyish face broke into a winsome smile that Amelia found irresistible, so she agreed to meet him in the stables after lunch.

She was warmly greeted by Beulah when she returned to her room, and the maid helped to unpack the clothing she had taken on her short trip. As she was hanging her violet dinner gown in the closet, her eyes fell on a small black bag on the closet floor, her father's medical bag which he had carried on rounds for more years than Amelia could remember.

She lifted the bag out and onto her bed and sat down with her memories. The leather was soft and smooth from wear and smelled of saddle soap, for her father had always kept it meticulously clean. Inside were still the medicines and instruments essential to a doctor's art. She closed the bag and sat clutching it to her chest, as if to recall her father and hold him to her. She felt an aching void reopen inside her, for she had always been closer to her father than anyone else, and when he had died, she had lost the best friend that she had ever had. She had loved her mother dearly, but there had never been that unspoken rapport, that instant understanding of one another that she had shared with her father.

And that was what she wished for in the man she married. Not only a lover, but also a friend with whom she could confide her most secret thoughts and wishes and have them respected and understood, the way her father had.

Her thoughts turned unwillingly to Matthew Laurence, and she knew that even though her whole body ached with love for him, she could never have that kind of relationship with him, even if he were not engaged to the awesome Diana Barrington. She could never marry a man who was anything less than totally honest with her. Her mind kept repeating that, but her heart cried out against it, for never in her life had she met anyone who had affected her as Matthew Laurence had, and she cursed her fate that he had not turned out to be the man for whom she had hoped.

She knew that she would be better off with a man like Philip who, although he did not stir her emotions as Matt did, would at least be reliable and one she could trust. Then she stopped in amazement, wondering where the idea of marriage to Philip had come from, for she had never contemplated it before. With a shake of her head, she thrust that eccentric thought from her mind and taking a deep breath, went into the parlor to face Ursula's wrath.

Maude and Ursula were already seated at the luncheon table, and Amelia kissed the dry skin of Ursula's proffered cheek before she took her seat.

"You're looking well, Aunt. I hope the last few days have been pleasant for you."

"They were very boring, actually," Ursula replied with a sniff. "No one around with whom to play a decent hand of cards and only Beulah for company."

She shook her head sadly, and Amelia couldn't suppress the rebellious thought that of all the women in the room, she found Beulah's company the most enjoyable.

"And after what Maude has told me, I can see that I should have gone along to give you guidance, Amelia. Swimming at a public beach? Outrageous! Did your mother teach you no sense of propriety? And your choice of costume for the ball is quite unacceptable, but we now find ourselves faced with two impossible choices. Wear the shameless outfit or insult Lady Caroline. How could you do this to me, Amelia, after all I've done for you?"

Ursula's gnarled fingers gripped the head of her ebony cane, and for a moment, Amelia thought her aunt was going to swing it at her.

Amelia pressed her lips together tightly to prevent an angry retort, counted to ten silently and then replied diplomatically, "I'm truly sorry to have caused you any embarrassment, Aunt Ursula, and I do appreciate your many kindnesses to me. However, I'm sure that in the midst of all the extravagant and exotic costumes for the ball, mine will appear quite tame."

Her placating words had the desired effect.

"Well, we can only hope." Ursula sighed dramatically, her fit of anger deflated, and the remainder of their luncheon passed in uneasy silence.

Amelia was glad of an excuse to escape the tense atmosphere of the suite as quickly as possible. She changed into her riding clothes and hurried to meet Bernard at the stables. His eagerness to be off was undisguised, and he had their mounts saddled and ready.

As Amelia settled into the saddle, he issued a challenge. "I'll race you to the entrance gates!"

The pair galloped down the curving avenue between the tall stately palms that lined the thoroughfare, whooping and laughing as they rode, with bicycles and pedestrians scattering at their approach. They reached the large columns of the entrance gate in a dead heat and pulled up their horses to a decorous walk as they headed north toward the doctor's house.

The two were so engrossed in Amelia's account of Aunt Ursula's disapproval of her costume that they did not see the two men on horseback waiting in the shadows of the trees ahead of them. As Amelia and Bernard approached, the men spurred their horses, rode directly in front of them and grabbed their bridles.

Amelia's horse reared in fright, and it took all her strength to keep her seat. It was not until her horse had calmed that Amelia recognized the two as the pair who had followed them in St. Petersburg. She looked fearfully at Bernard, but he showed no sign of fright.

"I assume you gentlemen want something. Our money or our lives, perhaps?" His voice was steady, and the only emotion it revealed was that of irritation at having his ride interrupted.

"Very funny," snarled the larger of the two men, a corpulent man with a bullet-shaped bald head. "You just shut your mouth. We'll do the talking."

His partner, a short muscular man with a greasy handlebar mustache pulled a revolver from his pocket and leveled it at Bernard.

"You better pay real close attention, kid," the fat man continued. "You already had one warning and still you ain't paid nothing on your account. The boss is getting impatient. He wants his money now."

"I told you before that I hadn't that kind of money, and nothing has changed now," Bernard replied coolly and indifferently and Amelia was amazed at his composure.

"You got a rich ma and a rich brother. You coulda got the money from them. Looks like now we're just gonna have to hold you for ransom to get the money back," the fat man threatened.

At this, Bernard put his head back and laughed heartily. "Do you realize what a favor you would be doing my family if you put me out of their way? Why, I've been nothing but an embarrassment and thorn in their sides since I came into my inheritance. They'd certainly never pay to get me back!" He laughed again, shaking his head at the outrageousness of the idea.

The fat man looked hesitant. "He may be bluffing," he muttered to his partner, "but he could be on the level, too. We better check with the boss about this."

Then he turned back to Bernard. "But don't forget, Mr. Fraser, we'll be getting the money back from you, one way or another, so you can expect another visit real soon!"

The pair released the horses and turned and rode away.

"Are you all right, Amelia?" Bernard asked. "I'm really sorry to have brought you into this."

"I'm fine, Bernard," Amelia fibbed, gripping the reins hard to stop her hands from trembling, "and very impressed with the way you handled the situation."

"It's only a temporary reprieve, I'm afraid. They won't be so easily discouraged next time."

"I hope there won't be a next time." She couldn't suppress a shudder. "What awful characters! What do you plan to do about them?"

"Right now, dear girl, there is not much I can do, except pray. I've told you I refuse to bankrupt Mother for the likes of them, although she, angel that she is, would spend every pound she has to save her worthless son."

"You certainly fooled those two thugs."

"Yes, but for how long?"

They continued their ride in thoughtful silence, their earlier exuberance dampened by their encounter, but as they approached Dr. Winston's, their youthful good spirits returned.

Sarah answered the door. "Why, Amelia, Bernard! What a lovely surprise. I haven't seen you for days."

"We've been on a shopping expedition to St. Petersburg," Amelia explained. "But now that we've returned, I wanted to thank Dr. Winston for taking such excellent care of me when I was ill with food poisoning."

"Oh dear." Sarah looked disappointed. "William's in Clear Water delivering a baby. It could take hours."

Her disappointment was insignificant compared to the look on Bernard's face. But he brightened appreciably at her next words.

"But I was just about to have tea. Won't you come in

and join me? Company would be lovely, especially *healthy* company." She giggled delightfully as she stood aside for them to enter.

She ushered them into the drawing room, and Amelia caught her breath at the beauty of it. It had the same high ceilings to which she was accustomed, but there all similarity ended. Instead of the dark colors and heavy fabrics that were the fashion of the day, the room was an open expanse of light.

"Oh, Sarah, what a magnificent room! If I lived here, I would spend all my time right here, it's so lovely," Amelia exclaimed, turning in all directions to take in every detail.

Tall French doors and a large picture window opened onto a panoramic view of the bay. The room itself with its cream-colored walls and highly polished oak floors was filled with the afternoon sun. The delicate draperies, the Aubusson carpet, and the upholstery of the graceful Queen Anne furniture were all in the softest hues of yellow and cream. And everywhere Amelia looked were beautiful plants: ficus trees in shining brass jardinieres, gossamer maidenhair ferns, and hanging baskets of trailing ivy.

"Why, it's like a conservatory."

Even Bernard was impressed, although his scrutiny was more of Sarah than her surroundings.

"Thank you," the younger woman replied, "but I can take no credit for the greenery. Gardening, both indoors and out, is William's hobby."

As Sarah served them tea, Amelia thought the room a perfect setting for Sarah with her flaming red hair and russet silk dress. Sarah's complexion paled noticeably under her freckles as Bernard recounted what had transpired on the road from the Belleview. She had seen his condition after he had been beaten, so she knew how rough these people were in their dealings. Amelia thought she detected more than just polite concern and wondered if Sarah was in love with Bernard. She hoped so. It would be refreshing to see the course of love run smooth for someone.

Chapter Fifteen

Bernard and Amelia returned to the Belleview in the gathering twilight, keeping their horses at a slow trot and watching the road for any signs of ambush. They breathed easier when they entered the hotel gates, for they felt it less likely that they would be accosted on the hotel grounds.

After leaving their horses with the stableboy, they walked slowly toward the hotel proper, enjoying the vivid hues of the sunset. They parted company in the lobby as Amelia stopped to check the mail, and Bernard hurried to inform his mother of his latest meeting with the delightful Sarah.

The desk clerk shook his head politely when Amelia inquired for her mail, and she felt disappointed and homesick because she had been hoping to hear from Dr. Will and Aunt Beth. Lost in thought, she did not see the tall stranger behind her, and as she turned, she bumped into him.

207

"Oh!" She colored, embarrassed at her clumsiness. "Please forgive me."

The sauve middle-aged man whom she had almost knocked from his feet removed his hat and gave her a dignified bow. He was handsome in a bold, swarthy fashion, and the streaks of gray in his dark hair gave him a distinguished look.

"Of course, Miss. This is an unexpected pleasure to literally run into such a charming guest of the hotel. Please allow me to introduce myself. I am Edward Rousseau. I have seen you before with Mrs. Hagarty, and I assume you're here for the season also?"

Amelia had always been shy about talking with strangers, but she did not want to be rude, especially after she had almost knocked the gentleman down.

"Do you know my aunt, Mr. Rousseau?"

"Everyone in Chicago knows Ursula Hagarty."

He flashed a wide smile which displayed his large white teeth.

"But I've never seen you in Chicago, have I? I'm sure I would have remembered such a pretty face."

His unctuous flattery made Amelia uneasy, but she felt she must respond politely. After all, he was a friend of Aunt Ursula's.

"No, I've never been to Chicago. I'm Amelia Donelly. My mother was Aunt Ursula's sister. Now if you will please excuse me, my aunt is expecting me."

"Please give her my regards, Miss Donelly, and I hope that we shall meet again."

He tipped his hat to her, and Amelia had the uncomfortable feeling that his eyes followed her up the stairs, but she did not have the temerity to turn around to see.

Ursula and Maude were in a better mood when she returned to the suite than when she had left it.

"Oh, Amelia, Philip was just here and he had the most wonderful news." Maude was gushing with enthusiasm.

"You'll never guess," she teased.

Before Amelia could open her mouth for a response, Ursula broke in impatiently. "Of course, she won't, you silly girl, so go ahead and tell her."

The fact that her two normally placid relatives showed excitement over the news was enough to pique Amelia's interest.

"The hotel's opera company is going to present their own special production of *Der Rosenkavalier* tomorrow night and Philip is going to take us all! Isn't it marvelous!"

Maude was actually dancing about the suite in her enthusiasm, but Amelia was disappointed at the news. She was no fan of opera herself. Although she and her parents had attended the symphony concerts regularly, neither of her parents had cared for opera, and she was ignorant of the art form.

Soon, however, the enthusiasm of her relatives as they chattered away like children over operas they had attended in Chicago and famous singers they had heard began to take effect. The opportunity to study something new was always exciting to her, and she listened eagerly to learn all that she could.

When the conversation lagged, Amelia remembered Edward Rousseau.

"By the way, Aunt, I ran into"—Amelia smiled at the literal meaning of her words—"an acquaintance of yours from Chicago in the lobby who asked that I give you his regards. He's a guest here, too. His name is Edward Rousseau."

Maude gave a pathetic gasp, and Ursula's dark eyes flashed angrily at the mention of his name, as she gripped her ebony cane like a weapon, shaking it at Amelia with more strength than Amelia would have thought she possessed.

"You must have nothing to do with this man, Amelia!

He has caused this family more pain than I could ever tell, and I do not ever again want to hear his name mentioned in my presence—or in Maude's. Is that clear?"

"Yes, Aunt Ursula," Amelia stammered, amazed and curious at the vehemence in her aunt's voice and Maude's pallor simply at the mention of the man's name.

Something was very strange here, but the venom and finality of Ursula's tone convinced her that it would be foolhardy to press either of them for information. Clearly this subject was closed.

Tense and subdued, they awkwardly resumed their discussion of the upcoming opera.

That night as Amelia prepared for bed, she pondered over the extreme reaction that Edward Rousseau's name had created. Just as she was wondering how to find out more about him, Beulah entered the room with an armful of clothing she had laundered and pressed after Amelia's trip to St. Petersburg.

"Beulah, if I ask you something, will you not mention it to Aunt Ursula or Maude?"

"Sure, chile, ole Beulah can be quiet as a grave when need be. What you wanna know?"

"You've been Aunt Ursula's maid for a long time now, haven't you?"

"Sure, since Miss Maude was a little girl, but that ain't no secret." She laughed.

"But that's not my real question, Beulah. What I'd like to know is what can you tell me about Edward Rousseau?"

Beulah turned abruptly from the bureau where she was placing the neatly folded undergarments. Her dark eyes were wide with fear. "You don't want to open up that hornet's nest, Miss Amelia. I never saw a woman so mad as Miss Ursula was at that man. She woulda killed him if she'd had the chance! No sirree, you best leave that subject be."

"Beulah, the man's a guest here at the hotel! If I'm not supposed to speak to him, I think it's only fair that I know why. He isn't the most pleasant man I've ever met, but somehow he didn't seem a horrible villain either. Please tell me."

Beulah stood for a moment, obviously caught between two loyalties. After several long minutes, she reached a decision. "Miss Ursula would skin me alive if she caught me talkin' about him, but I guess you being family, you got a right to know."

Beulah moved to the door that connected Amelia's room to the parlor, opened it a crack to see if anyone was there, then closed it gently. Then she crossed the room, lowered her bulk into the chair next to Amelia, and continued in a husky whisper. "It all started 'bout twelve years ago, the year Miss Maude had her comin' out party. This Mr. Rousseau had been at the ball— Miss Ursula saw to it that every el'gible bachelor in Chicago was there—and he started calling on Miss Maude. He was a han'some young devil with his dark good looks. He didn't have much money, but he had a good position at his bank and lots of promise, so when he ask Miss Maude to marry him, Mr. Sinclair and Miss Ursula, they didn't say no.

"So not six months after the comin' out ball, they gives another party to announce the engagement of Miss Maude and Mr. Rousseau. Miss Maude was the prettiest and happiest I ever seen her that night. But not two months later, her heart is broke. That rascal done 'loped with another woman, an older woman so ugly I don't see how a man could stand her, but with enough money to buy Chicago if she want it.

"Mr. Sinclair and Miss Ursula was so mad they wanted to take him to court and throw him in the jailhouse. Only thing that stopped 'em was poor Miss Maude. She was so heartbroke and pit'ful, they didn't want to cause her any more pain. So they let it all drop.

"For months, Miss Maude never come out of her room, and for a long time after that she never went out in public. She was so afraid she'd see somebody who'd remember how that man made a fool of her. And that, chile, is why nobody mentions the name of Edward Rousseau in this fam'ly. And if you is as smart as I think you is, you won't mention him neither!"

"Poor Maude," Amelia exclaimed. "I think I know exactly how she must have felt."

She didn't see the long hard look Beulah gave her with her eyes narrowed thoughtfully. She was thinking of the pain of Maude's broken heart—and her own. She felt guilty that she had not been friendlier toward her older cousin. The two of them had so little in common that it was difficult for Amelia to relate to Maude very well. She had been so impatient with Maude's frequently spoiled and whining attitude, but now she understood the lack of joy in Maude's life.

Dear God, she thought, *Don't let that happen to me. I don't want to be a dried-up loveless old woman at thirty.*

"Good night, Miss Amelia."

Amelia had forgotten that Beulah was still in the room.

"Good night, Beulah," she answered, "and thank you for telling me. I'll keep it our secret."

Amelia went to her bureau and unearthed from beneath her lace handkerchiefs the rosewood music box that Matt had given her. She carefully wound the brass key and opened the lid, watching the tiny gears revolve

212

as the tinkling music filled the room.

The inscription read, "The heart that has truly loved never forgets." Had Maude forgotten loving Edward Rousseau? And would Amelia ever forget her love for Matthew Laurence? She snapped the lid shut, stopping the gears, but the music continued in her mind, even into her dreams.

As she dressed for the opera the following evening, Amelia remembered what Beulah had told her. It was hard to imagine Maude as a flirtatious young girl engaged to be married and it was even more difficult to imagine Maude as Edward Rousseau's wife. There was something about the man that made Amelia shudder now when she thought of him. Surely Maude was better off without him.

Amelia was very pleased with her new dress of midnight-blue velvet. She had been saving it for a special occasion, and tonight would probably be as special as any nights remaining during her stay at the Belleview. She pinned the delicate white violets that Philip had sent her to the bodice of her gown and pulled on her long white gloves, buttoning the three tiny pearls at each wrist.

Amelia always enjoyed new experiences and tonight would be her first opera. Lady Caroline and Bernard had told her the story of *Der Rosenkavalier* at tea that afternoon, at some points even acting out the parts between them. Amelia knew that it was a comic opera, but she doubted that even the most skilled performance tonight could match the hilarity of her impromptu preview this afternoon.

She prepared herself as well as she could for the possibility that Matt would be there with Diana and decided that she must not let that ruin her evening. Only a few more weeks she reminded herself, and then back to Asheville and reality, and perhaps then when she thought of Matthew Laurence, he would seem more like a character in a book that she had read and less like a part of herself that had been torn from her.

She entered the parlor as Philip knocked at the door.

"Good evening, Amelia," Philip bowed gallantly. "You are looking even more beautiful than usual this evening. I am a fortunate man indeed to share your company."

Maude cleared her throat behind Amelia, standing hopeful of a compliment, too. Her dark gray gown emphasized the shadows under her eyes, and her hair, although artfully arranged by Beulah, was limp and dull. Amelia, remembering Beulah's story of the cruel Rousseau, went to Maude and embraced her.

"Let me fix your flowers, dear," Amelia suggested, taking the spray of stephanotis from the shoulder of Maude's gown and pinning it in her hair. "There, that looks much more elegant."

"You look very pretty tonight, too, Maude," Philip added.

Her cheeks flushed with color at his words, and she did look almost pretty.

When Ursula joined them, their party proceeded down the stairs, through the lobby and into the ballroom, which had been filled with chairs for the performance.

As they were taking their seats, Amelia heard Maude catch her breath sharply, and she looked up to see Edward Rousseau a few seats away. He nodded to Amelia and smiled, but Amelia turned to answer a question Ursula had asked and was saved the problem of an appropriate response.

The house lights were lowered and the orchestra began its overture. The curtain rose on the elegantly furnished Viennese apartment of the Princess von Werdenberg. The handsome young Octavian was on his knees before her declaring his love and was abruptly interrupted by the arrival of the princess's fat and comical cousin, Baron Ochs. Octavian disguised himself as a maid and the lecherous baron flirted with him.

The baron had come to ask the princess to deliver a silver rose to his future bride, Sophie, daughter of the wealthy Faninal. The princess decided to have Octavian deliver the rose, and once she was alone she sadly sang about getting older, losing her beauty, and foolishly loving someone so young as Octavian.

Amelia was profoundly moved by the poignant "Was erzurn' ich mich denn?" and retrieved her handkerchief from the wrist of her glove to wipe the tears from her eyes. As she lifted her head, her eyes met Matt's, who was sitting opposite her on the aisle. She tried to tear her glance away, but his eyes held hers and would not let her go. She felt the tears continue to slip down her cheeks, but she made no move to wipe them away, and she was so confused that she no longer knew whether she was crying for the princess or for herself.

The spell was suddenly broken as the house lights came up and made her blink, and it was only then that Amelia realized that it was Hunter and not Diana who sat at Matt's side. Her view was blocked as people streamed up the aisle for the intermission, and when the aisle cleared again, both Matt and Hunter were gone.

Her mind could barely follow the rest of the opera, and it was only at the rim of her consciousness that she saw the plot end with Octavian and Sophie united in love. Her eyes were drawn again and again to the empty chair across the aisle, but Matt did not return.

"Wasn't it marvelous, Amelia?" Maude bubbled on about the music as she clung to Philip's arm. "Mama has decided we may celebrate the performance by having champagne in our suite. Why don't you ask Lady Caroline and Bernard to join us? I know how fond you are of them, especially Bernard."

She gave a high-pitched giggle and batted her eyelashes at Philip, making Amelia think she had been sampling the champagne already.

It was a welcome diversion, though, so Amelia sought out the Frasers and issued the invitation. When they reached the suite, Amelia was immediately aware that Ursula must have planned this in advance, for not only was there champagne, but also a light buffet supper waiting for them. Amelia tried to concentrate on the lively discussion of the opera and the merits or faults of the singers, but she could not erase the picture of Matt and the look in his eyes from her mind. She forced herself to pay attention as Philip sat beside her and began to speak.

"I enjoyed it so much before when we dined together, Amelia, that I would be honored if you would dine with me again tomorrow night."

"You are very thoughtful, Philip. I would enjoy that."

She gave him a smile, for he always seemed to come to her rescue when her thoughts seemed ready to engulf her. She noticed again his classic blond handsomeness and wondered why she couldn't be sensible and fall in love with someone like Philip instead of a rogue like Matthew Laurence.

"Wonderful!" he exclaimed, and she found his enthusiasm embarrassing. She looked up to find Maude watching them closely and felt again a pang of sympathy for Maude as she remembered the poignant song of the princess.

Then she remembered her own prayer from the night before, "Dear God, don't let me grow old unloved."

Was it better to have someone to love her, even if she did not love him in return, than not to be loved at all? She returned her concentration to the attentive Philip.

Chapter Sixteen

A flurry of activities filled the following weeks: bicycling on the winding paths, horseback riding, deep sea fishing, teas and formal dinners. Amelia found herself constantly surrounded by Ursula, Maude, Philip, and the Frasers, but instead of feeling smothered by their attentions, she felt protected, for only once did she catch a glimpse of Diana Barrington, and Matthew she had not seen at all since the night of the opera.

Matt's absence left a void in her life that even constant activity could not fill, but Amelia knew that this emptiness was more tolerable than the unbearable longing she would experience if he were there in her sight but beyond her reach.

But she was too busy to be sad, and when her gypsy costume arrived from St. Petersburg, her natural youthful exuberance pushed her troubles to the background, and she eagerly anticipated the night of the Mardi Gras Ball.

The afternoon following the arrival of Amelia's costume, Lady Caroline visited the Hagarty suite for tea.

"My dear Mrs. Hagarty, you are so fortunate to have such an attentive daughter and niece. I have my son, whom I dearly love, but there is no substitute as one grows older for the care and affection of female kin. We all understand one another so well."

Her green eyes smiled kindly at Aunt Ursula, and Amelia watched in amazement as the old woman's manner softened visibly before her eyes.

"It was a pleasure to escort young ladies of such discriminating taste when we shopped in St. Petersburg. Their Mardi Gras costumes are so . . . sensible. Well, Amelia's *is* a bit colorful, perhaps, but quite decent."

At this point Caroline lowered her voice and leaned conspiratorially toward Ursula. Amelia had to strain to catch her next words.

"Do you know that there are women—one cannot call them ladies—here who plan to wear . . . Why I can hardly bring myself to say it." Lady Caroline paused and took a long sip of tea and a dainty bite of cake.

"Please go on, Lady Caroline," Ursula urged, captivated by her visitor's gossip, her eyes glowing with anticipation.

"Well"—Caroline's voice was barely a whisper—"I've heard that some of the costumes for this year's ball are to be worn above the knee . . ."

"What is this world coming to!" Ursula gasped.

"But that is not the worst," Caroline continued. "There is at least one other that is rumored to be quite—transparent!"

"Oh, my." Ursula sat back in her chair, weakened by the shocking news. "We live in a wicked age, Lady Caroline, a wicked age."

"That is why I say that you are so fortunate to have these two fine young ladies of such excellent taste and upbringing. I know that they make you very proud indeed. Now, please tell me all about the Palmers in Chicago. I haven't seen them in years."

Amelia struggled to suppress a smile. Caroline's strategy by now was clear to her. Amelia was certain that after their little *tête-à-tête* with Caroline today, Ursula and Maude would drop their disapproval of her costume. Now, aside from her longing for Matt, there was nothing to dampen her expectations of her first costume affair.

When the Tuesday night arrived, Amelia closeted herself in her room to give full attention to her dress. She enlisted Beulah's help in pulling tight the laces on the strapless corselet that cinched her already tiny waist and accentuated the rounded firmness of her young breasts. Because her skirt would be worn several inches above her ankles, Amelia pulled on sheer black stockings. She knew that a true gypsy would go barelegged and perhaps even barefoot, but her innate modesty would not allow her to be so daring. She compensated for the severe black stockings by wearing a pair of bright red high-heeled pumps of soft kid with straps to hold them securely across the insteps in case she felt like breaking into a gypsy dance.

Then she added layer after layer of ruffled petticoats of bright red taffeta that rustled when she moved. She blushed at her reflection when she pulled on the sheer white voile peasant blouse. Its long full sleeves were gathered at the wrists, but the plunging neckline exposed the cleavage between her breasts and accented her smooth shoulders and slender neck.

Next came the full black satin skirt cut in a circle so that it stood out about her waist like a wheel when she twirled. On the left side, the skirt was caught halfway to the hemline and tucked up to the waistband to expose the layers of carmine ruffles. Over the peasant blouse was added a velvet bodice in a bright floral design of black, red, and pink. The fitted bodice laced snugly just beneath her breasts.

Beulah brushed Amelia's long thick hair so that it flowed down her back almost to her waist. She pinned it back behind her right ear, and in that ear, Amelia wore a large gold hoop. Then Beulah tied a small black kerchief at an angle over Amelia's brow and stepped back to view the effect. For once the talkative woman was unable to find the words she needed to express her approval, so she made do with an emphatic nod. Amelia picked up the beribboned tambourine that completed her costume, tapped the flat of it against her hip and twirled around the room. Her eyes sparkled and her cheeks glowed.

"Oh, this is fun, Beulah!" she exclaimed, and thanked the old woman with a hug. "I think I'll just stay a gypsy after tonight and run away with the first tribe I find!"

Beulah was shocked. "What a terr'ble thing to say, Miss Amelia. Don't you know they eats little chil'ren?"

Beulah's eyes were wide with disapproval and she shook her head. "Don't know what's got into you lately, chile. You just go, go, go all the time like you's trying to run from the devil. You don't fool ole Beulah with this gypsy talk. What you need is to settle down and marry some nice man who can take care of you right, like Mr. Philip."

Beulah's observations were too accurate for comfort, but Amelia had already made up her mind not to let anything spoil her fun tonight. She turned to face Beulah with her hands on her hips and her feet set apart, looking every inch a Romany princess.

"I think I'll find me a dark handsome gypsy prince, with a golden ring in one ear and a knife in his boot, and we'll travel the world together in a painted caravan earning our living by performing exotic gypsy dances."

Amelia whirled about the room to illustrate.

"And then when I grow old and fat, I'll buy me a crystal ball and tell fortunes from town to town," Amelia said teasingly.

"Hrumpf!" was Beulah's only comment, and she left to see if Maude needed any last-minute assistance.

Amelia joined Maude in the parlor to show Aunt Ursula her costume.

Ursula's eyes narrowed as she viewed the breathtaking gypsy princess before her, but her only comment was kind. "You look very striking, Amelia. I'm sure you'll have plenty of partners to choose from tonight."

Amelia admired Maude's costume. The plain homespun gray dress with its starched white apron, neckerchief and cap suited Maude's dark coloring and the severe lines of her face. She looked almost pretty and her eyes glittered with excitement.

When Philip arrived, all three of the women were enchanted by his costume. He wore fitted breeches tucked into the tops of his high cuffed boots and a full white linen shirt open to the waist. A bright red sash encircled his waist and held a vicious-looking cutlass. A black patch rakishly covered one eye and his blond hair was topped by a wide-brimmed black hat with a long white ostrich plume.

"Oh, Philip, you look perfectly splendid!" Maude gushed as she circled around him to see the full effect.

Philip executed an elegant bow, pointing one booted toe and sweeping the large hat before him so that the ostrich plume dragged the floor.

"Thank you, ma'am," he replied. "I will be the envy of every man there tonight, because I will have a beautiful woman on each arm. And if they both promise to dance with me," he teased, "I'll show them where my treasure's buried."

Maude beamed with pleasure, while Amelia tied her

small black mask over her eyes and they were ready.

"Have fun, children," Ursula instructed them. "I know you will be late, so I won't wait up for you. I will plan to hear all the details tomorrow."

There was already a huge crowd of people in the ballroom by the time the trio entered, and Amelia told Philip that she wished to sit for a while and take in all the costumes.

As she watched the partygoers, she saw characters out of both history and fiction: Cleopatra with Marc Antony; John Smith and Pocahontas; Siegfried and Brunehilde; George and Martha Washington; a frontiersman in coonskin cap with his pioneer wife; a fairy princess with a handsome prince; a large white rabbit with Alice in Wonderland; and coming directly across the floor toward her was the regal Queen Elizabeth with her frizzled carrot-red hair and elaborate farthingale. Beside her trotted an Indian brave in full war paint, the fringed leather of his jacket and trousers flying as he hurried to keep up with the queen.

"My dear, you are fabulous!" Lady Caroline exclaimed. "You must have gypsy blood to wear the costume so well. You make me wish for a violin player so that I could cross your palm with silver to see you dance. But where are the others?"

Amelia nodded to the dance floor where Philip and Maude were engaged in a sedate waltz. Then she giggled. She had never seen a large white rabbit waltz before, but there he was, whirling Alice away right in front of her.

"Your costumes are wonderful," Amelia told them. "And you don't even need a mask, Bernard, with all that paint on your face."

"It does rather take me back to the day that we slipped away from Nanny in the nursery and got into Mother's face paints. Unfortunately, I was all too easily recognizable then, and Nanny warmed our behinds with a hairbrush and sent us to bed without tea!''

Amelia laughed, because although Bernard was her senior by a year or two, so many times he still seemed like a mischievous little boy.

Then her laughter died in her throat as she saw the couple standing in the doorway to the ballroom. It was Matt and Diana. Matt wore no costume or mask, just his elegant evening clothes that suited him so well, but Diana was another matter. She was dressed in a daringly diaphanous costume of shimmering fabric that clung revealingly to every curve of her body. A silver crescent moon was nestled in her upswept hair and her bare arms and shoulders were dusted with silver glitter.

"Well, well," Amelia heard Lady Caroline chuckle behind her, "the goddess of the hunt, and it looks like she's already bagged her first quarry from the unhappy expression on the face of her escort."

Amelia was grateful at that moment that Philip asked her to dance. She whirled into his arms with a flourish of red petticoats and gave him her complete attention, using all her powers of concentration not to glance toward the couple who still stood near the door.

She danced with Philip many times and with Bernard. But she was somewhat taken aback when a tall, dignified Sir Walter Raleigh asked for the honor of a dance in a clipped British accent. Then she recognized Hunter behind the mask. She was on the verge of refusing when she admitted to herself that Hunter could not be responsible for his employer's misconduct and also that he had always been kind to her. She accepted with a smile.

"I haven't seen you for a while, Miss Donelly. What have you been doing with yourself?" Hunter inquired politely.

"Oh, a great number of things."

Amelia was determined to sound enthusiastic in case

Hunter reported their conversation back to Matt.

"Just the other day we went out into the Gulf several miles, so far that we could not see land, to go deep sea fishing. I caught grouper, the largest fish I've ever seen. That evening the chef broiled it for our dinner, a most delicious . . ." Her voice dropped as they waltzed by Diana and Matt and her eyes caught Matt's over Diana's glittering bare shoulder. Amelia tried to wrest her eyes away but could not and was saved from breaking into tears only by Hunter's elegant and graceful turn as he steered her toward the other end of the ballroom.

Collecting her wits about her once more, she picked up the threads of their conversation. "And you, Mr. Hunter, what has occupied you since I saw you last? Are you having many days off to do as you please?"

"No, as a matter of fact, I've had no time off at all since I saw you on the dock that first time. Mr. Laurence and I have spent every waking moment on the matter that brought us here, and it doesn't look as if it will soon be finished."

Hunter's face, usually inscrutable, looked tired and careworn. Amelia wondered what business could create such fatigue and worry—and then another thought struck her. If Hunter was telling the truth—and she had no reason to doubt his word—then Matt had not spent all his time with Diana. Her spirits soared, only to dive again as she reminded herself that he still was engaged to marry the woman, and he would have the rest of his life to spend with her.

When the dance was over, Amelia led Hunter to introduce him to Lady Caroline and left them engaged in reminiscences of England, while she went off in search of Bernard, wanting him to meet Hunter, too.

Looking out the doorway into the corridor, Amelia saw Bernard standing between two vaguely familiar figures. One was dressed as a policeman and the other as a clown. She was about to approach them when the larger of the pair grabbed Bernard's arm, wrenched it behind his back, and shoved him toward the stairwell that led to the basement. Amelia looked around for help, but not seeing anyone, decided to follow them. If she could find where they were taking him, then at least she could come back for assistance.

She was glad that she had left her tambourine with Lady Caroline and that the soles of her kid pumps were soft and made no sound. She moved as quietly as she could to prevent the rustle of her taffeta petticoats as she descended the stairs that led beneath the ground floor of the hotel.

The Belleview's basement was unlike any she had ever seen. The hotel stood on squat brick columns a few feet above ground level, and the basement consisted of large bricked passageways that had been cut into the ground below the hotel to facilitate the movement of food and linens beneath it.

Amelia kept out of sight behind one of the columns as the sinister pair dragged Bernard halfway down one of the passageways and threw him roughly up against the brick wall. Amelia stayed in the shadows, but close enough to hear every word.

"We told you we'd be seeing you again."

The man dressed as a policeman was speaking in growling menacing tones, and Amelia suppressed a gasp of recognition as he removed his hat and mask. He was one of the men who had accosted them on the road to the Winstons.

"The boss has decided to give you one more chance to pay your debt," the man continued. "Since you don't seem to have no ready cash, the boss is gonna let you work off what you owe. All you gotta do is a little job for him, and all your IOU's will be returned to you."

Bernard stood up to his full height, looking the man

straight in the eye, and Amelia silently applauded his courage.

"What kind of work did your employer have in mind?"

"Just a small simple job, really. All you have to do is kill Matthew Laurence."

Amelia's cry of astonishment was drowned out by Bernard's angry retort. "What! You must be crazy! I'm no murderer. You can bloody well tell that to your boss!"

"Now don't be too hasty here, Mr. Fraser. At this point, what it seems to boil down to is your life and possibly the life of that redheaded woman of yours or Laurence's. Take your choice. I'd be all too happy to use you as an example of what happens to men who don't pay their debts. You better take a day or two to think it over. You can give me your answer day after tomorrow at three o'clock on the road where we met before. And remember, not a word of this to nobody or you're a dead man for sure."

The pair shoved Bernard hard against the wall again and then ran swiftly down the corridor where they were swallowed up in the darkness. Amelia ran from her hiding place to Bernard's side.

"Amelia! What are you doing here? Don't let them see you," Bernard whispered loudly, and pushed her along the corridor in the opposite direction from where the pair had disappeared.

Amelia was shaking with fright, but not for herself. "What are you going to do, Bernard? They've threatened to kill you! And why do they want Matthew Laurence dead?"

"I don't know, Amelia, but I do know that you must stay out of this. You've seen how they operate and how dangerous they are. I don't want you or Mother involved. Oh God, I guess you are involved—'that redheaded woman.' That must be you—or Sarah!"

By now they had climbed the basement stairs and stood in the hallway outside the ballroom. The gaiety of the music and voices from the ball was an ironic contrast to the seriousness of their plight.

"Don't talk nonsense, Bernard. I'm you're friend, so naturally I'm involved. And as for 'the redheaded woman,' why they have no reason to harm either Sarah or me."

Amelia wished she felt as confident as she sounded. The men did, of course, know that Amelia could identify them, but there was no time to worry about herself now.

"I'll do anything I can to help. Just tell me how."

"The only thing that might be of help to us now would be to know why they want Matthew Laurence dead. If we knew that, we might be able to figure out who the leader of this gang of scum is."

"I know Matthew Laurence. I could talk to him and see if I can find out why they want you to kill him," Amelia was surprised to hear herself say.

Bernard was equally surprised. "I didn't know you two were acquainted. But this may be just the break we're looking for. Would you speak to him, Amelia?"

Amelia felt her heart pounding rapidly as she contemplated a meeting with Matt. Her pride told her never again, but her fear for his life and Bernard's made her realize that this was something she could not refuse. She grabbed Bernard's hand and dragged him into the ballroom.

"He was here a minute ago. I'll find him and talk with him now."

But when they re-entered the room, neither Matt nor Diana was anywhere to be seen. Amelia left Bernard with Caroline and Hunter and started off in search of Matt. She checked the lobby and the hotel verandas and finally in desperation climbed the stairs to his suite. She knocked frantically at the door, calling his name.

The door opened wide and there stood Diana Barrington.

"Come in, Amelia," she invited with a forced feline smile. "I've been intending to have a talk with you for a long time, and now will do nicely."

Chapter Seventeen

Amelia did not wait to be asked again. She hurried into the room, and Diana closed the door behind her.

"Where's Matt?" Amelia insisted. "I must talk with him right away."

Diana walked languidly to the liquor cabinet and poured herself a snifter of brandy. Her silvered skin glittered in the dim light, and as she stood before the fireplace, the light from the embers silhouetted her curvaceous body in the transparent dress. But Amelia was too distracted to notice Diana's immodesty.

"Where is he?" she begged.

Diana laughed a low, throaty chuckle. "My, you are the impatient one, aren't you? But you might as well relax, girl, because I don't know where he is. But what I do know is that when he returns, it will be I who is here waiting for him and not you."

Amelia shook her head in frustration. "You don't understand—"

"On the contrary, I understand all too well, and it's time you came to understand a few things, too. Matt is in love with me and is going to marry me, and none of your little country girl tricks or wiles will make a whit of difference in that. You're a sneak, Amelia Donelly. While my back is turned, you flirt with and entice my fiancé with your so-called innocence, but you don't fool me for a moment. I know what you're up to and I want you to understand that I will fight to the death if necessary, to keep what is rightfully mine. So be warned. If you know what is good for you, you will go as far away as possible from the Belleview and as quickly as you can, and don't even look back."

Amelia stood momentarily stunned by what Diana had said. Then anger and pride flared within her as the woman's audacity registered. Her voice was forcefully controlled as she replied, "How dare you threaten me! And what do you know of me that you could presume to judge my character or my motives?"

Amelia fought for self-control, wanting more than anything to throw herself at Diana's smirking face and scratch her eyes out. But she knew that she couldn't waste time with Diana now when Matt and Bernard's lives were at stake.

"I don't want your precious Matt, because I've been taught to honor promises and the truth, and it seems he honors neither, but I must speak with him on a business matter of the utmost urgency—"

Diana cut her off. "Wrong again. As far as I am concerned, you have no business with Matt of any kind, and if you insist on seeing him, you'll pay dearly. I'll see you dead—" She stopped abruptly as Matt entered the door of the suite. "Why, hello, darling. When I lost you at the ball, I decided to wait for you here. It will be much more comfortable—and private—as soon as Miss Donelly leaves. We were just having a little chat."

Diana purred her words at Matt like a kitten.

"I can imagine," Matt said wryly. "But you may as well go to your room, Diana. The Mardi Gras is over."

Amelia's heart surged with hope as she grasped the possible meaning of his tone and words, hope that his engagement with Diana was finished.

He turned to Amelia. "Please stay." His tone was brusque, but his eyes begged her. "Hunter will be here in a moment if that will make you more comfortable."

Diana walked to the door and laid her hand on Matt's cheek. Standing on tiptoe she kissed him firmly on the lips. "The ball may be over, darling, but that is all. I'll talk to you tomorrow."

She slid her hand down from his chin until it rested possessively on his chest. Then with a last sensuous caress, she left.

Amelia had stood uncomfortably with her eyes averted, trying to ignore the agony she felt when she saw the two of them together. She had not seen Matt knock Diana's grasping hand away. She raised her eyes to find Matt looking sadly at her, and she felt certain that her momentary hope had been in vain. She stood deathly pale in the firelight.

"What is it, Amelia? Here, please sit down."

He pulled a chair close to the hearth and led her to it. She was shaking uncontrollably from fear and anger. Matt placed more wood on the fire and coaxed it into a roaring blaze. He poured a snifter of brandy for Amelia and thrust it into her hands.

"Drink it," he ordered, "all of it. No substituting tea this time."

Amelia obeyed, and as the fiery liquid and the blazing fire warmed her, she relaxed enough to stop shaking. But Matt could still read the terror in her eyes. He drew a chair opposite her and sat down so that he could see her face. At that moment Hunter entered the suite, saw the couple, muttered an apology and turned to leave, but Matt stopped him with a request to stay.

"That is, I want you to stay if it is all right with Amelia," Matt amended.

"Yes, please."

Amelia was glad of his presence. She knew that his quick mind might be of help in the present dilemma and that his presence in the room would prevent her from saying or doing something she might later regret.

"Now, Amelia," Matt said gently as Hunter seated himself nearby, "tell me what's wrong."

The tears raced uncontrollably down Amelia's cheeks as she was forced once more to face the terrible facts that had brought her here, and once again she found one of Hunter's large white handkerchiefs thrust into her hands.

"They want you dead, Matt." She sobbed.

Hunter and Matt exchanged a knowing look as Amelia wiped her eyes with the handkerchief.

"Who wants me dead?" he asked softly, trying to calm her with the tone of his voice.

Amelia took a deep breath, knowing that if she did not stop crying, she could be of no help to either Matt or Bernard.

"We're not sure," she replied carefully. "All we know is that the same people to whom Bernard Fraser owes his gambling debt want him to kill you in order to cancel what he owes them. He has been warned that if he doesn't do this, he is the one who will die."

She looked at him searchingly and her love for him stabbed through her with a searing pain. She knew he could never be hers. But even if she could not have him, she would never wish him harm, and the thought of his dying made the tears start again. He looked into her eyes, and the hunger she felt for him burned inside her.

She started as he took both her hands in his and held them gently.

"I don't know who would want to kill me. That is, I do not know him by name, but I must be getting very close to that information if he is getting so desperate."

Amelia's face was a picture of bewilderment, so Matt attempted to explain. "Hunter and I have been investigating a land fraud scheme that has its origins here in Florida. We've discovered what may be a connection between this illegal activity and the questionable lending practices of those ruffians Bernard Fraser has had dealings with."

"Bernard has to let them know how he plans to do it by the day after"—She glanced at the clock on the mantel whose hands showed two o'clock—"by tomorrow, Thursday afternoon. If he hasn't agreed to kill you and hasn't a plan ready for their approval, they made it very clear that he would be the victim."

She neglected to add that the "redheaded woman," be it Sarah or herself, was in danger, too. For now, her sole concern was the man who held her hands.

"I think the best thing for me to do would be to talk with Bernard. Hunter?"

Hunter gave a nod of agreement.

"Perhaps you could arrange for Hunter and me to meet with Bernard tomorrow. I have an idea or two that might at least buy us some time and may even force the person behind all this to show his hand. Will you set up the meeting for right after lunch tomorrow, Amelia?"

"Of course," Amelia agreed. "But where? Do you suppose Bernard is being watched?"

"That is a definite possibility, my dear," Hunter interjected. "But if we meet in the Fraser suite, we should be able to slip in and out without being seen unless, of course, the villains are hiding under the bed."

A smile crinkled his bright blue eyes and Amelia smiled in response.

She was acutely aware that Matt still held her hands in his, and at that moment he gave them a reassuring squeeze.

"Thank you for the warning, Amelia. It is more than I deserve, and I promise you that I will make this up to you, no matter what it takes."

She could not meet his eyes for fear that her tears would begin again. She reluctantly pulled her hands from his and stood to leave. Matt walked her to the door and gazed down at her, but again she avoided looking at him. Instead she said good night to Hunter and slipped out into the hallway. She hurried down the corridor toward her room, but this time she could not resist a backward glance. Matt stood in the doorway, but the light of the room was behind him and she could not see his face. She looked back again as she entered her room and he still stood there. She wanted with all her heart to race back down the hall and fling herself into his arms, but she knew the foolishness and futility of those thoughts. She entered her room and locked the door behind her.

She slept fitfully that night, awakening once with a scream stifled in her throat and her body bathed in a cold sweat of fear for Matt and Bernard. She forced the nightmares from her mind, but in their place came the leering face of Diana Barrington and remembrance of the warnings she had given Amelia in Matt's suite.

Amelia felt the yawning emptiness inside her from her parents' death and intensified by the fact that the one man whom she loved could never be hers. She could not imagine never seeing him again, but that was what would happen once she left the Belleview. She prayed that his plan for dealing with the threat against his life and Bernard's would work. Even if she were never to see him again, the knowledge that he was alive and well somewhere in the world would comfort her for the rest of her life.

Finally, exhausted from the excitement of the ball and the tension of her encounter with Diana and with Matt, Amelia fell into a deep and dreamless sleep.

She was awakened late the next morning by Beulah as she opened the draperies on the French doors to admit the brilliant morning sun. Amelia squinted against the light, sat up in bed and stretched as Beulah placed a breakfast tray across her lap. On the tray was a single red rose with a red satin ribbon and a small card.

Amelia's heart began to beat rapidly as she opened the note, remembering the roses that Matt had sent her just a few weeks ago. But she was disappointed to see Philip's signature on the card with the question, "Would the beautiful gypsy princess care to run away with a wild buccaneer?"

Another morning she might have enjoyed the facetiousness of his courtship, but today she had too much to worry about to banter words with Philip. She hurriedly ate her breakfast, bathed, dressed in her riding habit and made her way to the Fraser suite.

Bernard looked as if he had not slept at all and was toying with his breakfast. He looked visibly relieved to see Amelia and poured her a cup of coffee as he waited to hear what she had learned from Matt.

"Matt and his man Hunter want to meet with you here this afternoon. Matt said he has some ideas that might be helpful. You see, he and Hunter have been investigating a land fraud operation, and they think they must be close to discovering the person behind all this, especially in light of the task you've been assigned."

Amelia shuddered as she thought again of how casually the two thugs had talked of murder.

Lady Caroline, looking as fresh as if she'd gone to bed with the sunset, joined them.

"Good morning! How are my favorite youngsters today? Why, Amelia, whatever is the matter? You haven't had another 'accident,' have you? You're as pale as a ghost."

"No, Lady Caroline. I only wish it were that," Amelia responded.

"Wait," Bernard interrupted, "I'd better tell her. Mother, I think you should sit down. This isn't a pretty story."

Caroline, all her previous sparkle extinguished by the gravity of Bernard's tone, pulled Amelia down beside her on the sofa as she prepared for Bernard's explanation.

"Mother, do you remember the men who followed us in St. Petersburg?"

Caroline nodded.

"I didn't tell you because I didn't want to cause you any more worry, but they threatened me the day we returned to the hotel. Amelia was with me on our way to see Sarah. They were going to hold me for ransom, but I assured them the family would be so glad to be rid of me that they wouldn't pay."

"Why, Bernard!" his mother exploded. "What a horrible thing to say about your own flesh and blood! You know we'd do anything to keep you out of harm's way!"

"Of course, I know that, Mother dear," Bernard replied patiently. "The point is that *they* don't know it, so it kept me from being kidnapped. However, my reprieve didn't last very long. The same two were at the ball last night and they told me that they have a job for me to do to cancel my debt."

"Oh, that's a wonderful idea, Bernard, and I'm sure

the work will be good for you." His mother beamed at him.

Ever patient with his mother's flights of reasoning, Bernard plodded on. "The job they have for me is to kill Matthew Laurence."

"Good God, Bernard, you can't be serious?"

The reality of the situation was finally beginning to take hold in Caroline's mind.

"Of course you told them that you wouldn't do it?" she insisted.

"In words of which you would not approve, Mother, but their alternative was my life and that of 'my redheaded woman' if I do not kill Laurence."

"They can't be serious! Surely they don't mean . . ."

Lady Caroline looked from Bernard to Amelia and back again for assurance but found none.

"Amelia went to Laurence and told him of the threat—"

"Amelia? Went to Laurence? Do you know him, girl?"

Caroline looked at her questioningly, but Amelia could not meet her eyes, afraid of what her own might give away.

"Oh, I met him briefly on the train on our trip south," she answered as offhandedly as she could.

"Anyway," Bernard continued, "Mr. Laurence and his man, Hunter, believe that whoever wants him dead is the same person whom they are seeking in connection with their investigation of land fraud. Matt has some ideas of how to deal with this and wants to meet with us here this afternoon. Does that meet with your approval, Mother?"

Lady Caroline looked thoughtful. "I must say that I was very impressed with Mr. Hunter last night. Coincidently, I learned that he and your father were at school together, Bernard. And from all that I've heard of Matthew Laurence, I'm sure he will be a formidable ally. Yes, by all means, inform them that we will meet with them here. But what about the authorities? Shouldn't we notify them?"

"Let's discuss that this afternoon after we see what Mr. Laurence has in mind. If he is on the trail of someone, we don't want his quarry scared off, and the best way to protect me and my redheaded woman"— Bernard grinned at Amelia—"is to catch whoever is behind all this."

Amelia studied Bernard's boyish vitality which emanated from the top of his thick brown hair to the ends of his long slender fingers that held his coffee cup, and she prayed fervently that he would be spared. And she thought of another brown-haired man whose temples were sprinkled with gray, and she wondered if she would be able to continue living if anything were to happen to him. And then to her ardent prayer for his life, she added a prayer of confession of her own sin of coveting that which was not hers.

"Cheer up, Amelia," Bernard broke into her thoughts. "We're not finished yet. In fact, I'm sure we can make these people sorry they ever chose to tangle with us. We've a long fighting tradition in this family. Father was at Sandhurst, you know."

Amelia smiled at his enthusiasm, for Bernard seemed to view the whole problem as a kind of lark. She hoped his optimism was warranted. Perhaps when they all met together they really could come up with a plan to foil the villains in their midst.

Caroline, not wanting to dwell on unpleasantness, veered the conversation to other matters. "I noticed Philip Sheridan was very attentive to you at the ball last night, Amelia. And he was quite upset when you disappeared. If Bernard hadn't told him that you'd returned to your room with a headache, I do believe he would have organized a search party on the spot."

Caroline looked at Amelia inquisitively, and Amelia knew what she was implying.

"Philip is a very good friend, Caroline, to me and to Maude and Aunt Ursula, but that is all."

Caroline chuckled. "That may be all there is as far as you're concerned, my dear, but, believe me, I've seen that look in a man's eye before, and platonic friendship is not what he has in mind."

"Mother, don't badger Amelia about her private life," Bernard said. "She's upset enough about all this other mess without having to deal with the amorous intentions of Philip Sheridan."

Turning to Amelia, he added, "Do you suppose Sheridan could shed any light on this problem?"

"I seriously doubt it, and definitely the fewer people who know about our plans, the greater chance they'll have of success."

"Well, sitting about all morning fretting will get us nothing but a good case of nerves. I say we should all go riding. I see Amelia's dressed for it. Shall we?" Lady Caroline looked to them for consent, then retired to her room to don her riding habit.

"Your mother is quite a lady," Amelia commented.

"Yes, she is. And if I live to get out of this mess, I shall spend the rest of my life trying to make up for the pain I've caused her. I went rather wild after Father died, and it's taken me too long to grow up. Now I only hope I can live long enough to enjoy my maturity."

Amelia's stomach tensed into knots. Their meeting this afternoon and the possibility for the success of Matt's plan would determine whether two lives, both dear to her, would go on.

Chapter Eighteen

After a brisk ride on the bluffs along the coast, Amelia and the Frasers ordered a light lunch in the Tiffany Room. The hall was almost deserted; many revelers from the night before were still sleeping off the effects of their merrymaking. Although both Caroline and Bernard kept up a cheerful banter throughout the meal, Amelia noticed that they, like herself, barely touched their food. Their preoccupation was with the upcoming meeting and the lives dependent on its outcome.

When Amelia returned to her room to change out of her riding clothes, there was a soft knock on her door and Maude entered. Amelia again felt a twinge of guilt because she did not spend more time with Maude. She wished that she had more in common with her cousin, so that being in her company would be easier on both of them, but Maude was so often quiet and withdrawn that sometimes Amelia felt that she knew her less and less instead of becoming better acquainted.

"Philip has been here asking for you this morning, Amelia. Have you seen him?"

"No, I've been riding with the Frasers. But I do need to see him to apologize about slipping off without saying good night."

Her eyes glanced at the red rose Beulah had placed in a bud vase on her bureau, and Maude's eyes followed hers.

"Flowers from Philip?" she asked, but her voice was so devoid of tone or feeling that Amelia could not tell if she was jealous or simply curious, and she hadn't the time to find out, for the meeting in the Fraser suite would begin soon.

"Please excuse me, Maude, but I must change clothes quickly. There is someone I must meet in just a few minutes and I have to get dressed."

"Are you meeting Philip?"

Amelia paused for only a second. She knew she could not reveal anything about the true nature of her meeting, so perhaps in this case a small white lie would be acceptable.

"Yes, I am and I must hurry. I'm sorry, Maude," she spoke soothingly as she ushered her to the door. "I'll talk with you later."

"But you forget, Amelia dear, you promised to tell Mama about the ball last night. She's been waiting to hear from you."

"Yes, I know." Amelia cast about desperately for a way out of her dilemma. "Tell Aunt Ursula that I will fill her in on all the glorious and gaudy details at dinner this evening without fail," Amelia begged weakly as she gently edged Maude out of her room.

She closed the door behind Maude and leaned her forehead against the doorframe for a moment, wishing she could understand her unusual cousin. But she had no time for worrying about Maude now.

She threw off her riding clothes and put on a fresh shirtwaist and skirt. She didn't have time to put up her hair again, so she brushed it and tied it back with a black velvet ribbon. Her reflection in the mirror was deathly pale and her bright blue eyes were wide with anxiety. She pinched her cheeks to give them color and left her room by the hallway door, avoiding the parlor because she didn't have time to delay with Maude again.

When she reached the Fraser suite, she knocked softly and the door was opened instantly by Rose. The first person she saw as she stepped into the room was Matthew Laurence, who stood by the fireplace, his elbow propped casually on the mantelpiece. Hunter was seated in a chair before the fire, and Lady Caroline and Bernard sat on the sofa.

"Good afternoon, Miss Donelly." Matt's voice was cool and impersonal as he motioned to the chair next to him.

"Please forgive me for keeping you waiting, but I had difficulty getting away from Maude," Amelia said, still breathless from hurrying.

She sat down in the chair Matt had indicated. Matt's nearness made her blood pound in her ears, and although she kept her eyes averted from him, her body was very aware of him. All of her senses were intensified by his closeness, and she could even hear the leather of his riding boots creak as he shifted his weight. She felt his eyes on her, but kept her gaze riveted on her hands clasped tightly in her lap.

Hunter cleared his throat and spoke. "Mr. Laurence has asked me to fill you in on the investigation that we have been conducting over the past few months into a spurious land investment scheme. We have had the Pinkerton Agency trying to track down and identify the head of this organization and to discover where the money disappears once it has been bilked from unsuspecting investors. So far we have not been able to trace anything or anyone to the top. One connection that we have made, however, is between whoever is behind the land fraud and the moneylenders that have threatened Mr. Fraser.

"When Miss Donelly reported to us that these moneylenders want Mr. Laurence dead, we knew that we were on the right track, and that we must be getting very close for them to make such a desperate move. Actually, they have played right into our hands, for they have presented us with a scenario in which we can expose the top man in their organization. Our plan is a dangerous one, but then so is the element with whom we are dealing."

He paused and surveyed the room to be sure he had everyone's attention before he continued, "This is our plan. Mr. Fraser is to report back to the two hooligans who threatened him that he has arranged a fatal accident for Mr. Laurence. It is to occur when Mr. Fraser invites Mr. Laurence and me to accompany him on a wild turkey shoot. Mr. Laurence will be 'fatally' injured by an accidental blast from a shotgun."

"Oh, no!" Amelia could not contain the involuntary cry that escaped her. She began to tremble and then felt Matt's strong hand placed reassuringly on her shoulder. His kindness toward her made her want to weep. Why did he make it so difficult for her by seeming to be so caring? It would be so much easier if he simply ignored her. Now she felt she understood a new meaning of the term "killing with kindness." She pulled her attention reluctantly from the pressure of his hand and concentrated on what Lady Caroline was saying.

"But he won't really be hurt in anyway, will he?"

"Not if we are very careful, plan well, and follow those plans to the letter," Matt assured her, appearing to take his role as intented victim in stride. "Continue, please, Hunter."

"It will not be difficult to rig a shotgun with blank shells, and I have already consulted our thespian troupe in residence for the necessary 'bloodshed.' They have assured me that it is gruesomely realistic. After the accident has been staged, we will carry Mr. Laurence to Dr. Winston's. This part, a fraudulent death certificate to be offered as proof, I will leave to you to arrange." He gestured to Bernard, who nodded his consent.

"The success of the entire operation revolves around this part," Hunter continued. "When Mr. Fraser agrees to set up the accident, he must do so only under the stipulation that he be allowed to meet the man to whom he owes the money. He must insist that this man personally return his IOU's to him."

Hunter turned to Bernard. "You must understand that by doing this, Mr. Fraser, you are placing yourself in a great deal of danger. They will agree to this only if they are sure they can dispose of you so that you would never be able to identify their leader. But we plan to have the Pinkertons and the local authorities following your every move, so that we can not only close in and protect you but also capture the man we're after at the same time. Does anyone have any questions?"

Silence reigned in the room as all involved pondered the seriousness of the proposed plan. A small slip-up at any point along the way could mean the death of both Matt and Bernard.

Finally Lady Caroline spoke. "It's a sensible plan to me. The only way that we can remove the danger to Bernard and Mr. Laurence is to identify the principal in this scheme. Yes, there is danger involved, but not as much danger as there would be to both of you if we do nothing. I suggest that Amelia and I be present on the hunting trip. The more witnesses there are to the 'accident,' the more credibility it will carry."

"An excellent suggestion, Lady Caroline," Hunter

agreed, and gave her an admiring glance.

"The tricky part will be making them take me to their boss," Bernard said.

"It may be less tricky than you think," Matt entered the discussion. "You see, knowing the way these people work, I imagine that once they have used you to get rid of me, they will find it necessary to dispose of you also, so there will be no trail leading back to them. Your insistence on meeting their boss will probably be quite to their liking, if I have judged these characters correctly."

"What about the death certificate?" Hunter inquired. "Will there be any problem in getting the doctor to go along with us on this?"

Bernard shook his head. "As long as the authorities are aware of what is happening, I believe Dr. Winston will agree to a temporary deception. He was quite angry when he saw how those chaps roughed me up before. I think he'll be glad to do his part to put them behind bars. I personally will fill him in on what has happened and ask for his support."

"Very good," Hunter continued. "Now all we need to do is set a timetable. Bernard, your meeting with these villains is scheduled for tomorrow afternoon, Thursday, right? Then I suggest we set our hunting trip for the following Monday. That will give us a few days to confer with the authorities and alert the Pinkertons. In the meantime, except for Miss Donelly's association with the Frasers, which is common knowledge and therefore unsuspicious, I suggest the rest of us have no contact with one another except for Bernard's invitation to hunt. We must do nothing that raises any doubts or questions, and since we do not know with whom we're dealing, we must say nothing to anyone."

He paused and leveled a steady gaze at Amelia. "And

that includes your relatives and Philip Sheridan, Miss Donely."

Amelia nodded and glanced up to find Matt looking at her searchingly. She wondered what he was thinking, then realized that he must be thinking of her relationship with Philip. She felt the color rise in her cheeks and lowered her eyes to avoid his stare. All she could think of when she looked at him was how empty her world would be if anything happened to him.

A sudden anger at her fate erupted. In the space of a few short months her beloved parents had been taken from her. And then when it seemed she had found a love to fill the void in her life, she had discovered that that love belonged to another. She felt her rage at the unfairness of life building inside her and knew that she could not sit quietly in the same room any longer with a man she loved so fiercely and not give herself away. She rose so quickly that she startled Lady Caroline.

"What is it, Amelia?"

"Forgive me, but if we are finished here, I must get back to Maude. I'm afraid I walked out on her rather abruptly and I don't want to make her suspicious. Please excuse me."

Steeling herself not to look at Matt again, she hurried from the suite. But she knew she could not go back to face Maude yet. What she needed was a long brisk walk to exorcise her anger. As she ran down the stairs to the lobby, she saw Philip standing at the desk. But before she could turn down the west corridor and slip away, he had seen her.

"Amelia," she heard him call, and she knew that she had no choice but to stop and speak with him.

"Good afternoon, Philip, and thank you for the rose. I'm sorry I didn't have a chance to say good night last night and I do appreciate your escorting me to the ball—" She stopped abruptly for she realized that she was babbling. She took a deep breath, warned herself to slow down and began again. "Now if you'll please excuse me, I was just heading out for a much needed walk. I haven't been getting enough exercise lately."

"A splendid idea," Philip said. "May I join you?"

The last thing she wanted now was company, but unable to think of a plausible reason to say no, Amelia had no choice but to agree.

As they walked down the west corridor together, she observed that Philip looked very handsome in his golfing tweeds, and that his fine blond hair had been bleached almost white by his hatless hours on the golf course. His face was deeply tanned and contrasted sharply with the lightness of his gray eyes. Amelia thought again what a handsome man he was and wondered why she couldn't fall in love with someone like Philip instead of the ineligible Matthew Laurence. At the thought, her anger flared again, and her stride became so brisk that even the long-legged Philip was well pressed to keep up with her.

As they left the hotel, Amelia ran down the west portico stairs and turned right down the avenue. Her unbound hair was flying and the vigorous exercise brought a healthful glow to her cheeks. She attracted many admiring glances, including Philip's, but she was oblivious to everything but the need to be rid of her anger and frustration. At last they reached the bridge at the hotel entrance, and Philip suggested that they enter one of the small shops for something cool to drink.

Feeling somewhat abashed at the pace she had set and not a little winded, Amelia agreed.

They walked leisurely through the gift shops, and Amelia made a mental note to return the next day with some change to buy picture postcards to send to Dr. Will and Aunt Beth. When they reached the confectioner's shop, they sat at a small bistro table and ordered sodas.

"Well, Amelia," Philip asked as they waited to be served, "have you decided yet what you are going to do?"

Amelia looked startled, wondering if Philip had been reading her thoughts about Matthew Laurence. Then she relaxed as she realized he was referring to an earlier conversation they had had.

"Yes, I have," she answered firmly. "As soon as the season is over, I'm returning to Asheville to stay for a while with Dr. Will and Aunt Beth. I shall continue to try for entrance to medical school, and if that fails, I shall go into teaching. I have more than the necessary requirements to teach high-school science, and if that's the closest I can come to medicine, well . . ." She ended with a shrug and a smile.

Philip looked stunned. "You can't be serious," he said. "Surely the best place for you would be with your family, with your Aunt Ursula and Maude?"

Amelia shook her head. "No, they have both been very kind to me, but we are still basically strangers, even though we are related by blood. Dr. Will and Aunt Beth are really the only 'family' I have left now, and my place is with them."

"The season is still young, Amelia. There may be something yet that will change your mind."

Amelia looked away, embarrassed by the warmth in his voice and remembering Lady Caroline's remarks. She changed the subject to the safer topic of last night's ball as they drank their sodas. Amelia was afraid that Philip might refer to the card that he had enclosed with the rose he had sent her, but he didn't and she was relieved, because she wouldn't have known what to say. He was a very pleasant and attractive man, but her heart was irrevocably, if futilely, committed to another.

Their return walk to the hotel was unhurried. In place of her earlier anger, Amelia was overcome with a feeling of trepidation. She feared for Matt and Bernard, and now in light of their danger, she began to re-evaluate her own series of accidents: the snake, the poisoning, the stairs. She was only half listening to Philip and replied absentmindedly to his questions as her mind whirled about for a motive for someone to harm her.

If she had lifted her head to study the rows of windows as they approached the hotel, she might have noticed one slightly parted curtain and wondered whose eyes were watching them from the shadows. And had she seen the madness in those eyes, she would have known without doubt that she had a reason for her fears.

Chapter Nineteen

"Really, Amelia, you promised that we would spend more time together, and yesterday we saw you hardly at all."

Maude's voice was too soft and low-pitched to be called a whine, but its effect was the same. Instantly Amelia felt guilty for both the neglect and deception of her relatives. Today, she told herself, she must really make an effort to be a better guest.

"Now, Maude, that's not entirely fair," Ursula countered. "We had a perfectly lovely evening last night when you girls gave me such a magnificent description of the ball. It was almost as if I had been there myself."

"No, Maude is right, of course," Amelia said, "and today we must plan something together. Aunt Ursula, what would you like for us all to do once we've finished breakfast?"

"To be perfectly frank, my dear, as soon as I've eaten I intend to go straight back to bed. My rheumatism is acting up today, so as much as I would like to be included, don't plan your activities around me."

"I'm sorry you're not feeling well. Would you like for me to stay in and read to you?" Amelia asked.

"It's sweet of you to offer, but Beulah will keep me company. You two young people plan something on your own."

Maude spoke up quickly before her mother could change her mind. "I know what I would like," she stated in a tone that accepted no compromise. "I want to go riding with you and Lady Caroline, Amelia. Remember, you promised me weeks ago on the island that I could."

"That sounds like an excellent idea," Ursula said. "Aside from the obvious benefits of fresh air and exercise, you will also be developing some very valuable social contacts. One can never have too many of those in life."

"Yes, Mama," Maude replied obediently, and her eyes sparkled with the excitement of a child at the prospect of ice cream.

"It's settled then," Amelia said. "Perhaps I could have Beulah take a note down to the Frasers' suite to set a time for us to meet at the stables."

Ursula gave her approval and Beulah was dispatched with the note. She returned with a reply before the three had finished breakfast, and Amelia and Maude hurried to change into riding habits in time to meet Lady Caroline at ten o'clock.

Amelia had to struggle to keep her mind on Maude and her constant stream of small talk, gossip about the guests, and plans for what she would do when they returned to Chicago after Easter. Amelia knew that in just a few hours Bernard would be meeting with the pair who had threatened him, and she prayed that he would be convincing in his story.

As they waited at the stables for the grooms to bring

their mounts, Diana Barrington appeared. Her kelly green riding habit complemented her blond prettiness, but her face was suffused with rage when she saw Amelia. She strode toward her threateningly, smacking a gloved palm with her riding crop.

"So, Miss Donelly, I see you failed to heed my advice. Well, don't say I didn't warn you. Anything that happens you have brought upon yourself."

"You're threatening me again, Miss Barrington. There are legal consequences for that, you know."

Amelia refused to be bullied by the blond tyrant.

"Nothing that Daddy's army of attorneys couldn't handle. Perhaps you've heard the expression that all's fair in love and war? Be advised, my dear Miss Hillbilly Donelly"—Diana's beautiful face contorted into an ugly mask—"this is war!"

She turned as the groom brought the horses and walked toward the horse Amelia was to ride.

"Do you really think you can handle Satan, here?" She ran her hand down his flank as she continued condescendingly, "There are strong men here who can't control this horse."

Amelia stood dumbfounded, not knowing what to reply to the woman's rudeness.

"I'll have you know, Miss Barrington," Maude interjected in Amelia's defense, "that my cousin is an exceptionally fine horsewoman. And if you don't believe me, ask Lady Caroline."

Caroline had joined the group and was studying Satan with an experienced eye.

"He's a magnificent animal and he is spirited. Be careful with him, Amelia." She turned as if she had not known Diana was there. "Oh, good morning, Miss Barrington. Are you joining us?"

"No, thank you, Lady Caroline, I've had my ride already this morning."

Her tone to Caroline was fawning, quite unlike the manner in which she had addressed Amelia. Her father's money had bought her everything she had wanted, but it had not been able to purchase her a title, and Diana was in awe of the aristocracy.

"But I have warned Miss Donelly about Satan, Lady Caroline. There are men here who won't ride him."

Amelia found herself steaming with anger at the woman's pomposity. She approached the horse that Maude had been petting, hiked her skirt to put one booted foot in the stirrup and threw her leg across the saddle. As she settled her weight across the horse's back, it screamed in anguish and reared on its hind legs.

"Steady on, Amelia!" cried Lady Caroline, placing herself in danger under the rearing front hooves to reach for the bridle, but before she or the groom could grasp the reins, the horse had bolted headlong down one of the bridle paths along the bluff.

Amelia felt pain burn across her face as it was lashed by pine branches overhanging the path. She pulled with all her might, trying to stop the horse, but he only ran faster, and it took all the strength she possessed just to stay in the saddle. Her arms were aching and felt as if they would pull from their sockets, and her knees were beginning to weaken and loosen their grasp of Satan's sides.

Suddenly Satan turned off the path and plunged down the bluff. Amelia was whipped and battered by the undergrowth as the horse plowed through. He reached the foot of the bluff and raced along the soft sand of the shoreline. With an agonizing scream, he reared again, and Amelia felt herself flying through the air. She landed heavily in an expanse of soft white sand, which cushioned her fall and probably saved her life.

She lay stunned, for the fall had knocked the breath from her lungs. As she finally gasped for breath, she saw

Satan, standing docile as a lamb not twenty feet away from her. Even the arrival of Caroline, Maude and the groom did not cause the lathered black beast to move.

Maude and Caroline raced to Amelia as the groom went to retrieve Satan.

"Oh, Amelia!" Maude's face was deathly white. "Are you hurt?"

"Only my dignity." Amelia grimaced as she rose and brushed the sand from her riding skirt. "If he had thrown me anywhere other than this sandy patch of beach, it might have been a different story."

"I can't imagine what caused him to bolt like that," Caroline mused. "He is a spirited horse, but I've ridden him several times myself, and he's easily controlled with a firm hand."

At that point the groom walked over, holding something gingerly between the thumb and index finger of his right hand.

"This here was the trouble, ma'am," he spoke to Amelia, looking visibly relieved that she was unhurt.

He held up the item for their inspection. It was a large spray of sandspurs, a weed whose burrs had wickedly long spines and grew in abundance in the area.

"This was under the saddle blanket, and when you sat down on it, it dug these sandspurs into Satan's back."

"But how in the world did they get there?" Lady Caroline insisted.

The groom shrugged. "We check all the blankets carefully to make sure there's not a problem like this, but that don't mean that sometimes something don't slip by. 'Course, there's always the possibility som'un put it there on purpose. There was lots of you round that horse afore the lady got on. Coulda been one o' you."

"Well," sputtered Maude, "of all the nerve!"

"I ain't blamin' nobody, ma'am, jus' trying to figure how it coulda happened."

The groom offered Amelia his horse and remained behind to rub down Satan and walk him back to the stables.

"Up you go, my girl," Lady Caroline encouraged. "The best thing after a fall like yours is to get right back on. Besides, we must get you back as quickly as possible after such a fall, and horseback is the fastest way. Oh, dear!" Caroline peered in distress at Amelia's face. Angry red welts and scratches rose where the branches had lashed her. "And we must get some salve on those cuts, too," Caroline clucked solicitously.

Amelia's face burned from the beating she had taken as Satan had plunged through the underbrush, and her legs were weak from her frightening ride, but she knew that Lady Caroline was right; the longer she waited to ride again after her experience, the harder it would be. So she smiled gamely and remounted.

The three women set off at an easy canter, but brisk enough to make conversation difficult, so Amelia was able to spend the time reflecting on her latest "accident." Her deliberations of yesterday had proved fruitless as to why anyone would harm her, but now, still ignorant of the motive, she knew she must be cautious, and against her nature, distrustful of those around her.

But who would want to hurt her and why? The nagging question returned. The tall imperious Diana came to her mind instantly, her threats echoing in Amelia's ears. But Amelia reminded herself that Diana had been in Chicago when the first two accidents occurred. Or perhaps the first two events were just that, accidents, and the fall and the throw from Satan had been Diana's doing. But why? She had what she wanted. Why would she jeopardize herself by trying to harm Amelia?

Who else might wish her harm? The ruffians who

were after Bernard? But they hadn't been near the stables, and even if they had, of what importance could she be to them? Aunt Ursula? She admitted that Aunt Ursula could be crotchety and domineering, and she might even resent having to assume responsibility for her sister's child, but somehow she could not picture Ursula as a true villainess of the sort it wouldtake to plan the misfortunes that had befallen Amelia.

Matthew Laurence? The possibility that Matt might wish her harm seared through her as a physical pain. But was it possible that he considered her a threat to his relationship with Diana and wanted her out of the way? Was his kindness to her just a way of keeping her off guard? Although there was a ring of logic to that reasoning, Amelia cried out silently against it with her whole heart. Surely no one so kind and gentle as Matt had been could wish her harm. Her thoughts began to turn in circles, and she found herself feeling dizzy and ill.

Lady Caroline noticed that Amelia's color was not good. She brought her horse to a halt and spoke, "I believe you've had quite enough for one morning, Amelia. We will return now at a walk. Let me know if you need to stop and rest."

They returned slowly to the stables and dismounted. Amelia staggered slightly as her feet touched the ground and the landscape spun around her. A groom caught her before she fell, and she felt herself being transferred to another pair of strong arms. She looked up into the cool gray eyes of Philip Sheridan. She tried to insist that she was perfectly capable of walking, but even the formation of a few words took too much effort. With a sigh, she closed her eyes to make the world stop spinning and laid her head upon Philip's broad shoulder.

"Keep still, Amelia, I'll carry you to your room."

He called to the groom. "Bring Dr. Winston as quickly as you can."

Again Amelia felt the need to protest, but she did not have the strength to speak. Philip held her firmly, but gently, in his arms, and his long stride carried them smoothly across the grounds and into the hotel. In what seemed like seconds she was in her own room on her own bed. From the comfortable darkness behind her eyelids, she heard Philip speak and felt his lips brush gently across her forehead.

"I'll leave you here in Beulah's care, my dear, and the doctor will be here soon."

Then Maude's voice pierced her consciousness. "Really, Philip, the groom could have carried her, and it would have created less of a scene. How could you . . ."

But her voice trailed off as the connecting door into the parlor was closed, and the next thing Amelia was aware of was Dr. Winston's touch as his fingers probed her skull.

"Hmmm," he murmured as he found what he sought, a large bump on the back of Amelia's head. "Gave your head a good crack when you went sailing off that horse, didn't you?"

Amelia's eyes flew open. "Concussion?"

He was checking her pupils carefully. "Perhaps just a slight one. I suggest you stay awake for the rest of the day just in case."

With gentle hands he applied a soothing ointment to the scratches and welts on her face. "Fortunately these cuts are not deep and should heal without scarring. Now, I'll set up a schedule for someone to be with you so you don't doze off, then I'll come back to check on you after dinner. Rest all you can, but don't sleep. Understood?"

Amelia nodded. She pulled herself up to a sitting position and Beulah fluffed the pillows behind her. The doctor was replacing his stethoscope into his black leather bag.

"You know you're lucky you didn't break your neck. In fact, it's something of a miracle that you didn't break at least one bone from the way Lady Caroline described what happened."

He sat back down on the edge of the bed, held her hand in his and looked deeply into her eyes. "I know that you've had a very bad shock from your parents' deaths, Amelia, and I also know that that kind of loss can make some people very depressed, even suicidal. This is the second time in just a matter of weeks I've treated you, and it makes me wonder if your accidents might not be self-induced. Are you that unhappy, my girl?"

The kindness in the voice of the crusty old doctor made the tears well up in Amelia's eyes. Here was someone she felt she could confide in, but what could she tell him? If she told him that she feared someone was trying to harm her, would he think that her grief had affected her sanity? Then she was struck with a shattering thought, What if the doctor was right? What if her grief over her parents' death and the impossibility of her love for Matthew Laurence had sapped her will to live without her even being aware? Her blue eyes widened in horror at the idea.

"There now." Dr. Winston patted her hand in his best bedside manner and said reassuringly, "I doubt very seriously that someone as intelligent as you would not be aware if you were severely depressed. You've probably just had two very unlucky events. In any case, you must be more careful from now on. Sarah and I have grown quite fond of you, and we would be very upset if anything were to cause you harm."

Amelia smiled at the warmth and friendship of his words.

"Now, I believe Beulah and Philip have elected to take the first shift in your care, so I leave you in very good hands. I'll be back after dinner."

He gathered up his bag and coat and hat and left the room. Amelia could hear the low murmur of voices in the parlor, and in a few seconds Philip entered and pulled a low chair alongside her bed.

"I'm relieved to hear that you're going to be fine, Amelia, and I feel very fortunate to have you as my captive audience for a few hours. It seems I don't see you as often as I would like, although I'm very sorry for the circumstances that have given me this chance. You really gave me quite a scare. I was waiting for my horse to be saddled when the three of you came riding in. But I must say that you're already looking much better. Shall I read to you for a while?"

"Yes, Philip, I would enjoy that. There's a copy of *Sense and Sensibility* on the shelf by the window there and my place is marked."

Philip took the book from the shelf, and as he opened it, a piece of paper fluttered to the floor. Without looking at it, he picked it up and handed it to Amelia. It was the note of apology Matt had sent her after that embarrassing night in his suite. Philip found where she had marked the book and began to read, but Amelia heard nothing.

All she was aware of was the longing in her heart for a man she could never call her own. She slipped the note beneath her pillow, thinking that later she would tear it into pieces and throw it away, but knowing full well that she would be unable to force herself to do so. Although it caused her pain to remember, the note and the music box were all she had of Matthew Laurence and she would keep them forever. She would treasure them like all the memories of him she had stored away in her heart against the day when she would never see him again.

She glanced at Philip and forced herself to smile, but her thoughts were of another, and if wishing could make it so, Matthew Laurence would have been the one sitting beside her bed.

Chapter Twenty

When Dr. Winston returned after dinner that evening, Amelia felt fresh and rested and all signs of dizziness had disappeared.

"You are progressing beautifully, Amelia. The swelling has all but disappeared from your facial lacerations, and all your vital signs are good."

He folded the earpieces of his stethoscope and placed it carefully in his bag, a gesture of her father's that Amelia had observed countless times.

"You can resume most of your normal activities now, but you must avoid any strenuous exercise for the next few days. And if you find yourself feeling depressed or unhappy, come and talk to me, my dear."

"You are very kind, Doctor. I feel fortunate to have such good care." Then she paid him her ultimate compliment. "My own father could not have cared for me any better than you have done, and I am very grateful."

He was pleased with her comparison, knowing it to be her highest praise, and his parting kindly smile had been reassuring. Amelia had breathed a secret sigh of relief, for she had been afraid that she would be unable to attend the fateful hunting expedition on Monday which would determine Bernard's and Matt's futures.

Lady Caroline stopped in on her way to dinner to visit briefly, but Maude was also in the room, making open discussion impossible.

"Amelia, dear," Caroline said, "I don't want to tire you, but Bernard wants me to ask if you will ride with him to Dr. Winston's tomorrow. He thought the doctor might want another look at you and also that the fresh air and a visit with Sarah might do you good."

"How thoughtful," Amelia murmured, trying to keep from giggling at the faces Caroline was making behind Maude's back to let Amelia know that this was part of the overall plan and that things were on schedule.

"Please tell him yes for me," Amelia said, making a few faces of her own to let Caroline know that she understood.

Maude, oblivious to their charades, ushered Caroline out.

Left alone, Amelia again had to face the dilemma of several inexplicable accidents and the growing fear that someone was trying to harm her. She had no definite suspect but an entire range of disconcerting possibilities.

As she played cards with Maude and Ursula that evening, Amelia found herself watching Ursula closely for any telltale signs that might indicate a desire to injure her. But she looked in vain, for Ursula, enjoying a temporary respite from her aches and pains, was warmer and more charming than Amelia had ever seen her.

Maude seemed kinder and more animated than Amelia remembered, and besides, she had never expressed any sort of animosity toward Amelia. No, Amelia was almost certain that danger lay in other quarters.

The next morning, Beulah brought in a note from Bernard with Amelia's breakfast. They had been invited to have luncheon with Dr. Winston and Sarah, and Bernard would drive her in one of the hotel's buggies at eleven o'clock.

Feeling no ill effects from the previous day's fall, Amelia looked forward to her meeting with the Winstons and Bernard. She stood at the open French doors to the small balcony and looked out across the hotel grounds. Her heart lurched as she recognized Matt trudging toward the stables, and longing and desire welled inside her with a force that frightened her. She shook herself mentally, reminding herself of the futility of such a love, but the emotion she felt for him was not one to be erased by cool reason or common sense, and she wondered if she would carry this hunger for him with her for the rest of her life. She had never experienced feelings of such intensity, a yearning not only for the embrace of his strong arms but also for the companionship of his intelligence and wit. The turmoil of her emotions exhausted her and left her feeling empty and drained, and suddenly the day was not as bright as it had seemed before.

If she truly loved him, she reminded herself, she would be concerned more with his happiness and less with her own. And if it took Diana Barrington to make him happy, then she must accept that and go on. She couldn't allow the fact that he would never love her to paralyze her to the point that she neglected her own life. She would do everything that she could to save him for Diana, and then she must go about building a life of her own, even if it would seem empty and colorless without Matthew Laurence to share it with her.

Promptly at eleven she waited at the carriage portico for Bernard, and he appeared almost immediately in the buggy. His boyish appearance and cheerful demeanor belied the seriousness of their outing, but Amelia was glad for at least a momentary respite from serious thoughts.

Their drive to the Winstons was unhurried and pleasant. The day was sunny and mild, and Bernard, in markedly good humor at the prospect of seeing his beloved Sarah, kept Amelia laughing with outlandish tales of his school days at Harrow. Amelia was almost sorry when they arrived, for they would now have to consider the sober situation which confronted them and ask the Winstons to help with their plot.

Sarah answered the door and ushered them immediately into the cozy dining room where luncheon was being served. Dr. Winston's gardening skills were evident even here, for centering the table and filling the bay window were pots of jonquils, tulips, crocuses, and hyacinths.

"Oh, how lovely!" Amelia exclaimed, and her eyes misted with tears, for the flowers reminded her of the spring borders her mother had tended about the big house in Asheville, the home that she had sold so hastily and now would never be hers again.

"They are beautiful, aren't they?" Sarah agreed. "William has to pamper the bulbs to get them to bloom and flourish this far south, but we both agree that they're more than worth the trouble."

Dr. Winston joined them, greeting them courteously and at the same time studying Amelia with professional scrutiny.

They enjoyed a relaxing and pleasant meal, exchanging news of local events. But once the table had been cleared and coffee had been served, Bernard turned to the serious business at hand. Starting from the time he had been followed by the two characters in St. Petersburg and progressing through their encounter on the Clear Water Road, Bernard narrated all that had transpired since he had first been assaulted by the usurer's agents. Calmly, with a composure that Amelia admired and Sarah adored, he related their ultimate threat the night of the Mardi Gras Ball.

Both Dr. Winston and Sarah listened intently, neither showing any outward emotion except for the clattering of Sarah's coffee cup as her unsteady hand placed it in the saucer. But when Bernard continued to tell of the plan that Matt and Hunter had proposed, the doctor's face crinkled in thought, and Sarah's freckles stood out starkly against the pallor of her skin.

"That is the entire story, sir," Bernard addressed the doctor, "except for my meeting with them yesterday. They have agreed to the 'accidental' death of Matthew Laurence, and will take me to their boss. In exchange for a look at the death certificate, he is to return my IOU's. That is when the authorities are to move in and arrest him. We don't want to ask you to go against your code of ethics, but it is imperative that we have a death certificate that will seem authentic. Will you help us?"

Sarah watched her brother closely, holding her breath while she waited for him to answer. Dr. Winston leaned back in his chair, his fingers clasped before him on his checkered waistcoat. After what seemed several long minutes he spoke, "Bring Mr. Laurence here immediately following the accident. We'll send for the constable, which would be the logical course of action in an accidental death anyway. I'll confer with the constable, and as long as he is aware of what is happening, I see no reason why I couldn't give you a death certificate. As long as it is not registered at the court-house and is destroyed once these villains are captured, I can't see a problem with that."

Sarah sprang from her chair and embraced her brother. "I knew you wouldn't let them down." She beamed. Then the blood drained from her face again as she asked, "But what happens to you, Bernard, after your IOU's are returned?"

"That is when the authorities move in and make their arrests, and this whole troublesome business will be over with and I can get on with my life." Bernard smiled at her reassuringly. "And now, if you ladies will excuse us, there is another matter about which I must confer with Dr. Winston."

"Of course," Sarah replied. "Come, Amelia, I'll show you our garden."

Sarah led Amelia through the wide double doors that opened onto the veranda that encircled the house. Amelia had noticed that most of the homes in Florida were built with these encircling porches with wide overhanging roofs to protect them from the sun, and that most rooms had large double doors that opened onto the porches to catch the prevailing breezes. The day was warm, but pleasantly so, and Amelia wondered what it would be like here in the heat of summer. Then she dismissed the thought, for it was unlikely that she would ever see Florida again once the season at the Belleview ended.

They descended the wide steps into the back garden and Amelia caught her breath at the beauty of it. Like the Belleview, the Winstons' home was on a bluff overlooking the sparkling waters of Clear Water Harbor and the green strips of barrier islands that lay between them and the Gulf of Mexico.

But unlike the Belleview, the lawn of the Winstons had once been an oak grove and even now the rolling lush green grass that descended to the edge of the bluff was almost completely shaded by magnificent old oaks that had been gnarled and bent by the onshore winds over the years. Many of the oaks had wide wooden benches built around their trunks, but the others were surrounded by banks of azaleas in shades from white to pink to the deepest purple. Even the rhododendron of the Blue Ridge could not compare to the colorful display of these flowers.

"Oh, Sarah, it's like a fairyland! I've never seen such beautiful colors. With a garden like this, you must want to spend all your time out of doors."

"This is William's hobby, an escape from the pressures of his practice. When things get too much for him—a patient isn't doing well or someone dies—he comes out here and putters about with his flowers until his perspective is restored."

They walked down one of the brick paths that crisscrossed the lawn and were bordered by beds of bright Transvaal daisies, moss roses and white alyssum. As they sat on one of the benches under the oaks, Sarah pointed out Dr. Winston's small grove of citrus trees.

"Most of the winter crop is gone, except for the Valencia oranges, which are delicious for juice. And William had good luck this year with a new grapefruit strain, called a Duncan, that was developed north of here in Dunedin. It's full of seeds, but it's the sweetest grapefruit you'll ever taste."

Suddenly Sarah became very quiet and Amelia knew that her mind had returned to the dilemma that Bernard faced. She placed her arm around Sarah's shoulders and gave her a warm hug.

"Try not to worry, Sarah. I'm sure that everything will work out fine." Even as she said the words, she wished she could believe them herself.

"Thanks, Amelia. I wish I could feel as optimistic as

271

you, but to be truthful, if anything happened to Bernard, I don't believe I could bear it."

Slow tears rolled down her freckled cheeks. "I've never felt this way about anyone else before, but if a day goes by that I haven't seen Bernard, it seems empty and drab, and the days that I do see him seem wonderfully happy and full," Sarah confessed. "Have you ever felt that way about anyone, Amelia?"

Amelia longed for the opportunity to share her feelings about Matt with someone, and she knew that Sarah would be a sympathetic listener. But she also knew that her love for Matthew Laurence was a secret she would carry to her grave, because she could not stand the pity of others if she told them of her unrequited love. If she could not have her love, at least she could have her pride, so instead of answering Sarah, she simply shook her head.

"Well," said Sarah, standing and shaking out her skirts, her innate common sense restored, "let's go see what the gentlemen are up to."

And as they walked arm in arm back up the brick path to the house, Amelia envied Sarah the security of Bernard's love. She hoped for their happiness, but the torment of her own loneliness filled her with an anguish that could not be ignored.

When she returned to the hotel, Amelia found a message from Philip inviting her to dine with him that evening. She felt tired and out of sorts, but remembering his kindness to her after her fall from Satan, she knew that she owed him the courtesy of complying with his request, so she sent Beulah off to his rooms with an affirmative answer.

Then after what seemed too short a nap, she bathed and dressed in her gown of midnight-blue velvet. She sighed as she realized she would never wear this dress for Matt, would never see the light of approval and admiration in his eyes that she so longed for. She was so preoccupied with her thoughts that she did not see Beulah's worried expression as the old woman studied her in the mirror while pinning up her hair into a smooth chignon of reddish gold.

Amelia winced as the brush touched the bump on the back of her head, the only physical reminder of her accident.

Accident? she thought. Her mind again searched for possible suspects and motives, and again she encountered only blank walls and dead ends instead of answers.

Remembering all the bad things that had happened to her since she had arrived at the Bellevicw made Amelia feel suddenly vulnerable and very frightened. There was no one to whom she could turn for reassurance or protection. And if someone actually had been trying to hurt her, would they stop now that they knew they had frightened her? Or would they continue until they actually injured her—or worse?

She absentmindedly took her shawl and bag from Beulah and went into the parlor to meet Philip, who was visiting there with Maude and Ursula. His welcoming smile and obvious pleasure at seeing her were a balm to her troubled mind, and she gave him a radiant smile in return.

Philip was more charming than he had ever been that evening at dinner. He told Amelia quaint and amusing stories about his family and life in Chicago and listened attentively when she responded with events of her own life in Asheville. But after the dessert plates had been removed and the waiter had filled their demitasse cups, he became very serious, shifted his chair closer to hers and lowered his voice so that only Amelia could hear him.

"Amelia, I am going to ask you something tonight that I have wanted to ask since the first day I saw you. Until I met you, I had been completely satisfied with my bachelor existence, but now more than anything else in the world, I want you to share my life with me as my wife. I have asked your aunt for permission to speak with you and she has given it.

"Please don't give me an answer right away. I know that this has been a very difficult and unsettling time in your life and that making any major decision now is probably difficult for you. All I ask is that you give my proposal due consideration and take as much time as you need before you give me an answer."

He placed his hand over hers and the pressure of his grasp was warm and reassuring. Perhaps this was what she needed, she thought, someone to protect and take care of her. She didn't love Philip, she admitted to herself, but she cared for him and could make him a good wife. But would it be fair to him to marry him, loving Matt as she did?

"Thank you for the honor of your proposal, Philip." She smiled at him. "I will give it the serious consideration that it deserves and let you know my decision as soon as I can."

Philip threw back his head and laughed with boyish relief. "Well, at least I haven't been rejected on the spot, and I take that to be a very good sign."

After that, the subject was dropped, and their evening resumed its casual cheerful atmosphere. When Philip escorted her back to her suite, he raised her chin and softly kissed her good night. The kiss was not passionate, but to Amelia, it was the comfort she needed.

Watching the shadows that the dying embers of the fire threw on the ceiling, Amelia lay awake pondering the idea of marrying Philip Sheridan. It would be a life that most women would envy, and it would mean safety and security. Then she was struck by an ironic thought. It would also mean spending the rest of her life in Chicago, traveling in the same social circles as Mr. and Mrs. Matthew Laurence. Trying to sort things out was beginning to make her dizzy again. Why was it that every possible answer to her dilemma presented more dilemmas of its own?

Turning over and pulling the pillow firmly about her head to shut out the flickering light, Amelia finally fell into a fitful sleep.

Chapter Twenty-One

The pounding of torrential rains awakened Amelia early Sunday morning. The gloomy weather filled her heart with dread and fear, because the storm would probably postpone their plans for tomorrow's hunting "accident," and the delay would only prolong the agony of waiting. The thought of Matt dead, even a pretense of his death, was more than Amelia could bear. It was difficult enough to accept that he belonged to Diana, but if he were dead, there could be no hope that he would ever be hers.

Amelia shook herself back to reality. Matt could never be hers, but she still could not rid herself of the empty feeling in the pit of her stomach caused by the danger that Matt, that all of them, were in. What if those thugs thought Bernard was waiting too long and proceeded to kill Matt themselves, then what?

Dear God, she prayed, *please keep us all safe.*

But Matt's dark brown eyes appeared in her mind, and she realized that all her prayers were for him.

As she lay in bed, Amelia felt a twinge of guilt for neglecting to attend worship services. Her faith had never faltered in these past months, but as Ursula and Maude did not go into town to church on Sundays, Amelia had not been able to go unchaperoned. Deep in her heart she felt a longing to pray, to lay the whole terrible situation before God.

She dressed hurriedly. Although the rains would keep her from going to the Presbyterian Church in Clear Water, she could still attend the Mass that was held in the hotel chapel. The Roman Catholic service was unfamiliar to her, but her need and her own faith made the ritual meaningful and comforting. As she knelt with the congregation, she prayed fervently for Matt's and Bernard's safety.

Dearest Lord, she petitioned silently, *give me the wisdom to do what is right and good. Guide my heart, O Lord, to live my life the way You wish—*

Then the words could no longer come. The loss of her parents, the loss of Matt's love, the entire situation with Ursula, Philip, and now those awful men came crashing in on her, and the tears fell silently beneath her veil. As the priest passed her kneeling figure after the Mass, he did not speak a word, but gently laid his hand on her veiled head in benediction. With that single comforting gesture, Amelia felt an inner peace and knew that somehow everything would work out all right. *One step at a time*, she thought, *one step at a time*.

Passing through the hotel lobby to return to her suite for breakfast with Ursula and Maude, she stopped at the desk to inquire about the weather. The clerk assured her that the rain would end soon, although it would most likely be followed by a wind shift to the northwest and colder temperatures. He proved to be an accurate predictor.

By the time they had finished breakfast, the skies had begun to clear and the temperature fell. Ursula's rheumatism reacted severely to the shifting weather and she returned to bed in pain, while Maude disappeared into her room, complaining of a headache.

Amelia spent the afternoon curled up with a book in a chair before the fire, her feet snugly covered by an afghan, and a box of chocolates within reach. The comforting familiarity of this posture—the fire, the book, the chocolates—brought back pictures of home and Papa.

"One step at a time," the voice echoed again.

In the chapel this morning she had not recognized it, but now the advice was clearly linked with her father. How often he had told her, "One step at a time, my dear." Papa was there from her earliest memories of learning to ride Galen, her first pony, until she had begun applying to medical schools. How frustrated, how angry she had been at her father's advice to be patient. But how right he had been. If only she could tell him.

Amelia knew that this had to be her approach to life, especially now. First, she would see through tomorrow's charade to catch the villains who had threatened Bernard and Matt. Then with that out of the way, she would decide on an answer to Philip's proposal, with all its consequences.

She marveled at her own sense of calm, although it was more in character with the way she had been before her parents' deaths. Perhaps she was finally regaining her emotional equilibrium and would no longer be subject to the attacks of uncertainty and hysteria she had experienced so often since coming to the

Belleview. And perhaps finally accepting that Matt could never be a part of her life had something to do with it, too.

She retired early that night, and it seemed she had barely fallen asleep when Beulah was awakening her.

"Miss Amelia, it's four o'clock, and if you don't git moving, they's gonna leave without you."

Amelia threw back the covers and shivered as the frigid air in the room hit her. Beulah was building up the fire, but Amelia would be gone before the room warmed.

She dressed in thick woolen stockings, a turtleneck cashmere sweater, her riding skirt and boots. Braiding her hair and wrapping the braids in a crown around her head, she pulled on a red knitted cap that her mother had made for her. She was glad she had brought her leather cardigan jacket with its sheepskin lining, for even though she was in Florida, the temperature this morning was well below freezing. Grabbing her fur-lined riding gloves and a red woolen scarf, she gave Beulah a hug.

"You go on back to your warm bed, Beulah. You shouldn't have to get up again for hours."

"Ole Beulah's gonna do jes' that. And you, chile—" The dear woman's dark eyes shone with affection and worry for her young charge. "You take care to stay outta trouble for once, you hear? I'se getting tired of watchin' over you, and puttin' you to bed sick, and that doctor coming and going."

Although her words were gruff, Amelia knew there was love in them.

"I'll remember, Beulah," Amelia promised.

The hotel lobby was lighted and she found Lady Caroline and Bernard waiting for her. They, too, were dressed warmly and seemed amazingly calm, considering what the morning had in store for them.

"Our guide will be a Mr. McCracken, Amelia. Remember that he knows nothing about this and will have to be convinced that Matt is fatally injured. Otherwise the entire scheme might fail," Bernard warned her.

The three set off down the east corridor and out into the freezing air. The frozen grass crunched beneath their feet and the star-filled cloudless sky lit their way across the grounds to the lighted stable. There they met Mr. McCracken, who was instructing the groom in loading the wagon that would carry their gear to the sight of the turkey shoot.

Bernard made a point of handing McCracken his own special shotgun in its personalized case and seeing that it was stowed properly with the other equipment. The brass shells in his gun had been loaded with the necessary powder, but the shot had been removed and replaced with wadding.

Even though there was no shot, Bernard reminded himself, he had to be sure that his weapon was at least fifteen feet from Matt when he fired it, or it could still do him serious injury. As it was, the blast at fifteen feet would shred Matt's outer clothing, and Hunter's application of the theatrical bloodpack should make the accident appear gruesomely authentic.

Matt and Hunter appeared and handed their gun cases over to McCracken to be included with the gear.

"Great day for a hunt, isn't it, Lady Caroline? Maybe we'll bag us a big old turkey today," Matt joked.

"Oh, don't be too sure," Lady Caroline retorted. "Some of those turkeys are tough old birds, not worth shooting."

The others laughed with them, but Amelia stifled a gasp at their macabre humor, although she found that she had to admire their calmness and heartiness.

Only once did Matt look directly at her and nod a greeting, but Amelia merely said "good morning" and looked quickly away before he could read the longing in her eyes.

All her resolve of yesterday to put Matthew Laurence out of her heart and mind melted away. As from that first day on the train, his very presence stirred a desire in her that could not be denied, but that she must learn to control.

"Let's git agoing," McCracken shouted.

Horses were saddled for all the party except Amelia, who had volunteered to ride in the wagon with Mr. McCracken. When all had mounted, he headed the wagon south along the bluff toward the forested area where the wild turkeys nested.

The only sounds along the wagon road were the jingle of tackle, the soft clop of horse hooves in the sand, and the creaking of the wagon. In the soft predawn light, clouds of steam from the horses' nostrils were clearly visible in the cold crisp air. Even with a blanket tucked firmly around her, Amelia could feel the encroaching cold. She was only too happy when they reached their destination, a large clearing in an oak grove, and McCracken built a fire and passed around steaming cups of black coffee laced with brandy. Only then was she able to stop shivering.

McCracken showed Hunter, Matt, Lady Caroline, and Bernard the path to take to position themselves for firing as the turkeys awoke from their night's roosting.

"You go on without me," Amelia said. "I'm just along for the ride, for I could never shoot anything. I'll stay and keep the fire going and watch the horses."

McCracken, reacting exactly as the group had hoped and anticipated, said that he would stay with Amelia and the horses until the others had bagged as many of the fowl as they wished. Matt led the way down the path, his shotgun broken over his arm, and Bernard followed him. Lady Caroline and Hunter brought up the rear.

There followed a long period of harrowing waiting as Amelia sat and stared at the leaping flames of the campfire. The sounds of the departing hunters had faded in the distance. There were a few random reports of gunfire.

Then suddenly there was the explosion of a gun being discharged, a scream from Lady Caroline and the cry of a man in agony.

Amelia and McCracken threw down their coffee mugs and raced down the path. After about a hundred yards, they came upon Matt face down in the pine needles, his back a bloody mass, with Hunter bending over him. Bernard sat collapsed on a nearby log with his face in his hands and Lady Caroline's arms about him.

"I tripped," he said in a strangled voice, "and the gun went off by accident."

Amelia pushed Hunter aside. "Let me see if I can help," she insisted. "I've had some medical training."

Even though she knew the entire scenario had been prearranged, she was terribly shaken by the reality of it and carefully checked for Matt's pulse to make sure that he hadn't truly been injured. The tension in the air because of the danger of the situation and the knowledge that everyone's eyes, especially McCracken's, were on her intensified as her chilled fingers searched the warmth of Matt's neck. A strong healthy rhythm met her fingers and only then did she glance at Matt's back. If only they had not all had to go through this for McCracken's sake, but the scene had to be played through.

"Go back and bring the wagon," she instructed McCracken.

She did not want him to inspect the wound too closely, afraid that his experienced eye might detect their deception.

"We must get him to Dr. Winston's right away, and

even then, I don't think there's much hope. He's lost too much blood already, and his pulse is almost nonexistent."

The rough old Floridian native ran down the path as fast as his bandy legs could carry him, and Amelia regretted the necessity of deceiving him. Soon the wagon was creaking up the pathway, and Hunter and Bernard gently lifted Matt, eased him face down onto the wagon bed and covered him with the blanket that had previously been wrapped about Amelia.

Amelia climbed into the back of the wagon and settled down beside Matt for the long ride back to Dr. Winston's. McCracken climbed into the driver's seat, cracked the reins, and they started north at a terrifying speed.

Amelia looked down to see Matt's eyes open and his gaze upon her. He gave her a solemn wink, then furtively grabbed one of her gloved hands and squeezed it gently. A warm rush of emotion surged through her veins at Matt's touch. The situation was still dangerous, and the quality of their charade had yet to be proved, but somehow Matt's holding her hand comforted her and made her feel secure.

I should be the one to comfort him, she thought.

Then afraid that McCracken might see in their joined hands a clue to the deception, she attempted to break the bond. But no matter how she tried, Amelia was unable to extricate her hand from Matt's hold.

Hunter had ridden on ahead, so that by the time they reached the Winstons', the house was lighted and the doctor was waiting for them on the veranda.

"Bring him into the surgery," he instructed them, "and, McCracken, you'd best ride on into town and bring the constable."

Hunter and Bernard carried Matt into the house as McCracken turned the wagon in the drive, then headed north toward Clear Water Harbor.

Lady Caroline watched on the veranda until he was out of sight, then hurried into the foyer.

"He's gone," she called.

At that signal, all of them met in the drawing room where the shades had been pulled and the draperies tightly closed. Matt had removed his "bloodstained" jacket, and Sarah entered carrying a tray filled with coffee, cups, and hot ham biscuits.

"It will take him the better part of an hour to bring back the constable. We might as well relax as much as we can until then and get our stories straight," Dr. Winston suggested.

"The constable already knows the plan," Matt reminded them, "but we will have to go through the motions for McCracken's sake. We'll ask that he question McCracken, Lady Caroline and Hunter first. Then those three can return to the hotel, while Dr. Winston prepares the death certificate for Bernard. Then Bernard can escort Amelia back when he returns. I, of course, will remain in hiding here until it is time to follow Bernard.

"Lady Caroline, will you and Hunter please impress upon McCracken that he is not to speak of the accident to anyone? Use the excuse that next of kin must be notified first. However, if any of these characters try to force answers from him, God forbid, at least he will tell them what we want them to hear."

Amelia sat quietly listening to Matt's instructions and wondered if his concern for Diana prompted them. She thought of how she would feel if she were to hear that anything had happened to him and remembered how he had looked lying face down in the pine needles. She shuddered, then felt the comforting pressure of Matt's arm about her shoulder.

"This time tomorrow it will all be over and we can be

concerned with happier things," he assured her.

She read the warmth in his eyes and again felt an urge to throw herself into his arms. Struggling mightily to maintain her self-control, she realized that time and distance would be the only things to cure her of her undeniable longing for him.

They finished their coffee in silence, the gravity of the day's business weighing on their minds. Suddenly the sound of wagon wheels on the gravel of the drive sent the entire group into motion. Matt and Dr. Winston disappeared up the stairs, and quick-thinking Sarah grabbed their coffee cups and whisked them away into the kitchen. She was returning with extra cups and fresh coffee as the constable and McCracken were ushered in by Amelia.

First Constable Deckett climbed the stairs to speak with Dr. Winston. When he came down a few minutes later, he asked Hunter and Lady Caroline to join him in the waiting room for questioning. When they returned, he told McCracken that the three of them were free to return to the Belleview, and to remain there in case he needed to reach them for further questions.

Then he asked to speak privately with Bernard. Lady Caroline embraced first Bernard and then Amelia and said she would see them when they returned to the hotel. She thanked Sarah, gave her a motherly hug, and left with Hunter and McCracken.

"We'll leave Matthew's horse for you to bring back, if you will please, Amelia," Hunter said.

Amelia nodded and closed the door behind them.

"Well, so far so good," she announced to Sarah, who had collapsed in a chair by the fire.

"Yes," she replied, "but I'm afraid the most dangerous part is yet to come."

Bernard, the constable, and Dr. Winston came in to fill their coffee cups. The doctor handed an official-looking envelope to Bernard. "This is what they want to see. When do you deliver it?"

"I'm to meet them at the entrance to the Belleview at dusk. They are supposed to take me to their boss then so he can return my IOU's. Constable Deckett will have his men and the Pinkertons in position so they can follow us and make the arrests. So to avoid suspicion, I think Amelia and I should return to the hotel right away."

Dr. Winston nodded. Then to Sarah's surprise and delight, Bernard took her in his arms and kissed her soundly.

"As soon as this nasty business is behind us, I have a question I'd like to ask you, my dear."

"I'll be here," Sarah replied softly.

Bernard and Amelia mounted their horses and headed south toward the Belleview. The morning air was still frigid and they set a brisk canter to keep warm. Suddenly two men rushed from behind the trees and grabbed the reins of their mounts.

"Bernard!" Amelia screamed, terrified as she recognized their assailants as the men who had stopped them on the road before.

"What the hell!" Bernard shouted, trying to free his mount by turning the creature around so that he could plant his boot firmly in the face of one of the thugs, but the sudden appearance of the man's revolver stopped him.

The gun spoke for the men, for without a word, they dragged Amelia and Bernard roughly from their horses Amelia struggled against their grip, but to no avail. Within seconds her hands were bound, her mouth was gagged and her eyes blindfolded. She stumbled as she was moved forward, but the brute picked her up and pushed her again. The last sight she had seen was Bernard receiving a vicious blow to his stomach and a knee in his face. Hearing no more sounds of a struggle, she knew that he had not escaped.

She was shoved a few more paces into the woods where she was lifted into an enclosed buggy whose stifling interior smelled of leather and fine cigars. It took off rapidly over the rough roads. Without the use of her hands and arms to steady herself, Amelia found herself tossed about like a rag doll, and she could feel the bruises forming on her body. She groaned in agony.

"Shut up!" a strange rasping voice barked.

She bit her lip, driven to silence by her captor. She did not know if Bernard was with her, but could only assume that he was.

As the carriage slowed to a steadier pace over smoother roads, its clatter lessened, and Amelia heard Bernard humming "Rule, Brittania" gamely under his breath. She knew then that he was with her, but could not tell how badly they had hurt him.

The strange rasping voice spoke again. "We decided not to wait until tonight for our meeting, Mr. Fraser, just in case you decided to get smart and call in friends to follow you. This way, we won't have to worry about being disturbed. It's a shame we had to bring along your little friend."

The carriage stopped. Amelia was lifted out, then escorted up a brief flight of steps. She heard a door close behind her and a rough hand removed her blindfold. Bernard stood next to her, blinking at the sudden light. As she looked about, she saw they were in the luxurious parlor of a private railway car. Their captors stood menacingly behind them. Then a door at the end of the parlor opened and Edward Rousseau appeared.

"What's the girl doing here?" he demanded angrily.

"They were together, boss. It was either bring 'em both or neither."

Rousseau's demeanor changed to that of a gracious

host as he turned to the two captives. "Well, Miss Donelly, Mr. Fraser, please be seated. It seems we have some unfinished business to take care of."

At Rousseau's signal, the two were thrust rudely onto a red plush settee as Rousseau sat gracefully across from them and smiled wickedly.

Chapter Twenty-Two

Edward Rousseau, elegant in a burgundy velvet smoking jacket, lounged back in his chair and drew heavily on a long Havana cigar. His two henchmen stood threateningly on either side of Bernard and Amelia, but Rousseau's demeanor was that of a gentleman entertaining guests. His manner was polite and cool, but Amelia could sense the danger that lay beneath his sauve exterior. Here was a man who did not like to be crossed and would deal ruthlessly with those who dared.

"I regret, Miss Donelly, that you have become enmeshed in this sordid business, for that now necessitates removing you from the scene, as well as Mr. Fraser."

He puffed languidly on his cigar, his brow wrinkled in thought as he watched the smoke curl above his head. Suddenly he gave a deep chuckle, rose to his feet and stood before Amelia. Taking her chin in his hand, he twisted her face first to one side and then the other, studying it carefully. Then he yanked her to her feet and stood her in the center of the room, raking every inch of her with his eyes. With a satisfied nod, he pushed her back to her seat beside Bernard.

"What I have in mind for you, however, will not be so permanent a removal as his. I have an acquaintance in Tampa who does a profitable business in the white slave trade. He owns a house in New Orleans where, even at your somewhat advanced age for the business, I am sure you will do well and be in high demand. Men like their women red-haired and feisty."

Rousseau laughed again, pleased with his inventiveness in disposing of Amelia. "And although your disappearance will be a mystery, who will there be to demand its unraveling? You have said you are an orphan, and I know some very substantive reasons why your dear Aunt Ursula might want you presumed dead."

Amelia's eyes widened in horror as the implications of what Rousseau had said became clear to her. She would spend the rest of her life in a brothel, and Ursula would make no move to find her because Ursula wanted her out of the way. Was it Ursula behind all the "accidents"? But why? That was a question to which she would never know the answer, and her sense of irony made her realize that, whoever had been trying to get her out of the way, Rousseau would now do their dirty work for them.

Beside her, Bernard called Rousseau a name she had never heard before, but she could tell by the flaring of Rousseau's nostrils and the blow given Bernard by the bullet-headed man that it was not complimentary.

"As for you, Mr. Fraser, now that you have so conveniently disposed of Matthew Laurence for me, I'm afraid I shall have to arrange a little 'accident' for you, too. It will all seem very natural. A sensitive young man

292

accidently kills a friend in a hunting accident and cannot live with his burdened conscience."

Once again Rousseau watched the smoke rings rise from his cigar as he contemplated Bernard's fate. Then he continued his narration of his plans for the young man. "So in remorse, he retreats to the woods where his friend died, and with a streak of poetic retribution, shoots himself with the same shotgun. What a double tragedy, people will say, but none, not even your lovely mother, will be the least suspicious."

Amelia almost blurted out that Caroline knew everything, but stopped herself just in time. She did not want to endanger Caroline's life, and such information would probably save neither Bernard or herself from the fates Rousseau had so gleefully planned for them.

Rousseau glanced with satisfaction at the death certificate one of his men had removed from Bernard's jacket pocket.

"Yes, it's too bad about Laurence, but he was nosing about too much in things that did not concern him. I have become one of the world's wealthiest men by selling worthless land to unsuspecting investors, and Laurence was just about to ruin it for me. He was a fine man, but he did get in my way."

As Rousseau was speaking, Amelia gazed through the partially curtained window of the railway car and observed with a jolt that the car was parked on the spur at the Belleview.

Rousseau followed her gaze and smiled a reptilian smile. "This car is almost completely soundproof and too far away from the hotel for anyone to hear you, my dear, so don't try to attract attention, for I promise you, it will be a futile endeavor, and also likely to make my good men here react rather nastily. It is almost lunchtime now. As soon as it is dark, you and Fraser will be gagged again and led to your separate destinies. In the meantime, you might as well relax and enjoy what little time remains for you."

Amelia sat in stunned silence, in a state of shock that their carefully conceived plan could have gone so far awry. No one would miss them until dusk, when Bernard did not show at the hotel gates for his rendezvous. By then it would be too late. Bernard would be on his way to a gruesome death and herself en route to a life that made death seem favorable by comparison.

And who would miss her? Certainly not Matthew Laurence who could now marry his Diana; and certainly not Maude who had never shown her any genuine affection, only the kindnesses born of duty and obligations. Aunt Ursula? If Rousseau were to be believed, Ursula wanted to be rid of her. Dr. Will and Aunt Beth? It had been so long since she had seen them that they seemed in another world and another life, and now she would never see them again. She bit her lip to hold back the tears. She would not give Rousseau the satisfaction of seeing her cry.

Suddenly she remembered Sarah and Lady Caroline and realized what Bernard's death would mean to them. The anger she felt at the unfairness of it all gave her a sudden rush of adrenaline, and she knew that she must use all her wits to do anything she could to help them escape. She struggled helplessly, trying to wrest her hands from their bonds.

"Chin up, old girl," Bernard whispered to her. "We're not beaten yet."

Amelia gave him a grateful smile and shifted her weight to ease the pain in her arms. She winced as the ropes chafed against the burn marks on her wrists.

Rousseau appeared oblivious to their discomfort. One of the two guards left and returned, bearing a luncheon tray which Rousseau attacked with relish.

"I apologize for not offering you the traditional 'last meal,' my boy," he said to Bernard. "But I do not want to arouse the suspicion of my staff by ordering extra food. As far as they are concerned, you two have never been here."

When he had finished the meal and wiped his mouth meticulously with the damask napkin, the guard removed the tray, and Rousseau rose and stretched.

"Since this promises to be a very busy evening, I'm sure you two will excuse me if I retire for an afternoon rest. You are welcome to nap if you can. But don't try anything foolish. My men are well-trained and very loyal. You would only make things harder on yourselves."

He exited through a door which Amelia could see led to an enormous and luxuriously appointed bedroom.

As the long minutes stretched into even longer hours, Amelia did everything she could to fight the panic that she felt rising inside her. Surely there was something she could do that could help them to escape this deadly situation. She cast about for any possibility, but bound and guarded as they both were, she knew they had no chance of getting away. Rousseau had been too clever for them.

To keep from going insane with fear, she thought of her parents and tried to recall every memory that she had of them from her earliest remembrance. The scenes rolled through her mind like a magic lantern show, and she found herself calmed by the memory of their love. Her memories led her into a kind of trance, and it was with a start that she saw that the slant of the sunlight coming through the partially curtained observation window indicated that the afternoon was waning. Dusk could not be too far away. It would be dark before anyone raised the alarm and where would they be then?

Suddenly the quiet of the car was shattered by a command. "If you value your lives, don't either of you move!"

Amelia thought that her fear was causing her to hallucinate, for she heard Matt's voice as if he were standing at her elbow.

Immediately the room exploded with uniformed men, two of whom kicked open the door to Rousseau's bedroom and dragged him from his bed. Others grabbed the two guards, disarmed them and led them away in handcuffs. Then there was Matt kneeling at her side, untying the bonds that held her hands behind her back, and Hunter was leaning over the back of the settee, releasing Bernard.

With a cry of joy and relief, Amelia threw her arms about Matt and wept. "How ever did you find us?" she sobbed.

Matt sat on the settee and drew her on his lap, holding her close and wiping her tears with his linen handkerchief. Never had Amelia felt safer or more at home than she did now in his arms.

"Luckily I was watching you and Bernard leave from the upstairs window at Dr. Winston's this morning. I saw them take the two of you and head toward the Belleview. But by the time I ran downstairs and mounted one of Dr. Winston's horses, you were gone."

Matt muttered a furious curse as he caught sight of the angry rope burns on Amelia's wrists. "He will pay dearly for this, I promise you, Amelia."

"But how did you find us if you couldn't follow us here?" Amelia asked.

"Rousseau must have hoped to allay suspicion by having your horses returned to the stables right after lunch. When the groom alerted us that your horses had come in, Constable Deckett brought his tracking dogs and they led us here to Rousseau's private car. We assembled the group that was to have followed Bernard this evening, and as soon as everyone was in place, we moved in."

Matt, still holding Amelia in his arms, turned her face to his, looking deep into her tear-filled eyes. "Other than these burns, did he hurt you in any way?"

The fierceness in Matt's eyes as he asked the question made Amelia flinch, but she shook her head and felt herself gathered tightly into Matt's embrace.

"I would have killed him if he had."

It was said quietly and without emphasis, but Amelia knew from the set of his jaw and the tone of his voice that it was no idle threat.

She looked up to see Bernard grinning down at her and became instantly aware of the impropriety of her position. She jumped from Matt's lap, blushing and flustered.

"Are you all right, Amelia?" Bernard asked.

He looked even younger and more vulnerable than ever, but after today's ordeal, Amelia knew that Bernard had hidden strengths that few, with perhaps the exception of his mother and Sarah, were aware of.

"I'm glad they caught Rousseau and his crew, but after what he said today, prison's too good for him. I'd like a crack at him with my shotgun!" Then Bernard turned to Matt and Hunter. "Thank you both for everything you've done to help us. If you hadn't shown up when you did, I'd have been a dead man, and Amelia's fate would have been worse than death."

Matt looked at him questioningly, his face dark and menacing, and Bernard shook his head. "I'll tell you all the gruesome details later. Now I think we should get Amelia back to her family and get word to Mother and Sarah that we're both safe."

A short walk through the rose gardens returned them to the hotel lobby, where Bernard thanked Matt and

Hunter again and hurried to his mother's suite where she and Sarah awaited him.

Hunter informed Amelia that the authorities would probably have questions that they would want to ask her tomorrow, but Matt insisted that for now she return to her room to rest.

Before Amelia could say a word of thanks, she felt herself gathered up in a pair of strong arms and lifted off the floor in a crushing embrace. "Amelia, we've been frantic with worry! Thank God you're safe!" Philip set her gently on her feet and held her at arm's length to make sure she was unharmed. "Ursula and Maude sent me down to see if there had been any word of you. I must take you to them right away so they won't worry any longer."

And with that, he grasped her elbow firmly and propelled her toward the stairs.

Amelia turned to say good-bye to Matt and Hunter, but was disappointed to see that they had already disappeared.

With all the excitement of a small boy who has retrieved his favorite plaything, Philip rushed her up the stairs toward the Hagarty suite. Throwing open the door, he escorted her inside with a flourish.

"She's safe!" he exclaimed. "Isn't it wonderful!"

He stood with his arm possessively around her shoulders, hugging her to him with delight.

Ursula raised herself painfully to her feet and walked to Amelia. She raised her hand and caressed Amelia's cheek. "We were so worried when you didn't return this morning, my dear, and then when all the policemen began swarming on the grounds, we had no idea what was happening. I've had Philip searching for you since lunchtime."

Amelia saw the concern in Ursula's eyes and wondered if it was sincere. She remembered what Rousseau had told her and thought that she could give little credence to the word of such a scoundrel. She looked across the room at Maude who had stood quiet and pale from the time they had entered.

"Bernard and I were kidnapped by Edward Rousseau."

She heard Maude draw her breath in between her teeth with a hissing sound.

"Rousseau is behind a land fraud and extortion scheme that Matthew Laurence has been investigating. Matt and Bernard set a trap for him, one that Bernard and I became caught in ourselves, but Matt found us in time, and by now I would guess that Mr. Rousseau is safely behind bars and likely to remain there for quite a long time."

Ursula gave a nod of grim satisfaction. " 'The mills of the gods grind slowly, but they grind exceeding small,' " she quoted with a gloating smile. "The man deserves everything coming to him and more."

Suddenly Amelia felt tired and faint, and she sagged against Philip as her legs crumpled under her. Philip gathered her in his arms and carried her to her room. Beulah came bustling in behind him.

"You is going straight to bed, chile," she commanded as she turned back the covers on the bed, then added another log to the fire. "You been out gallavantin' since before light, an' that ain't no way for a lady to behave."

Beulah shooed Philip out of the room, closed the door behind him, and began pulling off Amelia's riding boots. For once Amelia let her exhaustion win out over her independence, and she allowed Beulah to undress her, pull on her warm gown and tuck her snugly in bed.

The last conscious thought she had before falling into a deep sleep was of Matthew Laurence and the warmth of his embrace when he had rescued her from Rousseau.

Chapter Twenty-Three

Amelia blotted the brief note carefully before slipping it into its envelope and sealing it. On the front of the envelope she wrote in delicate script, "Matthew P. Laurence." As she propped the envelope against the inkwell on the desk, she began to shiver in the early-morning cold of the room. She added more fragrant logs of orangewood to the fire, stirred the embers until flames licked the new wood, then curled up in the armchair before the fireplace, drawing her dressing gown of soft blue wool closely around her and tucking it about her feet.

Sleepily, she watched the pink and violet streaks of dawn illuminate the eastern horizon outside her window, observing that the air was still bitterly cold and crisp. The sky deepened into shades of carmine and rose.

"Red sky at morning, sailors take warning." Amelia thought of the old adage, then dismissed it. She would not be sailing anywhere today, and as for her luck, she felt very fortunate indeed after yesterday's near catastrophe.

She turned her attention to the flickering flames, mesmerized by their dancing flares, staccato pops and sibilant hisses. She did not look up when Beulah entered with a tray of hot coffee and croissants.

Beulah started to speak, but noticing the faraway expression on Amelia's face, remained silent. She placed the tray on the table beside Amelia and left the room as quietly as she had entered.

The aroma of the steaming coffee broke into Amelia's consciousness, and she poured herself a cup, sipping its warmth gratefully as her thoughts returned to Matthew Laurence. She had wanted to thank him in person, but she knew that the strength of her feelings for him were kept under better control at a distance. Instead, she had composed a carefully worded note of gratitude for his part in her rescue yesterday.

She still blushed when she thought of how shamelessly she had thrown herself at him in her excitement at being released, and she hoped that he had attributed her exuberant response to relief and had not looked further to see the love for him that consumed her. If she could not have his love, she assuredly did not want his pity.

Amelia tried to force Matt from her thoughts. Now that the threat to his life and Bernard's had been disposed of, she knew that the time had come to deal with the next dilemma in her life: whether or not to accept Philip's proposal.

She remembered Philip's elation at finding her safe yesterday and told herself that she would, without doubt, have a long search to find another man who would love her as he did. She knew that he would do everything within his power to make her happy and that she would never want for anything.

Anything, that is, except Matthew Laurence. Hugging her knees to her chest, she felt again his strong arms as they had gathered her to him yesterday; she remembered the heat of his breath against her hair as he had held her close.

She had always valued her ability to understand others and how they felt. She felt in her heart that Matt cared for her; all the signs were there. But reality contradicted that. If he loved her, would he still be engaged to the stunning Miss Barrington? Slow tears trickled down her cheeks as she thought of the empty days and years ahead of her without Matt.

An hour later she awoke, cramped and stiff from sleeping in the chair, the coffee and croissants cold beside her on the tray. Her eyes fell on the envelope on her writing desk, and she knew that she should dress and deliver it before luncheon.

She stood and stretched the cramps from her muscles and tried to shake her depression. She remembered how her father had taught her to look on the positive side and count the good things in her life when she felt unhappy, but this morning her mind went blank when she tried to think of anything good.

She dressed listlessly, picked up the envelope and left the room. When she reached the lobby, she approached the desk clerk. "Would you please place this note with Mr. Matthew Laurence's mail?" Amelia requested.

The clerk looked surprised. "Don't you know, Miss? Mr. Laurence collected all his mail before he left this morning," he informed her.

"Left?" Amelia gave him a puzzled look.

"Yes, Mr. Laurence, Mr. Hunter, and Miss Barrington all left this morning in Mr. Laurence's private car."

Gone, Amelia thought, and the word screamed through her mind. Gone. Forever. And without a single word of good-bye. That should prove conclusively how little she had meant to him. She must have wanted so much for him to love her that she had imagined all his kindnesses toward her.

"Miss Donelly?" The clerk looked at Amelia with concern, for the young woman's face had turned deathly pale and she stood as if in a trance.

"Thank you," Amelia murmured.

Slowly, she tore the carefully composed note into tiny fragments and dropped them one by one into the wastebasket at the end of the lobby desk. Then she turned like a sleepwalker and went to one of the sofas at the far corner of the lobby where she sat, unaware of anything around her except that Matthew Laurence had gone out of her life forever.

She had known that it would happen eventually, but she had hoped to have time to prepare and steel herself for his leaving. But now he had gone and taken Diana with him, and if anything proved to her that she was of no import to him, the very fact that he had not even managed a polite good-bye brought it home with a vengeance.

Oblivious to the time, Amelia sat silently, engulfed by an overwhelming sense of loss. It was as if all her senses and emotions had gone numb.

This must be what it's like to die, she thought, *and the absence of all feeling is worse than any pain I've ever experienced*.

Her eyes finally focused on the tall case clock across from her and she realized that it had been over two hours since she had left her room. Dragging herself to her feet, she climbed the wide stairs back to her room, never noticing the desk clerk who watched her anxiously, shaking his head sadly at the obvious despair of the beautiful young guest.

Not wanting to face anyone yet, Amelia entered her room by the hallway door to avoid the parlor. Throwing herself face down on her bed, miserable, yet unable to cry, she fell asleep.

A noise in the room awakened her, but she had been so deep in sleep that she could not rouse herself to see what it was. She lay semiconscious, aware only that it was still daylight because of the brightness of the room.

Suddenly she felt a wet cloth clamped over her face. As she gasped in surprise, she inhaled the familiar odor of chloroform. Frantically, she struggled with all her might to throw off the cloth, but it was held firm by her assailant, and it covered even her eyes so she could not see who held her. She could feel the anesthetic taking effect, and her desperate efforts to free herself became weaker and weaker. Slowly, she slipped into a black whirlpool and lay still.

The murmur of voices broke through her consciousness first. One at a time she began to identify the speakers. First Dr. Winston, then Aunt Ursula, Philip, Maude, and Beulah. They spoke in hushed tones, and the fog in her mind prevented her from understanding what they were saying. Like an underwater swimmer striving to break the surface, her mind struggled to clear itself, but she drifted in and out, only now and then aware of the whispering voices around her bed.

As awareness slowly returned, so did the knowledge that Matt had gone for good, and she was suddenly sorry that she was not dead. She drifted back into oblivion gratefully.

When she opened her eyes, the room was filled with early-morning light. Dr. Winston slept in a chair beside her bed, looking rumpled and exhausted.

"What happened?" She attempted to speak, but produced only a rasping whisper.

It was enough to jolt Dr. Winston from his light slumber. He examined her carefully, smiled his assurance, and sat down on the side of her bed, patting her hand. Then his expression sobered as he said, "It looks as if you've had another 'accident,' my dear. Only this time, we can be sure it was no accident."

He pointed to a table across the room where Amelia recognized her father's open medical bag, the one she had brought with her for sentimental reasons. Beside it stood an almost empty bottle of chloroform and next to that lay a small white cloth.

"Evidently Beulah scared off whoever it was. We found the cloth by the door opening into the hallway. Luckily for you, Beulah tried to come in to waken you for lunch. She discovered that the door connecting your room to the parlor was locked. By the time she came out into the hall and entered by the other door, whoever had attempted to put you to sleep permanently had vanished. I've notified Constable Deckett, and I have also informed him of the other attempts on your life. It seems we're dealing with a very devious and dangerous personality, Amelia. Do you have any idea who it might be?"

Amelia shook her head weakly in bewilderment. There was a myriad of possibilities, but none of them made any sense to her at all. She remembered Rousseau's vague reference to Aunt Ursula, but dismissed that as absurd. Whoever had tried to kill her had the strength of an ox; it couldn't have been feeble Aunt Ursula. Could it? Her failure to accurately gauge Matt's feelings toward her now made her suspect everyone around her, too.

Dr. Winston sensed her distress. "Try not to worry about it now, Amelia. We'll discuss it when the full effects of the anesthetic have worn off. In the meantime, Constable Deckett has suggested that someone stay with you at all times, if possible. Whom do you feel you can trust the most?"

"Beulah," Amelia answered without hesitation.

"My choice exactly." Dr. Winston nodded in agreement. "I'll make the arrangements with Mrs. Hagarty. I'm sure there will be no problem. She is most distressed over all this and anxious to do anything she can to help."

He pulled on his suit jacket and straightened his tie. "You can be up and around as soon as all effects of the anesthetic are gone. Just be careful of that small chloroform burn on your cheek. You're fortunate it didn't damage your eyes. And be careful in all other respects, too. We don't want any more 'accidents.'"

He gave her a warm smile and another reassuring pat.

"Sarah will be over tomorrow to visit you. She has some special news she wants to share."

After the doctor left, Amelia lay back on the pillows. She felt helpless and alone. Matthew Laurence had left her life as abruptly as he had entered it, and now she knew without reservation that someone for some unknown reason was trying to kill her, and there was no one to whom she could turn who she could trust or depend on. All she wanted to do was to bury her head in her pillow and cry, but she could almost hear her father's voice, the way it had admonished her so many times as she was growing up.

"Wallowing in self-pity won't help and it can sometimes make the problem seem bigger than it is. The best solution is to *do something*. Take a walk, chop wood, clean your room, but don't just sit there and pout, girl!"

Amelia smiled to herself, remembering how her father would stride about the room, waving his long arms as he made his pronouncements.

He was always right, she thought. Being active did help, if for no other reason than it took her mind off her problems.

She threw the covers off the bed and stood, a little

wobbly and with an uneasy feeling in her stomach, but she knew she would only become more depressed if she stayed in bed. She walked to the balcony door and opened it. A warm breeze from the southeast filled the room. She marveled at the vagaries of the Florida weather. She was in the midst of dressing when Beulah entered.

"I owe you my thanks again for rescuing me, Beulah. Dr. Winston said I might be dead now if you hadn't scared off whoever was in the room."

"Jes' wish I could get my hands on that devil. I'd wring his neck, that's what I'd do, goin' round hurtin' he'pless young wimmin."

Amelia suppressed a smile at the word "helpless." She didn't like to think of herself as such, but she had certainly been helpless in that situation.

"If what you did to that snake is any precedent, Beulah, I'm sure that whoever it was will stay well clear of you!"

Amelia had finished dressing and was combing her hair.

"Jes' where you think you goin, young lady?"

"It's a beautiful day, Beulah, and I'm going to take a walk to help clear this stuff from my head."

"Hrmpf!" was Beulah's only comment, but Amelia could tell by the width of her smile that the old woman was happy to see her recovered and on her feet.

The paths and roadways about the hotel were filled with people walking and bicycling in the warm sunshine. Amelia stood on the veranda and surveyed the activity about her. Surely she would be safe in all this crowd. Nonetheless, she started violently when someone grasped her elbow, and she turned to find Philip at her side.

"I intercepted Beulah as she was leaving the suite to

accompany you. She told me she was to meet you here, but I persuaded her that I could be trusted as your guardian. Are you certain you've recovered enough to be out?"

His look of concern seemed genuine, and Amelia regretted the circumstances which caused her to view everyone with suspicion.

"Thank you, Philip, I feel fine now, and I will enjoy your company for a walk. I need lots of fresh air to clear the stench of chloroform from my nostrils."

Philip offered his arm and they walked slowly down the palm-lined avenue toward the shops at the entrance gate. Before they reached the entrance, Philip stepped off the avenue and led her down a path to a bench overlooking the water. He brushed it off carefully with his handkerchief and offered her a seat. Settling down beside her, he kept his gaze on the distant horizon, but Amelia could tell from his expression that he saw nothing, but was thinking of serious matters.

"I know I promised not to press you about an answer to my proposal, Amelia, but this attempt on your life, and all the other things that have happened to you that in retrospect may not have been accidents, put my question in a very different light."

He turned toward her and his eyes were brilliant and piercing. "I want to take care of you and see to it that nothing harms you, and I can do that best if you will marry me. We could be married right away, and I could take you away from here and whoever is trying to harm you. You could go back to Chicago with me where you would be safe."

Amelia's pulse quickened at the mention of Chicago, because that was where Matt was, or at least probably would be in a few days' time. Would she ever be able to keep him out of her thoughts?

She forced her attention back to Philip, who had

grasped both her hands and held them in his, his eyes searching her face for an answer. She looked into his soft gray eyes and saw their love and concern. He was without question a handsome and caring man. Being his wife would be a pleasurable and easy life. And the instinct for survival within her told her that to marry him might keep her safe. At the same time, her good common sense told her that she was in no emotional state to be making a decision that would direct her course for the rest of her life.

"I am touched and honored by your concern, Philip, but it would be unfair to you for me to give you an answer yet."

"But, Amelia, for your own safety, I must get you away from here as quickly as possible. You're running a terrible risk by continuing to expose yourself to the person who means to harm you."

Philip spoke fervently with more emotion and force than Amelia had ever witnessed in him. Did he know something that she did not?

"Philip, do you have any idea who wants me dead or why?"

He turned his classic profile and stared at the distant water, waiting what seemed just a fraction too long before he answered. "Of course not, Amelia! Wouldn't I have alerted the authorities if I had any such information, not only out of my love for you but also out of my duty as a lawyer? All I know is that this person, whoever it is, is here, and therefore, I must get you away from here as soon as possible."

His logic was irrefutable, at least the portion that suggested she leave the Belleview, but she could not make a lifetime commitment on the basis of what might be only a temporary threat. She had to have more time.

"Give me another week. I promise that I will give you

my answer by next Wednesday. That will give me time to recover from the shocks of the last few days and to think more clearly.

"Now"—she retrieved her hands and stood—"we'd better return to the suite, or Beulah will have a search party out after us."

Chapter Twenty-Four

"I know it seems sudden, Amelia, but Bernard has been offered a wonderful position in Ocala, and he must report there as soon as possible. I want to go with him, so the wedding will be on Monday. Will you come?"

Sarah placed her cup and saucer on the tea tray and waited for Amelia to answer.

They sat shaded from the warm afternoon sun on the hotel's veranda. Amelia's gaze rested on the blue waters of the harbor, but she saw nothing. Instead her thoughts were focused on two more people who would now move out of her life and whom she might never see again. She had not realized how dear the practical Sarah and boyish Bernard had become to her until she thought of their leaving. Fighting back an impulse to cry, Amelia rose from the wicker rocker and hugged Sarah.

"Of course I'll come. You didn't really think I would miss something so special, did you? Now, tell me all about Bernard's new job."

"There's a place called Green Hills Farms in Ocala. It's about a hundred miles north of here in the center of the state. The main interest of the farms is in breeding, raising, and training race horses. The farms just changed owners, and Bernard has been asked by the company that bought it to assume the management position. He's always said that horses are all he really knows, so he jumped at the chance. And it's very peaceful and beautiful there, rolling hills and lots of grazing meadows, plus a lot of citrus growing, too."

Amelia thought that she had never seen Sarah so animated or so pretty. Her lovely heart-shaped face, framed by wispy curls of her dark auburn hair, glowed with happiness, and there was a new sparkle in her large hazel eyes.

"But what will Dr. Winston do without you? You've been his assistant for so long."

"William will miss me, of course, but there are any number of eligible ladies in the community who will be more than happy to assist him with nursing duties. It will be good for him. He might even find himself a wife."

Sarah gave Amelia an impish smile. She radiated joy and contentment, and Amelia wondered what it must be like to have life take the course that one wanted.

"But what about you, Amelia?" Sarah interrupted her thoughts. "Have you any clues as to who tried to chloroform you? I've been so worried about you. In fact, it doesn't seem right for me to be so happy when you are in fear for your life."

Amelia shook her head. "I met with Constable Deckett for over an hour this morning, explaining not only what had happened with Rousseau, but also the incident with the chloroform, and even the other events that may or may not have been accidents. But if he has any ideas, he didn't share them with me. I honestly believe that he is as much in the dark as I am. None of it makes any sense."

She still did not know who wished her dead, and time was running out. She had only a few more days before she must give Philip an answer as she had promised, and she still was vacillating.

The practical, logical side of her nature that her father had so carefully trained and nurtured told her that she would be a fool not to marry Philip Sheridan. Not only would marriage to Philip remove her from whatever or whoever endangered her life, but it would also assure her a life of ease and luxury, with dependence on no one but Philip, who loved her enough to indulge her every whim. There were many women who would do anything for such an opportunity for security, wealth and social position, not to mention the fact that Philip was a most attractive, well-mannered and pleasant man.

But there was another side to Amelia that cried out in anguish at the thought of marriage to a man she did not love. This part of her wanted to spend the rest of her life alone if she could not share her life with the one man she truly loved. She sighed deeply and looked up to find Sarah watching her closely.

"What is it, Amelia? I can tell something is troubling you. Wouldn't you like to talk about it? Maybe I can help."

Sarah looked so worried that Amelia felt guilty at spoiling Sarah's happy plans with worries about her. She longed to share her dilemma with Sarah, but she was afraid the practical-minded young woman would scoff at her hopeless infatuation with a man she would probably never even see again. Instead, she steered the conversation to a safer topic. "It's just that I will miss you both."

315

"Then you must plan to come and visit us often," Sarah invited sincerely.

"I would love to do that, but at this point I have no idea where I will be going once the season ends. But enough about me. Tell me all about your plans for the wedding."

The two young women launched into a spirited discussion of fashion and etiquette, unaware of the pretty and animated picture they presented on the veranda of the Belleview. They attracted many admiring glances from passing guests, and their infectious laughter and merry voices prompted smiles on the faces of those who heard them. The only somber note to the afternoon was the watchful presence of Beulah, sitting inconspicuously in the shadows, a solemn reminder to Amelia of the threats upon her life and the real possibility that her unknown assailant might strike again.

The day of Sarah's wedding was warm and bright with the cloudless azure sky a perfect backdrop for the outdoor ceremony. Amelia arrived early to help Sarah dress, and through the open window of the upstairs bedroom, they could hear the guests in the garden below greeting one another as they arrived.

Amelia marveled at Sarah's tranquillity. She moved serenely about the room in her beribboned chemise and petticoats, as if she were dressing for a weekly church supper instead of her own wedding. Her dress of forest-green silk was spread out on the bed, and its matching three-quarter length traveling coat hung on the closet door.

"How can you be so calm, Sarah? I would be shaking in my shoes right now."

Sarah smiled at Amelia affectionately. "No, you wouldn't, Amelia, not if you were sure, as I am, that you are doing the right thing. I've known Bernard since he came to Florida over a year ago, and although he has done some foolish things, I understood why, and my love for him has grown each day. He's the only man I've ever met with whom I want to spend the rest of my life. No, when your own wedding day comes, believe me, if you've made the right choice, you won't be nervous either. Only so happy that you feel you could die from it. Now will you stop being so nervous and please help me with my hair?"

Is that the way I'll feel if I decide to marry Philip? Amelia asked herself as she helped Sarah to arrange her thick auburn curls in a bouffant coronet and secured it with silver combs. She watched with amusement as Sarah dusted her face lightly with powder in a futile effort to conceal her freckles.

Sarah then slipped the green silk dress over her head and turned for Amelia to fasten the long row of tiny buttons down the back. The yoke of the dress was fashioned of silk illusion with a high band at the neck edged in cream-colored lace. The same lace trimmed the tucks in the bodice and the flowing illusion of the elbow-length sleeves. A triple rope of creamy pearls, a family heirloom and gift from the groom, complemented the dress perfectly. A bouquet of ivory tea roses and early orange blossoms with streamers of matching ivory satin ribbons tied in lover's knots, also a gift from Bernard, lay on the dressing table.

It took all of Amelia's resolve not to cry at the scent of orange blossoms. Matt had so insinuated himself into her life that there were now hundreds of simple things, like smelling orange blossoms, riding a train, hearing a waltz, or eating an orange, that would forever remind Amelia of the love she had lost.

There was a light knock on the door and Dr. Winston, looking ill at ease in his formal gray cutaway, entered. He looked at Sarah, calm and beautiful in her wedding gown, with brotherly pride and a suspicious hint of moisture behind his gold-rimmed spectacles.

"Everyone is here, Sarah, including Pastor Dean. Are you ready?"

Sarah nodded and embraced Amelia, who slipped out to join the other guests.

Amelia was glad that the weather had cooperated with Sarah's plans for the day. She had been in Florida long enough to appreciate how fickle the Florida sun could be. But today it beamed brightly on Dr. Winston's enchanting garden. The previous cold weather had not dimmed the beauty of the blooming azaleas that banked the boundaries of the lawn. The guests lined the curving brick pathway that led to the rose arbor where Pastor Dean stood in his black clerical robes and immaculate Geneva collar.

Bernard, looking younger and more vulnerable than ever, watched the house, anxious for his first view of Sarah, as if he were afraid she might not make an appearance. He grinned with delight at Amelia, and she felt a stab of shame at envying him such happiness.

Lady Caroline approached, threw a kiss to her handsome son with her tiny gray-gloved hand, then linked her arm in Amelia's. Her tailored dress and coat of dove gray made her look every inch the aristocrat she was. Her face shone under her wide black hat swathed in soft gray tulle.

"I've always wanted a daughter," she whispered, "and Sarah will be a perfect wife for Bernard. She'll help him keep his feet on the ground."

The entire crowd hushed as Dr. Winston and Sarah stepped out of the house and descended the path toward the rose arbor. Amelia's eyes filled with tears and Sarah passed her in a blur. The short ceremony from the Book of Common Prayer took only a few minutes. Then the couple was surrounded by the guests offering best wishes and congratulations.

Buffet tables had been set up under the oaks, and these were promptly loaded with platters of food provided by women from Sarah's church. The chef at the Belleview had sent a three-tiered wedding cake, beautifully decorated, and iced between the layers with his own special filling of fruits, nuts, and raisins. William had even arranged for a photographer to take pictures of the cake cutting.

When the guests had finished eating, Dr. Winston toasted the couple with champagne. Then Sarah disappeared into the house to don her hat and traveling coat. The buggy that would take them to the station in Clear Water Harbor for the trip to Ocala was already loaded with their luggage and waiting for them in front of the house.

The couple raced from the house beneath a rain of rice and good wishes and climbed into the buggy as the guests gathered to wave good-bye. Sarah searched the crowd until she spied Amelia, then as the buggy started, tossed her bouquet directly into the hands of her startled friend.

Amelia felt Lady Caroline's arm about her shoulders and looked up to see the woman watching her with a dancing twinkle in her eyes.

"It looks like you're the next bride, my dear. In fact, I'll bet you a sixpence you're married before the season ends. Now," with her disconcerting habit of changing topics midstream, she continued, "let's go see if there's any of that excellent champagne left."

That evening Amelia sat curled in the big armchair before the fire in her room, Sarah's fragrant bouquet in her lap. She wasn't superstitious enough to believe in signs, but she couldn't help thinking that this was an indication that perhaps she should accept Philip's proposal. It was Monday night and she had promised him that he would have her answer by Wednesday. She knew that saying yes was the logical answer, but her love for Matt and the complications of living in Chicago held her back. She knew that it was a big city, but she also realized that both Matt and Philip moved in the same circles of Chicago's social elite. There would be no avoiding an occasional meeting with Matt and Diana, and each time would renew the pain that she had hoped that absence and distance might ease.

But Amelia also knew that she had to be practical about her future. Now she faced dependency on Ursula, but her aunt was old, and Amelia had no assurance that Ursula would provide for her in her will. As for Maude, there was still the possibility that Maude might marry, in which case she certainly wouldn't want a young female cousin hanging about.

She knew that she could return to Asheville and Dr. Will and Aunt Beth. She had received their letter inviting her to do just that. But she didn't feel right putting an added financial burden on them while she tried for medical school. Even if she managed to stretch her meager inheritance to see her through her medical training, she realized she would never have enough money to set herself up in practice. And she was realistic enough to know that it would be difficult to find a bank willing to lend money to a female physician.

Her one real hope had been Matt's promise of help in establishing an investment portfolio to maximize her income. But Matt had gone out of her life without a word, and she could only assume that he had taken his offer with him.

There was always teaching, but Amelia rejected that with a shudder. She thought of the teacherage in

Asheville where the female secondary teachers were required to live. They were not allowed to marry, and the rules and regulations they were made to observe were legion. She saw herself at thirty, much as Maude was today, and she knew that teaching was not an option she could choose.

With a terrible sense of finality, Amelia knew that she had no choice but to accept Philip's proposal. It was not a question of love, but of survival. And he was handsome and kind. Perhaps she could learn to love him if she tried. Tomorrow she would tell Aunt Ursula and Maude of her plans, and on Wednesday she would give Philip his answer as she had promised.

As she arose to climb in bed, she placed Sarah's bouquet on her dresser. It looked as if she would owe Lady Caroline that sixpence, she thought as she pulled the covers around her. Before the season ended, she would be Mrs. Philip Sheridan III. The fragrance of roses and orange blossoms filled the room as she drifted off to sleep.

Chapter Twenty-Five

"Marry Philip!"

Maude dropped the silver coffeepot onto its service tray with a clatter, breaking the serenity of their luncheon. Ursula jumped at the noise, but showed no sign of surprise at Amelia's announcement.

"I know that I'm of age and therefore don't need anyone's permission, but as a matter of courtesy, Aunt Ursula, I felt I should inform you before I accept Philip's proposal."

Amelia spoke haltingly, disconcerted by Maude's startled reaction to her announcement that she would marry Philip

"Philip told me that he had already spoken to you before he asked me, and—" Amelia tried in vain to continue.

"Mama! You never said a word to me about this!" Maude interrupted, her face pale and her expression ugly and contorted.

"No, I didn't," Ursula replied frostily. "There are some things that are not necessary for you to know. Now please be still and let Amelia continue."

Maude pressed her lips tightly together and sat with her hands clasped so firmly in her lap that the knuckles glowed white. Amelia could feel the growing tension in the room and was dismayed by Maude's evident displeasure at her news. She had hoped to include Maude and Ursula in her plans for a formal church wedding, but now she realized that perhaps a simple ceremony in the home of a justice of the peace might be a wiser course of action.

"I told Philip that I would let him know tomorrow," Amelia went on. "He wants us to be married immediately and return to Chicago. He believes I will be safer there."

As she spoke, Amelia remembered the attempts on her life with a feeling of unreality, as if they had been a bad dream. Then forcing her mind back to the matter of her marriage, she went on, "I will suggest it be a simple ceremony, perhaps just a civil one. But of course I will want you both to be there," she added hastily.

Maude sat unmoving, a blank look frozen on her face. Amelia tried to catch her eye to smile and ease the tension, but Maude would not look at her. Poor Maude, Amelia thought, it must be difficult to have been jilted in her youth and now to find herself growing old with no suitors. No wonder she resented the idea of Amelia's marrying. Well, perhaps Ursula could deal with her.

"Excuse me, please, Aunt, Maude. We can talk more about this after I've talked with Philip tomorrow."

"I'm very happy for you, my dear," Ursula replied, but her expression belied her words. Her eyes were on Maude who still sat as if in a trance.

Eager to escape the strained atmosphere of the parlor, Amelia returned to her room. She wanted to write to

Dr. Will and Aunt Beth about her news, but as she tried to explain to them why she was marrying Philip, she could not find adequate words and threw down her pen in frustration.

Feeling a need to put as much distance as possible between herself and the unhappy women in the next room, she changed quickly into her riding clothes and went to the Frasers' suite. Perhaps Lady Caroline was missing Bernard and would be glad for a chance to ride.

Dour-faced Rose answered the door and asked Amelia to be seated, while Caroline called from her dressing room that she was changing into her riding habit and would join her in a few minutes.

The two women walked unhurriedly to the stables, enjoying the warmth of the sunny day and the touch of spring in the air. The scent of orange blossoms from a nearby grove wafted on the breeze to them and reminded Amelia of Sarah's wedding bouquet and Lady Caroline's prediction. Unwillingly, she also remembered her carriage ride through the orange groves with Matt. Would she never be free of him?

She returned her thoughts dutifully to Philip, cataloging his virtues as if counting sheep. She longed to tell the older woman who had so befriended her about her decision to marry Philip, but she knew it would be unfair to Philip not to tell him first.

Amelia was surprised by Lady Caroline's behavior when they reached the stables. Caroline ordered a horse saddled for herself, and then set about saddling Amelia's horse for her. As Caroline checked the saddle blanket carefully, Amelia was reminded of her throw from Satan and the worry over who wanted to harm her surfaced from the depths of her mind where she had tried to confine it.

When Amelia's horse was saddled to Lady Caroline's satisfaction, the two women mounted and started off on the trail that edged the bluff south of the hotel. The tide was out and a variety of sea birds, including terns and sandpipers, filled the sand flats. A great blue heron poised on one leg, not moving even when the horses passed, and a graceful long-billed curlew with bright cinnamon wing markings soared overhead.

The women made desultory comments about the scenery, until Caroline, in one of her characteristic conversational shifts, asked, "How do you feel about horses, Amelia?"

Amelia laughed. "What a bizarre question! I love to ride, of course, but other than that, I really haven't given horses much thought."

"How would you feel about running a breeding farm?" Lady Caroline persisted in her strange line of questioning.

"First, I have absolutely no qualifications for such a job. Bernard's the one who knows horses, remember? And if you're looking for an investor, I'm definitely not qualified."

"Hmm." Caroline looked thoughtful as they walked their horses along the shore.

"Forget the horse farm. How would you feel about living in Florida the rest of your life?"

Amelia laughed again. One of the things she loved about Caroline was her unpredictability. "The few months I've been here have been beautiful, and I'm sure it would be pleasant to live here year round. But there's not much chance of that for me, I can assure you."

She thought of Chicago and its long cold winters, so different from the milder climate of Asheville and the semitropical Florida.

"Why would you ask such a question?"

The dancing twinkle returned to Caroline's merry green eyes. "Oh, just making conversation. I'll race you back to the Belleview. The loser buys tea!"

As Amelia urged her horse on, Caroline's questions were forgotten, and she was amazed to find herself half a length ahead of Caroline in returning to the hotel. Handing the reins to the grooms, the two friends walked arm in arm back to the broad veranda at the entrance, settled comfortably in the large wicker rockers, and ordered tea. In moments a linen-covered table with silver tea service and sandwiches and cakes was set before them, and they spent a pleasant hour reviewing the highlights of yesterday's wedding.

As they rose to leave, Caroline embraced Amelia.

"Have dinner with me tonight, won't you? It's going to be lonely without Bernard for a while."

"Of course," Amelia agreed. "I'll meet you in the Tiffany Room at eight."

Reluctantly, she returned to her lonely room to try again to write the difficult letter to Dr. Will and Aunt Beth.

At ten o'clock when she returned from dinner, the letter was still unwritten. Amelia simply had not been able to find the words to explain why she was marrying a man she did not love. Almost immediately there was a soft knock on the door that connected her room to the parlor.

When she opened the door, Amelia was surprised to find a smiling Maude waiting there.

"I'm glad you haven't gone to bed yet, Amelia," Maude said, standing on the threshold. "Could you come to my room for a moment? There's something I would like to show you."

"Certainly," Amelia said, relieved that Maude no longer seemed upset with her. "I'll be there as soon as I've put away my gloves and shawl."

A moment later Amelia crossed the parlor and entered the open door of Maude's room. Maude stood looking out the window, her back to Amelia, her posture the same ramrod stiffness Amelia remembered from their first meeting.

"Close the door, please."

Maude's voice sounded strangely controlled, and Amelia closed the door and moved into the room.

Maude turned and Amelia saw a glint of light on the nickled barrel of a small derringer. Its double barrels stared at her like two black eyes.

"This is what I wanted to show you, Amelia dear."

"Good heavens, Maude, put that thing away before you hurt someone!" Amelia exclaimed.

Maude's eyes glittered with a hard look and she laughed harshly. "Poor innocent little Amelia. You don't understand. I intend to hurt someone. You, to be exact."

Amelia's mind struggled to assimilate the incomprehensible situation before her.

"You still haven't figured it out, have you?" Maude's upper lip curled into a grotesque smile. "The rattlesnake in your room, the poison on the island, your fall down the stairs, your fall from Satan, and the chloroform? You have more lives than a cat, dear cousin."

Maude's whining tone had modulated into a harsh sneer. "But now your luck has finally run out. You will be very dead when I've finished with you this time."

"But why, Maude? What have I ever done to you?"

As she spoke, Amelia thought of crying for help and looked about for some means of escape, but even as she looked, she knew that at that range Maude could shoot her before anyone could answer her cries. Her only chance was to keep Maude talking in hopes that Aunt Ursula or someone, anyone, would appear.

"What have you done to me? You've taken the two things in life that mean the most to me—Philip Sheridan and Grandfather Sinclair's money."

Amelia shook her head. Maude's accusations made no

sense. Maude in love with Philip? And Grandfather's money?

"Yes, I do plan to marry Philip, but I have nothing to do with Grandfather's—"

Maude's barking laugh interrupted her. "You just don't know about it, that's all. Grandfather changed his will right before he died leaving everything to you. He felt so sorry for you because you had no inheritance. He knew Mama and I were taken care of with Hagarty money. Mama's had Philip protesting the will from the moment she found out, and they didn't want you interfering, so they decided to keep it from you as long as they could. But now you won't get any of the money or Philip either!"

She leveled the derringer at Amelia's heart. Amelia's hurt at Philip's deceit was overridden by her desire to stay alive. She had to convince Maude not to shoot her. "You won't get away with this, Maude. You'll be put in prison and won't have the money or Philip for yourself."

"Ah, but you're wrong, Amelia. I will claim that after the attempts on your life, I became concerned for your safety and Mama's and mine, so I purchased this gun for protection."

She held out the tiny derringer with its pearl grips for Amelia's inspection, then aimed the double barrels again at Amelia's heart. "And then tonight you burst into my room without knocking, and I, thinking you someone who meant to harm me, shot you in the dark. It was not until I turned on the lights that I realized I had killed my own dear cousin. I will be absolutely distraught." Maude laughed her cackling laugh again, and Amelia could see the madness gleaming in her eyes.

Amelia knew that she must keep talking, that every minute she could keep Maude from shooting increased the chances of Ursula or Beulah coming in to find them. But her mind went totally blank as she cast about for what to say to the madwoman who confronted her. Then she had an inspiration.

"I don't believe you were really responsible for all my accidents, Maude. There was no way you alone could have accomplished all that."

Maude bristled with pride. "It was all my doing, mine alone," she bragged. "The rattlesnake was easy. I just had one of the local urchins catch me one and put it in a mason jar. When we returned from dinner that night, you were asleep in the bathtub and I simply turned it loose in the bathroom.

"While the chef was preparing our picnic for our island outing, I slipped some rat poison from the kitchen into my skirt pocket. It was an easy matter to sprinkle it in your food before I served it to you. If it hadn't been for Matthew Laurence's arriving so unexpectedly, that would have been the end of you.

"And it was I who pushed you down the stairs that day. And I who managed to sneak the sandspur beneath Satan's blanket while you were talking with Miss Barrington. But the most creative of my schemes was the chloroform. That would have appeared as a neat suicide, if Beulah hadn't interrupted me. As a doctor's daughter who had assisted her father many times with anesthesia, you, overwhelmingly saddened by the untimely deaths of your parents, would have appeared simply to have chosen the most logical and painless method of killing yourself."

Amelia could tell from the look of terrible purpose on Maude's face that she had finished with talking.

Maude extended the gun at arm's length, but not close enough for Amelia to try to reach it.

"But this time, dear cousin, there is no way out. We've talked—"

Suddenly the door into the parlor slammed open against the wall with a mighty crash, and as Maude turned toward the sound, the derringer discharged. In an instant Amelia saw Matt with Beulah close behind him. Matt threw himself across the room, lunging at Maude, and the gun fired again. Then, as if in slow motion, Matt and Maude crumpled to the floor and both lay still as blood formed a crimson pool beneath them.

"Oh dear God, they're both dead!" Amelia screamed, and the room was swallowed up in darkness.

Chapter Twenty-Six

Amelia was roused by the acrid odor of smelling salts. She found herself lying on the sofa in the parlor and looked up to see Lady Caroline hovering over her anxiously, waving an open vial back and forth beneath her nose. Hunter, his usual ruddy face startlingly pale, entered the parlor from Maude's room, closing the door firmly behind him.

Amelia pushed away the smelling salts, sat upright and grasped Lady Caroline's hands. "Are they—" She could not force herself to say the words, hoping if they remained unspoken, what they meant would not be true.

Caroline looked at Hunter questioningly.

"Dr. Winston has been called," he said. "I'm afraid there isn't anything he can do for Miss Hagarty, but Matthew is at least still alive."

"Thank God," Amelia breathed. "But shouldn't someone be with him?"

She rose to go to him, but Hunter laid a restraining hand on her shoulder. "Mr. Carlisle, the manager, is trained in first aid. He's with him now. And we can't move Miss Hagarty until the Constable arrives. You must stay here, Miss Donelly. It's not a pretty sight."

His voice was gentle, but the intent of his words was strong. Weakly, Amelia resumed her seat. Only then did the full realization that Maude was dead strike her, and her first thought was of her aunt.

"Aunt Ursula, does she know? Perhaps I should go to her."

Shaken and on the verge of hysteria, Amelia felt that under the horrible circumstances, she ought to be doing something, not just fainting away like a heroine in a bad novel.

"Beulah is with her, dear, and for now, I would imagine she would not want to see anyone else. There really isn't anything you can do until Constable Deckett arrives, unless you feel like telling us what happened."

Lady Caroline, looking terribly upset but well under control, sat down and motioned for Amelia to join her. Amelia, pale and unsteady, sat next to her.

"It was Maude all along who was causing the accidents."

Amelia shook her head bewilderedly, still unable to comprehend the depth of Maude's hatred. "She was jealous of me because of Philip Sheridan. She knew that we were to be married—"

"What in heaven's name are you saying, girl? You, marry Philip? You can't be serious!" Lady Caroline would have continued, but she was dumbstruck.

Amelia almost giggled at the absurdity of Caroline's reactions. That Maude was a murderer had caused her nary a blink, but Amelia's impending marriage to Philip had stunned her. Amelia gained control of her fluctuating emotions and continued her story.

"And she was also ranting crazily about Grandfather Sinclair leaving his entire estate to me. She wanted to kill me, she said, so she could have Grandfather Sinclair's money and Philip to herself. I think she had gone completely mad, although she was still very clever. She had planned to make my death look like an accident, of course. And it would have, if Matt hadn't come along. Why was he there? I thought you both had returned to Chicago."

She looked at Hunter in helpless confusion, overwhelmed by all that had happened and terrified for Matt.

Dear God, she prayed silently, *please don't let him die*.

Hunter's voice intruded on her prayers. "We were in the lobby checking back into our suite, when Beulah came running down the stairs. As soon as she saw Matthew, she ran to him, grabbed his arm, and cried that Maude was going to shoot you. Matthew took the stairs three at a time with the redoubtable Beulah close on his heels. When he entered Maude's room, she either shot him intentionally or the gun went off accidentally because he startled her. What happened after that, we can only guess until after Matthew regains consciousness, unless you can tell us what happened?"

Amelia shook her head. "I'm not sure. It all happened so fast, and I was so stunned to see Matt that everything else was a blur until I fainted. Poor Maude, to be so unhappy, and now—" Amelia voice choked with tears.

"Poor Maude indeed!" Caroline exploded in disgust. "She's been trying for months to kill you, Amelia, and tonight she almost succeeded! And almost succeeded in killing Matt—"

Once again words failed Lady Caroline, and Amelia thought for a moment that the woman was going to weep, but her staunch British spirit would not allow that. Lady Caroline, her composure restored, took charge. She put her arms comfortingly around Amelia and spoke to Hunter. "Randolph, you had better see how Matthew is faring. I'm going to get Amelia's night clothes and take her to my suite. She can sleep in Bernard's room tonight."

Amelia sat as if in a trance as Caroline gathered her belongings from her bedroom. Everything that was happening was still wrapped in a dreamlike aura of unreality. She jumped, startled from her reverie, when Caroline spoke in a brusque no-nonsense tone that allowed no contradicting.

"Come along, my girl. What you need is a nice hot toddy and a warm bed, and my Rose makes the best toddies west of England."

She gently helped Amelia to her feet, led her to the corridor and down the hall. In Bernard's old room, she helped Amelia out of her dinner gown and into her warm flannel nightdress.

The angular and unsmiling Rose was kneeling at the fireplace, heating a poker in the burning embers. When it glowed red hot, she thrust it into a mug on the hearth beside her, withdrew it, then handed the cup of steaming liquid to Lady Caroline.

Caroline placed the cup in Amelia's hands. "Drink it down, girl, every drop!" she ordered.

As Amelia complied with the command, a faint memory in the back of her mind detected the bitter aftertaste of a sleeping draught her father used to prepare for his patients, but before she could put a name to it, her eyelids drooped, and Caroline was taking the cup from her and tucking the covers round her.

"Poor darling," Amelia heard Caroline murmur, her last conscious thought before the sleeping potion took effect.

* * *

It was noon before Amelia had awakened the next day, and even then it had taken several cups of strong coffee to chase the cobwebs of the sleeping draught from her mind. Lady Caroline had sent Rose to Amelia's room to gather her clothes, and now all of her belongings, including her father's black medical bag, were in the room that Bernard had occupied.

Amelia was once again dressed in mourning, a black velvet-trimmed shirtwaist and black bombazine skirt, which emphasized the shining red-gold of her hair and the pallor of her complexion. She sat unmoving in the parlor of Lady Caroline's suite, her hands clasped and head bowed in fervent prayer for Matt's life.

Hunter had informed her a few moments before that Matt was still unconscious. Dr. Winston had removed the bullet from his shoulder and he had lost a great deal of blood. He lay now in the suite that he and Hunter had shared before, hanging tenuously to life. He had come to help her, and if he died, it would be her fault. She longed to go to him and watch at his bedside, but she knew that she must first face Philip, and most difficult of all, Aunt Ursula.

Rose interrupted her thoughts. "Mr. Sheridan here to see you, Miss. Shall I show him in?"

Amelia sighed and nodded. It would be better to be done with this quickly.

Philip entered the parlor and Amelia was shocked at his appearance. He looked like an old man. His shoulders were slumped and his characteristic self-confidence gone. He stood just inside the doorway, twisting the brim of his hat nervously in his hands.

"I don't know what to say or where to begin . . ." He had difficulty speaking, stumbling over his words, and he kept his eyes fixed on the floor, unable to look at her in his shame.

Amelia felt pity for him, even though a part of her was enraged that he had kept the knowledge of her inheritance from her.

"Please, sit down, Philip. Rose, take Mr. Sheridan's hat and bring him a brandy."

Rose sniffed disapprovingly, but took Philip's hat, then went to the sideboard and poured the amber liquid in a snifter. She handed it to Philip and withdrew.

"Perhaps the best place to begin would be at the beginning," Amelia prompted him gently.

Philip downed the brandy in a desperate gulp. Then gazing out the window of the parlor, refusing to meet Amelia's eyes, he spoke, "When I first came to Florida in January, it was to inform Mrs. Hagarty that Jeremiah had changed his will right before he died, leaving everything, except the house where Ursula and Maude lived, to you. Mrs. Hagarty was outraged. She was sure that his latest stroke had affected his mind, and therefore, his will could be contested. Even before I had met you, she convinced me that it would be kinder to you not to let you know about the inheritance, in case the courts ruled that the latest will was invalid. She insisted that you would not miss what you had never had.

"Later, after I had met you and had fallen in love with you, I knew that I could take care of you and that you would never need Jeremiah's money."

He paused awkwardly, then for the first time looked Amelia in the eye, pain and embarrassment evident in his expression. "No, I can't lie to you anymore, Amelia. In all honesty, I was afraid that if you knew you had the money, you would have continued to try for medical school and would have had nothing to do with me.

"And now I feel so responsible for all that has happened. I had no idea that Maude felt about me or her lost inheritance the way she did. If only I'd told the whole truth from the beginning, perhaps none of this

338

would have happened. Can you ever forgive me, Amelia?"

He was so genuinely distraught that Amelia could not stay angry with him. She felt that he had suffered already and, because he was not an insensitive man, would probably suffer more for a long time to come.

"Yes, Philip, you have my forgiveness. I cannot condone what you did, but I believe I understand your motives."

His expression cleared and a faint spark of hope glimmered in his eyes. "Is there a chance then that you will accept my proposal after all?"

Amelia shook her head. "I don't think that would ever be possible now, Philip. I am very fond of you, but I do not love you, and I could not pretend to. Especially since all that has just happened has proved what havoc deception wreaks."

His hope extinguished, Philip rose to leave. "I will be taking your aunt, and Maude, back to Chicago tomorrow. May I see you again before I go?"

"No, Philip," Amelia said firmly, but kindly. "I think it best that we not see each other again until the trauma of all this has eased for both of us. Perhaps then it will be possible for us to meet again as friends."

For a long instant he studied her face as if committing it to memory, then without another word, he turned and left the suite.

Amelia felt emotionally drained after her meeting with Philip, but she knew that, although she dreaded the confrontation, she could no longer delay seeing Aunt Ursula. Her feelings for the woman were a conflicting mix of pity over the death of Maude and anger because she had kept the contents of Jeremiah's will secret and had tried to take from Amelia what her grandfather had intended for her.

As Amelia knocked on the door of the Hagarty suite,

her eyes searched the west end of the corridor for any sign of activity outside Matt's rooms, but the hallway was deserted.

When the door opened, Amelia found herself engulfed in Beulah's embrace. Tears streamed down her ebony cheeks and she was unable to speak.

"Thank you, Beulah, for saving my life. That's three times you've come to my rescue, so I owe you thanks thrice over. But I'm so sorry about Maude."

"Poor Miss Maude, but she bought her own troubles," Beulah replied sadly.

"May I see Aunt Ursula? Is she up to talking to me?"

"She's in a bad way, chile, but you go on in. Maybe you can help."

Amelia knocked softly at Ursula's door and entered when a weak voice called, "Come in."

She was unprepared for the old woman's appearance. Ursula was sitting up in bed, her shoulders covered by a black shawl, and her fine white hair was elegantly coiffed, but her previous pink-and-white unlined complexion had suddenly caught up with her age. Her face was wrinkled and jaundiced, and for the first time Amelia noticed patches of brown age spots on the formerly flawless skin.

Ursula did not cry, but her entire demeanor exhibited the lassitude of someone who had lost the will to live. She motioned feebly to a chair beside the bed, and Amelia sat down.

"I'm glad that you are unharmed, Amelia."

Amelia was touched by Ursula's genuine concern, especially since she had just lost her only child.

"I'm very sorry about Maude, Aunt Ursula."

She wanted to say more, but words were inadequate to express her feelings.

"My poor baby." Ursula sighed. "She must have been very mad indeed to try to kill you. And I never even guessed that she was so infatuated with Philip. They had always seemed just good friends, ever since they were children. But Maude always kept to herself, even as a child, and I never really knew what she was thinking. And after Edward Rousseau broke their engagement, she became even more solitary and reclusive. I had hoped that by inheriting Father's fortune she would attract suitors, marry and have a family. That is the only reason I contested the will. Believe me, Amelia. Maude needed all that wealth to draw men to her, while you attract men like moths to a flame. I'll drop the suit now. I have no need for Father's money. I only wanted it for Maude."

Amelia nodded, not knowing what to say. She realized, knowing her aunt, that this was as close to an apology as she would ever receive. But she could feel only pity for the poor woman, wracked by physical and emotional pain, so she rose, kissed the dry wrinkled cheek, and turned to leave.

"Thank you for your care since Mama and Papa died, Aunt Ursula. I am grateful for the many things you have done for me. I won't see you before you leave tomorrow, but perhaps someday we will meet again and under happier circumstances. Lady Caroline has invited me to stay with her until the season ends. Then, in light of my inheritance, I will decide where to go from here. Good-bye."

She stopped in the parlor long enough to say a tearful farewell to Beulah, then returned to Lady Caroline's suite to await news of Matt.

Chapter Twenty-Seven

A rumpled and haggard Dr. Winston was drinking tea with Lady Caroline when Amelia entered the suite.

"Ah, there you are, my dear. I've been inquiring about you. I was wondering if you were fit enough after your terrible experience last night to help me with a bit of nursing. Sarah's replacement is working out well enough so far on routine matters, but this case requires some expert care. What do you say?"

Amelia knew that he must be needing someone to care for Matt, and her emotions ranged from joy at the opportunity to look after him to fear for his life.

"Of course, I'll be happy to do whatever I can. I assume you're referring to Matt. Is he conscious yet?" Her voice wavered with anxiety.

Frowning, Dr. Winston shook his head. "Not only is he still unconscious, but it appears that there may be some infection developing from his wound. His temperature has been rising gradually, so he will have to be carefully watched. Are you sure you're up to it?"

"I'm perfectly all right, I assure you, and taking care of Matt is the least I can do after he risked his life for me."

"Excellent!"

Dr. Winston replaced his cup and saucer on the tea tray and took one last small cake, which he popped into his mouth whole and swallowed with a gulp.

"Just one request, please. Cover up or get rid of that black. It's no color for a sickroom."

"Yes sir," Amelia agreed.

She went to her room, found the starched white pinafore that she had worn when assisting her father, and put it on. Memories of her father and his practice flooded her mind.

Dear God, she prayed, *help me to remember all he taught me so I can help Matt. Please don't let him die.*

Then making an effort to subdue her personal feelings, she checked the mirror to make sure that her hair was neatly secured and joined Dr. Winston.

"Much better," he said as he surveyed her trim appearance. "Now we can go relieve Mr. Hunter, who has been keeping watch."

"Please tell Randolph that I have tea here for him," Lady Caroline requested.

She used the name with a casualness and familiarity that caused Amelia to look at her curiously. She remembered that Caroline had called Hunter by his first name last night, too. In fact, Amelia had not even known Hunter's given name until last night, and she wondered how Lady Caroline had come to be on such intimate terms with Matt's valet.

But these musings were forced from her mind as she followed Dr. Winston through the parlor of Matt's suite and into his bedroom. Matt lay in the middle of the large bed with its ornately carved headboard of cherrywood, the afternoon sun streaming in on his still form. His skin was waxen and his thick dark hair a stark contrast to the crisp white pillowslips. His upper torso was bare, except for his right shoulder, which was swathed in heavy gauze bandages.

With an efficiency that belied the furious pounding of her heart, Amelia placed the inside of her wrist against his forehead and felt the fever which burned his body. She longed to look into the depths of his soft brown eyes, but his eyes were closed, and for the first time she noticed his thick brown lashes against the pallor of his cheeks.

"Have Mr. Carlisle send for me if there is any change, Amelia. In the meantime, all we can do is watch and pray."

Dr. Winston wearily gathered up his coat and medical bag, patted her shoulder comfortingly and quietly left the room.

Amelia brought a basin of cool water and wiped Matt's face and upper body in an attempt to lower his temperature. His quiescent form, formerly so vibrant and strong, filled her with melancholy, and she struggled to maintain the objectivity necessary to be alert to her duties. She checked his pulse and found it reassuringly normal, then drew the large armchair beside the bed.

Although it was frightening to know that his life was in danger, she forced his danger from her mind and indulged herself in the opportunity to study him more closely. She would paint these pictures of him in her memory, so that for the rest of her life she would have them to treasure and remember.

She knew that her own life had taken a critical turn last night. The decision to marry Philip had been discarded, and a life of independence and wealth had been given to her. Perhaps, she thought, the inheritance was to make up for not having Matt. For now she knew that she could never love anyone else, and that she would devote the rest of her life to the practice of medicine, giving to others the love and care she would have lavished on Matt, if fate had not decreed that he belong to another.

Abruptly she realized that she had not seen or heard anything of Diana since Matt's return. Did that mean that Diana had not returned with him? Perhaps she had traveled on to Chicago to prepare for their approaching marriage. Surely Hunter had wired Diana of Matt's wound. Would she now arrive to relieve Amelia of his care? Amelia shuddered at the thought of another encounter with the arrogant and haughty Diana.

The hours passed and she watched the vivid colors of the sunset fade over the Gulf before closing the draperies to keep out the night chill. Matt continued to run a fever, but at least it went no higher. He still showed no signs of regaining consciousness.

Hunter entered the room and spoke softly, "Caroline has dinner waiting for you. I'll keep watch while you eat, and Dr. Winston will be here after dinner to check on his patient. You run along now."

Amelia gave Matt a last anxious glance, but she knew that no one would care for him any better than Hunter, who seemed to love him like a son. So she smiled her thanks and returned to Lady Caroline's suite.

As she was removing her apron and washing up for dinner, she remembered Hunter's referring to her friend as simply "Caroline," and thought it strange that the unfailingly correct Hunter should speak of a woman and an aristocrat so familiarly. Perhaps the horror of last night had drawn them close, much like the camaraderie of soldiers on a battlefield.

Rose was removing the domes from the serving plates

as Amelia entered the parlor. Her mouth watered with hunger at the smell of the food, and she realized that she had not eaten since dinner the night before. Lady Caroline gestured to the place across from her at the table and Amelia sat down. Rose served the plates with generous helpings of roast beef and Yorkshire pudding, then Lady Caroline bowed her head and said grace.

"Lord, for the food we are about to receive, make us truly thankful. Support Ursula Hagarty with Your love, and send the healing power of Your Holy Spirit upon Matthew Laurence. Amen."

Amelia fought back tears and smiled at her friend. She felt extremely fortunate to know someone like Lady Caroline who truly cared about others and was always willing to help them. She had readily and enthusiastically accepted Amelia as if she were one of her own family.

"You must be starved, my dear," Caroline observed. "You do justice to this marvelous roast beef, and while we dine, I'll tell you a little story."

Amelia was used to Lady Caroline's unusual conversational shifts, but never before had she heard her tell a story, so she listened attentively and curiously.

"Over twenty-five years ago, about the time I was first married, my husband told me of a close school chum of his, Lord Weybridge, with whom he had spent many happy hours hunting and drinking. He no longer saw Lord Weybridge, though, because about a year before our wedding, Lord Weybridge had married. His bride was a beautiful woman whom he loved beyond measure. It was not one of your typical aristocratic wedding arrangements for money or title, although Lady Weybridge had both. The reason for Lord Weybridge's separation from his friends, however, was not his marriage, but its tragic circumstances. You see, shortly after their wedding, Lady Weybridge developed a very serious and mysterious illness. It took many different forms and symptoms, and they never knew how or when it would strike. The only constant factor in the disease was that whatever form it did take, it was accompanied by a bizarre butterfly-shaped rash across her face.

"Time and again Lady Weybridge became so ill that the doctors did not expect her to recover. Often she would lapse into a coma for no identifiable reason, and days later just as inexplicably regain consciousness. Through all of this, Lord Weybridge remained devoted to his wife. Together they consulted the best medical minds in Europe and America, but found no hope for a cure.

"When they had been married about ten years, Lady Weybridge finally died from her strange illness, and her husband slowly went out of his mind. He began drinking heavily, and he neglected the family estate to the point that it became unproductive and ramshackle. After five years of this increasingly worsening drinking, his younger brothers offered to take over the estate while Lord Weybridge came to America to a clinic for alcoholics. They had hoped he could conquer his drinking problem and return to England to run the estate himself.

"Lord Weybridge agreed. At this point nothing mattered to him anyway. His lovely wife had been everything to him, and with her gone, life had no meaning. The family saw him off to America, and he was to have been met in New York by someone from the clinic. However, after the ship had docked in New York, the clinic's administrator wired the family and said that their representative had been unable to locate Lord Weybridge. The family hired special detectives, who searched everywhere for him, even checking the morgues and the hospitals, but he had disappeared without a trace. For over a year the family searched for him before they finally and reluctantly concluded that he must be dead.

"What the family did not know was that Lord Weybridge had left the ocean liner in New York and gone straight to Grand Central Station where he caught a train headed west. He had not had a drink during the entire crossing. This had given him the confidence to believe that perhaps he could start a new life for himself in California, away from all the memories and reminders of his beloved wife.

"However, when the train reached Chicago, he remembered that the last time he had been there was to visit specialists with his wife. It was also Christmas Eve. The holiday and all his painful memories were too much for him. He left the train and went to the nearest bar. It was a bitterly cold day, and he had left his overcoat, baggage and most of his money on the train. Whoever found all that must have simply kept it, for the family was never notified.

"He proceeded to get falling down drunk, and he would have died in the below freezing weather if he had not literally run into and knocked down a warm-hearted young financier who took him home and gave him a job."

"Hunter!" Amelia cried in astonishment.

"More precisely, my dear, Randolph Hunter, four-teenth Earl of Weybridge. I thought I recognized him, but I was not sure until the day of the meeting that we had here in this suite. You left before the others, and as we began reminiscing about England I knew that was who he had to be. He admitted it when I questioned him, but asked that I not let anyone else know. Even Matthew had not known it until that time.

"I encouraged him to inform his family, but he thought it would not be fair to his brothers who have run the estate all these years. However, I convinced him that he at least owed it to his mother to let her know that he is still alive. So he wired them and was surprised and gratified to receive word from his brothers insisting that he return to England to resume his title and control of his lands. He plans to leave as soon as the season here is over."

Lady Caroline paused in her narrative and blushed like a schoolgirl. "And I will be returning with him to become his wife."

"How wonderful! Dearest Caroline, I'm so happy for you."

Amelia jumped from her seat and embraced the older woman affectionately.

"But what about Matt?" she asked as she sat down again. "Whatever will he do without Hunter who's been his best friend?"

Lady Caroline's eyes resumed their dancing twinkle. "Matt will be married soon, and although I know he'll miss Randolph, I'm sure his new bride will keep him good company."

Lady Caroline ignored the crestfallen expression on Amelia's face and asked Rose to serve dessert.

"We must finish quickly now so that you can return to your nursing duties."

Amelia could barely swallow the chocolate mousse for the lump in her throat. Here were two more beloved friends who would soon be moving out of her life, probably forever. And Matt would definitely be married in the near future. The pain of that thought made her abandon it. Then she remembered that she was an heiress now and could afford to visit England if she wished, but there would be several long years of medical school before she would be free to travel, if then.

She excused herself from the table, donned her white pinafore again, and returned to Matt's room to relieve Hunter. He would probably always be Hunter to her, she thought. She couldn't imagine calling him Lord Weybridge. Suddenly she remembered what he had said to her the first day she had met him on the pier.

"You will discover, Miss Donelly, that the grieving will go on for a long time, but one must still enjoy life, despite the pain."

Now that she knew his story, the words had more meaning for her, and they gave her hope that perhaps she would be able to survive life without Matthew Laurence after all.

But when she entered the room and saw him lying there, still and helpless, the pain welled in her so strongly that she wanted to cry out against it. Dr. Winston had finished his examination and was replacing his stethoscope in his medical bag.

"The fever's broken. Now if he would only regain consciousness, I'd say he has an excellent chance of pulling through."

"I appreciate your care, Doctor," Hunter said with a telltale huskiness in his voice. "The boy is like a son to me—" He couldn't say more, but brushed his eyes quickly with the back of his hand and left the room.

Amelia listened carefully to Dr. Winston's instructions and promised again to let him know if there was any change. After the doctor left, she settled again in the large chair by the bed. She gazed hypnotically at the flickering blue-and-gold tongues of flame in the fire that Hunter had built and thought about the story that Lady Caroline had just related to her.

Gradually, she became aware of someone's eyes on her, and she glanced at the bed to find Matt's eyes wide open and focused on her face. Before she could make a move to call Dr. Winston, Matt spoke. His voice was soft, but every word was clear and strong. "I love you, Amelia."

Chapter Twenty-Eight

Amelia stared at Matt in wonder and disbelief. Then she moved quickly to his side to check his temperature, thinking that his fever had returned and caused him to be delirious. But he brushed her ministering hand away, grasped her arm with his left hand and drew her down on the bed beside him.

"Please listen, Amelia. There are some things I must tell you."

The pleading look in his eyes melted her heart, but her professional training would not let him endanger himself.

"You mustn't talk yet, Matt. Let me send for Dr. Winston. When he has said it is safe for you to do so, then you can talk to me all you wish. But for now, you must lie still and stay very quiet."

She placed her fingers against his lips as he began to protest. "No objections. I promise when you are well enough I will listen to whatever it is you have to say."

In response, he held her hand against his lips and gently kissed the tips of her fingers before he released her and nodded his agreement.

With her blood pounding in her ears, Amelia sped out the door and down the corridor to Lady Caroline's rooms to tell Hunter to send for the doctor. Her pulse was racing from the excitement of Matt's regaining consciousness and his declaration of love for her. She did not know what he had to tell her, but for now all she cared about was that it appeared that he was going to be all right.

"He's conscious!" she announced happily as she burst into Caroline's parlor. "Call Dr. Winston."

"Thank God," Hunter uttered sincerely. "As soon as I've arranged for the doctor, I'll go to Matt."

There was an unaccustomed huskiness in his voice, and he excused himself to blow his nose noisily into one of his large white handkerchiefs. Caroline placed her arms around him and smiled up into his narrow aristocratic face.

"You see, my darling Randolph, I told you that he would be fine," she beamed.

Amelia slipped quietly from the room. They had already forgotten she was there.

When Amelia re-entered Matt's room, his eyes were once again closed, but now he seemed to be in a light sleep, not the deep unconsciousness he had previously experienced. Being careful not to awaken him, she reassured herself as she saw that his breathing was deep and easy and his color was beginning to return to its normal ruddiness.

She stayed at his side until Dr. Winston returned, but Matt did not reawaken. When the doctor arrived, she excused herself and returned to her room. Hunter would spend the night with Matt, sleeping in the large armchair by the bed as he had done the night before.

Exhausted from the emotional strain of her cousin's death and Matt's injury, Amelia threw herself fully clothed on the bed, pulled the comforter around her and went to sleep.

Rose and Lady Caroline awakened her the next morning, the first with her breakfast tray, and the other with the news that Matt had slept peacefully through the night and was now sitting up and eating solid food.

"Now that he is conscious, Constable Deckett will want to speak with him. He thought it would be best if you are there, too, Amelia, so he can question you both at the same time. He will be here within the hour, so you'll need to hurry," Lady Caroline said.

Amelia rushed through her breakfast and bath. She rejected her black mourning clothes and wore instead a simple dress of deep teal blue with a wide Bertha collar of linen edged with white crocheted lace. Her hands shook with the excitement of seeing Matt again, and finally Rose took Amelia's hairbrush from her and arranged her hair herself.

When she entered Matt's room, Constable Deckett was already there with Hunter and Matt. Amelia avoided Matt's eyes, afraid that he would read too easily her love for him in them. Hunter brought her a chair, and the constable asked her to begin by telling what had happened the night Maude died.

"I had just returned from dinner with Lady Caroline," Amelia began nervously, "when Maude knocked at my door and asked me to come to her room. She said she had something she wanted to show me."

Painstakingly, Amelia recounted the evening, remembering almost word for word the conversation that had taken place, almost as if it had been burned into her mind. When she recited the list of ways in which Maude had tried to kill her, Constable Deckett broke in for the first time. "That woman must have been stark raving mad. Someone has truly been watching over you, Miss, to have protected you from these attempts on your life. Sorry to interrupt. Keep on, please."

Amelia continued. When she came to the point in her story of Matt's entrance, she became confused and said that everything had happened so fast at that point that she really could not give an accurate accounting.

"Mr. Laurence, are you sure you feel well enough to fill us in on what happened next?" the constable asked.

Matt was propped up against the pillows, looking pale and weak, but he nodded his agreement and began in a weakened voice that strengthened as he related his story. "Hunter and I were downstairs in the lobby when Beulah, Mrs. Hagarty's maid, came charging down the stairs, a wild and frightened look in her eyes. When she saw us, she ran to me, grabbed my arm, and started pulling me toward the stairway. She said that she needed help, that 'Miss Maude was goin' to shoot Miss Amelia.' When I heard that, I ran upstairs as fast as I could and burst into Maude's room."

At this point Matt leaned back on the pillows and closed his eyes, and Dr. Winston moved quickly to his side, but Matt waved him away with assurances that he could continue.

"The door slamming open must have startled her," he said, "for as she turned toward me, the gun went off and I was hit in the shoulder. Then I saw her turn the gun on herself and threw myself across the room at her in hopes of disarming her. But I couldn't reach her quickly enough. You know the rest."

Constable Deckett thought Matt had finished and started to speak, but Matt cut him off with what sounded like a low growl. "However, Constable, had I known then what I know now"—his eyes burned into Amelia's —"if Miss Hagarty had not killed herself, I think I would have done it for her."

He lay back on the pillows once more, pale and exhausted.

"Thank you, Mr. Laurence, that's all I need for now. Looks like a clear case of suicide to me. Saves the state the cost of a trial for attempted murder, though. However, we will need to call you and the others involved as witnesses at Rousseau's trial."

Placing his notebook back in his coat pocket, he turned to leave. "Sorry I had to disturb you like this, Mr. Laurence. I hope you're feeling better real soon. Good day."

Constable Deckett shook hands with Hunter, bowed to Amelia and left.

Amelia looked anxiously at Matt, who lay still and quiet with his eyes closed.

"Don't worry, Miss. I'll look after him for now. Perhaps you could come in after lunch," Hunter suggested in a whisper.

Amelia nodded and returned to her room with Matt's rich baritone voice still resonating in her mind with his condemnation of Maude.

Poor mad Maude, she thought, to have killed herself like that.

Trying to shake the gloom from her spirit, Amelia went to the window and pulled aside the heavy curtain to let the sunshine in. The day was bright and sunny, and as she stood looking out across the hotel grounds, she saw Beulah and Philip assist Ursula onto the northbound train that waited by the hotel's main entrance. She was filled with an inundant sadness. She had hardly known Aunt Ursula, but Philip had loved Amelia and been her friend, and dear old Beulah had been like a mother to her. Tears misted her eyes as she let the curtain fall, and she wondered if she would ever see any of them again.

After lunch with Lady Caroline, she returned to Matt's room. He was asleep again. Hunter left quietly and Amelia settled herself in the chair by the bed, feasting her eyes on Matt. She noticed that his breathing was regular and his color had improved after his ordeal with the constable.

He awoke midafternoon when Dr. Winston stopped by to check his progress.

"You're doing splendidly," the kindly doctor assured him as he changed the bandage on his shoulder. "There is no sign of any infection now, so a few more days of bed rest, and you can gradually be up and about."

"Just one question," Matt said. "I have some things I need to speak with Miss Donelly about, but she refuses to listen unless I have your permission to talk. What do you think?"

Dr. Winston studied him over the top of his gold-rimmed spectacles which had slipped down the bridge of his nose.

"As long as you don't overtire yourself, and I believe Amelia can recognize those signs, I think some conversation would be all right. I'll be in again this evening."

As she closed the door behind the departing Dr. Winston, Amelia began to tremble. What if Matt told her something she didn't want to hear, like the date of his wedding to Diana Barrington? Having been so close to him the last two days had been heaven for her. And now she was afraid that she was going to have to become accustomed all over again to his going away.

"Please sit here, Amelia." Matt gestured to the left side of his bed, and Amelia sat obediently, anxious to have the ordeal over.

"You must promise not to say anything until I finish. Agreed?"

Amelia nodded, for the tightness in her throat had

increased to the point that she knew she would cry if she tried to speak.

"When I came to the Belleview in January, it was for two reasons. The first you know—to uncover the perpetrators of the land investment fraud. The second you don't know, because unfortunately Diana appeared on the scene and you jumped to all the wrong, but logical, conclusions before I had a chance to explain."

He shifted his weight, drawing Amelia closer to him as he spoke. "You see, I had allowed myself, out of sheer boredom, pressure from my mother and lack of good sense, to become engaged to a woman whom I did not, and do not, love."

Amelia couldn't believe what she was hearing. She looked at Matt incredulously, wanting to ask a dozen questions at the same time, but his expression warned her that she was not to speak yet, so she sat expectantly, trying not to hope for the words she wished to hear.

"So the second reason for coming to the Belleview was to take time to think clearly about what I wanted to do with my life, and how I might best break off my engagement with Diana.

"Then I met you, Amelia, and I knew for the first time in my life what real love is. My hands, however, were tied when Diana arrived, for she asked that I give her at least until after Mardi Gras before breaking off our engagement. I think she truly believed that she could change my mind. That was why I couldn't tell you or explain, not to mention the fact that you wouldn't let me talk to you anyway."

"It was exactly what you deserved—" Amelia began before remembering her promise of silence.

Matt pulled her even closer to him, then resumed his explanation. "Diana had promised to leave after the ball, but she is a very spoiled and stubborn young woman and refused to do so. I couldn't take her back to Chicago then, because by that time we were deeply involved in our plan to trap Edward Rousseau. As soon as he had been arrested, however, Hunter and I took Diana as far as Jacksonville, where we placed her on a Chicago-bound train. The woman is out of my life for good now."

Amelia attempted to picture anyone being able to make Diana Barrington do what she did not wish to, but the effort was too much, and she returned her full attention to Matt.

"On the way back from Jacksonville, we stopped in Ocala to inspect the breeding farms, Green Hills, that my agents had purchased for me. I believe you know my new manager, Bernard Fraser?"

His eyes gleamed mischievously. Amelia started to speak, but he raised his hand in warning. "Remember your promise."

Amelia nodded, but by now excitement and happiness were welling up inside her until she felt she would explode with joy.

Matt continued, "We were returning here when Beulah found us, and you know the rest of that story. What you may not know is that the reason for my return was to ask you to marry me. I love you, Amelia, and if you will do me the honor of becoming my wife, I will cherish and care for you as long as I live."

A long stillness grew in the room, and Matt's face became troubled when she did not answer.

"Please say yes, Amelia."

Amelia grinned wickedly. "I promised not to speak until you finished. Are you finished?"

Matt reached out with his good arm and pulled her against him. "Only with talking," he murmured in her ear.

"Then my answer is definitely yes." Amelia sighed before his lips crushed hers.

Amelia tapped softly on Matt's door the following morning and entered quietly. The draperies were still drawn and the room was dark, but the overwhelming sensation was the scent of lavender that caressed her nostrils, reminding her so strongly of her mother that for a moment she thought she had stepped into another world.

She glanced quickly toward the bed where Matt slept undisturbed by her entry, then noticed another figure that had risen from the chair at his bedside.

"Amelia?" A feminine Southern drawl spoke her name. "I'm Catherine Laurence."

The petite figure of Matt's mother approached her and embraced her affectionately and unhesitatingly. The warmth of the gesture and the smell of lavender filled Amelia's heart with joy. Catherine stepped back, keeping a firm grip on Amelia's hands, to examine her from arm's length. The two women were bonded instantly by their love for the man who lay still and silent on the bed.

"Matt wrote to me about you weeks ago, but none of his descriptions have done you justice. You are beautiful."

"Oh, Mrs. Laurence—" Amelia began to protest.

"Hush, my dear. Let's go somewhere where we can talk. Hunter will be here shortly if Matt awakens."

The women left the suite to breakfast on the veranda. Amelia and Catherine had immediately established a comfortable rapport, and their conversation lasted long into the morning, ranging from stories of Matt's childhood to the recent events at the Belleview.

"There is one other matter I must discuss with you

before your wedding, Amelia."

Catherine's voice had become solemn and her expression almost grim. Amelia, frightened that anything would spoil her new-found happiness, was almost afraid for the older woman to speak. In fact, Catherine was having great difficulty doing so. She self-consciously rearranged the flatware, took a sip of water, and nervously cleared her throat. Finally Amelia could stand it no longer; whatever it was, she had to get it over with.

"Please, Mrs. Laurence, what is it?" she begged.

Catherine took a deep breath. "I have no daughters of my own, so I've never had to broach this matter, so I really don't know how to begin," she stammered. "However, since your own mother isn't here, I feel it is my responsibility to, well, to inform you of certain, uh, aspects of married life of which you are unaware."

She stopped in surprise as Amelia, Catherine's intent finally dawning on her, laughed in relief. "Dear Mrs. Laurence, you are so kind, but that won't be necessary. You forget that I am a doctor's daughter with a degree in science. I've studied both anatomy and physiology, so your instruction isn't needed in my case."

She smiled and embraced the older woman. "I'm sure that as long as Matt and I love each other, that we'll have no difficulties with that 'aspect,' as you call it."

Visibly relieved at her reprieve from such a chore, Catherine rose from the table and held out her hand. "Come with me. I've brought you a dress at Matt's request, and I'd like to show it to you now."

The evening before their wedding, Matt and Amelia sat before the fire in Lady Caroline's suite awaiting the return of Hunter and Caroline from dinner. Catherine had already retired in expectation of tomorrow's busy schedule.

"There is one thing that worries me about our marriage, Amelia." Matt's voice broke their companionable silence, and Amelia looked at him in alarm.

"What is it, Matt?"

"Since you so graciously agreed to honor me by becoming my wife, you haven't mentioned one word about medical school. Surely a goal that has been so important to you for so long hasn't just disappeared. Don't you think we ought to discuss it?"

Amelia groped for the appropriate words, and as Matt watched the emotions play across her face as she searched for an answer, he pulled her into his arms, burying his face in her hair and speaking softly into her ear. "Don't be afraid to be honest with me, Amelia. We must always tell one another the truth."

Keeping her eyes on the dancing flames of the fire, afraid to look at Matt for fear that he would not like what she was about to tell him, Amelia took a deep breath and began. "I love you, Matt. You must know that, and I want to be your wife and have your children, but I want to be a doctor, too. I don't think I could ever give up that dream—not even for you."

The minutes lengthened and Amelia found herself holding her breath, waiting anxiously for Matt's reply. Suddenly he grasped her by the shoulders and held her at arm's length so that he could see her eyes as he spoke.

"I know you are well aware that it's a difficult path that you have chosen for yourself?"

Amelia nodded solemnly.

"And that even if you are able to overcome admission barriers, that you will meet with prejudice and perhaps even animosity from both professors and fellow students?"

Again Amelia nodded.

"And that even should you overcome those obstacles that a practice with a female doctor might have very few patients, at least as a start?"

"But, Matt, I have to try! How will I know if I don't try? I can't *not* attempt it because I know there will be difficulties. I can prepare myself for the possibility that I might fail, but I could never live with myself if I didn't even try!"

Matt studied her face, his own grave and unsmiling. Finally, after what seemed endless minutes, he spoke, "And that, my darling Amelia, is why I love you as I do. Try for your medical school. Finances are no problem now. And be prepared to battle prejudice and ignorance. But also know that you won't be battling them alone. I'll be there beside you every step of the way. I promise."

By now Amelia was truly speechless, and Matt took advantage of her silence to kiss her as she deserved.

Easter Sunday was the last day of the season at the Belleview. The next day all the guests would depart for their respective homes or spring or summer resorts. Amelia's trunks were packed and ready in her room, and the porter would arrive soon to take them to the train. Her traveling clothes were laid out on her bed.

Lady Caroline, resplendent in Easter finery, watched as Rose helped Amelia dress.

"It looks as if you owe me that sixpence, my girl. But even so, here's one for your shoe. Although I must admit, I never saw a bride who had less need of good luck."

Amelia laughed and caught the coin her friend had tossed to her. Sliding off one satin slipper, she placed the small coin in the toe of her shoe before donning it again.

How fortunate she was to have such a friend, Amelia thought. During the last three weeks, she and Caroline had become even closer than before, for in all the preparations for the wedding today, Caroline had acted as a surrogate mother, advising and supporting, and even calming prenuptial jitters.

The ceremony had been delayed until Matt had recuperated from his wound, and this gave his mother time to alter her own wedding dress to fit Amelia. The simplicity of the white dress inset with rows of Belgian lace and its high lace collar and flowing sleeves accented the willow slimness of Amelia's graceful figure. And now as Caroline watched Rose adjust the full tulle veil over Amelia's coronet of roses and ivy, she had to admit that Matt knew exactly what he was doing when he had asked his mother to bring the dress.

Amelia was ready. It was only a few minutes now before she would become Matt's wife. There was a knock on her door and Caroline leaped to open it. Standing on the threshold was a middle-aged couple looking shy and slightly embarrassed. When Amelia saw them, she gave a cry of welcome and threw her arms about them.

"Dr. Will! Aunt Beth! How wonderful, and what a surprise!"

Dr. Will calmly disentangled himself from Amelia's embrace, and kissed her solemnly on the forehead. "Your parents would be very proud of you, my girl. Wouldn't they, Beth?"

His wife smiled and embraced Amelia again. "We're so happy for you. I know you're going to be very happy, especially with so considerate a husband. Mr. Laurence thought you should have someone to give you away, and since you have no family, he thought of us. He even sent his private car to Asheville to bring us here. And because the hotel closes tomorrow, he's arranged for us to stay with Dr. Winston for a few days' vacation before returning home."

Amelia was deeply touched by Matt's thoughtfulness. She kissed Aunt Beth and Caroline, who left to join the other guests in the lobby.

"Are you ready, my girl?" Dr. Will asked.

"You probably wouldn't believe me if I told you that I've been ready for a long, long time," Amelia teased, remembering a January morning on a southbound train.

She lowered her veil over her face and linked her arm through Dr. Will's. Rose handed her bouquet to her, an aromatic cascade of white roses, stephanotis, lily of the valley, and baby's breath. Then Rose kissed her cheek shyly and smiled.

"Good luck, Miss Amelia."

As Dr. Will and Amelia descended the wide stairs to the lobby, the hotel orchestra played a stately wedding march. The guests stood on either side of an aisle that led to an arch of greenery before the French doors. Pastor Dean, Matt, and Hunter as his best man stood waiting for her. Lady Caroline stepped forward to act as her attendant.

Amelia's voice trembled with emotion during the vows, but Matt's was strong and sure. When the minister pronounced them man and wife, Matt gathered her into his arms with an enthusiasm that brought applause from the guests. Then to the strains of Handel and Mendelssohn they recessed to the Tiffany Room for a wedding banquet and dance.

As Amelia sat at the head table next to her husband, she was sharply aware of her parents' absence and wished that they could have lived to share her happiness. But she could not be unhappy today. She remembered a line from Tennyson's "Ulysses", "Though much is taken, much abides."

Yes, she thought, she had suffered great losses, but she had been given so much, too.

Then she looked around the room and thanked God for her many blessings, especially her wonderful friends. Bernard and Sarah had come from Ocala. They would be her neighbors whenever she and Matt resided at Green Hills. Dear Aunt Beth and Dr. Will had come all this way for her. Catherine, whom she had already come to love, reminded her so much of her own dear mother. Kindly Dr. Winston who had tended both her and Matt, would also be going to Ocala to start a new practice there. And then there were Caroline and Hunter. She and Matt would be sailing with them to England where the newlyweds would attend the wedding of Lord Weybridge and Lady Caroline before continuing their own European honeymoon.

Bright sunlight streamed through the windows, illuminating the faces in the room. Matt stood next to her, his glass raised in a toast to his bride, and all the others joined in, as Amelia basked in the warmth of their love. The season at the Belleview had come to an end, but Amelia knew her life was only beginning.